ONE
GOLDEN
SUMMER

TITLES BY CARLEY FORTUNE

ONE GOLDEN SUMMER

Carley Fortune

BERKLEY ROMANCE
New York

BERKLEY ROMANCE
Published by Berkley
An imprint of Penguin Random House LLC
1745 Broadway, New York, NY 10019
penguinrandomhouse.com

BERKLEY and the BERKLEY & B colophon
are registered trademarks of Penguin Random House LLC.

Book design by Ashley Tucker

Library of Congress Cataloging-in-Publication Data

Names: Fortune, Carley, author.
Title: One golden summer / Carley Fortune.
Description: First edition. | New York : Berkley Romance, 2025. |
Identifiers: LCCN 2024051020 | ISBN 9780593638910 (trade paperback) |
ISBN 9780593638934 (ebook)
Subjects: LCGFT: Romance fiction. | Novels.
Classification: LCC PR9199.4.F678 O54 2025 |
DDC 813/.6—dc23/eng/20250103
LC record available at https://lccn.loc.gov/2024051020

First Edition: May 2025

Printed in the United States of America
1st Printing

The authorized representative in the EU for product safety and
compliance is Penguin Random House Ireland, Morrison Chambers,
32 Nassau Street, Dublin D02 YH68, Ireland, https://eu-contact.penguin.ie.

To the lake, to the hills, to the sky

ONE
GOLDEN
SUMMER

PROLOGUE

A great photograph makes you think you know the subject, even if you've never met. A great photo reaches out and pulls you inside the moment, so you can feel, smell, and taste it. And this, by all accounts, is a great photo.

I stare at it, and just like that, I'm seventeen.

I hear them across the bay. It's the end of summer, and those three voices are as familiar to me as the weight of the camera between my hands. The older boy is calling out to the other two—his brother and the girl, who lie on the floating raft in their bathing suits, sunny-side up.

I've been at the cottage since the end of June, watching them swim and flirt and fly around the lake in their yellow speedboat. Each of them is beautiful. So sun-kissed and free.

They climb into the boat. The oldest drives. His brother and the girl sit in the front. I stand on the edge of the dock, adjusting the aperture.

It happens in the shortest blink of time.

I hear the boat. Their laughter over the engine. I look up to see them heading toward me. I bury myself behind the lens. They enter the frame.

Click.

1

FRIDAY, JUNE 13

They are five of the most stunning women I've ever seen. It has nothing to do with the lighting or how much time they've spent in hair and makeup. It's the genuine smiles on their faces. The fan is blowing, the music is loud, and the photo editor *oohs* as she watches the images load onto my laptop screen. I don't need a glimpse to know they're spectacular. I can feel it with every press of the shutter.

I'll crash later, alone in my empty condo, but right now I'm in my element. When I'm behind a lens, I can draw out a sly grin or a slight tilt of the chin. I'm in command. It's one of the reasons I've been working so much lately. I *need* this feeling. The buzz of a perfectly humming set is my high.

The youngest woman is in her twenties, the eldest in her seventies, and none of them are professional models. It took time to earn their trust when they arrived at my studio. If anyone understands how nerve-racking it can feel to have your photo taken, it's me. Now, the women dance and pose in bathing suits without a shred of self-consciousness. Their stretch marks, wrinkles, and cellulite are on display, emblems of their lives given due reverence in each frame.

"It's going to be impossible to make selects," Willa, the photo editor, says once we wrap. We're standing shoulder to shoulder, scrolling through the images on my computer. The best will run in *Swish*, a weekly style magazine that debuted this spring. "There are so many great shots, Alice."

"I'm glad you think so," I say, beaming. I've never worked with Willa before, and I want to wow her. *Swish* is distributed in the country's largest paper, and it's all my industry friends can talk about. This is my first gig for the magazine, and I want to nail it. Magazine work doesn't pay very well, but it's far more creative than what I get to do with my commercial clients—it's also increasingly rare.

I pause on a shot of Monica, a new mom who was the most nervous of the group. Her head is thrown back and her arms are flung out. It's a moment of pure joy.

"We have two weeks for you to file," Willa says.

"No problem." This will be a low-touch edit. The assignment brief described it as a "refreshingly real" swimwear shoot with "regular people" showcasing the looks. It's another reason I was excited about the job: no aggressive photoshopping. "I'll just fix the flyaways and blemishes. It'll be fast."

"Well, you might have to do a little more than that." Willa lowers her voice. "I want to keep it authentic, but let's say the lumps and bumps are more like a *suggestion* of cellulite. I'm sure you can work your magic."

My smile vanishes. I've collected enough euphemisms for digitally altering the female body to fill a thesaurus. I've been told to make women look more flattering, appealing, engaging, enticing, attractive, and flat-out more fuckable. But I've never been asked to *suggest* cellulite.

"I thought you wanted this to be *refreshingly* real," I say calmly, like I'm not ready to throw my camera at the wall.

"I mean, yes, *absolutely*." Willa goes on. "It's great having different body types represented, but let's just clean it all up."

I don't bat an eye behind my tortoiseshell glasses. On the surface, I'm the picture of polished professionalism. I've quieted my auburn curls into a sleek ponytail. My makeup is minimal but effective. There isn't a single chip in my ruby red nail polish. But underneath, I'm crumbling.

It's not the first time I've been asked to do something I disagree with. Being a freelance photographer means I sometimes need to bend, compromise, and push my beliefs or vision to the side to please clients. It just happens more often than I'd like at this stage in my career.

"It's your call," I tell Willa, heart sinking. "It's your magazine."

I'm not a combative person, but even if I were, I'm too worn down to argue. It takes a lot of energy to be *on* all day, and I've been on for so long, I suspect my off button is broken.

And it's not just me who's noticed. I met Elyse, my brilliant instructor turned mentor and now friend, for coffee last week, and she told me I looked like a ghost. I'd had the dream the night before—the one where I'm being chased—and I was even more drained than usual.

"You excel at capturing inner light," she'd said. "But I worry you've lost your own. Get it back, Alice. I want to see you shine." Elyse told me to slow down.

For the first time ever, I ignored her advice. Work is what's kept me together these past six months. Or at least I thought so. But as soon Willa leaves, exhaustion slams in. I sit on the floor of my studio, rubbing my fingertips against my temples. I've taken on so many assignments to keep busy, but I took this one for me. And it backfired.

What I need is a night off. Just one night where I don't curl up with my laptop and color correct until my eyes burn. A few solid hours in which I pretend deadlines don't exist, where I can forget about the group show in August, and the look of concern that flashed across Elyse's face when she saw me. I need an evening where I definitely, one hundred percent will *not* think about Trevor, and that night is tonight. I'm going out with my big sister.

Eventually I peel myself off the floor. I'm locking up when my phone vibrates with a string of texts. I know it's her before I check the messages. Heather almost exclusively sends texts in multiples.

PUT ON YOUR PARTY SHOES! I just scored us a table at Jaybird.

Wait, do you even own party shoes?

I'll buy you a pair on my way to pick you up.

I'm typing out a reply when another message lands. But this time it's not my sister.

2

I t's a message to the Everly family group chat from my father.

Nan is in an ambulance.

My grandmother Nanette Everly—Nan to all, not just her grandchildren—has always been my biggest champion. I was a toddler when she identified my creative streak, and she nurtured it like one of her peony plants. When I was six, she took me to the Art Gallery of Ontario for drawing lessons. We sat among the Henry Moore sculptures, sketch pads on our laps, experimenting with shadows and shapes and lines. She taught me how to use a sewing machine when I was eleven. She gave me my first camera in high school. I've always tried to emulate her poise, the way she makes everyone around her feel seen. Nan's more practical than a road map and has a knack for making the best out of a bad situation. I admire her as much as I love her.

So when she falls in dance class and shatters her hip, drinks with my sister turn into a sleepover at Sunnybrook Hospital. As Nan undergoes an emergency hip replacement, I wipe my schedule clean so I can help her recover. I'm the best option. My father is in the middle of jury selection, and Heather has even less spare time. She's a lawyer like Dad *and* a single parent. Our younger twin siblings, Luca and Lavinia, are . . . well, they're Luca and Lavinia. I love them endlessly, but they're twenty-four and still take being the babies of the family seriously.

The morning Nan's released from the hospital, Heather comes with me to help take her home.

"You girls have other things to do than dote on me," Nan says as we guide her into the house with her new walker. For an eighty-year-old who had surgery thirty-six hours ago, she looks good. She gets her short white hair set once a week, is always smartly dressed, and has stayed active. Her posture is immaculate. I find myself pulling my shoulders back whenever I'm in her presence, even now.

"Not at this moment," Heather says. "But I'm due in court this afternoon."

"I, on the other hand, will be at your beck and call," I tell her.

Nan frowns. "I hate to think of you stuck here with me, Alice. You should be out living your life."

"What life?" Heather mutters under her breath.

"I'm happy to stay here," I say, ignoring my sister. "You know I love this house."

Nan lives in Leaside, a leafy neighborhood in midtown Toronto. During those first hectic years after the twins were born, Heather and I slept at Nan and Grandpa's on the weekends more often than we did in our own beds. Our home was a few streets over, but I loved this house best. The plump peonies that line the walkway. The homemade paisley curtains over the leaded glass windows. The doorbell that tolls as if announcing a newlywed couple. You can hear its thunderous ring in every corner of the redbrick Georgian, but to me, it's the sound of calm and quiet. No screaming babies. No overwhelmed mother. A bedroom of my own.

"Let me do the stairs by myself," Nan says sharply when Heather takes her elbow.

It's not like Nan to be snippy, but I get it. She's been living on her own since Grandpa died twenty years ago, and she guards her independence like a dragon. Plus, she was supposed to leave for an Alaskan cruise next week. I'd be prickly if I were in her shoes, too.

"Poor Nan," I whisper as she navigates her walker over the threshold.

Heather shakes her head. "Poor you."

"We'll be fine."

After a good night's sleep, Nan will be back to her optimistic, high-spirited self.

But three days pass, and Nan grows even crankier. I've never seen her so low. On the morning the cruise sets sail without her on board, her silence is as brooding as the clouds that darken the western sky. She hasn't even touched her crossword puzzle. When rain pelts the windowpane, I glance at her. Nan loves a good, "bracing" storm, but not a glimmer of interest brightens her face. I'm caught off guard by how old she looks. It sneaks up on me sometimes—that her hair is white and not gray anymore. And then I remember the peonies.

I run out of the house in my pajamas with a pair of scissors, but the flowers are already bent over, dozens of pink and white heads kissing the mulch, beads of water clinging to their ruffled petals. Under normal circumstances, Nan would be out here in her housecoat before the first drops fell—she prefers the flowers in a vase to seeing them droop like this. I snip quickly, but when I return to the house, my arms full of fragrant blossoms, wet hair plastered to my cheeks, she looks at me vacantly and says, "I didn't realize it was raining."

I need to fix this.

~~~

When Nan lies down for a nap after lunch, I sit in the same spot I used to as a kid: at the top of the staircase, staring at the wall of family photos opposite the banister. My niece's first step. Luca and Lavinia's high school graduation dinner. Nan and Grandpa at their best friends' cottage in Barry's Bay. They used to visit John and Joyce there every year. It's Nan's favorite place in the world. I spent just two months at the lake, but it left a mark on me, too.

I turned seventeen that summer. For my birthday, Nan gave me a camera—a very good SLR. I shot frame after frame, teaching myself, trying to get better. I put the best photos in an album that I gave to Nan on our last day at the cottage. I find it now on the basement shelves, and sit on the red carpet, legs crossed beneath me.

Even before I open the cover, it comes back to me. My first time away from home. My first taste of freedom. Two months of waking to sunlight bouncing off the lake and rippling on the ceiling. Diving off the dock, then swimming beneath the surface as far as I could. Barbecues on the deck. Permanently damp hair. Art projects in the boathouse. Red life jackets. Canoe trips. Picnics on the island. The Harlequins I'd sneak from Joyce's stash. Coconut sunscreen and watermelon slices and my terry cloth bathing suit cover-up. The kids across the bay. And their yellow speedboat.

I flip through photos of shorelines and treetops, wildflowers and rocks, the twins, their heads bobbing in the water, almost impossible to distinguish. There's one I took of myself in the bedroom mirror, my hair sopping wet. I thought it was clever: Alice through the looking glass.

Most are photographs of Nan. My original muse. Nan reading on a hammock, the twins tucked into her sides. Nan mend-ing a rip in Lavinia's shorts, her glasses perched on the tip of her nose. Nan paddling a canoe, waving at me onshore with an incandescent smile.

On the very last page is the photo that started it all.

I slide it from its sleeve and study the faces of three teenagers in a yellow boat. From the moment I took it, I've been chasing this kind of perfection in an image. The emotion. The movement. The sense of timelessness. A whole summer of practice, and I got this shot on one of my last days at the lake. I still can't believe how well I captured them. Even now, I can smell the gasoline, hear their hollers across the water.

The older boy is at the steering wheel and the younger one stares at the girl, who's smiling into the wind. The light is gorgeous, but not because I've bent it to my will. There's a naivety to the image, a lack of artifice. It's been years since I've seen it, but for some reason, I still feel deeply connected to these three kids, preserved in never-ending summer.

The photo is the first chapter of my origin story, the beginning of my love affair with photography. It launched me on the path to becoming the person I am now.

I flip back to the picture of Nan in the canoe with her star-bright smile, and an inkling of an idea begins to take shape. A way to cure Nan's blues and get her out of the house. A change of scene. Fresh air. Endless skies. Glittering water.

A second trip to the lake.

Our return to Barry's Bay.

3

WEDNESDAY, JUNE 18

I find John Kalinski's number in Nan's address book. I haven't seen John since his wife's funeral more than a decade ago, but I remember both him and Joyce well. They were entwined in my grandparents' lives.

John sounds happy to hear from me. "Stay the whole summer if you want," he says when I ask about renting the cottage for a couple of weeks. He tells me he's been thinking about selling it for years—the place is empty.

The offer catches me off guard—both John's unexpected generosity and how appealing a two-month hiatus from my life sounds.

When I relay the conversation to Nan over afternoon tea, she doesn't react with the excitement I expect. Instead, she's silent for a long stretch of time.

"John assured me it was okay with him," I tell her. "He can't visit the cottage at all. He'd prefer if someone was staying there."

And then she smiles—*really* smiles—for the first time since her hip replacement.

I do the math. I check my bank account. I pore over my invoices and am surprised to find that I've already made more than I did all of last year. The silver lining of the breakup is that I've been relentlessly productive.

I think about my last conversation with Elyse.

You're even paler than usual, Alice. You look like a ghost. I'm worried about you.

I can afford to take a break. More importantly, maybe I can't afford not to.

Everything falls into place after I call John and tell him that yes, we'd love to stay at the cottage until the end of August.

I manage to postpone many of my assignments and help find other photographers to cover the rest. I track down a physiotherapist in Barry's Bay who can see Nan, and her post-surgery checkup goes well. John gives me the name and number of the guy who's looking after the cottage for the summer—he has a spare set of keys.

"If you need a hand making the cottage more comfortable for Nan, I'm sure he'd be able to help," John tells me.

As I dial the number, I find myself sinking back into memories of Barry's Bay. Saffron sunsets. Fireflies twinkling in the dusk. The heat of the dock's sunbaked wooden planks underfoot. A red-roofed cabin shaded by evergreen boughs.

The daydream ends with a record scratch when a man's voice booms through the line.

"What the hell are you doing?"

"Um . . ."

There's more shouting, now muffled. I check my screen to make sure I've dialed the right number, and yes.

"Excuse me? Hello?"

I'm about to hang up when the voice says to me, "This is Charlie Florek."

"Charlie, hi. This is Alice Everly calling."

I hear the metallic *thwack* of metal on metal. A hammer, maybe.

"One sec," Charlie says, annoyed, and then: "For the last time, Sam, will you kindly fuck off? You're going to ruin it."

I hear a disgruntled reply, and then Charlie says to me, "Sorry, who is this?"

"Alice Everly. I'm staying at John Kalinski's cottage this summer." I try to talk over the ruckus in the background. It sounds like he's on a construction site. "Is this a bad time?"

There's a long pause, raised male voices, and then the noise stops.

"No, I'm good. Apologies for that." Charlie clears his throat. "Hi. Alice, right?" It's a nice voice. Deep with a scrape of sandpaper over his *r*'s.

"Right."

A thing about me: I once broke my wrist in ninth-grade gym class and spent twenty-four hours gritting my teeth against the pain until I finally told my mom I *might* need to see a doctor. I don't like asking for help, or being an inconvenience, or wasting anyone's time. This phone call incorporates all three—Charlie is clearly in the middle of something.

So I rush forward, getting it over with. "John said you might be able to help me out. I have a list of things I need to do at the cottage for my grandmother. She's just had her hip replaced, and I—"

Charlie cuts me off. "How are you?"

"Excuse me?"

"'*How are you?*'" says Charlie, sounding amused, "is typically what you ask someone after '*Hello*.'"

"I'm fine, thank you," I say, slightly thrown. "Anyway, my grandmother—"

Charlie interrupts me a second time. "I'm good, Alice. Thanks for asking."

"Right." My face heats. I can't remember the last time I was chided. "That's good. That you're good. We're both good."

Another thing about me: When I'm not holding my camera, I can find it hard to speak up. In my loud, chaotic family, with strangers, with pushy art directors . . . It's one of the reasons why I love shooting so much—it's the only time I feel like a certified badass.

I clear my throat, trying to get back on track. "As I was saying, there are a few things I need to have done at the cottage before we arrive, and I was hoping you or someone you know could help. I have a list." I fetch my notebook and begin reading off the bullet points. "Grab bars, moving furniture, moving out the rugs—"

"Alice." Charlie interrupts me yet again.

I inhale, annoyance growing. "Yes?"

"Take a breath. I can feel your anxiety all the way in Barry's Bay."

"I'm trying to be conscious of your time," I say, channeling my most professional, together self. The Alice I am behind the camera. "I simply want to ensure everything is suitable for when I arrive with my grandmother. If you're unable to assist me, that's quite all right. But perhaps you know someone who can."

A low chuckle fills my ear. "Don't worry. I'm *quite* happy to *assist*. John gave me a heads-up about your grandma's surgery. I'll take care of everything. Text me that list of yours, and I'll *ensure* everything is *suitable*."

I blink. "Are you making fun of me?"

"Wouldn't dream of it," he says, but I can hear him smiling. No, not smiling. *Smirking*. "Just get yourself up here, Alice. Something tells me you need some time at the lake more than I do."

The hammering resumes in the background, and Charlie curses.

"See you soon, City Girl."

And then he's gone.

The evening before Nan and I leave, I go back to my condo to pack. When the elevator opens at my floor, I find the cardboard box I left in the hallway still sitting there. Trevor keeps making plans to pick up his stuff and then canceling. The remains of a four-year relationship come down to a copy of *The Minimalist Entrepreneur*, wireless headphones, and a stray dress sock. I nudge the box inside with my foot, though I'd rather shove it down the garbage chute.

Not that it would help me forget. Every corner of this place smacks of Trevor. When he moved in, we appointed it in whites and beiges, marble and glass, everything sleek and minimal. It never used to feel so hollow—it used to feel like home. Now everything is a reminder of how much I conceded to him. The pristine white sofa we bought one Sunday after brunch—I wanted something soft and smooshy, but Trevor loved its clean lines. The Carrara tulip dining table with the uncomfortable chairs he picked out. It's where I was sitting when he broke up with me. He'd made dinner that night. It was six months ago, and I can still smell the coq au vin—I'll never eat it again.

I don't know how to make you happy, Alice. Do you?

I've just zipped my suitcase when the buzzer trills. Heather arrives in a cloud of strong perfume and carrying a suspicious orange paper bag that she shoves at me.

"For you."

Heather calls shopping her unguilty pleasure, and she's always buying me clothes. The back of my closet is stuffed with bandage dresses and low-cut blouses, courtesy of my big sister.

I peer inside the bag, pushing aside the tissue paper to reveal emerald silk. "What is this?"

"Don't look so disgusted. It's a dress."

I pull it out and raise a brow. "It's a *tiny* dress."

"Minuscule." Heather grins, and it's like a camera flash. My sister has always been beautiful, but her smile is so radiant it's almost startling. "Green's your color, Turtle, and if you don't put it in your suitcase, I will."

One of the ways I revolt against my red hair is to *never* wear green. Most of my clothes are neutral, with a few hints of blue. A rare splash of yellow. I set the bag on the counter, promising nothing.

Heather and I have identical hazel eyes, but our similarities stop there. Heather's an unrepentant show-off; I prefer going unnoticed. She has our dad's height, confidence, and coffee-brown hair, which she wears in a sharp-angled bob—part of her courtroom intimidation tactics. I get my library-soft voice and auburn curls from our mom. Heather's the rebel; I'm the good girl. She's impulsive; I'm a planner. And, unlike me, she's completely uninhibited.

Both she and Dad are showboats. Luca and Lavinia are the same. At the last family get-together, my baby brother stripped off his shirt at the table to display a tattoo of a lion, a turtle, a flamingo, and a monkey across his chest, and Lavinia handed out invitations to her Muppets-themed burlesque.

I always thought I took after our levelheaded mom. But in December, when the ink had barely dried on the divorce papers, she moved across the country to British Columbia. We'd grown up hearing stories about the season she spent picking and packing cherries in the Okanagan Valley in the late eighties. The old VW van. A friend named Cinnamon. Camping in the fields. That version of Mom seemed as far-fetched as bedtime fairy tales. That is, until she announced she'd reconnected with Cinnamon and was going to work at a biodynamic vineyard in Kelowna. Our homemaker, homebody mother now lives two thousand miles away, pouring glasses of pinot noir and viognier in a tasting room overlooking Okanagan Lake.

"How's my niece?" I ask my sister.

Heather got married young. Became pregnant young. Got divorced young, too. I lived with her for a couple of years after the split, when my niece was just a baby. Heather was determined to tackle both law school and a newborn. Bennett is thirteen now.

"Don't use my daughter as a distraction technique," she says, marching to my bedroom with the shopping bag. I hear her open my suitcase. "I'll need photo evidence of you wearing it," she calls.

I scowl at her when she returns.

"What? You'll look hot in that dress."

"Nan will be so appreciative."

Heather squeezes my waist, which is currently covered by a white-and-blue-striped nightshirt, and I swat her hands away.

"What are you doing?"

"Just checking to make sure there's a body under all that cotton. I'd forgotten."

"Ha. Ha."

A line appears between her dark brows. "I'm serious. Don't let yourself disappear just because Trevor's gone."

I flinch at my ex's name, then silently berate myself for being fragile. I wonder if it would be easier if he hadn't moved on so quickly.

Heather's face softens. "Show that dress a good time, Ali. You both deserve it."

"We'll see."

She looks at me like I'm hopeless, then kisses my cheek. "I've got to go. Bennett's at a friend's tonight, and I'm meeting someone."

"Which one?"

Heather's too busy to date, but she has a short roster of friends with benefits.

"He's new. Just in the city for a night."

"Ah."

It's another way Heather and I differ: I've never slept with someone I don't love. I can't fathom having a one-night stand. But since I have no intention of throwing myself into another relationship for a long time, if ever, I may need to rethink my strategy.

"That sounded like a very judgy *ah*," Heather says.

"No judgment. Only reasonable sisterly concern. Be careful, okay?"

"Always." Heather wraps her arms around me, guaranteeing I'll smell like vetiver for the rest of the night. "I'll see you soon, okay?"

"In just a few weeks." She's bringing Bennett to the cottage to spend a week with Nan and me. I can't wait. Three generations of Everly women under one roof is my idea of heaven.

"And you're coming back to the city for the show, right?" she asks.

I wince.

Elyse is about to open a gallery on Davenport, and *In (Her) Camera* is her first exhibition—it's also the first major show I've been asked to participate in. It was a pinch-me moment: my former photography instructor, a woman I worship, wanting to represent me. Then she told me which photo she wanted to display, and I felt ill. But how could I say no when everyone knows that

Elyse Cho has impeccable taste? It's been many years since she was my teacher, but I have yet to find equal footing in our friendship. I still see her as my superior in all ways.

"We'll see," I tell Heather. "I'm not sure I'll be able to swing it."

A perk of heading north for the summer is that I have a good reason to avoid the opening night party.

"Turtle," Heather says. "You *have* to come back."

"Sure," I say, ushering her to the door. "Love you, Lion."

"Love you more."

When she's gone, I open the photos from the swimwear shoot on my laptop. They're due tomorrow, and I've already edited them. Twice. In one version, the women have been "smoothed" the way Willa wants. In the other, I've removed a few pimples and tidied the flyaways, but I haven't touched the cellulite.

I love photography. I've been shooting professionally for more than ten years, and I feel lucky to earn a living this way. But I thought if I proved myself, I'd reach the point where I'd be working to achieve my own vision, not someone else's. That's why I took this assignment. Like most magazines, *Swish* doesn't have the big budgets that come with ad campaigns—Willa promised they make up for it by giving contributors more creative runway.

I think about what Elyse would do. She understands the realities of collaborating with photo editors, but she *respects* artistic vision. I sigh and shut my laptop. I still have one more day to decide which photos I'm going to send.

My phone vibrates with a text.

Charlie: Everything's ready for you, City Girl. Keys are in the outhouse.

City Girl? I may not be prepared to take a stand with my work, but I can do something about *that*.

Me: Thank you.

Me: But for the record, my name is Alice Everly.

Charlie: Noted. I look forward to meeting you, Alice Everly.

4

FRIDAY, JUNE 27
FIRST DAY AT THE LAKE

It's the last Friday in June, and Southern Ontario is fleeing to the lakes. Traffic is heavy. It's going to take us well over four hours to get from Toronto to Barry's Bay, a blink-and-you-miss-it town on the north end of Kamaniskeg Lake.

Nan has been quiet since I turned off the 401 and began heading north. With the city, suburbs, and exurbs behind us, her attention is fixed on the view outside. First fields and farmland. Now forests and fresh water. We drive over the Burleigh Falls bridge, and she sighs at the sight of the rapids. We're on a single-lane highway, and traffic is almost at a standstill, so I peel my eyes from the road and take in the cascading white water.

"It's funny how little has changed," Nan murmurs.

She's dressed, as always, in a crisp white collared shirt and trousers, a polite string of pearls adorning her neck, and rose pink Chanel lipstick. Everything about her appears precise, almost stiff, a striking opposition to her playful personality. But my life-loving Nan is still not herself. I get the sense that she's not here with me but rather lost in past trips to the cottage. It's been a decade since her last visit.

My timer goes off. I took notes at Nan's last doctor's appointment. I've also read an entire internet's worth of postsurgical-care articles. Bed exercises. Short walks. Icing. She isn't supposed to sit for long stretches, so I'm pulling over every hour so she can move around.

"I need to find a spot where we can stop for a bit. Can you do those calf squeezes the physiotherapist showed you until I do?"

I feel her blue eyes on me. "You've got me in these compression socks already. I'm fine, Alice. I'm not going to die of a blood clot in the next ten minutes."

Not on my watch, she won't. "Please just do the calf squeezes, Nan."

She lowers her glasses. "You're not relaxing."

"I am. I'm very relaxed." In truth, I've been up since five, checking and rechecking my packing list.

Nan hums and then turns her head, gazing out the window once more.

We're squarely in cottage country now. Billboards advertise live bait and tackle, campgrounds and cabin rentals, marinas and river rafting. Yellow signs warn drivers of deer and turtle crossings.

We stop at the Kawartha Dairy in Bancroft for ice cream cones. She has orange-pineapple, and I get Bordeaux cherry, and we eat them in the car as we embark on the last leg of the journey. The highway runs through sharp granite rock faces, and rivers and marshes glint under the early summer sun. The farther north we go, the thicker the woods and the lighter the traffic, but we're at the tail end of vehicles. Some pull boats. Others have kayaks or canoes strapped to the roof. These hours stuck in a car are a rite for cottagers—the pilgrimage from city to lake, a ritual passed from one generation to another, along with a love of fresh air and big skies, and a tolerance for jumping into chilly water.

My family didn't partake in the custom. The summer Nan brought Luca, Lavinia, and me to the lake sixteen years ago was my first taste of life outside of Toronto. I savored every drop. John and Joyce were traveling that year. Dad was tackling one case or another, and my grandmother wanted to give my parents a break. Heather refused to leave the city, so Nan took the twins and me with her to Barry's Bay. I remember the town being small—a world away from the dense neighborhood where we lived.

"There it is," she says as we round the edge of a cliff. "The big end of Kamaniskeg Lake. We're almost there."

I gasp at the massive expanse of blue and the small islands dotting its surface.

As we approach Barry's Bay, water shines on one side of my car; the bustling Pine Grove Motel stands at the other. Ten minutes later, we're on Bare Rock Lane, a bumpy stretch of road surrounded by dense forest. Slices of lake flicker between branch and bush out the window. There's a KALINSKI sign nailed to a maple at the end of the driveway, a dirt path that leads to a dark brown log cabin.

Nan sighs when it comes into view. It's a classic cottage, built in the twenties, set on a wooded hill over Kamaniskeg. It has a stone chimney and a merry red tin roof with matching shutters. The window boxes are planted with poppy-colored impatiens. It looks like the kind of place where only good things happen. I park next to a neatly stacked row of firewood.

"Would you like me to help you out?" I ask Nan, noticing her hands are folded tight in her lap.

She shakes her head, her eyes not leaving the cottage. "I think I'll just sit here while you find the keys."

I climb out of the car and breathe it all in. Sun on cedar. Moss on rock. The unpolluted freshness of country air. The sounds of lake life. Waves lapping against the shore. A chain saw in the distance. A chipmunk scampering through a patch of wild strawberries.

Twigs and dry pine needles crunch under my feet as I walk to the rear of the house, looking for the outhouse, where Charlie said I'd find the key. Seeing no sign of it, I make my way around the other side of the cottage. I'm greeted with a view of the lake. It's an overwhelmingly large pool of clear water, so spectacular I stop to marvel for a moment. But I don't see any sort of shed.

I return to the car. "Any idea where the outhouse is?"

Nan frowns. "I didn't think there was one—not that I can remember, anyway."

I circle the building and still can't find it. "Crap," I say to the blue jay observing me from the limbs of a birch. "Crap," I say to the spruce and maple.

I pull my phone from my pocket and call Charlie. He answers on the first ring.

"Hello, Alice Everly," he says, drawing my name out slowly, roughing up the *r* in Everly. It sends a pleasant zing down my spine.

"Charlie, hi. We just got to the cottage, but I can't seem to find the outhouse."

"I'm good, Alice. How are you?"

"Magnificent," I say flatly. What's with this guy? "And you?"

"Better now that I've heard from you."

I roll my eyes.

"Where are you right now?" he asks.

"Beside the woodpile."

"And what are you wearing?"

My cheeks flash hot with anger. "Are you serious?"

He chuckles. "Not usually. Though in this case, I'm asking about your footwear. The trail to the outhouse is pretty overgrown."

I glance down at my sandals. "I'll be fine."

"Walk to the back door—the one facing the bush."

I do as Charlie says. "All right."

"Look up the hill."

The slope is covered in brambles and leggy saplings. Through the thicket, I spot a small wooden shed with a thatched roof just a few meters away. No wonder I couldn't see it—it's practically camouflaged. It probably hasn't been used in half a century.

"You could have picked an easier spot for the key," I say.

"There have been a couple of break-ins around the lake—kids looking for booze, probably. I didn't want to leave the key under the mat. But if you need assistance, I can be there in five."

"That won't be necessary," I say.

"Your call. See you soon, Alice Everly."

"What do you mean by *soon*?" I ask, but he's hung up.

I stare at the outhouse, hands on my hips. Despite what Charlie thinks, I'm not the kind of city person who can't cope without a doorman and a Starbucks within a one-block radius. I pride myself on being self-sufficient. A problem solver—never the problem. The friend you'd call if you needed help moving or fashioning a seahorse piñata for your niece's sixth birthday. I'm *that* friend. Competent. Reliable. And I can cope with anything, including being dumped by the man I thought I'd marry. Including his getting engaged two months after that. And I can certainly fetch a key from a shed, even one that looks like a prop in a horror movie.

So I climb the hill. The trail isn't overgrown; it's nonexistent. I push aside branches, ignoring the sting of something scratching my shins. There's a wood latch on the outhouse door, and when I turn it, it swings open, almost knocking me to the ground.

It's so dark inside all I can make out is a white plastic toilet seat set on a raised platform. I squint into the black, and then I see a magazine rack fixed to the wall and a stack of old issues of *Cottage Life* on the ledge beneath. I feel around until my fingers hit a small piece of metal. But then I hear something behind me. I look up, and four sets of beady eyes stare back at me. Racoons.

If there's one thing a Torontonian knows about wildlife, it's to never get in the way of a mama raccoon and her babies. The big one begins making a low growling noise and I spin on my heel, losing my balance and falling out the door. With an *oof*, I land on a rock.

I brush myself off, hissing, and limp back to the cottage, cursing Charlie's name.

"Everything all right?" Nan calls from the car.

"Just a minor run-in with some furry neighbors. I'm okay."

"You're bleeding."

I inspect my legs, and sure enough, I'm bleeding. My shins are covered in red welts, and burs have attached themselves to my nice linen shorts.

Effing Charlie Florek.

Inside, the cottage is almost exactly as I remember. The knotted wood walls are stained a deep honey brown, and the furniture is mismatched—a two-seater sofa, a floral armchair, and a leather recliner I remember sinking into when I was a teen. Strangely there's no coffee table—I swear it used to be a trunk with puzzles and games inside. There's a gorgeous stone fireplace, iron tools standing on a rack beside a box of kindling and newspaper, and Joyce's bookshelf, still filled with her paperback drugstore romances. The cottage is perched just above the water, and the entire front of the space is glass. I stand there, shaking my head at how beautiful it is.

And just like that, I'm seventeen again, dressed in a terry cloth bathing suit cover-up with a camera strapped around my neck. I'm free from Trevor, from *suggestions of cellulite*, from the sense that I haven't taken a photo that feels like *me* in months. I stare out the window, and I can see eight-year-old Luca and Lavinia leaping off the dock and a yellow speedboat ripping across the water.

But then I blink, and I'm returned to my thirty-two-year-old body. I stare at the empty bay, wondering if there's a way to go back.

I help Nan navigate the walker into the cottage, ignoring her request to do it on her own. She looks around the living room, eyes fluttering. I squeeze her hand.

"Think we can manage two months here together?" I ask.

She nods but says nothing. Her eyes land on the bookshelf, and I watch her swallow.

"I think I need a tea," Nan says, moving toward the kitchen. She drinks a cup of orange pekoe (one milk, one sugar) every afternoon around three. It's almost four now.

"Let me do that," I offer.

She swats at me. "I'm not incapacitated, Alice. I can put the kettle on. And I'm supposed to do as much as I can independently. Doctor's orders."

"Okay." I eye the giant rug in the living room. It's a tripping hazard and sure to give Nan's walker issues. So much for Charlie taking care of everything. "I'll get the rug out. Let me know if you need anything."

The cottage faces south, and the sun has turned it into a sauna. My hair is curling at the nape of my neck once I've pushed the couch and chair off the rug. I kneel at one end so I can roll it up, but the thing is fixed in place.

"Alice?" Nan calls.

"What's wrong?" I spring to my feet and rush into the kitchen to find her holding a sheet of paper.

"Have you seen this?"

She passes me the page.

"It was on the fridge," Nan says.

The edge is frayed, ripped from a spiral-bound notebook, and both sides are covered in black ink. When I've finished reading it, my ears are ringing.

I've been dreaming of spending a quiet summer on the water. I've pictured long walks and sunrises, midafternoon swims and cozy nights with a book. I've imagined peace and rest and catching up on work.

But I didn't anticipate Charlie Florek.

5

Alice Everly (not City Girl),

I know you appreciate a list, so here's what I've taken care of to <u>ensure</u> the cottage is <u>suitable</u>:

- *All area rugs and runners have been removed, except for the big one in the living room. I've taped it down and it shouldn't give your grandma any trouble. I've also shifted the furniture, so she has clear paths to the kitchen, porch, bathroom, and bedroom.*

- *I've taken out the trunk that John uses as a coffee table so there's more space for her walker. You can find the games, puzzles, and a deck of cards on the shelf in the closet of the second bedroom. I'll bring you a couple of small end tables soon.*

- *I've added grab bars to the bathroom and anti-slip strips to the shower stall. Did you bring a seat for her to use in the shower? They sell them at the drugstore in town, if not. I've also installed a raised toilet seat. John insisted on covering the cost of all this stuff, so no need to pay me back.*

- *I made up the largest room for your grandma. I've taken out one of the nightstands and shifted the bed to one side of the wall to give her more space.*

- *I've put night-lights in her bedroom and throughout the cottage so you can both move around safely in the dark.*

- *I also shuffled stuff around in the kitchen so that day-to-day items are easy for her to reach.*

- *This place gets hot as balls. There's a fan in your grandma's room but let me know if you need one. I have a spare.*

- *Boat is in. Gas tank is full.*

- *There's a Tupperware container of cheese and potato pierogi in the freezer in case you need an easy dinner tonight.*

- *(How impressed are you right now? Text me a picture of your face.)*

                                                              —*Charlie*

On the reverse side, there's a list of odd jobs he'll be doing for John: replacing a loose step to the lake and adding a railing, cutting back some of the brush, re-staining the dock. He's left info about the fireplace, the Wi-Fi, and the water (drinkable, from a well). And then a final note: *John asked me to take care of you and your grandma, and I promised I would. Lucky you: We'll be seeing a lot of each other this summer.*

I stare at the letter. Even his sloppy penmanship seems flippant. This man is *very* sure of himself. I feel a tiny pinch of envy.

"This is ridiculously detailed," I mutter.

"I'd say we have a guardian angel," Nan says, sounding brighter than she has all day.

I scan the letter again and snort. A fallen angel, more like it. *How impressed are you right now? Text me a picture of your face.*

"I'd say our angel has a big opinion of himself."

We do have the pierogi for dinner. They're homemade, and they're obnoxiously delicious.

"You know I made those curtains over the sink?" Nan calls as I'm washing the dishes.

The kitchen is tucked to one side of the cottage, a little closed off from the rest of the space, but the window has a great view of the woods. I've cranked it wide open, along with every other window in the cottage. Charlie was right: It's hot as balls in here.

"It looks like your handiwork," I say to Nan, examining the yellowing eyelet fabric strung on a tension rod.

"Joyce's sewing was dreadful. Couldn't even mend a seam. I hemmed all of John's pants."

"I'll wash the curtains tomorrow," I say. "I might be able to get them a bit brighter."

"You should—"

"Hang them in the sun, I know." Everything I know about caring for fabric and clothing is because of Nan. She can remove any stain, and she's a wonderful seamstress.

"Should we start a puzzle?" I ask after I've cleaned up. We spent many nights puzzling here after the twins went to bed.

Nan's standing at the bookshelf, holding a glass jar of matchbooks.

"What's that?"

Her smile is sad. "Memories."

I cross the room, and she passes it to me. I fish a matchbook out. It's navy and silver, with the name of a restaurant I don't recognize on the front flap and a Toronto address written on the back.

"They collected these to light the fire?" I guess.

"No. It was a game your grandpa and John used to play. They'd hide a matchbook every time they visited each other. These are the ones your grandpa hid here. There's probably some still squirreled away."

That sounds safe. I narrow my eyes and look around the room. The rafters would be a good hiding spot. There must be a ladder somewhere.

"Alice," Nan says, and I turn my attention back to her. "You don't need to hunt out the matches. We'll be fine."

I set the jar back on the shelf, deciding not to agree with that.

Nan stares at it for a moment longer, at the decades of friendship contained within it. It must be hard for her—coming here after all this time, without Grandpa, without Joyce.

"You're going to have a great summer, Nan. I'll make sure of it." I've found a choir she can join. There's a regular euchre night at one of the churches.

"I know you will." She pats my shoulder. "I want you to have a great summer, too. Let your hair down. Do something stupid. Do something *selfish*."

"I'm spending two months on a lake with no plans except to hang out with my dear grandmother. How much more selfish can I be?"

"You've invited your niece for a week to give your sister a break," she says.

My brows furrow. "So?"

"And you're paying for Luca and Lavinia's car rental when they visit for your birthday."

"I haven't spent much time with the twins this year," I say. "I don't want it to be a hassle for them to come." I'm not sure they would unless I covered the cost. Financial responsibility eludes them. I'm pretty sure our dad still pays their rent. Not that I'm complaining—he helped me with the down payment on my condo.

"You've booked me in for my hair appointments," Nan says.

"Every Monday."

"And you've found a physiotherapist in town."

"She comes highly recommended. And I've got the newspaper delivery set up so you can do your crossword." Nan says it keeps her brain sharp, but she's addicted to the satisfaction of completing it, which she never fails to do. Her brain needs no sharpening.

"You've been very considerate of my needs, and I'm thankful. But I don't want you playing nurse to me all day. What are you going to do for yourself?"

"I have some editing work to do."

"That's not what I mean."

"I'm going to relax."

"And what does that look like?"

"Well . . ." I pause. "I'll read, swim, take some photos." I say it like it's a question.

"And what else?"

I shift my weight. Now that I'm here, the thought of filling an entire summer of empty days seems daunting. When was the last time I didn't have a schedule? "Does there have to be more?"

She smiles. "I don't know. You tell me."

Nan loves to keep busy. She golfs, sings in multiple choirs, makes butter tarts and peach jam for church fundraisers. When Heather and I stayed with her as kids, she kept our hands and minds occupied, too. She taught us how to weed the flower beds and water the hanging baskets. We decorated cakes, cross-stitched birds and butterflies on scraps of fabric. We learned how to sew simple cloth bags and knit hats for the twins. I loved it all, but Heather was easily frustrated. She claims she doesn't have a single artistic bone in her body, but it's not true. The way she structures an argument is its own kind of poetry.

"You know," I say as Nan settles into her armchair, "I haven't sewn anything in ages."

She holds up arthritic fingers. "That makes two of us. I miss it. Remember your graduation dress?"

"Of course." It was midnight blue with a ribbon at the nape of the neck that cascaded to my waist. "Maybe we should do another collaboration this summer. Your expertise and my hands." A project to keep us busy.

Nan smiles. "Do you have something in mind?"

"We should start with something easy." I mull. "We could make new curtains for the kitchen?"

Her eyes spark, and I feel warm from the inside out.

"Curtains, yes," she says, surveying the space. "This whole place has become a little weary, hasn't it?"

"It's . . . rustic." The furniture has seen better days, but I don't mind. John's cottage is cozy, lived in. The antithesis of my apartment.

"We could freshen it up," Nan says. "It wouldn't take much. Curtains. Pillowcases. A new tablecloth." She looks at the rafters. "What do you think, Joyce?" Nan does this sometimes— talks to dead people, my grandfather usually. Her eyes return to me, decisive. "We'll need a sewing machine."

"Done," I say, though I have no idea whether I can get one in town, or whether online retailers would ship here. We're kind of in the middle of nowhere.

"And fabric," Nan adds. "Stedmans used to have a good selection. We'll start there."

"Do you think John will mind? Maybe I should ask first?"

Nan scoffs. "John wouldn't notice if we painted the walls hot pink."

I laugh. Grandpa was like that, too. "So, what do you think? Should we start in on a puzzle?"

"I don't feel like I have it in me tonight." She yawns. "It's been a long day. I might just head to bed and read."

I move her walker into place and kiss her on the cheek.

"Sweet dreams, Alice," she says. "And remember . . ."

I smile. Because until this moment, I'd forgotten how every day ended the summer I was seventeen.

"Good things happen at the lake," I finish.

She nods once. "Good things happen at the lake."

Even with the windows thrown open, the cottage is still sweltering, so I take Nan's words of wisdom literally and put on my striped one-piece and a white cotton caftan. It has pretty blue embroidery at the neck that matches my bathing suit. I bought it not knowing how I'd spend my summer but sure that this dress would be involved.

I pour sparkling water over ice and wander through the screened porch and out onto the deck, where an ancient-looking triangle dinner bell hangs next to the door. I'd forgotten about it, but as I run my fingers over the metal, I have a flashback of Luca standing on a stool and whaling on it until Nan told him to cut it out.

The deck is a wooden platform that rests on a rocky ledge over the water—a prime perch for admiring the view. It's even more beautiful than I remembered. Open water stretches for more than a mile straight ahead, with the green hills of the western and eastern shores on either side. The sky is an endless swirling canvas of lavender and rose against dusky blue, reflected on the lake's flat surface.

Stairs run from the upper deck down to the dock, which travels out from the rocky shoreline. An aluminum boat with three benches and a small motor is tied to one side. I think I can remember how to drive it. Nan made me get a boating license before we came when I was a teenager—not that I've used it since then. There's a short sandy strip of beach, and the boat-house sits beyond. It has a stone base, a second-floor loft, and a small deck over the water. I set my towel and caftan on the back of a red Muskoka chair and sit at the end of the dock, my feet dangling in the water.

Not sure how deep it is, I slide in rather than jump. It's like slipping into the sunset. Here I am, days away from my thirty-third birthday, in the same spot where I swam as a teenager, when my eyes began to open to the vastness of the world beyond my own.

"Go explore," Nan told me when she gave me the camera sixteen years ago.

And I did. I photographed every angle of this shoreline. I tromped through the bush and documented birds and bugs, mushrooms and moss. I snapped pale green lichens clinging to rocks and the wildflowers that grew along the contours of the driveway. Columbines and lilies and asters. I'd pick bunches of them for Nan, and she'd arrange them in a striped ceramic milk jug. I shot that, too.

I haven't stopped exploring. My camera has been my pass-port, my permission slip to see new places and meet new people, safe behind my lens.

I float on my back, arms spread, and stare at the dimming

sky, the deepening purple and red. I'm not sure when I start crying, only that I'm overwhelmed with how big the galaxy is and how insignificant I am.

Six months ago, I thought I had it figured out. Work, boyfriend, condo: all sorted. And then Trevor dumped me, and I spiraled. I didn't understand what I'd done wrong when I tried so hard to do everything right. I took on one job after another, needing some sense of control. When, two months after our breakup, he told me he'd met someone else, that they were getting married, I signed on to even more work. Headshots. Weddings. Creative work for car companies and banks. Before Nan's fall, I hadn't had a day off in nine weeks.

It's been the busiest season of my career, but far from the most fulfilling. I've built my reputation on giving clients exactly what they want—my collaborators trust me to get the job done without headaches. I told myself if I worked hard enough, I'd reach the end of the rainbow and be rewarded with a windfall of artistic freedom. But the rainbow never ends. I'm stuck.

After my swim, I wrap myself in a towel and fold into the Muskoka chair, breathing in the sweet evening air and attempting to forget about my Toronto problems. I scan the cottages around the bay. There's a big white house on top of a hill with a Jet Ski resting on a lift and a floating raft. Next to it, a small A-frame. They're probably less than two hundred meters away, and both are familiar. It's where the teenagers from my photo dived and swam and hung out for hours. I can picture them jumping into the water. Laughing. Flirting. Arguing. I envied them. Unburdened. Free. *Happy*.

A few minutes pass before two kids appear on the dock of the A-frame. As they cannonball into the water, one after the other, I feel like I've slid back in time, watching a reel from my past play before my eyes.

The unmistakable taunting of siblings travels across the water. They're younger than the trio I spent my summer observing. They swim toward the floating raft at the white house next door and climb up the ladder. I laugh as the girl pushes the boy into the water. They clamber back onto the raft and begin a game of who can jump the farthest.

I relax into the chair, shutting my eyes as I listen to their happy squeals. I'm used to the din of the city. I grew up with the white noise of traffic and sirens as my bedtime lullaby. But I forgot how much I love the serenity of the lake. I breathe deeply, letting it fill my lungs.

I stay like that until the kids have dried off and gone inside, and there is nothing but the lapping of water and the laughter of adults from somewhere on the bay.

But then I hear it.

The motor is so loud it disrupts the tranquility even before it's in sight.

I straighten as a boat angles around the bay. I blink a few times, covering my mouth. Maybe I have fallen through time. Because the boat is yellow.

And it's coming straight for me.

6

It's zipping across the water, leaving a stripe of foaming white in its wake. My heart races as it gets closer. There's only one person inside, but all I can make out is that it's a man with light brown hair. As he passes the dock, he lifts his hand. It's the universal greeting on the lake, not because he knows me. I wave back and then jump at the sound of its horn.

Aaaah-whoooo-gaaaaah!

It's the most absurd sound, and I know it. I heard it dozens of times when I was seventeen.

The boat cuts across the bay and slows in front of the white house with the floating raft. The engine stops. The man ties it to the dock and climbs out, but it's too dim to tell if he's one of the boys from my photo. I lose his shape as he heads up the hill. If it were morning, when the sun hits the shore, I know I'd be able to see him more clearly. I remember how that house glowed like a beacon in the early hours of the day.

I stay there for a moment, and then I dart up to the cottage two steps at a time. I fling my towel over the clothesline that's strung between two white pines, throw on my caftan, and race inside.

I'm not sure why I packed the photo except that I wanted it with me. I find it tucked in the pages of my notebook.

And there it is—the same boat, sixteen summers ago, when three teens formed its crew. It's not just the shade of yellow that makes it distinctive. It's old—it would have been vintage even when I took the photo—with brown vinyl seats and a bow curved like a duck bill.

I stare at the three passengers, the sun glowing on their cheeks and shoulders. The girl faces the wind, one hand in her wet hair, trying to hold it out of her face. There's a towel around her torso, gold bathing suit straps peeking out of the top.

The younger of the boys is cute, gangly in the way of quick-growing adolescents. He wears a T-shirt and is staring at the girl like no one else in the world exists. I spent enough time watching them to know the older boy is his brother. He's gorgeous and tan and is looking at his sibling with a happy, satisfied smirk. I liked to imagine having a boyfriend like him.

It was a fluke I got the shot. An unlikely combination of luck and timing. I'd been shooting Luca and Lavinia as they played in the water. I'd heard the motor and looked up through my lens just as they zoomed by.

I immediately checked the camera screen to see what I'd captured. As soon as I saw the photo, I was hit with a sense of purpose I'd never experienced before. I was meant to be a photographer.

I called it *One Golden Summer.*

It was the standout in my portfolio when I applied to my photography program. Elyse was one of my instructors, and years later, she told me it was the reason I'd been accepted—that it showed I had promise, an eye for emotion, a knack for drawing the viewer into an image. Maybe it's because I wanted to be in that boat with those kids so badly.

The eight weeks I spent in Barry's Bay were a turning point. I often felt invisible as a teenager, but behind a lens, invisibility became my superpower. With a camera, I discovered a place in the world where I thrived. I'm a better photographer now, but the way I shot back then, standing on the edge of the dock, had a purity I'll never recapture. I was doing something just for myself.

Maybe this summer could be a turning point, too.

I grab my laptop and lie stomach down on the bed, scrolling through the two versions of the swimsuit photos. I flick back and forth between the ones with the smoother thighs and stomachs, and the more honest version.

Sixteen years ago, I sat on this very bed, dreaming about being friends with the kids across the bay, hoping they'd notice me and say hello. I waited all summer for an invitation that never came. But I'm not seventeen anymore—I'm days away from my thirty-third birthday.

I think of how I've spent my entire career saying yes.

I think of all the beautiful, intelligent women in my life I've heard complain about everything from their thighs to their eyelashes.

I think of all the times in my life when I've stayed quiet because it was more comfortable than speaking up.

And I do something new.

I submit the photos I like.

After the email *swoosh*es away, I jump off the bed and head to the kitchen, bringing the yellow boat photo with me. I tack it to the fridge next to Charlie's note.

It's a reminder of where it all started. No editing. No artificial lighting. No compromises. One moment of joy, captured for all time.

My eyes drift to Charlie's letter. I pull it from its LIVE,

LAUGH, LAKE magnet and read it for the fourth time today, stymied by his self-satisfaction, his extreme thoughtfulness, and the last bullet point on his list.

How impressed are you right now? Text me a picture of your face.

I feel like I've been thrown into a game I don't know the rules to. Is he *flirting* via to-do list? He sounded roughly my age on the phone, and cocky. Does he want my photo, or is he joking? I know there's a breezy, quippy middle ground between *purely platonic* and the *melding of souls*, but it's not familiar turf. I'm a soul melder through and through. I've never been good at flirting—and I've *never* gone for cocky.

As I pin the note back on the fridge, I catch my reflection in the window. I've let my hair air-dry after the swim, and now it's a cacophony, tumbling over my shoulders in an outrageous collection of swirls and curves and bends. I wear it straight so often that I barely recognize the woman who stares back at me in the glass. It's not that all this unruly auburn is unattractive—it just doesn't feel like me. I'm a homebody at heart, a classic Cancer. But my hair is fire, sucking up attention like oxygen.

Maybe it's because I'm still energized from filing the photos to Willa that I take out my phone and do something I never do. I lift my chin to the light, stick out my tongue, and snap a selfie. I send it to Charlie. A minute later, I swear I hear a deep laugh drifting across the lake on a warm breeze.

My phone lights with a text just as I've lain down in bed.

Charlie: I assume you found the keys.

Me: And a family of raccoons.

Charlie: I was expecting a thank you for my hard work and kindness.

Me: Thank you.

Charlie: Say it like you mean it.

Me: Are you always this infuriating?

Charlie: No.

Charlie: Usually I'm worse.

I fall asleep fighting back the smile pulling on my lips.

7

have the nightmare again. I'm in the stairwell of my condo building, running up one flight, then another, heavy footsteps following me. When I finally reach the top, I find no door, only a black rotary telephone. I pick up the receiver and dial with shaking fingers, but I can never make my voice work.

I open my eyes to the sound of my ringtone, thinking I'm in Toronto. But then I track the water out the window, the green paint-chipped dresser, and the Algonquin Park poster on the wall. Groggy, I answer the phone.

"I can't run these, Alice," Willa says by way of greeting. I sit up, immediately awake. "I'm sorry to call you on the weekend. But I wanted to give you time to fix things. I appreciate what you're trying to do. It's noble."

"I'm not trying to be noble. The photos are exactly what was asked for originally."

"They're good," Willa says. "But too many lumps and bumps

will distract readers. This is supposed to be about the bathing suits."

"I don't think you're giving your readers enough credit."

"Trust me," Willa says. "I'm only asking for a little bit of polishing and a few nips and tucks."

"Nips and tucks?" Suddenly I feel sick. Nips and tucks were *never* part of the conversation.

"I'll show you what I mean. I've marked a few areas to slim down. Nothing major. We'll keep it tasteful. I'm sending the files to you now, okay?"

The email lands as soon as I hang up.

Willa has annotated the photos with red circles around various body parts and instructions.

Smooth, trim, erase.

I pinch my nose between my thumb and middle finger. I can't deal with this now.

"Is everything okay?" Nan asks, glancing up from her iPad when I shuffle out to the living room. She's always got a memoir on the go.

"Of course," I say, kissing her. "Everything's perfect." The last thing Nan needs to worry about is my professional angst. "Who are you reading about?"

"Ina Garten. It's called *Be Ready When the Luck Happens.*"

"A good motto for a photographer," I say.

I duck into the kitchen and see that Nan hasn't fixed herself anything. "Can I make you breakfast?"

"You might be able to fool someone else, but I know when you're hiding something," she calls to me.

"Just work stuff. Orange marmalade?"

"I'm thoroughly capable of making that myself," Nan says as I drop two slices of bread into the toaster.

"But you don't have to," I call back. "That's why I'm here."

"I hate being a bother," Nan says when I set a plate of toast in front of her.

"I know." I'm the same way. "But you're not a bother. I like helping. It makes me feel useful."

I return to the kitchen to make my own breakfast. I eat the same thing every morning: two eggs, scrambled; a slice of buttered multigrain toast; and one cup of coffee with steamed milk. "Speaking of which, I'm going to make a meal plan for the week. I'll go into town for groceries and see if I can find us a sewing machine. Any requests?"

"Scotch."

Technically, Nan can have a drink, but I don't want her to take another fall. "I'm not buying scotch."

"You're no fun," she says, but there's no bite in her tone.

"I'm a little fun." I think of the selfie I texted Charlie Florek last night.

In the light of day, I can't believe I sent it, and I can't deny the rush it gave me. But I'd rather sass Charlie behind the safety of a screen than meet him in real life. There's a chance he'll show up this morning with the end tables he promised to bring. *We'll be seeing a lot of each other this summer*, his letter said. So once Nan is settled in a patio chair on the deck with her crossword, I pull my hair up and escape to town.

I park beside a black Porsche at the grocery store and roll my eyes at such a blatant display of wealth in a working-class village of twelve hundred people. I'd bet my Pentax the owner is from the city. I scan the other shoppers, wondering whether I could pick out who's local and who's an out-of-towner. Bearded lumberjack dude in plaid, addressing the teenage boy refilling the green beans by first name: local. Blonde with the Tiffany bracelet interrupting to ask whether the store carries harissa paste: cottager. It strikes me that Charlie might know the lumberjack. He might *be* the lumberjack.

I'm choosing from the baskets of local strawberries when I spot a tall man with a head of short golden-brown hair. Even with his back to me, he's magnificent. My gaze travels over the colossal set of shoulders stretching his blue T-shirt, down to the red bathing suit on his bottom half. His calves are like slabs of concrete—thick and tan and toned. Bodies like this are meant to be rendered in white marble and displayed in a Florentine piazza. He picks up one basket of pickling cucumbers, examines it, and then exchanges it for another. I slide beside him, reaching for an English cucumber with a quiet "Excuse me."

The man jumps as if I've sprung out from behind a bush wearing a clown mask. I squawk, leaping back, and my elbow collides with the field tomatoes. I lose my grip on the cucumber as the tomatoes fall to the floor. *Plop, plop, plop.* I kneel, cleaning up my mess, and he crouches beside me to help. I catch a glimpse of big hands and bronzed forearms.

"Thank you," I say, glancing up to find myself confronted by a pair of pale green eyes and one of the most remarkable faces I've ever seen.

And that's saying something. I come across a lot of exceptional faces in my line of work—so many that I've become indifferent. It's not that I don't appreciate beauty. I do. But classic good looks don't excite me. I'm far more interested in the features we don't typically see on the screen and in advertising campaigns.

But *this* face.

I feel this face in my body. In the twitch of my hands, which desperately want a camera between them. I *need* to capture this face.

There's the odd color of his eyes. The way his eyebrows are tapered slashes across his forehead, a touch darker than the hair on his head. His lashes are fringes of feathered gold. He has a mouth made for kissing; his lips are full and pink and pouty. His jaw is squared off, befitting someone who headlines a superhero franchise and bench-presses small cars for sport.

It's not just that he's handsome—it's that nothing about him is too perfect. His nose is slightly crooked, as if it's been broken. Fine lines fan out from the corners of his eyes. He's sporting a day's worth of tawny stubble, like maybe he didn't get enough sleep last night. I think of twined limbs glowing in the moonlight. He looks like sex.

He's doing a similar inspection of me, a corner of his grin slowly lifting. My mouth has gone dry, my skin stovetop-hot, and I can't seem to pull my eyes from his. I chew on my lip. Maybe I could ask to photograph him . . .

But then he smiles, and the gods of summer must be smiling, too, because a matching set of dimples appears in his cheeks, startlingly boyish and sweet.

It slips past my lips before I can stop it: "Whoa."

His eyebrows lift.

I scurry to my feet, dropping the bruised tomatoes in my cart while more words continue to tumble from my mouth. They might be *thank you* and *tomatoes* and *bye*. Before he can say anything, I steer my cart toward the next aisle with the speed of a NASCAR driver, cucumber abandoned, just as awkward as I was at seventeen.

8

As Nan watches me unbox the sewing machine I bought at the hardware store, I tell her about my horrifying run-in by the cucumbers. The Nan I know would have tears of mirth falling from her eyes. But she only shakes her head, the barest hint of amusement on her lips.

"Should we go into town later and hunt for fabric?" I ask, hoping to perk her up, but she turns me down.

"Tomorrow. I'm still feeling a little slow today. I think I'll take a nap after lunch."

"You're going to have to be a patient teacher. I haven't sewn since high school."

I loved using Nan's Singer. There was one pattern I made over and over, a 1980s Laura Ashley dress I found in Nan's stockpile, with overall-like straps, roomy square pockets, and very little shape. I wore it with blouses and plaid shirts underneath. I thought it looked romantic. But by the time I entered my senior year of high school, I'd become aware of how the DIY dresses made me stand out. I overheard a classmate calling me a freak and switched to jeans and T-shirts the following day. I still dress to go unnoticed.

"You'll pick it right back up," Nan says. "It's like riding a bicycle."

I cut her a look, and she wrinkles her nose. I was never any good at riding bicycles.

"Well?" I stand up, evaluating the makeshift workstation I've set up on a card table by the windows.

"That'll do," Nan says. "You know, Joyce always thought it looked like too much of a hunt camp in here." She gestures to the paper cutouts of fish that hang over the windows, the year and species of the catch written in lead pencil. *Lake trout, '84. Bass, '03. Pike, '91.*

"I think they're kind of cool." Cottage history, as told by fishing trips.

"I don't mind them, either." She points to one. "I caught that pickerel. Joyce wanted to paint the walls white, brighten everything up, but John wouldn't hear of covering up the wood."

And *everything* is wood. Floors, walls, ceilings, kitchen cupboards, furniture. A rainbow of brown. The only touches of femininity are the Harlequins and the floral armchair. Nan sees me eyeing it.

"That was Joyce's spot."

"Maybe we do florals," I say, thinking aloud. "Make it more like Joyce."

Her eyes flicker. "Sounds like a plan."

When Nan lies down on the screened porch sofa, I change into my bathing suit and caftan and grab a wide-brimmed straw hat. I burn like birch bark, going from pale and freckled to red and freckled, with no stop at tan in between. I pack a canvas tote with sunscreen, a snack, my notebook, and my old Pentax.

In my final year of university, a group of students organized an exhibition of our work in an empty storefront in the West End. We thought we had talent. Knew it, really. My best friend, Oz, swiped our prof's overstuffed Rolodex—an antiquated object even then, its position on his desk an obvious brag—and sent an email to every gallerist, buyer, collector, and journalist in the thing. I sold my first piece, a print of *One Golden Summer*, to an art buyer for one of the big banks whose CEO came from generations of cottagers. I spent the hundred dollars on a vintage Pentax K1000 after Oz talked the seller down by twenty-five bucks.

Now the image hangs somewhere in an office tower downtown, and Oz and I don't speak.

But I still have the camera. I still love it. The thing is built like a tank, almost indestructible—even the light meter still works. I mostly shoot digital, but I love film, love the nostalgia it imbues, the intimacy. The feel of this camera in my hands, the curves of its body, is more familiar to me than any man. It's seen me through my final year of university, through boyfriends and breakthroughs and breakups. It's seen me grow up.

"Don't rush home," Nan tells me, lifting her head off the pillow as I'm leaving. "I'll be fine on my own."

"Call me if you need anything, and I'll come back as soon as I can."

She waves a hand, shooing me away.

I fetch a red life jacket from a hook inside the boathouse. There are two empty slips inside, and a wooden staircase that leads to the room over the top. It's been a long time since I've driven a boat like this, but starting it is easier than I thought. With two mighty tugs on the cord, it chortles to life. I twist the handle, and with a jolt, I'm off. Nervous, I do a few practice loops in front of the cottage. My steering is jerky at first, the throttle a little touchy, but soon I'm gliding across the water, a broad smile on my face.

I zoom past the big white house with the yellow boat, but there's no action outside. The kids at the cottage next door are swimming. I head south, around one bend and another, past a woman and a small dog on a paddleboard, past a cottage with a small seaplane, past water trampolines and dock slides and a man floating on an inflated moose, a beer in one hand, living his best life. He waves, and I wave back. This, I decide, is my ideal form of socializing.

Networking is crucial in my profession, where survival comes down to relationships. Cocktail parties and opening night receptions. Show my face. Stay relevant. Manage more sophisticated small talk than a singular *whoa*. I flat iron my hair, pull it into a low ponytail, put on something black and chic. Minimal makeup, except for red lips and nails. I usually wear contacts, but I'll opt for my tortoiseshell glasses. It's a brand. A stylish, tasteful suit of armor. I get nervous before events, and I have to fake smile my way through a lot of small talk. I can't stand the posturing—the subtle (and not-so-subtle) ways people signal their success or attempt to interrogate mine. The armor helps.

Slowing down, I navigate around a small island across from a cliff in a narrow neck of the lake. If my memory can be trusted, this is the spot where Nan took us to jump into the water. Luca and Lavinia scurried up with a couple of older kids, and they dropped off the edge like two tin soldiers. I wanted to do it, too, but I chickened out.

We picnicked on the island that day, but now it's tricky to find a place to tie the boat. I hop out into the shallows and guide it toward a stump that I can loop the rope around. There's a fire pit and a couple of empty beer cans that I'll gather up before I leave, and a rock under the shade of poplars that I spread my towel on.

I bite into an apple as a pair of Jet Skis stop in front of the cliff, two people riding on each. They drop anchors, strip off their life jackets, jump into the water, and swim to shore. I can tell from their voices that they're in that in-between stage, not kids anymore but not quite adults, either. Seventeen or eighteen, maybe. Two boys, two girls. They climb to the top and throw themselves over the edge, laughing when their heads bob back up.

I watch them do it again and again, climbing and then jumping, one after another, with a pang in my chest. It's sadder than longing, softer than envy.

I think about the girl I was at seventeen. Untamed hair. Baggy dresses that swallowed me up. Painfully shy.

It didn't help that I had a bombshell of an older sister. Heather and I shared a room, and I'd study her as she zipped herself into clothes that showed off her curves, applied glitter to her eyelids, and slicked on lip gloss that made her mouth shine like vinyl. She was so much more *adult* than me. She was having sex. Teenage Alice had never been kissed. I couldn't even manage a smile in my crush's direction. When I discovered Joyce's stash of Harlequins at the cottage, I read the naughty bits over and over. But it was the fantasy of being irresistible that hooked me.

Back then, I felt like I could disappear and no one would notice. Not my dad, who was in the early days of starting his own firm and rarely at home. Or my mom, who was left to handle the chaos on her own. She'd fly around the house, arguing with Heather about the length of her skirts, stopping the twins from pummeling each other. Some nights she made three dinners— one for the twins, another for Heather and me, and something special for her and Dad. She called me her "good girl" and always passed me with a quick kiss on the head. But I missed her, even when we were in the same room. I miss her even more now.

It wasn't until university, when I met Oz and a group of arty, weird, and ambitious photography students, that I felt like I belonged.

Now, one of the girls on the cliff notices me and shouts, "Hello," and I wave back.

"Wanna come hang out?" she yells over.

I laugh, though it's tempting. Teenage me would have been thrilled at the invitation.

"Thanks," I call back. "But I'm good."

And then it strikes me with an electric-bright bolt of clarity.

I'm almost thirty-three, and I *still* don't have my life figured out. I'm standing in the ashes of a four-year relationship that I poured my heart into, and my love of photography is slipping under a torrent of deadlines and compromises. But I don't have to reckon with any of that here. It will all be waiting for me in September. I think about what Nan asked me yesterday—about what I was going to do with my summer, and how I didn't have much of an answer. But I know exactly how I'd spend it if I were seventeen again.

The kids jump three more times before climbing back on the Jet Skis and taking off. The wakes crash against the shore, and then it's quiet.

I stare at the cliff. The thought of jumping off it makes my stomach plunge, but it's not *that* high. I could do it. I could do more than that.

I pull out my notebook, thinking of all the things, big and little and silly and *fun*, I would do if I were seventeen. I think of the photo hanging on the fridge at the cottage, the three kids I watched with awe. The boys, who somersaulted off the raft and went wakeboarding and waterskiing. The girl, who wore a gold bikini and swam across the lake. I think of how cool Heather was, how bold she's always been. Chewing on my bottom lip, I turn to a blank page and write.

1. *Jump off the rock*

2. *Wear a skimpy bathing suit*

3. *Read a smutty book*

4. *Throw myself a birthday party*

5. *Kiss a cute guy*

6. *Take one good photo*

7. *But also make a bunch of bad art*

8. *Learn how to do a backflip off the dock??? Front flip? A more elegant dive?*

9. *Take up a water sport. Paddle boarding? Wakeboarding? Waterskiing?*

10. *Go skinny-dipping*

11. *Make a new friend*

12. *Do something reckless*

13. *Ride a Jet Ski*

14. *Glittery makeup like Heather used to wear*

15. *Put on the green dress*

16. *Low-key drugs???*

17. *Sleep under the stars*

I'm laughing by the time I finish. It's probably the most embarrassing bucket list ever penned, and I doubt I'll accomplish half of it before the end of August. But it also feels radical—two months of adolescent freedom. And I know where to start. Luca and Lavinia are visiting for my birthday, and the twins love a party.

I spend another hour on the island, shooting a roll of film then taking a swim, before I pack my things and untie the boat. It's a short ride back to the cottage and my bathing suit is wet, so I throw my caftan at my feet and my hat on my head. I start the motor and pull away from shore, mindful of the fallen tree trunks and rocks beneath the surface.

And then I see a burst of yellow.

I'm so startled that I turn the throttle without looking where I'm going. There's an earsplitting scrape of metal, and I'm flung forward. My elbows hit the middle bench, my knees the floor.

Groaning, I slowly pick myself up and peer over the side. There's a rock just under the surface, and I'm stuck on it. I'm shipwrecked.

I hear the whir of another boat pulling alongside mine. The engine cuts.

"That was interesting," a wry voice says.

I push my hat off my face and find a familiar yellow speedboat floating a few feet away. In it is a man with celery-green eyes.

"It's you," he says, mouth arching. His dimples wink. "Whoa."

9

D o you need help?"
    I hear the words, but I must be in shock because all I
can do is stare. The man from the grocery store is here, shirtless,
in the yellow boat from my picture.

His body is absurd. It's big and broad yet tight and toned, and
it fills six feet of space better than any other body.

"Are you okay?" he asks.

I wrestle my attention back to his face, wondering if he's one
of the boys in the photo. That fierce jaw, those full lips, the upper one bowed and sweet—at odds with the mischievous grin
tugging at its corners. His strange green eyes are even brighter in
the sun. I blink before I get lost in them.

"I'm fine." I twist my arms around. Bruises bloom on both
elbows. Between the scrapes on my legs and this, I'm a disaster.
"Just a little banged up."

He leans over the side of his boat, inspecting the damage on
mine. "I think you'll be all right. You should be able to use an oar
to push off the rock." He meets my gaze, eyes shimmering like
this is all very funny.

I pick up one of the wooden oars with the confidence of

someone who knows what she's doing. But it's heavier than it looks, and I lose my grip, almost dropping it into the lake.

"I can help if you want," I hear him say as if smothering his laughter.

"No need."

Gripping the oar tight, I push against the rock and end up stumbling back a step. I hear a low whistle. I put all my strength into the next push and move the boat precisely nowhere.

"You sure I can't give you a shove?"

I glance over my shoulder. The man's pretty mouth is curved into a lazy grin, arms crossed over his superb chest. My gaze falls to the hard ridges of his stomach, to the waistband of his red bathing suit.

A laugh, and then: "Eyes up."

I immediately turn as scarlet as a rose on February 14.

His eyes wander to the flaming mass of hair tumbling out from under my hat. "That's okay, Red," he says. "I was checking you out, too."

I *hate* when people call me Red, though I never say anything about it. But there's something about the way he's looking at me, so smug and amused, that has me snapping back.

"Do. Not. Call. Me. That." I push and push with every muscle in my body. Nothing.

"I'd be happy to give you a hand," he purrs.

"You can keep your hands to yourself," I bite out, and then with one final push, the boat slides off the rock.

He claps slowly. "Well done, Red."

"Are you serious?" I glare at him from beneath the brim of my hat.

"Not usually."

Not usually.

I've heard those words before. I blink at him.

"Charlie?"

Dimples firing, he taps his temple with two fingers. "At your service, Alice Everly."

My cheeks heat at the way he says my name. The *Alice* is as smooth as melted butter, but *Everly* sounds like it's being scraped over his tongue.

"How do you know who I am?" I ask.

"You sent me your photo, remember? And that's John Kalinski's skiff you just crashed."

I wince.

"You're having quite the day," he says. "Destroying produce displays and crashing boats. Do you always wreak such havoc?"

"Hardly."

"I don't know," he says, his smile teasing. "You seem like trouble. I think I'll have to be careful when I'm around you."

"Don't worry," I tell him. "There's no need to be around me at all."

I give him a close-lipped smile that we both know means, *Now please leave.*

He lifts his brows in response.

With an eye roll, I sit on the bench and give the engine cord a tug, but the motor doesn't start. I give it another yank, and still nothing.

"I'd be happy to assist you." He doesn't add *City Girl*, but I can hear it.

"No, I'm good," I reply through clenched teeth. Of all the people on the lake to come to my aid, it had to be him. I pull the cord again. And again. And again.

"You might want to wait," he says. "Or else you'll—"

I try once more, and the engine falls silent. The smell of gasoline drenches the air.

I look at Charlie.

"Or else you'll flood the motor."

"You'll need to wait about twenty minutes before you can give it another go," Charlie informs me with a highly satisfied smile.

"You don't have to look so happy about this."

"Why not? Now I can give you a ride home." He winks. "It's not every day I get to stage a rescue."

I snort. "I'll wait it out, thanks. It's a gorgeous afternoon."

He studies me for a second, his gaze so direct I almost look away. When he speaks, all the teasing has vanished from his voice. "You can trust me to take you back to your cottage, Alice. Let me get the rope so I can give you a tow. Looks like you've had enough sun."

I follow his eyeline to my reddened skin. He's right. I'll need to slather myself with aloe vera later.

"All right." I acquiesce.

With abundant inelegance, I manage to row my boat next to Charlie's. As he tethers the vessels together with a length of nylon rope, my eyes journey down his biceps and sculpted forearms to his massive hands. He grins again when he sees me staring.

And then reaches for me.

"What are you doing?"

His smile cracks like lightning. "Lifting you on board."

In a flash, Charlie hooks his hands under my armpits and, without so much as a grunt, has me in the air. I reach for his shoulders with a yelp as he sets me on my feet. His skin is warm under my hands. I'm so close the brim of my straw hat touches his chest. He smells like sun and soap and something expensive and plantlike that I can't identify. I tilt my chin, and for a second, we both stare. Charlie looks down between us, to where my palms rest flat against his chest, and I take a sudden step back, dropping onto a seat.

Charlie chuckles. "Are you always clumsy?"

"Not really."

"Must be me, then."

I roll my eyes, and his smile broadens. "Don't worry, Alice. I have this effect on people."

He reaches over me, picking up a striped towel from the floor at my feet. His knuckles brush innocently over my calf, and I resist a shiver. He hands me the towel. "Throw this over your shoulders. You probably burn if you so much as look at the sun."

"I burn if I consider the possibility of going outside," I tell him, and his dimples appear.

Charlie starts the engine, and on the way back to the cottage, he points out a sandy bit of crown land that's nice for picnics. He drives with one hand on the wheel, like the boat is an extension of his body, knees turned to me, paying attention to the water as much as he does me.

"So you're here with your grandmother for the summer. Will you have any guests joining you?"

I look at him from the corner of my eye.

"Boyfriend? Girlfriend? Husband? Wife? Partner?"

"Subtle," I tell him.

"Not my forte." When I don't respond, he asks, "Maybe a distant cousin on your mother's side?"

"The wedding's next Saturday," I say, deadpan.

Charlie looks at me strangely. His dimples are in place, but something shifts in his eyes. "You're funny."

"I'm not really." I don't think anyone has accused me of being funny before.

"I disagree."

"Believe me," I tell him. "I'm the kind of person who, when I tell a joke, someone will say, 'That's funny,' but they don't actually laugh."

"You *are* funny." He says it like it's a revelation.

"And yet you still didn't laugh."

At that, he chuckles. The sound is deeper than the engine's rumble. It settles low in my belly, a feeling I quickly dismiss.

"So we've established that you're funny," he says.

I shrug.

"And single?" Charlie winks.

"Single. No boyfriend, girlfriend, husband, wife, partner, or questionable relationship with a distant cousin on my mother's side."

"It's the cousin on your dad's side I need to be concerned about, right?"

Before I can stop myself, I bark out a singular "Ha!"

Charlie grins like he's won a round, and the expression zings through me. I've seen the same smirk, on the same face, only it was sixteen years younger.

The realization knocks me over like a tidal wave. Charlie is the older brother from my photo, the one I wove elaborate fantasies about. My mouth falls open in slow motion, and I snap it shut before he sees me gaping. I flash several degrees hotter, suddenly nervous, suddenly seventeen.

"A summer with just you and your grandmother," Charlie says, jerking me back to the present. "That's unusual."

I blink at him, finding it difficult to get words past my lips, before coming up with, "Is it?"

"I'd say so."

I take a deep breath, pulling myself together. "We're close. The least I could do was get her out of her house."

Charlie's gaze travels my face; his brows are pulled together slightly. "That doesn't seem like the least you could do."

I hum, not fully agreeing. "She's family. I did what anyone would."

"I doubt that." His eyes find mine, piercing as lasers, as if he can see deep inside. It's unsettling. "I bet you're not like anyone else, Alice Everly."

10

I find myself studying Charlie as we pull up to the dock, trying to figure him out. Arrogant, definitely. Unpredictable, too. A loose cannon. The kind of guy I normally avoid. The Everly clan has ego, attitude, and drama aplenty. I don't need it elsewhere, especially not from men. Security. Safety. Comfort. It's what I *thought* I had with Trevor.

"How's your grandmother settling in?" Charlie asks.

"Okay, I think."

He waits for her to continue.

"She's more tired than usual after her surgery, but she's healthy. Her doctor says she's recovering well. I'm hoping being here will lift her spirits."

"Let me know if you need anything else. I'm happy to help."

I frown. "Why?"

Green eyes sparkle back. "Why not?"

"You don't know us."

"Let's just say I owe the universe a few good deeds." He raises an eyebrow. "And now you owe me."

I'm not sure if he means to be suggestive or if it's because his voice sounds like foreplay, but I find myself growing pink. "Is that so?"

Charlie cuts the engine, secures the back of the boat, and hops out to tie the front. When he's done, he stands over me, extending his palm. "Big-time."

I take his hand and climb out of the boat. But he doesn't let go. Goose bumps rise on my arms.

"Safely ashore," Charlie says.

"My hero."

My gaze lingers on the slash of his jaw and the stubble that covers it, before falling to the base of his tan throat. Here I am with the boy from my photo. Only he's all grown up. And so am I. My pulse quickens against my wrists.

Charlie tilts toward me with a wolfish grin. "Are you *blushing?*"

"It's sunburn." I let go of his hand and step back.

A delighted bellow bursts from his chest. "You tell yourself that, Red."

And there it is. *Red.* The reality check is impeccably timed.

I let out a growl, growing an even a deeper shade of crimson.

"I told you not to call me that," I snap.

"You're cute when you're mad." Charlie reaches out, flicking the brim of my hat.

I stare at him, stunned. "What's wrong with you?"

"Far too many things to list." He's smiling—impervious to my irritation or simply enjoying it. "I'll let you discover that for yourself another day. How about I take you around the lake? Point out the spots you need to be careful of."

"That's really not necessary."

He glances at John's boat. "I think it might be. Besides, we're neighbors. I'm just right over there." He points to the big white house across the bay, the place that once beckoned to me in the early morning sun.

"I think I'll pass."

"But why?" His forehead scrunches. I doubt he's been turned down once in his entire life.

"It's nothing personal. You're just not my type."

He puts a hand on his chest, as if offended. "I'm everyone's type."

I can't help it. I laugh. Loudly. This guy is *something*. Charlie blinks at the sound. Admittedly, I have a bloodcurdling laugh. Heather calls it my witch cackle.

"You know, some people consider boasting distasteful," I say.

"Nah." His eyes flash with mischief. "Not you, Alice Everly. You like it."

His voice is deep and rough. Somehow, he makes my name sound illicit. I imagine him whispering against my skin.

Alice Everly. Alice Everly. Alice Everly.

Nope. No. Not happening. I square my shoulders. "You have no idea what I like."

He smirks. "I think I have a pretty good idea. Let's not forget how we met," he says with a wistful sigh. "I remember it like it was only this morning. You, me, the cucumbers . . ." He leans close and whispers, "*Whoa.*"

He's teasing, but he's so ridiculous I'm not embarrassed. He's right; I don't mind it. If anything, I might like it. I'm not sure I've met such an unapologetic flirt before. But we have a whole summer ahead of us, and I've got to put a stop to it.

"You have a great face," I tell him.

He cocks his head. "Thank you, Alice."

"But there's an almost infinite number of great faces in this world, and I've seen *a lot* of them."

"Oh?"

"I'm a photographer. Faces are kind of my thing. And to be fair, yours is . . ." I squint into the sun, considering my word choice. "Remarkable," I say, looking at Charlie again. "You're handsome, obviously. You know that. The shade of your eyes: It's rare. You know that, too."

He squints at me. "Why doesn't that sound like a compliment?"

"It *is* a compliment," I tell him. "The first thing I thought when I saw you this morning at the store was that I wanted to photograph you. There's a kind of lived-in quality to your features that makes you interesting to look at."

Charlie is completely still. Aside from his throat moving with a single swallow, he's turned to stone.

"You have the perfect imperfect face. Hence the *whoa*." I tip my chin up, gathering strength. "But it's just a nice face. It's literally the last thing that would make someone attractive to me."

At first all Charlie does is stare, but then he grins. "Message received. Alice Everly: not into faces."

He moves past me and steps onto the end of his boat so he can haul in John's skiff. I watch the muscles in his back shift as he pulls on the rope. Charlie glances over his shoulder, catching me mid-ogle. Busted.

"More of an ass woman, then?" His smile is a brilliant display of straight white teeth and dimples.

I know I'm as purple as a beet, but something about him, his lack of modesty, makes me feel emboldened. "I was checking out your shoulders." My eyes drop to his backside. "But your ass is okay."

Charlie tuts. "It's exceptional."

I battle the smile that wants to bend my lips. Trevor was *nothing* like this. He was sincere, earnest to the point of being businesslike, but I always knew where we stood. Trevor was solid ground; Charlie is a sheet of thin ice. So it's bizarre how not awkward I feel with him. We're *sparring*, and it's *easy*. I'm not sure what he's going to say, and while it's slippery new terrain, it feels like I know how to skate across it.

"I'm not sure what to make of you," Charlie says as he kneels, tying John's boat.

"You don't have to make anything of me."

"I think I do," he says. "It's kind of *my* thing."

He reaches for my caftan and beach bag and sets them on the dock. I spot my notebook on the floor of the boat at the same time he does. It's exactly as I left it, folded open to the page with my bucket list.

"I can get that," I rush out. But it's too late—Charlie's climbing in to retrieve it.

"Allow me," he says. "Since I can't win you over with my *remarkable* face." He shoots me a pointed glance before picking up the notebook.

Please don't look. Please don't look. Please don't look.

He looks.

"What is this?" Charlie's brows ascend toward space. His gaze flicks to mine. His lip twitches.

"Just give it to me."

Charlie holds it out, and I lunge so quickly I almost fall into the water. He steadies me by the arm, smiling.

"Not a word."

He lifts his hands. "I didn't say a thing."

Charlie steps onto the dock just as I hear Nan's voice. "Alice, are you going to introduce me to your friend?"

I stare at the deck, where she stands with her walker.

"He's not my friend," I call back.

"Rude," Charlie says.

"Bring him up for tea."

Charlie turns to me, grinning. "Bring me up for tea, Alice."

11

A re you collecting handsome men today?" Nan asks when Charlie and I arrive at the top of the stairs.

"Just the one," I tell her. "Nan, this is Charlie Florek. He's looking after the property for John."

"Our spirited letter writer and handyman?"

"The very same."

Her smile blooms as she pieces it together. "And the gentleman from the grocery store this morning?"

"Yup."

Charlie folds his arms across his chest, smug. "She told you about me, huh?"

Nan's smile is wider than I've seen it since we arrived, encompassing every inch of her face—her lips, the skin around her mouth, the creases around her eyes.

"Nanette Everly." She sticks out her hand, and Charlie envelops it with his palm. "But everyone calls me Nan. Thank you so much for everything you've done around the cottage. I'm sure Alice has told you how grateful we are."

His eyes skate to me. "Actually, she left that part out."

"You're so dashing she must have forgotten herself."

"Now that you mention it, she did seem a bit flustered."

I meet his shimmering gaze with daggers.

"Make yourself comfortable, Charlie," she says. "And I'll fix us tea."

"I can do it, Nan."

"Nonsense."

"Please." I feel Charlie watching us. I don't want to fight in front of him, but Nan can't go back and forth between the kitchen and the deck easily. Nor do I want her to attempt it with cups of tea balanced on her walker. "Just let me."

"I'm more than capable, *dear*." She's being polite in front of company, but I know what it means when she says *dear* like that.

I open my mouth, but Charlie speaks up first. "My grandma fractured her hip a few years ago," he tells Nan. "Slipped in the snow. How did you manage it?"

"I wore the wrong shoes to dance class. My foot went right out from under me doing kicks to some silly old song."

"It was 'Dancing Queen,'" I say, sharing a look with Charlie that says, *We're not allowed to laugh at this.*

"Apparently not," Nan huffs.

Charlie's eyes widen. *But it's so funny*, they say.

"Why don't we all go inside," he offers, holding back a grin. "Alice needs to get out of the sun, and I wouldn't mind a comfortable chair."

Nan peers at me over her glasses. "She does look rather crisp, doesn't she?"

We get her inside, Charlie moving a floor lamp closer to the wall to make more room for her walker. I head to the kitchen to put the kettle on, almost gasping at the photo of teenage Charlie on the fridge. I pull it down and hide it under a stack of paper napkins in a cupboard. What a day.

"I grew up on the lake, but I live in Toronto now," Charlie is telling Nan when I return to the living room.

"What neighborhood? Alice is in the Junction."

"I have a condo in Yorkville."

Nan is in her armchair, with her pressed shirt and her pearls. Charlie is on the sofa, shirtless and barefoot. The contrast is just too good. I fetch my camera out of my bag.

Click.

Nan is used to my shooting and pays no attention, but Charlie's head whips around, a questioning look on his face.

I offer no explanation. "I'll find you something to wear."

One of the drawers in my bedroom dresser is full of cozy socks and faded T-shirts. I dig out the largest one for Charlie and change into a pair of yellow linen shorts and a sleeveless white blouse, then lasso my curls into a bun at the nape of my neck.

"Very impressive," Nan is saying to Charlie when I return. She's not easily impressed, nor is she one to needlessly flatter. Somehow, in the span of a few minutes, Charlie has managed to win my grandmother over.

Her praise makes him glow. He's shining like the sun, cheeks slightly flushed. He looks younger. He looks like the boy in my photo. "Thanks," he says. "I've worked hard."

I hand him the shirt, and he pulls it over his head. It's sky blue with BARRY'S BAY written across the chest beneath a loon, and it's obscenely tight through the shoulders and arms. Does he fight fires for a living? Does he fight crime? I glance at Nan, and we share a conspiratorial look.

"Tea will be ready in a few minutes," I say, taking a seat on the sofa next to him.

"Charlie was just telling me that he works on Bay Street as a trader."

I look at Charlie, picturing him in a suit and tie. Post-work cocktail parties. Hot women.

"That makes sense."

Charlie tilts his head. "Meaning?"

"You fit the bill." Cavalier. Confident. I bet he's competitive.

"That feels like an insult," Charlie says.

"You'll survive." I reach over and pat his leg but am not prepared for the heat of his skin beneath my fingers, or the way they want to explore his thigh, find out whether he's hot everywhere. I don't think Charlie is prepared, either, because as soon as I touch him, his gaze rockets to my hand. I snatch it back just as fast.

"I doubt anyone survives you," he says, lifting his eyes to me. They truly are magnificent, changeable in the light. A deeper bottle green than they were in the sun.

Nan sizes us up like we're dessert. "Oh, this is too good. Charlie, it's been a long time since I've seen someone ruffle Alice's feathers the way you did with the letter. It was a riot."

"The pleasure's all mine."

Nan hoots. *Hoots.* She's as happy as a clam—I can't believe it. I haven't seen her like this since before her fall. "Oh, I like you far more than the last one."

"Nan," I say, hoping to sidestep the subject of my ex. "It's not like that."

Charlie grins at me like a jungle cat. "Not yet."

Now she claps.

"Don't encourage him," I tell her, but I love seeing her happy. And I suspect Charlie's leaning into it, flirting to put on a show. It's a very believable act.

He tilts forward and whispers to Nan, "So what was wrong with the last one?"

"He was a real dud," she says. "So serious and fussy. I never once saw Alice laugh when they were together."

"Nan, please."

"It's true," she says to Charlie. "Dull as a chalkboard. Alice helped him with his business, and he had the nerve to break up with her." I shut my eyes for only a second, just long enough to keep it together in front of Charlie.

I don't know how to make you happy, Alice. Do you?

"I'm sorry," Charlie says softly.

"There's nothing to be sorry about." I stand, smoothing my hands over the front of my shorts. "How do you take your tea?"

"I don't," Charlie says.

"Pardon?"

"I don't drink tea," he clarifies.

Nan scoffs. "Everyone drinks tea."

Charlie turns to her. "How should I take it, then?"

For all his joking, I appreciate that he doesn't speak to Nan like she's a delicate old lady or a child.

"Sweet tooth?" Nan asks him.

"Not with this body."

"Just with a splash of milk, then."

Charlie turns back to me. "I'll take it with a splash of milk, thanks."

I retreat to the kitchen, a Trevor-shaped headache pushing against my temples.

"But don't I make *you* happy?" I asked just before Trevor walked out.

He'd given me a sad smile and kissed my cheek. "I think you really tried."

I thought Trevor was the one. But now he's engaged to a pediatric nurse named Astilbe, and I'm left facing the possibility that the only person I'll spend my life with is me.

Over and over, I keep falling. Over and over, I keep getting my heart broken. Everlasting love may have existed for my grandmother's generation, but I'm beginning to think it's a modern myth. Heather's divorced. My parents are, too. They pulled the plug on their marriage three years ago, right after the twins left home. I held out hope that the separation was temporary until the very end, when the divorce was finalized, and Mom changed her last name. She's Michelle Dale once more.

I blink away the tears and bring out the tea and cake.

"I imagine sabbaticals aren't common in your line of work," Nan says to Charlie as I hand him a cup. It looks like a dollhouse accessory in his hand.

I take a seat, noticing that he straightens slightly, like he's zipping himself together.

"Probably not. But I'm not common. I'm very good at what I do."

A few minutes earlier, I would have rolled my eyes, but I find myself studying Charlie, trying to determine whether there's something more to him than dimples and triceps.

"I imagine you are," Nan says, then gestures to me. "Alice is a photographer."

"I've heard," he says, looking at me with a delighted quirk of his brow.

"She's very gifted. One of her photos has been selected for a big exhibition later this year. What's the show called, Alice?"

"*In (Her) Camera*," I tell her. "My friend owns the gallery," I say to Charlie.

"Don't downplay it, Alice. It's a stunning shot. Haunting."

Haunting. Yes.

It's a portrait of a woman, staring directly into the camera, chin tilted up. From a distance Aanya looks like a typical executive. Blazer. Bland chin-length blowout. But when you step closer, you can see the creases of her eye makeup, the flakes of mascara beneath her eyes, the exhaustion in her gaze. She looks defeated. She was the CEO of a major telecom, and I shot her for a magazine profile. Three days later, Aanya was ousted in a corporate coup. It's without question a powerful image, but there were other photos she and I liked far better—ones where the lighting isn't so harsh, where she looks tired but determined, that felt truer to who she is. I tried to convince the photo editor to choose one of them, but he selected an image that suited the story the magazine wanted to tell.

Maybe that's why it bothers me so much. Someone else decided how Aanya showed up in the world. Or maybe it's because I didn't argue my case with the photo editor hard enough.

Elyse loves the portrait. She looks at Aanya and sees strength and resilience. I see my own weakness.

Including it in the show makes a statement about who I am as a photographer. The portrait is good; great even. But it doesn't feel like me. In truth, I'm not sure what *me* feels like anymore. Aside from the photos I snapped on the island earlier today, I don't remember when I shot just for myself, without worrying about acing an assignment.

"When is the show, Alice? I don't think you mentioned," Nan says now.

"It runs from August until the end of the year."

"You'll have to go back for the opening," she says. "I wouldn't mind a few days here on my own."

"It's not a big deal, Nan. I don't want to leave you." Which is only part of the truth. I'm happy to have an excuse not to see the photo in the gallery.

Nan narrows her eyes. "I'm not a child."

I feel Charlie looking between us. "I know," I say quietly. "That's not it."

"You can't blame Alice for not wanting to leave the lake in August," Charlie says. I glance at him, grateful. He lifts his teacup in my direction before turning to Nan. "You know, I think I remember you from when I was growing up. You and your husband visited a lot, right?"

It's an elite distraction. Nan lights up like a Christmas tree. "We came every summer. John and Joyce were our closest friends."

Charlie squints. "John said it's been a long time since you've been back. He asked me to let him know how you're doing—said you haven't spoken in a long time."

I whip my head in Nan's direction. I didn't know that.

"People change." She keeps her eyes set on Charlie as he sips his tea. He hasn't touched the cake. "Now tell me, what are you doing to keep yourself busy this summer? I imagine a man like you would get bored quickly."

"I don't really believe in boredom," he says. "I know a lot of people in Barry's Bay. I've got my boat. The Jet Ski. I have some projects to do around here for John. And I'm building a tree house."

"A tree house? Do you have children?" Nan asks.

Charlie shakes his head. "My brother and sister-in-law are expecting their first in October, two days before my birthday." His voice has gone soft. "I'm throwing them a big party next month. My take on a baby shower. The tree house is my gift." His voice catches, and he blinks, caught off guard by his emotions.

I jump in quickly, trying to ease what's just come up for him. "What newborn baby doesn't love climbing ladders?"

"Alice," Nan chides. "It's a nice thought."

But Charlie looks at me, like I somehow knew he would, eyes glimmering as if he's ready to play. "I thought I'd stick a bassinet inside, so the baby doesn't disturb my sleep. I might need some help getting it up there, though. You game?"

"I'm in. We should add a rocking chair, too. That way your brother and sister-in-law will be comfortable."

"Genius," he says. "They don't need proper shelter."

"Or running water."

Charlie chuckles, and his eyes fall to my mouth and pause there. It's because I'm smiling, I realize. A big, toothy grin that pulls at my cheeks. He suddenly gets to his feet.

"I should probably head out. Thank you for the tea. I'll bring those end tables to you tomorrow," he tells Nan. "I'll leave my number in case you ever need anything when Alice isn't around."

"Speaking of," Nan says with a devious smile. "We're celebrating Alice's birthday next week. July 1. Her brother and sister will be here. Why don't you join us for dinner?"

"You don't have to come," I say to Charlie as I walk him down to the dock. "It's just going to be a little party, but my siblings are *a lot.*"

"I like *a lot.*"

"There'll be feather boas and tiaras and glitter," I say. I have a vision for the night, and Charlie doesn't fit into it.

"That's good news," he says, coming to a stop on the dock. "I look fantastic in a tiara."

"But it's Canada Day," I say. "You probably have plans."

Green eyes bore into mine. "If you don't want me to come, Alice, just say so."

I chew on the inside of my mouth. I don't know what I'm going to get with Charlie. He's like the mystery roll of film I once discovered under the lining of my bag. I had no idea what I'd find on it.

He sticks out his hand.

"What are you doing?"

"I get the sense I haven't made a good first impression, so let's start over. I'm Charlie Florek."

I frown, and he beams back at me.

"And you are . . ." he prompts.

"I'm Alice Everly?" I say, putting my palm in his.

Charlie squeezes it firmly, giving it a shake. His smile draws out his dimples. "And *you* are Alice Everly."

Alice Everly. Alice Everly. Alice Everly.

I should pull my hand away, but for some reason, I don't. I let him hold my small hand in his large one.

"Rumor has it that you're throwing a big party on Canada Day, Alice. The whole lake is talking about it."

I think of the boy in my photo, and the girl who wanted to hang out with him. I think of the way Charlie made Nan giggle.

"You should come," I tell him. "I think I can put up with you for an evening."

Charlie smiles, and it's so genuine I struggle not to do the same.

"Don't look too happy," I tell him. "You'll have to wear your own shirt."

"No guarantees."

He drops my hand, and mine feels so much colder. Charlie steps into the boat with grace, pulls the T-shirt over his head, and tosses it to me. "Wear it to bed, Alice. Picture me in your dreams."

I wrinkle my nose, but it only makes him laugh.

"You're . . ." I don't even know what he is.

"Remarkable?" He throws me a grin, then unties the boat. He gets it started and then pulls away, his back to me, the sun caressing his skin.

"Oh, and, Alice?" he calls, looking over his shoulder. "About that list of yours. Consider number three your birthday gift."

I don't remember what number three is, but I *know* I should be embarrassed that he does. I stare at Charlie's yellow boat as it soars across the bay, clutching a shirt that smells like summer.

12

Read a smutty book. Number three.

Of all the people to have seen my silly list, it had to be Charlie. I throw my notebook onto the bed and pick up the Barry's Bay T-shirt to take it to the laundry. I lift it to my nose without really thinking, and Nan catches me.

"It smells weird," I tell her, and she gives me a knowing look.

I try to push Charlie out of my head, but Nan spends the entire evening gushing about him.

So handsome. Charming, in a devilish sort of way. Reminds me of Robert Redford in The Way We Were. *And those arms!*

She's chattier than she's been since we arrived. When she retires to her bedroom for the night, I go down a highly unadvisable vortex of vintage Robert Redford photos. My mind keeps drifting back to the moment on the dock, when Charlie turned to me and said, "If you don't want me to come, Alice, just say so." It's the way he looked at me, the way he knew what I was thinking.

Shaking my head as if I can knock him out of it, I text Luca and Lavinia.

Me: I'm going to throw a little party while you're here.

Luca: Who is this?

Lavinia: Why have you stolen my sister's phone?

Luca: You can't fool us, scammer. Ali hates parties.

After ten minutes of razzing, the twins settle down. They promise to bake a cake. We'll eat the leftovers for breakfast, the way Mom always let us when we were kids. Luca has already started a playlist. Lavinia is on wardrobe. I'm on decorations.

Sequins, Lavinia texts now.

Feathers, Luca replies.

Glitter, I write back. *Like Heather used to wear.* Number fourteen.

With some reluctance, I fill in the twins on Charlie.

Me: It'll be the four of us plus the guy who's looking after the cottage.

Luca: Is he hot?

Lavinia: Is he single?

Luca: Send us a photo immediately.

Lavinia: Do they have internet up there?

Luca: What's his name?

Lavinia: What's his star sign?

Me: Very. I think so. Don't have one. Obviously. Charlie. Don't know but big Leo energy.

Lavinia: Swoon.

Luca: Dibs.

Me: Calm down. He's kind of a jerk.

I press send on the last one, and then I feel bad. Charlie's arrogant, but he isn't a jerk.

Luca: So why is he invited?

Lavinia: OMG! Are you trying to keep us away from him??!!

Luca: You LIKE him!

Lavinia: You TOTALLY like him.

Two minutes later I have a call from Heather, demanding I fill her in on the "lake babe."

"I can't figure him out," I tell her after recapping my boating disaster.

"I bet that's driving you crazy."

It is. I keep inspecting the few pieces of information I know about him, holding each facet to the light, trying to make discordant pieces fit together.

"He's completely full of himself," I tell Heather. "But he's charming. He saved me today and went out of his way to get the cottage ready." I think of the way he spoke about his niece or nephew. "I have a feeling the bravado could be a front."

"Sounds like he has issues."

"Totally," I say, chewing on a nail.

Heather makes a short *mmm* sound, which means she's also thinking.

"Nan liked him," I add.

"Did she? Well, she's a good judge." She pauses. "A ripped cottage hottie who daylights as a trader . . . that's not your usual type."

"Oh, definitely not. I am *not* going there."

"But, Ali, your usual type hasn't really worked for you. Trevor—"

I cut her off. "I'm not interested in *any* type right now."

She ignores me. "You are a giver, and Trevor was a taker. You put all that work into his business, and he took it for granted."

Trevor has a small but successful letterpress company. When we started dating, I began shooting all his product samples and social media content. When things were busy, I helped mail out orders. I adjusted my own work schedule so I could man the booth with him at trade shows and referred my bridal clients to him. I pride myself on being a solid friend, a helpful sister, the good daughter. But for the man I loved? I would have done anything.

"And despite what you say," Heather continues, "you *do* have a type."

I brace myself because there's no stopping her once she's made her opening argument.

"Ever since Oz, you've been with these tidy, quiet sweater-vest guys."

Oz is one of those people who showed up at university on the first day fully formed, from the way he shot to the way he dressed. Ripped jeans. Plaid flannels. A pierced eyebrow. He played bass in a band and shot gritty, unflinching images of urban life. He was a great photographer. He still is.

"But just because they don't have tattoos, doesn't mean they're any different," Heather goes on.

But Oz *was* different. He paid attention to me and my work in a way nobody ever had. By second year, we were inseparable, using the darkroom together and watching docs in his Kensington Market apartment. I went to all his gigs. His family lived in Winnipeg, so he spent Thanksgivings and Easters with the Everlys. And I was secretly madly in love with him. There were so many fleeting moments where he'd look at me with affection, or when he told me no one understood him like I did, that I almost confessed. But I never managed it. Until that night in August.

It was the summer after graduation. Oz convinced me to come to a DJ night in a cramped, makeshift venue above a furniture store. We were dancing, and then his hands were on my hips, and then on my backside, and then we were kissing. When he was above me later that night, I thought my heart might split wide open. It was my first time, and it was with my best friend, the man I'd loved for years in silence.

Maybe things would have been different if I'd told Oz I'd never had sex. Maybe he wouldn't have slept with me. Maybe we'd still be close. When I asked the next morning when we should tell our friends about us, he looked confused, then remorseful. He told me he didn't see us as a couple, that it had been a onetime thing. I couldn't help it: I cried an entire river of tears while he held me. When I left his apartment, I told him I'd be okay, but I stopped returning his texts. I cut Oz out of my life.

"Ali, are you listening to me?" Heather asks.

I hum.

"I was saying that you need someone who supports you in the same way you support them. You need someone who gives as much as they get."

"I don't *need* anyone."

"You know what else I think?" my sister asks.

"That honeydew is the superior melon?" (Ew.)

"Obviously. You could use some bravado in your life."

I frown. "Meaning?"

"Make out with Charlie in his fast boat. Slather some sunscreen on those pectorals. Fool around in the boathouse."

"I'll pass."

"Ugh. You're hopeless. Then I'll come make out with him."

"You don't date."

"But I *do* have sex. Unlike you."

"Anyway," I grumble. "New subject."

"Fine. What are the details of your opening night? I need to clear my calendar and book us hair appointments. We should probably get our makeup done, too."

I shouldn't have told my sister about the show. She won't shut up about it.

"I'm not going," I say. "I'll be up here with Nan. She needs me here."

"Oh please."

"Just drop it," I say, though Heather won't be satisfied until I'm standing in Elyse Cho Gallery, sweating through my cocktail dress.

"I will not drop it. So it's not your favorite photo. Who cares? This is a big deal, Ali. It's the gallery's inaugural exhibition— there's going to be a ton of press."

"I care, and I'm not like you. I don't love the spotlight in the same way."

Lavinia is the actor, but all the Everlys crave attention. My father and Heather find it in the courtroom. Lavinia onstage. Luca behind the bar. My mom is more like me. We're the reserved ones, the introverts.

"I do not *love* the spotlight."

"Heather."

"The show could open a whole new world for you," she says. "You're always talking about how you want to shoot artier stuff. This is an opportunity to get in front of rich people who need arty shit for their walls."

"Arty shit?" What I don't say is that I think I've made a big mistake. If people like the photo, I'm afraid Elyse will want more like it, and that buyers will, too. I'm afraid I won't be able to say no, that I'll find myself on the wrong road, unable to find my way back.

"I mean it as a compliment," Heather says, then sighs. "I think you should put on your big-girl panties and one of your boring black jumpsuits, and just do it," she says. "And Charlie while you're at it."

Before I turn in for the night, I scroll through the photos I've snapped on my phone to see if there's anything worth sharing.

The best thing I've taken is a shot of Nan, looking out the window, her hands gripping either side of her walker. But I know she wouldn't want me to post it—she hates that she needs help. There's one of my feet in the water that I took on the island earlier today. The ripples on the surface have an interesting geometry. The tones look almost black and white. You can just make out my hair in the reflection of the lake, but you can't see my face.

I apply my go-to filters and post it with a brief caption. Lake, June 2025. I label all my photos this way. The subject, the month, the year. I do a quick scroll of my notifications before I shut my phone off for the night, but there's one from an hour ago that makes my heart skip.

charlesflorek started following you

13

As if conjured by Heather's will alone, an email from Elyse arrives the next morning. It's a draft invitation for the opening of *In (Her) Camera*—she wants my opinion.

"What are you scowling at?" Nan asks from across the table.

"Nothing."

She blinks at me over the rim of her glasses. "Alice. You are a wretched liar."

I really am. "It's just a message about the show."

"I was thinking I'd prefer to come with you than stay here," Nan says.

"All the driving on top of the event would be too much for you, Nan. Besides, I'd rather not leave the lake. You know I don't love being in a crowd or making speeches." Elyse has asked if I'd mind saying a few words at the reception.

Nan opens her mouth to respond but is cut off by a knock at the door.

It's eight a.m., and the air is cool. Mist swirls over the lake and the stones on the walkway glisten with dew. There's also a handsome man in a denim shirt on the doorstep. He has dark eyes, brown skin, a trim beard, a ballcap, and a pair of worn-looking steel-toed boots.

"Uh . . . hi?" I'm not my most eloquent when faced with gorgeous strangers first thing in the morning. I'm still in my jammies.

"I'm taking it that Charlie didn't tell you I was coming by." He has a grocery bag in one hand.

I shake my head, and he offers his free hand. "Harrison Singh. I'm one of Charlie's buddies."

"Alice Everly," I say, taking his calloused palm. His grip is strong. Everything about him looks strong. What do they put in the water up here?

"Charlie got tied up with something this morning, so he asked me to run these out to you on my way to work." He gestures to the black truck he's arrived in. There are two end tables in the back.

"Oh. Thank you. I'm sorry he had you up this early," I say, folding my arms over my chest. My skin is pebbling in the crisp air, and my shorts and cami are too skimpy for a stranger's eyes. "It wasn't urgent."

"I don't mind at all." The smile Harrison gives me is shy but definitely *interested*. I'm not sure what to do with that and find myself blushing in return.

Harrison passes me the bag. "Charlie also wanted me to bring you these. He said you forgot them at the store yesterday."

I peek inside. The bag is full of English cucumbers.

"What do you need all these cucumbers for?"

"I might whack Charlie over the head with one, for starters."

Harrison gives me a puzzled look.

"I'm just kidding. He thinks he's pretty funny, huh?"

"He does." He shrugs. "And he is. Let me bring these in for you."

I offer to help, but Harrison insists on carrying the tables into the living room. I introduce him to Nan, and she tries to get him to stay for coffee.

"I'd love to," he tells her. "But my grandfather will rip into me if I'm late."

"You work with your grandfather?" I ask.

"With my dad, too. We build houses."

As we're walking back to his truck, Harrison pauses, turning to me. "You're here all summer?"

"Until the end of August."

He nods slowly, his eyes catching on mine.

"Are you and Charlie . . . uh . . . dating?"

I make a face. "Not even close."

"Maybe I'll see you around, then? I'm usually at the Tavern on Thursday nights."

"The Tavern?"

"You don't know it? I thought you and Charlie were friends or something."

I cackle at that. "We just met yesterday."

"Oh. The way he spoke . . ." Harrison frowns, and it's adorable on him. "I figured you knew each other well. Anyway, the Tavern is Charlie's family's restaurant. Or, it used to be. Charlie and Sam sold it a couple years ago."

"Sam?"

"Charlie's younger brother."

"Ah."

"I could take you sometime? Food's good."

"Like a date?" I want to be sure about what's going on here. I'm wearing rumpled pajamas and my glasses. My hair is a hornet's nest.

With a nervous laugh, Harrison rubs the back of his neck. "Yeah? Or not. We could just have a beer. No pressure, obviously."

We stare at each other in awkward silence for a moment. I'm not sure why I'm hesitating. Harrison could be number five on my bucket list. He's more than kissable.

"Maybe," I say. "I'm a bit busy taking care of my grandmother right now, but I'll think about it."

Stedmans is a Barry's Bay icon. It's something like a general store—clothing, housewares, and office supplies on the main floor, and outdoor equipment and kids' toys in the basement. We bought all our puzzles here the summer I was seventeen. It's a rainy day, and it feels like half the town is inside, stocking up on beach towels and sweatshirts and board games. There is a trove of fabric in the back of the store, arranged by color, and florals galore—botanicals and calicos, ditsies and damasks.

"How are we going to choose?"

Nan narrows her eyes to assess the inventory. "Joyce loved blue."

"How did she feel about toile?" I pull out a bolt with a royal-blue pastoral pattern.

"I don't think she would have opposed, but I'm not sure it would suit the cottage."

"Too fussy?"

She hums a yes.

In the end, we decide on a blue and cream Liberty-style print, with dashes of orange, yellow, and green, for the kitchen and bathroom curtains.

We spend the rest of the day measuring and cutting and laughing over my clumsy use of the sewing machine foot pedal as I wind thread around a bobbin. While Nan naps, I set up a makeshift art studio for myself in the boathouse loft. When she wakes, she makes me practice sewing in a straight line, over and over, on a cheap piece of remnant we bought for this very reason.

"Straight enough?" I ask, bringing it over to Nan for inspection. She's resting in the armchair with her tea.

She peers at the stitching through her glasses, as if she's Coco Chanel herself. "You've got it," she says. "We'll start the curtains tomorrow."

Charlie: Harry asked me to put in a good word, so this is me putting in a good word.

Me: Noted.

Me: Strange that he thought your word would have sway with me.

Charlie: Strange that he didn't listen when I told him you were a redhead with a big mouth.

Me: A big mouth and a lifetime supply of cucumbers. Thank you for that.

Charlie: A thank you? From Alice Everly? Whoa.

Charlie: No reply? It's eleven at night. Surely you can make time for me.

Me: Time for what exactly? Don't you have someone else to bother?

Charlie: Is this your roundabout way of asking whether I'm single?

Charlie: You disappeared again.

Me: Goodnight, Charlie.

Charlie: Sweet dreams, Alice.

14

I wake to the sound of hammering across the bay and sunlight flooding my small bedroom. From my pillow, I have a clear view of the lake, Charlie's yellow boat included. I catch myself staring at it and throw back the sheet.

"I'm sorry I overslept again," I say to Nan as I pad out to the living room. She's in her armchair, turning through the pages of a photo album. "Can I make you breakfast?"

"No, dear. I fixed myself toast hours ago."

"What are you looking at?"

"Summers gone by." She smiles to herself. "This is from one of John and Joyce's first few years at the lake. Before children."

I stand over her shoulder. The picture is of my grandparents and Joyce sitting on the front steps of the cottage—John must have taken it. The three of them are so young.

"This would have been the late sixties," Nan says. "They hadn't built the deck yet. Or the steps to the lake. There was a little path through the bush to the water. There was no washing machine, so we cleaned everything in the sink. For years, John and Joyce spent almost all their time up here working. Your grandfather and I helped when we could."

"Charlie said something yesterday about you not having spoken to John in a long time."

Nan turns the page. "It's been a while."

"How long?"

She turns another page but doesn't answer for a several seconds. History clings to the corners of the room like cobwebs. "It's been years."

"Why? You were all so close."

Nan and David. John and Joyce. They'd known each other since childhood. They all grew up in Leaside, the same area where they would one day raise their families. My grandmother and grandfather started dating first, but only by a few weeks. Each couple had one boy, born within months of each other. Joyce and Nan were homemakers. John and my grandfather commuted downtown together; my grandfather worked in insurance, John in the head office of a department store chain. They were a unit. A four-sided structure. Until my grandfather died.

"Things can change when you lose people," Nan says. "But let's leave the past in the past, Alice."

I take the hint and go fix myself breakfast.

"I think I'll eat outside," I tell Nan. "Do you want to join me?"

She shakes her head, her eyes not leaving the photo she's studying. "I'll stay here for a while longer."

"I'll help you with your exercises when I'm done, and then we can start the curtains?"

"No rush. I'm not going anywhere."

I watch her for a moment. I hate seeing her so down.

"I love you, Nan."

She glances up at me, blinking. "I love you, too."

Nan is buried in another album when I finish eating, so I wander down to the lake with my half-finished coffee.

Sunlight dances on the surface of the water like sequins winking on a liquid gown. The unicorn pool floatie I bought in town yesterday is bobbing happily beside the dock. It's enormous, with a rainbow mane and tail, and a golden horn and wings. I also bought a moose and a loon—I have visions of Luca, Lavinia, and me lounging on the lake with piña coladas.

The hammering continues as I sip my coffee. I picture Charlie working on his tree house. I try to put him out of my mind, but each *thwack* has me imagining his smirk and shirtless chest. And then the drill starts. I retreat to the cottage and find my phone.

Me: Is that you making such a remarkable racket?

"Have you done your exercises yet?" I ask Nan when Charlie doesn't respond.

"I was hoping you'd forget."

But she folds up her crossword and gets started, complaining the entire time about how boring it is lying on her back and squeezing her butt. But I can tell Nan's already stronger than she was a week ago. After she's done, we begin our first sewing project.

Rod-pocket curtains are simple in theory. There's a lot of folding and ironing. I'm uncoordinated with the machine at first, but Nan helps me keep the fabric straight and gives quiet instructions.

A little heavier on the pedal. Now the backstitch. Good, Alice!

We're both grinning when I get one finished. Stiff, I move my neck from side to side.

"Why don't you go for a swim," Nan says, taking her crossword to the dining table. "You've barely been in the water."

I still haven't given the unicorn a ride.

When I'm changing into my bathing suit, I glance at my phone and find an unread text.

Charlie: Did I interrupt your morning, princess?

I feel myself smiling, imagine the word *princess* rasping out of Charlie's mouth, then throw my phone onto the bed.

I bring John's binoculars down to the lake and stand at the end of the dock, scanning the shoreline. Birches sloped over the water. Towels drying on deck railings. Flags flapping in the breeze. I pass over the A-frame and then Charlie's boat, and almost drop the binoculars as he appears in my view. He's on the deck. No shirt. Bathing suit bottoms. I shouldn't creep on him like this, but . . .

Whoa.

He walks down the hill to the water. I see when he sees me: A brilliant smile lights his face. I curse, quickly set the binoculars down, and dive into the lake.

I stay submerged as long as I can, eyes closed, letting the water fill my ears. And then I swim, from the dock and out, back and forth, back and forth. Legs fluttering. Arms arching. I don't stop until I'm short of breath.

Without a fraction of a glance toward Charlie's place, I dry off and attempt to board the unicorn. The thing is so massive and awkward, I can't get my weight centered. I fall off twice to the sound of Nan laughing from the deck before I manage to spread myself between its golden wings. It's shockingly comfortable. I close my eyes and cover my face with my arms. Seconds later, I hear the obnoxious roar of a Jet Ski whipping around the bay.

I hear it pass me once, twice, a third time, closer and closer. It slows somewhere nearby, and the engine stops.

"Lucky Pegasus."

15

I turn toward the voice and am unsurprised to find Charlie astride a yellow Jet Ski.

"It's a unicorn."

"Unicorns don't have wings," he says, eyeing me with a lazy smile.

"Pegasuses don't have horns."

He tilts his head in agreement, and then waves up at the deck. "Good afternoon, Nan."

"Nice to see you again, Charlie." She might as well be licking her chops.

He points to the binoculars.

"Spying on me?"

"I was bird-watching."

Charlie smirks. "See any noteworthy species?"

The unicorn or Pegasus or whatever it is squeaks as I try to prop myself up. I can only lean awkwardly on the thing's mane.

"Just a giant peacock."

"Text me next time you're nature-spotting. I'll be sure to put on a better show."

"I changed my mind—you're more like an oversized pest than a peacock."

He snorts, then holds out a spare life jacket. "Get on. Unless you'd rather keep riding that . . . thing."

"This *unicorn* is very comfortable."

He begins undoing his life jacket. "Is it?"

"What are you doing?"

"I'm joining you. Looks like there's room for two."

"There absolutely isn't."

"I guess we'll find out."

Charlie drops an anchor, and before I can compute the plethora of ridges on his chest and stomach, he dives into the water. I have no idea where he is until he surfaces right next to the unicorn. He grins up at me, and my stomach dips.

"Move over, Alice."

"Don't you dare."

Charlie sets a large hand on a wing and another beside my thigh.

"You're going to tip it over," I say, trying to scoot away from the edge.

"Maybe that's the point." He wraps his hand around my calf.

"You wouldn't," I say, eyes wide. "You're a grown—"

The word *man* is lost to my yelp as he pulls me into the lake. I get my head above water as fast as I can so I can splash him in the face.

"Oh, you don't want to start that," he says with a Peter Pan smile. We're treading water. Charlie moves in a circle around me, and I follow his orbit.

"You started it."

I splash him, and he swipes an arm through the water, drenching my face. I cough, and he moves closer.

"Are you okay? Sorry I—"

I splash him again, and he's so shocked, I cackle, loud and

ugly. But I stop when I see his expression. He's blinking at me, brows knit.

"What's wrong?" I ask, wiping water out of my eyes.

Charlie shakes his head. "Nothing. You just . . ." He clears his throat. "You have a great laugh."

We stare at each other for a moment, and then Charlie tips his head toward the Jet Ski. "Let's go. I'll show you around the rest of Kamaniskeg so you don't destroy John's boat on another rock."

"I—" My instinct is to say no, to stay safely onshore, but then I remember the list and that teenage Alice would have flipped if a cute guy gave her a Jet Ski ride.

So I change my mind. I do it for younger me.

We swim to the Jet Ski, and Charlie hoists himself up. He leans toward me, extending his hand, and pulls me up without any show of exertion. I straddle the seat behind him and buckle the life jacket. When the engine starts, I lock my arms around his waist. He smells sunny and gardeny and fresh, and it's an effort not to breathe him in more deeply, to figure out what that scent is.

"As nice as it is to be held by you, Alice, there are handgrips for you to hang on to."

I snap my arms back, apologizing.

"Just reach down and you'll feel them." Charlie glances at me over his shoulder. Beads of water garnish his lashes like dewdrops. His eyes are an impossible shade of green, almost golden in the afternoon sun. He's freshly shaven. His profile is stunning.

Click.

I wish I had my camera.

"Alice?"

"Sorry. I was just . . ."

"Ogling my *remarkable* face." Charlie's mouth curves into that smug setting I'm already familiar with. It's a hint of a smile, knowing and teasing, higher on one side than the other. Charlie's features speak for him. *Nothing fools us*, they say.

"Your eyelashes," I say, deciding to tell him the truth. It's not like his head can grow any larger. "The way the water clings to them is really pretty in this light."

Charlie faces me more fully, the cocksure expression evaporating. He frowns, searching my eyes. A thrill courses through me. I feel it in my ears, my fingers, my toes. It's spiked with fear, like I've accepted a dare.

"You're different," Charlie says.

I will my voice to stay steady. "I'm not sure that's a compliment."

"It's not an insult. Just a fact. I've never met anyone quite like you."

I don't have time to figure how I feel about *that* before he starts the engine. "You ready?"

I white-knuckle the handgrips. "Go slow."

Charlie's laugh rumbles between my legs, and that courses through me, too. "Not a chance."

He lifts his eyes to my grandmother, who watches us from the deck, a giant smile on her lips. "I'll have her back in one piece in about an hour, Nan."

That's the only warning I get before we're racing across the water. I hold in my breath, squeezing my knees tight to Charlie's hips.

"You okay back there?" he calls over his shoulder.

I turn my head, watching the cottages rush by. "I think so."

It doesn't take long for me to unclamp. I like the wind in my face, the water splashing on my calves. The view of Charlie's arms and bronzed neck isn't terrible, either.

I don't notice that I've sighed until Charlie calls back to me, "Enjoying yourself?"

"I am. It's weirdly relaxing."

He shows me the best passage around the bay, slows when we reach the larger island, and glances at me. "You've never been on a Jet Ski?"

"First time."

A corner of Charlie's mouth inches up. "Is that why it's on that list of yours?"

Ride a Jet Ski. Number thirteen.

I make a point of finding the buckle on my life jacket fascinating. But he ducks down so I'm forced meet his laughing eyes. "Any other firsts on there?"

There are tiny flecks of yellow surrounding his irises, and I glare at them. "That's none of your business," I say primly. "What you read was private."

"I'm only curious."

"Well, don't be."

Any trace of humor fades. "I'm sorry. I'm only teasing."

"Okay."

"My family was big into teasing," he says. "It's basically the Florek love language."

I mellow. "I don't speak Florek, so you'll need to translate."

"The one thing you really need to know is that we only make fun of people we like."

"What happens when you fall in love? Do you stage a roast? Gift wrap a rubber chicken?"

He chuckles. "There's that Alice Everly sense of humor. You'd fit right in."

As soon as the words leave his lips, his grin flattens. "Hold on," he says. "I'll show you the safest route around the island."

As he points out the areas that are hazardous for the blades of a motor, there's not a sliver of a smirk in sight. He glances at me over his shoulder to make sure I'm following, his gaze narrowed in concentration, and I wonder if there's a more serious person under the swagger. I'm usually quick to figure people out, but Charlie keeps surprising me.

Before we set off again, I point to the cliff across from the island. "I'm going to jump from that."

"I know."

"How do—" I cut myself off. The list. Number one. "Never mind."

Charlie studies me. "Want to do it now? I'll go with you."

My stomach knots.

"Are you scared of heights?" An earnest question.

"No."

We look at the rock face.

"So you're afraid of . . . ?"

"Dying."

"I won't let you die. Or get hurt."

I stare into his eyes and somehow know he means it.

"Whenever you're ready, let me know. I'll make sure you're safe."

"Good," I say, heart pounding. "Let's do it now."

I peer over the edge. "It's higher than it looks."

Charlie steps beside me. "All you have to do is jump. I'll go first. I'll be down there if anything happens."

My head snaps in his direction. "I thought you said this was safe."

"It *is* safe. But I'll still be there."

Staring back at the water, I take a deep breath, in and out.

"I'm turning thirty-three tomorrow. You'd think I'd be a little braver."

"I think the older we get, the scarier shit becomes."

It's kind of profound. I narrow my eyes. "How old are you?"

"Thirty-five." Charlie's voice is so grim I laugh, but it dies in my throat at his expression.

"Is it really so bad?"

"Nah." He sounds light, but there's a trace of something like sorrow in his eyes. "Every year we get is precious."

There's more to the story—I feel it in my gut.

I don't know Charlie well enough to pry, but every bone in my body softens with the need to place a grin back upon his lips. I take a few large steps back from the edge.

"What are you doing?"

"Isn't it obvious?"

Charlie's mouth opens, but he doesn't try to stop me. I stare down the granite ledge, fill my lungs, and then I run, launching myself off the cliff with as much force as I can. I hurtle through the air, arms circling.

It's over quickly. My smile breaks through the surface, and I plunge into the cool depths of the lake. When the downward pull eases, I flutter my legs, returning to daylight and oxygen. I spin in the water just in time to see Charlie jump. I'm laughing, pushing my hair out of my eyes, when he bobs up beside me. His grin shines like morning sun over the bay. The dimples. The creases hugging the corners of his eyes. The water running down his nose.

Click.

Charlie sends a gentle flick of water into my face. "So much for being afraid."

I splash back, exhilarated. "Race you to shore."

We jump twice more, the last time in tandem. Then we climb on the Jet Ski, and as my hair whips behind me, I try not to examine why I feel looser than I have in months, or the reason my cheeks hurt from smiling, or why my skin heats whenever my knee bumps Charlie's thigh.

When we get to the big end of Kamaniskeg, Charlie points out where, on still days, you can see the wreckage of the *Mayflower*, a paddle steamer that sank in a winter storm more than a century ago. He tells me how three passengers survived by hanging on to a casket.

"When it's windy, the whitecaps in this part of the lake can be dangerous," he says. Even now, when there's not much more than a breeze, waves disrupt the surface. Charlie turns to make sure I'm listening.

"Got it."

"It could be unsafe in John's little boat." He stares at me, unblinking.

"Okay."

He nods, satisfied, and then we're bombing across miles and miles of open blue. It's rough here, and Charlie goes fast. Once we make it to the mouth of a river, he drops the speed, and I breathe a bit easier.

"Sorry about that. But you would have felt the waves even more if I went slow."

"I'm all right," I tell him. And I am. If there's one thing I've learned today, historic paddle steamer wreckages aside, it's that Charlie knows what he's doing on the water.

We travel down the river, past a rope swing, to a bridge where a string of kids wait to jump into the water below. On the other side is a restaurant. A row of Muskoka chairs is lined up along the beach, where children are playing, and behind them are patio tables with red umbrellas. A band is setting up outside.

"That looks like a fun spot."

"It's called the Bent Anchor," Charlie says. He glances at me, and his eyes catch on my hair.

I reach up; the curls are a knotted nest. "How bad is it?"

He shifts to face me, and I ignore the brush of his leg against mine. "You look like you should be standing in an oversized shell."

"You're comparing me to Venus?"

"You have great hair."

I wrinkle my nose. "I don't know."

"You don't take compliments well."

"Not really."

"It looks like it can't easily be controlled," Charlie says. "It suits you."

I pull a face. "I usually wear it straight and pulled back," I say. "I prefer controlled."

"Controlled isn't you," he says. "You're unpredictable."

"I'm very predictable."

"I don't think so," Charlie says. "I think you're a wild card."

Just then, a strong breeze travels over the river, sending my hair across my face and into Charlie's eyes. We both reach to hold it out of my face at the same time, his fingers settling on mine. For a moment that seems to stretch for hours, he looks at me in that disconcerting way, like he can see not only into my soul but to a deeper place. A corner that's full of secrets I haven't learned yet. It makes me feel stripped to my essential parts.

"Told you," he says. "Wild card."

"You don't know me very well."

"Not yet." His eyes flicker down to my mouth, and then, catching himself, Charlie springs his gaze back to mine. He turns away, gesturing toward the restaurant, his voice a little ragged. "It's good. I can tell Harry to take you."

A second passes before I remember who he's referring to. His friend. Harrison.

"Oh," I say. "Sure."

"Is it cool if I give him your number? He's been asking for it."

"Yeah." I should sound enthusiastic. Harrison is cute. "So cool."

Nan is waiting for us on the deck, where we left her. I hand Charlie the life jacket and thank him for the ride.

"I'll see you tomorrow evening?" I ask.

"The big party." He fixes a dazzling grin on his face. "I wouldn't miss it."

16

Within twenty minutes of stepping foot into the Cut Above salon, Nan and I are up-to-date on every fresh piece of gossip circulating around the town of Barry's Bay. Who's retiring, which businesses are up for sale, the health and marital status of various members of the community. One stylist sets Nan's hair with rollers while the other mixes dye for a woman in a sundress and flip-flops. Nan's in good spirits—she switched out her walker for a cane, and we took a short walk in town before her appointment.

A black Porsche cruises past the window, and all the heads in the salon turn.

"There he goes," says the younger stylist.

"There who goes?" Nan asks.

"Charlie Florek." She sighs out his name, and I stare at her for perhaps a moment too long.

"I went to school with him," she tells me. "He's some kind of big banker in Toronto now."

"He still comes home, though," the older one adds. "Even after his mother passed."

I think of how pensive Charlie was when we were on the cliff and the way he spoke about life being precious. I've been feeling sorry for myself since Mom moved to BC, but she's only a phone call away.

"I'm sure you'll meet him soon enough if you're staying on Kamaniskeg Lake this summer," the younger stylist says to me.

"What do you mean?"

The pair exchange a look, but it's the woman who's getting her hair dyed who speaks.

"Our Charlie has always been a bit of a ladies' man. I taught him math all through high school and handed out tissues to more than one girl whose heart he'd broken. Sharp as a tack, though. I'll give him that."

My eyes travel to Nan. Her mouth is pinched.

"And from what I hear," the other woman adds, "he hasn't changed a stitch. A bit of a Casanova."

"Well, when you look like that . . ."

I feel woozy, like I've had too much sun.

Nan clears her throat loudly. "Let's give the man some privacy, shall we?"

The women glance at each other, but no one says another word about Charlie.

As we're working on the second curtain panel for the kitchen later that day, Nan pats my hand. "Don't worry about what those ladies said in town today."

"I'm not. I'm just not surprised." He's a playboy. It's exactly what I expected.

I lie on top of the sheets that night, staring out the open window. It's black on black, except for the moon's silver stripe on the water and the lights across the bay. Charlie's place shines brighter than the others. I stare at that orb of white as the time changes from 11:59 p.m. to midnight. Seconds later, my phone glows with a message.

Charlie: Happy birthday.

I roll over and face the wall.

I have the dream. I'm running up the stairs. Someone is be-hind me—I can hear their footsteps echoing in the stairwell. I reach the top, but it's a dead end with only a black rotary phone on a table. I pick up the receiver and dial, but I can't say a single word.

17

A drumroll of thunder and a string of texts from the twins greet me in the morning. They've sent them all after two a.m.

Luca: I'm so sorry, Ali. I have to pick up a shift tomorrow night. Or I guess tonight? One of the bartenders walked out, and I kind of need the cash.

Lavinia: I wish I could come. But I'm not comfortable driving all that way on my own. Plus we're really tight right now.

Luca: We'll make it up to you!

Lavinia: YES! As soon as you're back in the city!

Luca: HAPPY BIRTHDAY!!!

Lavinia: We loooove you!

Luca: You are sooooo old!

Lavinia: But never as old as Heather!

I stare at my phone in my storm-darkened bedroom. I should have guessed. Luca is notoriously unreliable, and Lavinia accepts it. We all do. You try looking at his face and being annoyed—it's like trying to stay mad at a puppy. And even though I'm disappointed, I transfer them $500. I don't want them eating Mr. Noodles for a month straight again.

Lightning flashes, and I shut the window. The lake, the sky, the shore—it's all gray. Even the raincoat yellow of Charlie's boat is muted in the murk.

Nan is asleep, so I fix myself coffee and eggs and take them out to the screened porch to watch the storm, nestled under a blanket. Rain dapples the lake's surface, but it's not falling heavily. We've already had a good soaking—the flowers in the window box look like they've been tromped on by garden gnomes. The Pegasus-unicorn has been tossed onto the dock.

The party supplies I bought in town yesterday are stashed in the far corner, so they aren't in Nan's way. Pink balloons. Multicolored streamers. Plastic tiaras. Glitter face gel and nail polish. My Sweet Thirty-Three was going to be the opposite of the dinner parties Trevor and I threw, when we spent our entire Saturday shopping and cooking. We used beautiful linens and plates and serving dishes, all in shades of cream and taupe, and there'd be a stunning arrangement from a flower shop in Leslieville. The lighting was immaculately dimmed. The music was classical. The candles flickered all night. Everything was just so. This birthday was supposed to be girlie and tacky and unpretentious. I wanted to see my younger siblings. I wanted them to want to spend a few days here with me. I wanted cake.

A memory surfaces from my seventeenth birthday. I was sitting on the dock with my diary, watching that yellow boat roar around the bay. I felt aimless. I had no idea what my future might look like. I remember writing, *Today I am seventeen, but sometimes I wonder if I even exist.* That evening, over slices of chocolate cake, Nan gave me a camera.

It was my starting line, the beginning of finding myself, my purpose, my place in the world, separate from my big sister and my parents. With a camera slung over my shoulder, dreams began to fill my head.

My phone rings, and my mother's voice fills my ear. She doesn't say hello; she just starts singing. A drop of liquid slides down my cheek. Mom has called to sing "Happy Birthday" every year since I left home.

"I miss you," I tell her when she's done. I haven't seen her since I visited her in BC three months ago, and I hate calling. The three-hour time difference makes it so that when I'm done with work, she's in the middle of her day. I don't want to bother her. After the twins were born, she was in perpetual motion, but she still shuttled Heather and me to piano lessons and soccer games, made all our Halloween costumes, checked over our homework. Every night, after the twins were asleep, she had "big-girl time" with Heather and me. Sometimes we read, sometimes we watched TV—it didn't matter what we did, it was always the best part of the day. I have no idea when she found time for herself. I figure she deserves that now.

"I miss you, too, honey."

"You're up extremely early."

"Yoga," she says.

The yoga is one of the many changes I tracked when I visited her in March. She'd chopped off her hair and let it go gray. There were no cardigans in her closet. No tennis whites. She wore chambray shirts to work and marshy green athleisure in her downtime. Her friends at the winery called her Meesh. She seemed more content, more at ease. But the mom I grew up with was gone. She's Meesh Dale now, not Michelle Everly.

"I'm sorry the twins won't be there to celebrate with you," she says.

"Me too."

Mom made every birthday special when we were kids, baking cakes from scratch and letting us eat leftover slices for breakfast the next day. I sniffle, then wipe my face and push the hurt away.

"You hanging in okay?"

"Yeah. I'm okay. I've got Nan."

"And cake?"

"Luca and Lavinia were supposed to bring the cake."

She laughs, and I know exactly what she's going to say next. "Never trust the twins with cake."

A smile forms on my lips. "How could I forget?"

Luca and Lavinia will never live down their fourth birthday party, when they were discovered up to their elbows in Mom's homemade Dora the Explorer cake before the guests arrived. I washed the twins off with a hose in the backyard while Mom tried to salvage what was left of Dora and Diego.

Mom sighs. "Thirty-three. How is that possible?"

"I really don't know," I tell her. It's been sixteen years since I was last at the lake, but it's almost like no time has passed. "Right now, I don't feel thirty-three at all."

The rain settles into a gauzy drizzle after we hang up, but as I watch the silver lake in silence, I decide I need to do something to shake off the lingering gloom.

When I need to clear my mind in the city, I run. I run until my thighs ache and my lungs burn and all I can focus on is putting one foot in front of the other. But I kind of hate it. I want to be enveloped by the trees and the mist, but I don't have the energy for even a slow jog, so I put on my coziest clothes and head down Bare Rock Lane, deeper into the bush, focusing on the moist air kissing my cheeks.

I pass a gravel driveway with a wooden sign nailed to a tree. FLOREK. I keep going until I hear the rush of a stream. I follow it into the bush, where a narrow path of wet leaves trails beside it. Here, the rocks are covered with deep green moss. Yellow-capped mushrooms grow at their bases. I trod through the forest, following the twists of the water deeper and deeper until I hear the snap of twigs somewhere to my left, and fearing a bear, I start singing the first song that comes to mind. I belt out "Dancing Queen" as loud as I can as I weave my way back to the road, half panicking and half laughing at myself.

As I return to the cottage, I have a moment of clarity: I'm going to bake myself a cake. Nan and I will eat it tonight, and then I will eat it again for breakfast tomorrow, just like I did when I was a kid.

Mercifully, the grocery store is open on Canada Day. The rain must have lured people away from the lakes, because it's packed. I'm surveying the baking section, holding a box of Funfetti cake mix in one hand and devil's food in the other, when I see someone approach in my periphery. I take a step to the side to give them space.

"Isn't it kind of sad to bake your own birthday cake?"

I jump at the sound of a deep voice next to my shoulder.

Charlie looks like he's just woken up. His hair is a little smooshed on one side, and his stubble has grown overnight.

"You scared me." I shove his shoulder but end up pushing myself back. He's that solid.

Charlie is dressed in a white crewneck sweatshirt with forest-green bands around the neck and sleeves, and—my eyes drop down the length of him—loose jersey pants. "Are those your pajamas?"

"No." His eyes glow with wicked intent. "I sleep naked."

"Of course you do."

"I thought your brother and sister were on cake duty." He looks up and down the aisle. "Or are they here, too?"

"No. They had to cancel. I'm not going to do the whole party thing."

"Are you uninviting me?"

"There's nothing to invite you to."

He eyes the boxes of cake mix.

"It would just be the three of us," I say.

"Three's plenty. You should see what I can do with just two people." He lifts his eyebrows, and I struggle to keep a straight face.

"I'll leave you and Nan to it, then."

"I should be so lucky."

Charlie takes the boxes from my hands and sets them back on the shelf.

"Hey," I protest.

"You're not making your own cake. It's too bleak."

"Then who's going to do it?"

He stares down at me.

"Not you."

"Yes, me."

"You're not serious." I look him over. "You can't bake."

"Oh, I can bake." Charlie takes a step closer. He bends down to my eye level and lowers his voice. "I can bake *all night*."

A laugh bubbles up in my throat and past my lips before I manage to school my features. I lean toward Charlie, our noses inches apart. His gaze narrows on me.

"I don't believe you," I say slowly. "I think when it comes down to it, you're all talk, no bake."

His eyes shine. "I'm going to a bake you a cake so good you'll be ruined for all other cakes."

"Prove." I prod a finger into his chest, and sweet hell, it's like poking a steel door. "It."

"Done. I'll see you tonight." He turns and begins walking down the aisle.

"Charlie, wait."

He pauses and looks back over his shoulder.

"Why?" I ask.

"Because I love defying expectations, and you, Alice Everly, seem to have a lot of them."

18

paint my toenails with sparkling purple polish and bedazzle my eyelids and cheekbones with silver glitter. I don't bother straightening my hair—it would curl in the humidity anyway. It looks like chaos, but I *feel* a little chaotic. I even put on the green scrap of a dress Heather packed in my suitcase. It's short and silky with spaghetti straps and cut low in the back. I don't have a bra that works with it, so I'm not wearing one.

I take a photo of myself in the bathroom mirror and send it to Heather.

What is happening up there??? she writes back. And: **You look HOT.**

I tell myself looking hot was not the goal. I've decided to defy expectations, too, including my own.

I feel sunnier than I did this morning. My phone has been lighting up all day with *happy birthday*s from friends. The twins sent me a video of an elaborate dance routine, involving high heels, cowboy hats, and a perplexing number of jumping jacks. Bennett's message included every tangentially celebratory emoji in the Unicode library. My dad recounted the day I was born, a story I can recite word for word. I also received a text from Harrison, asking me to dinner. I haven't responded.

I've just put the lasagna in the oven when Nan calls out, "He's here."

And sure enough, through the window, a black Porsche slithers through the bush. The rain has stopped, but fog hangs in the trees. It's like a car commercial.

"How do I look?" Nan asks, adjusting her tiara.

"Regal."

And she does. She's wearing her pearls and a tweed skirt and jacket set that she's had forever and will never go out of style. She's sitting straight as a pin, shoulders proud. I roll my own back as soon as I note her posture.

I open the door before Charlie knocks, propping it ajar with my hip. He stands on the stone steps, and for untold seconds, all I can do is stare. Charlie is wearing a suit. It's the color of the sky, an almost metallic gray. The top two buttons of his white shirt are undone. And he's holding a chocolate layer cake. For a heartbeat, he looks at me, just as stunned as I am.

"I baked," he says.

"So you did."

"You look . . ." He swallows. "Like a mermaid."

I glance down at myself. "This dress was a leap for me."

"It was a very good leap." His voice is rougher than usual.

I point at his car. "The five-minute walk was too much for you?"

"I didn't want to scuff my shoes," he says. "And I have a few more things in the car I couldn't carry. Do you mind taking the cake in for me?"

I do as he asks, then meet him outside on the pathway in my bare feet to see if he needs help. Water drips from the branches, onto the forest floor and tin roof. A drop lands on my shoulders. I stand there quietly, listening to the earthy song.

Charlie looks into the limbs of a birch. "I like it after the rain, too."

"It smells unreal." The air is thick and fresh, more fragrant, almost medicinal. It reminds me of Charlie. We breathe it in together, but then I feel his focus drift to me. "What?"

"Nothing. I just figured you were more of a city girl. City person," he amends when I arch a brow.

"Says the guy driving the Porsche."

He shrugs. "I like nice things."

I hum, gazing into the mist—it's draped over the water like a vaporous blanket. "It doesn't get much nicer than this, even for city girls."

Charlie doesn't reply, but when I glance at him, I catch an expression on his face that makes me pause, like he's seeing me for the first time.

"You didn't have to do all this," I say, gesturing to the bags he's holding. He's brought wine and a gift.

"My mom would have eviscerated me if I'd shown up to someone's house empty-handed."

Once we're inside, he gives my grandmother a kiss on the cheek. "Nice to see you, Nan." He passes her a paper bag. "This one's for you."

"What is that?"

Charlie and Nan look over to me.

"I asked Charlie to pick me up a bottle of scotch since you wouldn't." Nan pats him on the hand. "You're a good man. How much do I owe you?"

"Don't worry about it."

"Fiddlesticks."

He gives her a look that clearly means, *What are you going to do about it?* and then asks, "Would you like a glass now? I can pour one."

"Charlie," I say, but they both ignore me.

"Oh, that would be lovely."

I raise my voice. "Charlie."

They both glance in my direction. Charlie looks like he's been caught with his hand in the cookie jar.

"Can I talk to you in the kitchen?"

"Sure."

Nan passes him back the bottle and says, "I take it with a splash of water. No ice."

I shake my head as he crosses the room and follows me into the kitchen. I set the wine on the counter. It's not a big space, and it feels even smaller with him in it.

"It's not a good idea for her to drink," I whisper crossly.

"It smells amazing in here. What are you making?" He crouches down to peer into the oven. "Is that lasagna?"

Charlie looks up at me from beneath his lashes, and for a moment I forget I'm angry. He's down there and I'm up here, and . . . his lips curve, and I swear he knows exactly what I'm thinking.

"Yes, it's lasagna," I hiss, my ears going hot.

He stands and inspects the ingredients on the counter. "Caesar salad? Bruschetta?" He raises an eyebrow. "That's a lot of garlic. If this were a date, I'd be disappointed."

"Can you be serious for one second? What's with the scotch?"

"Your grandmother called and asked if I could bring her a bottle. She told me her doctor said it's okay if she has a drink. She also mentioned that you're a little overprotective."

"I'm just trying to take care of her."

"I get that, but she's eighty, Alice. She's earned the right to make her own choices about her health."

How can I argue? I hate when people infantilize older adults. "I guess a bit of scotch won't hurt," I grumble.

He leans down to meet my eyes. "If she gets trashed, I'll carry her to bed. There'll be no drunken falls tonight."

I huff out a short laugh. "I'm a lightweight. I make no promises."

"Then I'll carry you to bed, too." He gives me a patented smirk, and I pull a face, even though I'm picturing his strong arms holding me against his chest.

"I see I'm underdressed," he says.

"Huh?"

He taps the tiara on the top of my head. I'd forgotten it was there.

"Don't worry," I say, collecting myself. "I have one for you, too."

"Do I get sparkles?"

"Do you want sparkles?"

"I want sparkles." His dimples appear along with a grin that means trouble. "You can apply them anywhere you want, Alice Everly."

He says my name like nobody else has. Like it tastes better than other names.

Alice Everly. Alice Everly. Alice Everly.

"Lucky me."

Charlie passes me a gift bag. "Your birthday present."

There's no card. Just a book. It's a paperback romance, the best kind, with a busty heroine on the cover. She's in the arms of a ravenous-looking shirtless man and dressed in an emerald gown that falls off her shoulders.

"You've turned a very red shade of red," Charlie says. "It's cute."

"Shut up."

"Don't worry," he adds. "It's a good one."

"You've read it?"

"I flipped through it in the drugstore. Think of me when you get to page 179."

I immediately turn to the page, see the words *tongue* and *swirls*, then snap the book shut.

"You're incorrigible, you know that?"

"I do."

I examine the cover. It's called *Ruling the Rogue*. "You know," I say, holding the book beside Charlie's face, "there's a bit of a resemblance between you two."

"Oh, I know."

I bark out a laugh.

Charlie gives me a strange look.

"What?"

"The way you laugh," he says.

"I know, it's horrendous. My sister calls it a witch's cackle."

"No." He shakes his head. "I like it."

Charlie turns away before I can tell if he's joking. He pours Nan's scotch, pausing when he sees our flowery curtains. "Are those new?"

"They are. Nan seems to think John won't mind. She sewed the old curtains. It seemed fitting we make new ones."

Charlie tilts his head, confused. "You're sewing new curtains?"

"Yep. We're giving this place a facelift."

He squints. "Did John tell you he's been planning to sell? He won't get to enjoy your makeover."

"I know, but it's something for Nan and me to do together." I drop my voice. "She seems down lately." Charlie stares at me, an odd, puzzled look on his face. "Anyway, John's real estate agent will thank us."

He assesses me for another moment before pulling down a pair of mismatched wineglasses. One is delicate and etched with thistles, and the other looks like it was purchased at a dollar store.

"White or red?" he asks. "Unless you're a scotch drinker?"

"Not usually. I'll have red, please." He pours it in the prettier glass, and we bring the drinks out to the living room.

"Alice, you're the color of a geranium," Nan says.

I place a hand on my cheek.

"I hope you two didn't get up to anything untoward in the kitchen." She winks at Charlie.

"Fully PG," he tells her.

We sit on the sofa, and Nan pales when she sees the glass in my hand. She takes a deep, wavering breath. Charlie and I share a glance.

"Is everything okay?" I ask.

"That was Joyce's special glass." Her voice catches. "Alice will take good care of it," she says, looking at the ceiling.

I wait for Charlie to shift or look at his hands or show some other sign of being uncomfortable with Nan speaking to her dead best friend, but instead he raises his glass. "To Joyce." And then he looks at me, green eyes holding mine. "And Alice. Happy birthday."

We each take a sip, and then Charlie says, "John and Joyce were good to us when my dad died."

He's lost both his parents? I stare at Charlie's profile—it's all hard lines, no softness to be found. "I'm so sorry," I say quietly.

"It was a long time ago. I was fourteen." He says it like it's not supposed to hurt anymore, like the fourteen-year-old Charlie who lost his father is a different person.

"I remember," Nan says, and I tear my gaze away from him to look at her. "It was sudden, wasn't it? He was young."

A muscle flexes in Charlie's jaw. "His heart gave out while he was cooking at our family's restaurant."

"John and Joyce were both so upset," Nan says. "They were worried about you boys and your mom."

Charlie leans forward, resting his elbows on his knees. "Our mom was barely holding it together, but she had the restaurant to run, so Sam and I were alone a lot. Joyce stopped in almost every day when she was at the cottage. She'd bring us muffins and cookies and casseroles." He seems so unlike the person I was just speaking to in the kitchen. He's so still, so contained.

"That's Joyce," Nan says. "She was a wonderful person."

"She was," Charlie agrees. "And so is John. He'd take Sam and me fishing and talk to us about random stuff, but it helped to get out of the house, to have someone treat us normally. I probably would have partied a lot harder than I did if he hadn't popped around every time the music got too loud. He looked out for us."

Nan says nothing, and then Charlie straightens. "He's still a wonderful person."

They stare at each other.

"I'm sure that's true," Nan says, looking away.

"He asked me to tell you to call him. He asked me to tell you that he misses you."

Nan's eyes are becoming glassy, and I don't know whether to ask what in the world Charlie is talking about or bonk him on the shoulder for upsetting my grandmother.

"We'll see," she says.

I clear my throat, needing to put an end to this. "Charlie, is now a good time for glitter?"

I squeeze a dab of silvery gel into my palm and examine Charlie's face, carefully avoiding eye contact. I'm on the couch facing him, legs folded beneath me, but even with Nan across from us, it feels intimate being this close.

"Something wrong?"

I meet his gaze then. "I'm not sure it'll suit you."

Flecks of gilt in pools of green shimmer back at me. "Everything suits me. Quit stalling, Alice."

I tap my index finger in the gel and raise my hand to Charlie's face, trying to figure out which part of it is safest to touch. It's not the hard lines of his jaw or the laser focus of his stare that has me suddenly rattled; it's the fact that he's here, on my birthday, with a homemade cake and a gift that's now an inside joke.

Charlie's brows lift, and I realize I've been studying him for a preposterous length of time. I hear Nan shift and turn to see her reaching for her cane.

I immediately jump to my feet. "Do you need help?"

"I'm all right. Just need the ladies' room."

I face Charlie, alone. The quiet is too much.

"Music?"

I crouch beside John's very out-of-date CD collection. Yikes. I go with *The Definitive Rod Stewart*, and "Maggie May" begins to play.

"Rod Stewart?" he asks.

"Yup. Huge fan."

I sit beside Charlie again and hover a finger over his cheekbone. "You're not afraid of me, are you?"

"I'm afraid of getting glitter on your jacket."

Charlie laughs like he knows I'm full of crap and then shrugs off his jacket. He unbuttons his cuffs and rolls the sleeves of his shirt past his forearms.

"Better?" His gaze is a game of truth or dare.

"Uh-huh."

I press my finger lightly to the upper edge of his right cheekbone and slide it up toward his temple. I feel his eyes on me, but I repeat the stripe on his left side without meeting them. If he sees my hand shaking, he doesn't mention it.

"How do I look?"

I lean back to inspect my handiwork. Of course he can pull off glitter. "Pretty ridiculous."

He smiles. "I doubt that."

I leave Nan and Charlie to make the salad, and when I return to the living room, he's sitting on a dining chair in front of her, painting her nails with the purple polish. He's doing a terrible job, the tiny bottle cap ill fitted to his hands. I sneak past to get my camera. I take one shot of Charlie concentrating on Nan's manicure, her fingers in his, and another when they both look up at me.

"Has Alice told you that this isn't her first trip to the lake?" Nan asks when we're all seated around the table with plates of lasagna. Charlie's gaze shoots to me. "I brought her and her younger siblings for the entire summer when John and Joyce were traveling."

"She didn't mention that," he replies, eyes on mine.

"When I was seventeen." I give Nan a meaningful look. She hasn't said anything, but she must have connected Charlie with the yellow boat in my photo.

"Really? I would have been nineteen. I was here that summer."

"Then that makes three of us," I say.

"Huh." Charlie lifts his wine to his lips. He's still on his first glass, whereas I've had . . . um? Several?

We're almost done eating when I see that Charlie has painted a thumb purple. Something in my chest twinges.

"I thought I'd better stop there before I made a real mess of it," Charlie says when he catches me staring at his hand.

I smile, but my heart is beating faster than usual. It's probably the wine. It probably has nothing to do with the fact that despite our being an odd trio, the conversation hasn't died all evening. Or that Charlie is unpredictable in the best way. Or that I haven't laughed so hard in ages. Or how effusively Charlie praises my lasagna, calling it the most glorious combination of tomato sauce, noodles, and various cheeses. Or that he clears the table, three plates a time, then washes the dishes, refusing help.

He returns holding the cake, with a single candle in the center. I raise my camera, committing Charlie in a tiara and glitter, singing "Happy Birthday," to film.

It's a dark chocolate sour cream cake with chocolate buttercream, and sweet mother, it is good. I make an obscene sound when I take my first bite.

"You can *bake*," I say with my mouth full.

Charlie grins. It's a boyish smile, dimpled and delighted. It's his real smile.

"You made this?" Nan asks.

"It was my mom's recipe."

"It's incredible," I go on. "It's moist and rich, but not too rich. Or too sweet. It's like really, *really* good."

"Excellent," Nan agrees. "I'd love the recipe."

Charlie beams at my grandmother. "My mom would have been thrilled to hear that."

The twinge in my chest returns, only stronger now.

"I think she would have been thrilled *you* made it," Nan says.

I'm still gushing about the cake when a horn interrupts me.

Aaaah-whoooo-gaaaaah!

"Oh shit." Charlie looks at me, wild-eyed. "They're here."

19

W ho's here?" I ask. I rise from the table to look out the window.

The clouds have parted, leaving red streaks across a slate-blue sky. It's starting to grow dark, but there are countless boats on the lake, all heading in the same direction. Charlie's drifts just out from our dock, and there are two people inside. I glance at him over my shoulder.

"My brother and his wife."

"How lovely," Nan says.

Judging from the look on Charlie's face, he doesn't agree.

"What are they doing here?"

"Wreaking havoc. I'll go get rid of them."

"Whatever for?" Nan says, but he's already on his way outside.

We share a look.

"Go out there," she says. "Report back."

I do as I'm told and follow Charlie to the dock. As I'm walking down the steps, I hear him say, "You two are the worst busybodies."

"I have nothing to do with this," replies a deep voice almost identical to Charlie's. "It's all Percy. Though I don't hate the opportunity to make you sweat."

"I'm not sweating."

"No, you're *sparkling*," a woman says.

I step onto the dock, and all three of them look at me. I raise my hand. "Hey."

"You must be Alice," the woman says. It's too dim to see her very well, but I can tell she's a big-eyed brunette. She's also pregnant.

"That's me."

I stand next to Charlie at the edge of the dock. "Sorry," I tell him. "Nan sent me on a reconnaissance mission."

"I'm surrounded by spies, then," he says, but there's no bite to it.

"We're not spying," the woman says to me. "It's just that Charlie has been refusing to give up any details about the mystery girl across the bay, so I thought we'd come say hello ourselves and drag you out for a bit. Happy birthday, by the way. How was the cake? Charlie refused to give me, his pregnant sister-in-law, a taste."

I glance at Charlie.

"I know. She talks a lot," he says. "You forgot the part where you introduce yourself, Pers."

She waves. "Sorry. I'm Persephone, but please call me Percy, and this is Sam."

"Nice to meet you, Alice," Sam says. His hair is darker than Charlie's and a bit of a mess, but I can't see much more than that. "Happy birthday. Sorry for interrupting your evening. Percy would not be deterred."

"No need to apologize. It's good to meet you both." I give Charlie a pointed look. "It's such a nice surprise."

"They just drove up from Toronto today," he says.

"Charlie has been trying to keep you to himself," Percy tells me. "But he knows I've wanted a cottage friend, so I've come to claim you."

I let out a laugh. "What does that involve?"

"I thought you might want to come with us to see the Canada Day fireworks."

"Is that where all the boats are going?"

Sam nods. "It's pretty cool seeing the show from the water."

I look to Charlie.

"I'll go if you want to," he says.

"I do," I tell him. "It sounds like fun."

We join the parade of boats, and even though I've changed into sweats, it's chilly in the wind. Charlie and I are sitting at the front; Sam and Percy are in the driver and passenger seats. Nan almost pushed me out the door when I told her where I was going.

We swerve around a corner, and there are dozens of vessels bobbing in the water. There's a beach and a playground on one part of the bay and a causeway from the mainland out to a large island. Vehicles are parked around the shore, ready to watch.

"This is . . ." I look at Charlie and then back to the bay, a huge smile on my face. "So cool."

"I haven't been in ages. We used to come every year when we were kids."

Despite Percy saying she wanted to claim me, she and Sam move to the back of the boat while we wait for the sky to turn black. I sneak a glance at them. Sam is handsome like Charlie, but there's something softer about him. More boyish. Percy is sitting on his lap, and he's looking up at her with awe. He pulls her to his lips, kissing her softly.

"They're always like this," Charlie says.

I look at him with disbelief.

"Tell me about it," he says, but he's smiling. "How come you didn't mention that you spent a summer here?"

"It didn't come up." A half-truth. "But it was amazing. One of those formative teenage experiences, you know?"

"Sure." He stares at me for a moment. "It surprises me, though."

"Why?"

"Because I don't remember you."

I look up at the sky, where the stars are blinking to life. "I guess I'm not very memorable."

"Well, that's bullshit," Charlie says, and I turn back to him. "You know you're hot."

"I wasn't digging for a compliment," I say, a bit defensive. "It's just true. And it was especially true when I was seventeen."

"I don't buy that. We were neighbors. I'm sure I would have noticed you." The first firework whistles toward the sky, but neither of us turns to watch it. It bursts overhead, and the glitter on Charlie's face shimmers in reply.

"Well, I guess you didn't," I say, before a series of bangs echoes around the lake. I settle lower into the seat and lay my head back, watching blooms of gold flower into the night.

"You must have seen us," Charlie says. A dog with a bone. "We would have been on the water from dawn till dusk, and we weren't quiet. Why didn't you say hi?"

I can feel his gaze on me, but I don't look. I feel each firework in my chest.

"I was shy," I tell him. "I could have said hello, but I wouldn't have known what to say next."

"I can't picture you as shy."

I snort.

"Why is that funny?"

I turn my head to the side, and my breath catches. Charlie has his arms behind his head, one ankle crossed over the other, the picture of ease, but he's studying me with sharp intensity.

"It's funny because I'm the turtle."

Charlie looks appropriately confused.

"I have three siblings," I explain. "Heather is two years older. Luca and Lavinia are twenty-four." I can't remember when or why we came up with the animal thing, but it's fundamental to being an Everly child. "Heather is the lion, Lavinia is the flamingo, and Luca is the monkey."

"And you're the turtle."

"Right. My family is full of big personalities. Aside from my mom, they're all loud and opinionated and . . . I don't know . . . brighter than me? I'm the quiet one, the level head," I tell him. "And I'm still shy."

Charlie frowns and we both fall silent. I look back to the display of red and white fizzling above us.

"You're not quiet around me," he says slowly, a minute later, as if he's been thinking it over.

"No." I turn to him. There's something about Charlie that calms the part of my brain that constantly worries about saying the wrong thing. "But I would have been shy . . . back then, I mean."

But I wonder if that's true, or if I would have found him easy to be around when I was seventeen.

"I guess we'll never know."

"Did you have a nickname when you were younger?"

"Yeah," he says quietly. "My actual name is Charles. But my dad always called me Charlie."

"What were you like?" I ask.

Charlie shifts, propping himself on one elbow, facing me. "Terrible."

I laugh. "So basically the same?"

"See, that's why I like you."

"Because I make fun of you?"

"Because you're honest. And, for the record, I think you're very bright."

"It's the glitter," I tell him.

Charlie's gaze roams my face slowly. "It's definitely the glitter."

20

arrive at the Florek house the next morning bearing leftover chocolate cake. It's a lovely home, white with black trim and gabled windows on the second floor. There's a large porch and a detached garage with a basketball net hanging over the door. It's not cottagey like John and Joyce's place—the bush has been cut back around it, making way for lawns and gardens.

I knock on the door, assuming everyone is awake—the hammering started an hour ago. Percy answers in nothing but an orange bikini.

"Alice, hi."

"I brought cake."

"You are a dream." She gestures to her body. "Sorry about this. I wasn't expecting you, and it's too hot for real clothes."

I begin to stammer out an apology, but Percy takes the plate in one hand and my arm in another, and drags me into the house, padding toward the kitchen in bare feet, her dark brown hair tumbling down her back in loose waves. Mine is pulled into a bun at the nape of my neck. I'm dressed in black—pressed shorts, a thin belt, a sleeveless blouse, and leather sandals—and I feel stiff in comparison.

"Coffee?" she asks over her shoulder. "The boys are out bashing two-by-fours as if they know what they're doing."

"Sure."

I lean against the counter as Percy grinds fresh beans.

"You brought a camera," she says before I've had a chance to explain why I have my Sony slung over my shoulder.

"I'm a photographer."

She offers me a big smile. "I know. It's one of the few things I've managed to get out of Charlie. You've shot for my magazine before."

I raise my brows, surprised. "Where do you work?"

"I'm the editor of *Shelter*. You did an incredible shoot for us last year."

"Up in Muskoka." I remember. It was for a feature on the woman who modernized her family's resort while preserving its history. "The subject hated having her photograph taken."

"My art director mentioned that, but I couldn't tell from the shots," Percy says. "You must have loosened her up."

Her fiancé had stopped by when we were setting up, and her face brightened. After he left, I asked how they met, and she transformed into the person she probably is when she doesn't have a camera shoved in front of her face.

It was a good shoot. The art director was lovely. She and I drove up to Muskoka together and spent the night there. We took a canoe out in the morning so I could get some shots from the water and ended up chatting for a solid hour. I meant to reach out to her and see if we could work together more regularly, but I got too busy with other assignments.

"Do you always carry a camera with you?" Percy asks.

"Kind of. I thought you might like some photos from this summer, before the baby comes."

She tilts her head. "Like a maternity shoot?"

"Nothing as posed as that. Just some spontaneous stuff so you can remember this moment." Selfishly, I'm much more comfortable with strangers when I'm photographing them.

She grins. "That's so nice. Although I'm not sure anyone needs images of me in a bathing suit while I'm six months pregnant."

"You look beautiful," I say honestly. Percy has doe eyes, a light smattering of freckles that kiss her nose and cheeks, and a sweet nose. Separately, each feature is cute, but they assemble to make something more intriguing.

"All right," Percy says. "It would be nice to have some photos of this summer." She blows out a breath. "Before things get real."

I take the lens cap off my camera, slipping into photographer Alice mode.

"It's an amazing thing that your body is doing," I tell Percy, and she puts her hands on her stomach, smiling down at it.

"Or like something out of a horror movie."

Click.

She glances at me, surprised. "You really are gorgeous," I tell her, and she smiles again.

Click.

"Aha," Percy says. "You sweet-talk your way into getting a decent shot."

I laugh. "You got me, but I'm also telling the truth."

I take a couple more shots as she grabs four mugs from the cupboard and fills them with coffee, then set my camera strap over my shoulder as Percy passes me two.

"Let's go caffeinate the boys."

Percy leads me out to the deck, and we both freeze at the

sound of Charlie and Sam's raised voices. I glance at Percy, and she quickly wipes the alarm from her face.

"Brothers," she says. "They love each other, but they suck at communicating."

"What are they fighting about?" I ask as I follow her down the steps off the deck and around to the side of the house.

She seems to debate her answer. "Their lack of construction skills, probably."

I hear them before I see them.

"I don't care if you don't want to talk about it. You need to be prepared." They sound so alike I can't tell whether it's Charlie or Sam speaking.

"Fuck off, Sam."

So that clears that up.

I glance at Percy.

"Let's go break this up," she says.

Charlie spots us over Sam's shoulder and he says something quietly.

"I'm not dropping this," Sam replies.

Both men are in their bathing suits, Sam with a T-shirt and Charlie bare-chested. Sam is slightly taller, his wavy hair is longer on top, and his eyes are blue, but there's no mistaking them as siblings. Charlie casts him a hard look, but it dissolves when he looks at me. I think of the way he looked at me last night, glittering under the fireworks, and my heart beats faster.

After I got home, I checked off numbers four (*throw myself a birthday party*), fourteen (*glittery makeup*), and fifteen (*put on the green dress*) from my bucket list, and I stared at number five (*kiss a cute guy*). I felt invigorated, bright, like Charlie said.

This morning, I sent Harrison a message, telling him I wasn't available for dinner right now. And then I emailed Willa. I told her I wouldn't edit the photos as requested. I quoted the original brief ("a refreshingly real swimwear shoot") and explained that I wouldn't have taken the assignment if I'd known she wanted me to retouch the images so dramatically. There's a chance I've permanently damaged our relationship, but for once, the thought of someone being unhappy with me doesn't feel cataclysmic.

"You must be very brave to throw yourself to the lions like this," Charlie says to me now, nodding at Sam and Percy.

"There's a special place in hell for anyone who denies a pregnant woman chocolate cake," I tell him. "I brought Percy a slice."

I stare into the branches of tall neighboring hemlock and maple trees, where the frame of a large tree house sits. "So, this is it?"

"Impressive, isn't it?" Charlie says.

"Your ego?" I ask, still gazing upward. "Very. It's *immense*."

Charlie chuckles, and I hand him his coffee. I catch Percy and Sam looking at us. She's gaping, and he's wearing a lopsided grin.

"How do you put up with him?" Sam asks.

"I don't. I just haven't been able to get rid of him yet."

Sam glances at Charlie, who shrugs. "I told you she was ferocious."

"That's perfect for you," Percy tells him.

"We're just friends, Pers," he says.

For a few seconds, it feels like I've been shaken from a nice dream. Charlie's flirting doesn't mean anything.

Charlie looks to me. "Right, Alice?"

"Right." And it's for the best, I remind myself. Because this summer I'm focusing on me—and Nan. I'm not about to develop feelings for the heartbreaker across the bay. "Just friends."

"I doubt that," Sam mutters, and Percy elbows him in the side.

"Screw off," Charlie says.

Percy's stomach grumbles loudly, and she laughs. "This little guy must have heard about the cake."

"This little *girl*," Sam says.

Percy is shaking her head, but they're gazing at each other like there's no one else in the world who matters. In our four years together, Trevor never once looked at me like that.

I glance at Charlie. He's watching them with an expression that's almost sad. He sees me staring and smiles—but it's not his boyish grin, and there's nothing smug about it. It's a smile I haven't seen before.

"You have to sleep here when you finish it," I say, looking at the tree house again.

"*If* he finishes it," Sam quips.

Charlie cuffs him on the back of the head. "I told you I'd have it done in time for the party."

Percy looks skeptical. "The party is in three weeks." She turns to me. "You should join us, Alice. A bunch of our friends are coming for the weekend."

A house full of people I don't know. My eyes drift to Charlie.

"Come," he says. "I could use the backup."

"I doubt that, but I'll be there." I look at Percy. "I'll bring my camera."

"We better get back to it," Sam says, giving her a kiss on the cheek.

I watch Charlie climb the ladder up to the tree house, muscles flexing in his back. "I'll be over this afternoon to do a few things at the cottage," he calls down to me.

As I turn around, I hear Percy say to Sam, "Do you really think they're just friends?"

"You know how he is," he replies. A moment passes, and he adds, "But I guess there's a first time for everything."

21

Nan and I make curtains for the bathroom and covers for the throw pillows in the living room. We pillage Stedmans for more fabric. But unless Charlie's around, Nan is often melancholy or biting. She gripes through her physio exercises, even though they're clearly helping. She's moving more confidently with the cane, and we take careful strolls together along Bare Rock Lane. Each day we go a little farther. I try talking to her about why she and John aren't speaking, but she's deemed the subject a "private matter."

Thankfully, Charlie shows up every afternoon after he and Sam are done working on the tree house. I don't mind the hammering anymore. There's something wholesome about the sound of two brothers working together, even when I hear them bicker across the bay. Charlie does odd jobs around the cottage—raking fallen pine needles and fixing a loose step. He spends so much time here that I wonder if he's avoiding Percy and Sam. I can't get the way he looked at them out of my head.

On Wednesday, he escorts Nan to her first Stationkeeper Singers choir practice, and she returns with plans to team up with him for the community euchre night. On Thursday, he arrives in Sam's red pickup, the back full of lumber. He's going to build a proper railing for the stairs that lead to the lake so Nan can get down to swim. He sets up a table saw on the deck. His T-shirt lies in a heap beside it. He's wearing a black bathing suit and a pair of steel-toed boots. It *really* works for me.

We'll go for a swim when he's done, just like we did yesterday and the day before. I inflated the moose for Charlie, but he's claimed ownership of the Pegasus-unicorn. I swim along the shore while he floats, and then I join him, laying out on the moose. Yesterday we ended up talking for well over an hour, about our jobs and our condos and our favorite spots in the city. We discussed our families and our university years, the music we listen to, where we've traveled, the books we love best. I learned that Sam is a cardiologist and that Percy's working on a novel in her spare time. I found out that Charlie's last relationship ended after Christmas—he and Genevieve were together for a few months, and he was the one to break it off. I changed the subject when he asked about my ex—I don't want to bring Trevor to the lake. And Charlie gave me a vague answer when I asked what he and Sam had been arguing about the other day. Clearly he doesn't want to bring that to the lake, either.

I watch him now from the sewing table, my gaze drifting to his shoulders as he uses the saw, his bronzed skin glistening under the sun. Nan tells me I'm drooling.

"I am not." Salivating, maybe. I can't help it if Charlie insists on waltzing around without a shirt. So what if I sneak a few glances? I'm only human.

She looks at me over her glasses from her spot in the armchair, a queen on her throne. "I don't blame you. If I were a younger woman, I'd let him put his shoes at the end of my bed."

"There'll be no leaving of shoes. He doesn't see me that way."

"Oh please."

"He doesn't."

"He does," Nan says. "When you aren't staring at him, he's staring at you. It's like watching a tennis match."

"We're friends," I tell her.

Just friends, I remind myself.

"It's hard to work when you're staring at me like that," Charlie says when I bring him a glass of water.

"It's hard not to stare when you're sweating like that." Perspiration runs in rivulets down his chest. I follow it down the flat expanse of skin to his belly button and the line of hair that dips below. He's breathing heavily.

Charlie does a double take when he stops working to accept the glass from my hand. "That's new."

I'm wearing a yellow bikini that I bought at Stedmans earlier this week, after Willa got back to me about the swimwear photos. The email was two letters.

Ok.

No greeting. No salutation. I stared at the screen, a hand covering my mouth. And then I started to laugh. I might not work for *Swish* again, but I'd held my ground. No one is going to give me permission to be the kind of photographer I want to be except for me. I needed to do something to celebrate, so I drove into town and purchased a thirty-four-dollar string bikini (number two). It shows a lot more *everything* than I'm used to, but it's sweltering, and I feel emboldened.

"It's new," I tell Charlie.

"Make sure you stay in the shade," he says. His face is flushed. He rests his hands on his knees and bends over, panting.

"Are you all right?"

"Just out of shape."

"The state of your abdominals says otherwise." I put my hand on his shoulder. "I think it's time to quit. You've been in the sun all day."

I lead him inside, past Nan, who's snoozing on the screened porch sofa despite Charlie's ruckus. He pauses in the entryway to the living room, laying a hand on the wall to steady himself.

"Charlie?"

He stares at me, wide-eyed.

"It's just the heat," I tell him, and he gives me a look that says he doesn't believe me. He seems genuinely frightened.

"Here, sit." I take his arm and guide him to the couch, then leave him to get a cool facecloth. His head is in his hands when I return. I sit next to him and dab the cloth on the back of his neck.

"That feels nice."

Charlie closes his eyes, and I move the cloth to his forehead, then his temple, and his breathing begins to slow.

"This is embarrassing," he says after a moment, head still dropped.

"This is nothing. You read my bucket list. You've got to do a lot worse than mild heatstroke before you reach that level of mortification."

He turns his cheek toward me. His eyes meet mine, searching and serious. "Tell me why you wrote it?"

I hum. "Nostalgia?"

Charlie slowly sits up, leaning all the way back on the couch, his heading resting on the cushion, slanted my way. Waiting.

I chew on my cheek, thinking. "It's been a rough year. Being here made me think about the summer I was seventeen—and how I'd go back and redo it if I had the chance. I know when September rolls around, I'll have to face everything that's waiting for me in the city. But I want to leave it behind while I'm here—do all the silly things I'd do if I were seventeen again."

"And you love a list," Charlie says, voice gentle.

"Precisely."

For a moment, I slip into the pools of green in his gaze.

I crinkle my nose. "It's silly, right?"

He shakes his head. "I think I get it. If I could go back, knowing what I know now, I probably would."

"Really?"

"Sure. There are things I'd like to do differently. That feeling of being invincible. All of life stretching before you. Not to mention no sixty-hour workweeks."

"No bills. Or real responsibilities. No exes with fiancées named Astilbe."

Charlie smiles. "Specific."

"No compromising my integrity."

"No serious consequences," Charlie says.

"Exactly."

"Can I see that list again?"

My smile falters. "Didn't you get a good enough look at it?"

He makes a wishy-washy movement with his hand.

"Come on, Alice. I'm not going to laugh at you," he says, the twinkle returning to his eyes.

"You might."

"Okay, I might. But I won't think less of you."

And I believe him. I blow out a breath and fetch my notebook. Charlie reads it as I stand over his shoulder, arms crossed in front of me.

He glances up. "'Low-key drugs, question mark, question mark, question mark'?"

"I was the kind of girl people assumed wouldn't touch a joint. I was literally passed over more than once."

"What would you have done if you'd been offered a toke?"

"I would have declined," I say.

Charlie beams up at me. "You were a good girl."

"The goodest. What about you?"

"The opposite. I was reckless. Cocky. Jealous. Competitive. I was a little shit." There's no humor in his smile. "I guess not much has changed."

Hearing Charlie talk about himself like this pulls at something in me. I sit beside him.

"Charlie, I don't think there's enough room in an airplane hangar for your ego. But you're not a shit. I doubt you were back then, either."

"I was. It's probably a good thing we didn't meet when we were kids. I did a lot of stupid stuff to distract myself from how I was really feeling. You wouldn't have liked me."

"You lost your father when you were fourteen. I can't imagine how hard that was."

Charlie pins me with the full force of his stare. "Don't go soft on me now, Alice."

So I stare back. "If you want to talk about it, I'm here. I'm an excellent listener and a vault when it comes to secrets."

"I'm sure you are." His chest rises and falls. I can tell he's making a decision about me, weighing how much he can confide. I get the sense that he doesn't confide in many people, that he doesn't sit with his feelings very often as an adult, either.

"I had great parents," he says slowly. "My dad was a steadfast, serious guy, but he was also kind and thoughtful. He had this dry sense of humor. Sam is a lot like him. My mom was full of energy, always laughing. Everyone loved her. You just felt good being with her, you know?"

"Yeah," I say, looking at him. "I know."

"From a young age, I could tell they were so in love. Being around them felt safe." He scrubs a hand over his jaw. "They grew up together. They were friends first. And even though they worked their asses off at the restaurant, they made our time together count. My mom would cook these epic breakfasts . . ." His voice catches, and he clears his throat. "We were like one of those TV families. Almost perfect." My heart squeezes even before he says the words: "And then my dad died."

Charlie stares down at his hands. "I was fourteen, but Sam was only twelve. Our mom was a wreck. My grandfather gave me this talk about being the man of the house, and it scared the fuck out of me. I didn't know what that meant or what I was supposed to do or how to fix things."

"Of course not. You were a child."

He makes a sound like he doesn't quite agree. "I did everything I could think of. I helped at the restaurant and tried to make our mom smile and made sure I didn't fall apart in front of Sam. If you were the turtle of your family, I was the joker. The guy who didn't take anything too seriously, who didn't let anything bother him. It felt like, if I was normal, then they would be normal, too."

"And did that work?"

"Sort of. Sam curled up inside himself after Dad died, and Mom worried about him. I didn't give her reason to worry about me." His smile is so profoundly sad. "That's not to say I didn't piss her off."

"What teenager didn't piss off their parents?"

"I bet Alice Everly didn't."

"Busted. Heather was the rebel; I was the easy one. Although." I lean closer and lower my voice to a whisper. "In second grade, I stole a library book."

Charlie's dimples appear, and I'm overwhelmed with the need to keep them there, adorning his cheeks, to be the person who makes the joker smile.

"It was a children's encyclopedia of birds," I say. Charlie chuckles, and I feel exhilarated, like I'm jumping from a cliff into the lake. "It had all these colorful toucans and lorikeets on the cover, and I wanted to keep it forever. I ripped out the library card envelope, thinking I was brilliant. When my mom found it in my room, she made me return it to the librarian, tell her exactly what I'd done, and apologize. It was so humiliating, I never wanted to get in trouble like that again."

"And you didn't, I'm guessing."

"Nope. I was determined, even then."

"My brother was like that. Very by the book. The year after Dad died, Percy's parents bought the cottage next door to us. Sam and Percy became instant best friends. She talked nonstop and somehow pulled him out of his shell, helped him have fun again. They took care of each other."

I study him. "Who took care of you?"

He looks at me from the corner of his eye. "Our mom did her best, which was pretty damn good. And the chef at the Tavern, Julien, was always keeping an eye out. But I still managed to do a bunch of boneheaded stuff."

"Like what?"

"Partying." He pauses, and then adds, "Girls."

I think of what the women in the salon said last week. I think of what I heard Sam say, and what it implied.

You know how he is.

"I didn't have my first kiss until I was nineteen," I tell Charlie.

"I hope it was worth the wait." The look on his face is hysterical.

I laugh. "It was kind of a letdown. It was just a random guy during frosh week. But to be fair, my expectations were extremely high at that point."

His thigh bumps against mine. "I would have kissed you."

It knocks the air out of me. "What?"

"Back then," Charlie says, eyes glued to me. "When you were here that summer. I definitely would have kissed you."

"And what makes you think I would have wanted to kiss *you*?" I press my thigh into his leg.

His smile is treacherous. "Everyone wanted to kiss me."

I hit him on his concrete block of a shoulder, and he laughs. I love seeing him like this. Unburdened.

"We should do it together," I find myself saying.

He looks taken aback. "Kiss?"

"The list." I laugh. "You should have a seventeen-year-old summer with me."

Charlie's eyes brighten. "Yeah?"

He reads my list over again, lips moving silently. Then he digs his phone out of his pocket and snaps a photo.

"No problem," he announces.

"No problem?"

"Nope," he says. "You've already done a bunch of it. You jumped off the rock, threw yourself a birthday party." He arches an eyebrow. "And *that* is a very skimpy bathing suit. We can do this."

"We?" I say, smiling.

His eyes spark. They're aurora borealis green.

"You and me, Alice Everly."

22

Does this mean we have to go skinny-dipping together?"

I convinced Charlie to stop working and go for a swim. Now we're floating, Charlie on his Pegasus-unicorn, me on the moose. I'm getting so good at boarding the thing that I can wear my straw hat and caftan without worrying about falling off or being ravaged by the sun.

Charlie doesn't reply. His hands are joined behind his head, his legs spread on either side of the golden tail, feet dangling in the water. "Nah," he says after a moment. He looks like a deity of sunlight and water. It's an effort not to stare. "You can find someone else to kiss and get naked with." Charlie tilts his head to me, and I feel a spark of disappointment that I immediately smother. "Harry, for example."

"That's not going to happen."

"Why not? He too good-looking and kind for you?"

"I'm not interested in dating anyone right now."

Charlie smirks at that. "Just fucking, then?"

"What? No!"

"You're bright red, Alice."

"Shut up." I narrow my eyes at Charlie. "What about you?"

"What about me?"

"You mentioned your last relationship the other day. Was it a bad breakup?"

"Not really. I never imagined it going anywhere. It was fun for a while." Charlie's eyes are fastened to mine. "Yours was rough?"

I can do this. I can talk about Trevor without crying. "Brutal. You heard what Nan said. We were together for four years. We lived together. I didn't see it coming."

"Is that why you're immune to Harrison's charm—you're not over your ex?"

"No, that's not it." And as I say it, I realize it's true. If Trevor wanted a second chance, I wouldn't give it a split second of consideration. "I'm not sure I can invest in another relationship."

Charlie turns, propping himself on an elbow. "What happened?" His voice is so gentle. And because I haven't been able to confide in anyone without bursting into tears, and because he's easy to talk to, I do.

I tell Charlie all the ways we were compatible. We were homebodies. Serious about our work. Always reliable. We each ran our own businesses. We bonded over being both creative *and* organized. Two peas in a tidy pod.

"I grew up in a chaotic household," I say to Charlie. "There was a lot of love, but it was loud and messy—like living in a monsoon. With Trevor, things were calm. Quiet."

"Sounds dull," Charlie says, eyeing me while he drags his hand back and forth in the water in lazy strokes.

"No."

He raises his eyebrows like, *Really?*

"Maybe a little predictable," I concede. "Our friends called us the perfect couple. And I loved it."

What I don't tell Charlie is how much being a flawless girlfriend required. I'd try on outfit after outfit before our dates,

straightening my hair to a shine, making myself sleek and effort-
less looking. I started listening to classical music because Trevor
loved it. I made gourmet meals in our gourmet condo, and we'd
eat on our designer chairs, drinking red wine and discussing art
and work and Steve Reich. I loved all the things he loved. At
least, that's what I thought until the end.

I don't know how to make you happy, Alice. Do you?

"Why?" Charlie asks.

"Why what?"

I slant my head and find him studying me with a frown of
concentration.

"You said you loved being called a perfect couple. Why?"

"Because it's exactly who I wanted to be."

"There's no such thing as perfect."

"In theory."

"And if there were, it would be boring." He flicks his hand in
the water, sending a gentle arc of water over my toes. "And you,
Alice Everly, are anything but boring."

The compliment washes over me like a warm breeze.

"Trevor got engaged just two months after he dumped me,"
I say after a moment. "It felt like a second betrayal—I put so
much effort into his business, so much effort into us."

"I think you dodged a bullet," Charlie says. "He sounds like
an ass who didn't know when he had a good thing."

My lips part in surprise. "Thanks," I whisper.

"It makes sense," he says.

"What does?"

"You're acts of service."

My stare is blank.

"It's your love language."

"I'm sorry, are you citing romance self-help to me?"

"Not with that attitude."

I stifle my smile. "My apologies. Please, do go on."

"My mom had a copy of *The 5 Love Languages* in our house growing up."

"Which you read because . . ."

"Girls," he says.

"Naturally."

"Anyway, people often show love the way they want to receive it. You're acts of service. You show love by performing thoughtful acts, like helping your ex with his business and bringing Nan to the lake. But those gestures can go unnoticed or unappreciated."

It's like a gear locking into place in my brain. That *is* me.

He shifts onto his back, lacing both hands behind his head, and my gaze briefly catches on the flex of bicep as his elbows splay on either side of his temples.

"But the thing about love languages," Charlie says, "is it's not just about how we express love, but how we *receive* love. You need someone to do something for you that makes you feel loved. Someone to help you."

I shake my head. "I hate asking for help."

"That's because deep down, you want someone to see what you need before you have to ask."

"You're full of surprises, Charlie Florek."

A gust of wind has us spinning away from each other, but Charlie tugs on the rope that tethers us together so that he's facing me, his head near my feet. He wraps a hand around my ankle so we don't drift apart, and I hold on to his. It's tactical, but my body doesn't know that. My skin sizzles beneath his palm, sending a hot bolt up my calf.

"What's your love language?" I ask. "I assume teasing isn't included in the book."

The corner of Charlie's mouth lifts into a seductive smirk, and I'm certain his grip tightens on me. "Physical touch."

Heat ripples through me once more, settling between my legs. "Oh."

"Which brings us back to you."

"Me?" It comes out breathless.

The smirk grows. "You've back-burnered relationships, but what about sex?"

My cheeks flush again, but this time, I answer honestly. "I haven't got that sorted out yet. I know it sounds prudish, but I can't get my head around sleeping with someone I don't care about."

Charlie stares at me, no hint of the joker anymore. I like this about him—he has an instinct for when it's okay to play and when it's better to listen. He sees what people need the way I do.

"Anyway . . ." I smile. "Let's just say I've appreciated page 179 of *Ruling the Rogue* more than once."

Charlie's laugh bounces around the bay. "Good for you."

We look at each other, grinning.

"I used to think I'd settle down with someone," he says. "House. Backyard. Kids. A big, slobbery dog." He gazes at the shore, and the smile on his face makes me ache. I can see his fantasy as clear as a photograph. "I used to think I'd have all of it."

"Past tense?"

"Yeah." He seems to choose his words carefully. "I've realized I'm not built for something long-term."

"Resigned bachelor?"

"Something like that. The relationship my parents had, that my brother has—that cosmic, soulmate thing—it's not in the cards for me."

"Because you don't want it?"

There's a deep sadness in his gaze. "I *can't* want it."

I chew on my lip before I speak. I don't want to overstep. But Charlie's having none of it.

"Say whatever's on your mind, Alice."

"The way you looked at Sam and Percy the other day. You seemed . . . unhappy?"

"Do all your friends undergo such thorough scrutiny?" Charlie says, locking his eyes onto mine. "Or am I special?"

"I'm sorry. I just . . . Forget it." I let go of his leg and reach for the rope so I can pull myself toward the dock, but then Charlie speaks.

"They remind me of my parents."

I turn back to him.

"The way they look at each other," he says. "The way they touch each other constantly. How they whisper to each other. Even the way they make fun of one another. It's so much like my mom and dad."

"That must hurt."

"Sometimes," he admits. Creases form at the corners of his eyes when he smiles. "And sometimes it's really nice."

We watch each other in silence. The only sounds come from the lake. Water lapping against the shore, the distant hum of a boat circling the bay, the occasional soft *splash* of a pine cone falling into the water.

Charlie's expression turns as serious as I've seen on him.

"What?"

"You should give Harrison a shot," he says. "I think you'd get along."

I get along with you.

"You have more in common than you think," Charlie says. "He's just getting out of a relationship, too."

I've been under the impression that Charlie is something of

a playboy, someone who wouldn't turn me down for an innocent kiss if asked. It stings that he's trying to set me up with his friend. And not just a little. It stings enough to tell me I'm heading in a dangerous direction, straight toward a crush. It's trademark Alice Everly. Crush fast. Crush hard. Get my heart ripped out of my chest. I need to step away before it's too late.

"You're right," I tell Charlie with a grin that pulls my cheeks too tight. "I should go out with Harrison. A night on the town would be nice."

He blinks like I've surprised him. "Good."

"Great," I add. "I can't wait."

A muscle twitches in Charlie's jaw, and he looks out at the water.

Number five, here I come.

23

Holy shit." Harrison gapes at me when I open the door.

"Is it too much?" I say, looking down at myself. I've put on the green dress, but he's wearing jeans and a T-shirt, far more casual than me. He's shaved the beard and combed his hair, so it falls over his ears, a thick, shiny black. "I can change."

I texted him after Charlie left yesterday, asking whether he was free tonight. He replied immediately, and we decided on the Bent Anchor, the spot Charlie pointed out to me on the river.

"No way," Harrison says now. "You look amazing. Sorry, swearing at you probably wasn't the best way to say hello."

"Hello," I say, smiling. I forgot how lovely he is.

"Hi." He offers me his arm. "Shall we?"

We sit at a picnic table underneath a red umbrella on the sand, overlooking the Madawaska River. A bluegrass band is playing on the patio. Every so often, a boat or Jet Ski passes by, and the riders wave to children playing on the beach. The place has the ideal first-date alchemy: It's laid-back and the service is fast, and if you run out of things to say, there's enough to watch and comment on that you could survive the night without things getting awkward.

Harrison and I order barbecue chicken and ribs, and he tells me about working with his family, and that while he enjoys building houses, his true passion is pottery. We discuss glazing techniques and art and photography. I study his long fingers, thinking he must be good with them. My white wine comes served in a stemless plastic glass, filled to the brim, and when I'm on my second, I don't care that I'm wildly overdressed. The breeze off the water keeps the mosquitoes at bay, but I'm shivering once our food arrives, so Harrison fetches me a hoodie from his truck.

By all measures, it's a good date. But I keep catching myself thinking about Charlie and what it would be like if I were sitting across from him. Or how Harrison's sweatshirt smells nice enough—like it's just been washed—but Charlie's smell is more complex. I push the thoughts aside—only to find my mind wandering to him again.

At the end of the night, when Harrison and I walk to the parking lot, I study his profile. He's gorgeous. He's interesting. He has a nice mouth. But I can't summon any excitement over kissing him.

He leans a shoulder on his truck. "This was fun."

"Really fun," I agree.

"But we're not clicking, right? It's not just me?"

I wince. "No, it's not just you."

Maybe it's my fault there's no spark between us. I've spent the entire date thinking about Charlie.

Harrison is open and funny and creative. Why shouldn't the night end with his lips on mine? I wanted to kiss a cute guy—just for the sheer fun of it—and he more than fits the bill.

"But maybe if we . . ." I put my palm on his chest, but he rubs the back of his neck and looks to the side. I drop my hand immediately.

"I'm sorry. You're awesome, Alice. You're beautiful and easy to talk to, and I'll probably kick myself for saying this later, but tonight made me realize I'm not over my ex. And I can't . . ." He motions between us. "It doesn't feel right."

"I get it," I say. "If anyone understands bad breakups, it's me."

Harrison drives me back to the cottage, and when we turn down the driveway, my heart quickens. Charlie's car is here.

"Didn't know you were having company tonight?" Harrison asks, seeing the look on my face.

I shake my head. I turn to Harrison. "Do you want to come in?"

"I shouldn't. I have an early start tomorrow."

I reach for the door handle but then stop. "What's your take on him?"

"On Charlie?" Harrison frowns, as though it's a question he's never considered.

"Yeah."

"We've been buddies since kindergarten. He's basically the same guy he was when we were kids, although I've noticed he's a bit different these days."

"How so?"

Harrison thinks about it for a moment. "He's become a lot more serious. He used to be the guy who always brought the party. I guess we're all getting older."

I say good night to Harrison and open the door to the cottage, then gasp. I glare at Charlie. "What the hell is this?"

24

I look like the junk food aisle has been dumped on the floor. There are open bags of chips and popcorn. Gummy bears. Chocolate-covered pretzels. A jar of peanuts. A half-eaten chocolate bar sits on the end table beside Nan. Both she and Charlie have glasses of what I assume is scotch. Rod Stewart is blaring. Nan looks like she's fighting back laughter, and Charlie's dimples are so deep they swallow the lamplight. His hand is buried in the bag of gummy bears. His smile falls when he sees me in the doorway.

I look around, dumbfounded.

"How much scotch did you two have?"

Nan giggles in a way that I've never heard. "It wasn't the scotch."

And then I spot the green leaf on the wrapper of Nan's chocolate bar.

"Oh my god."

"It's not a big deal, Alice," Charlie says, getting to his feet. He's wearing jeans and a gray flannel shirt. His hair has some kind of product in it. He's made an effort.

"You got my grandmother *high*?"

"Don't freak out."

"Do *not* tell me not to freak out."

Nan snickers again. "You're in for some trouble, Charlie."

"So are you," I snap.

"Alice." Charlie again. "Back off."

I stare at him, gaping. "Excuse me? How could you sneak over here when I'm not around and bring my grandmother drugs?"

"I didn't sneak. She asked me to. It's a low dose. Very safe. And it's legal."

I look at my grandmother.

"I was curious if it would improve my sleep."

"Why didn't you tell me? I could have done something to help."

"I didn't want to worry you. You're already treating me with kid gloves." Her eyes are a little glassy and her tone is soft, but I bristle. I've only wanted to be helpful.

Charlie places a hand on my shoulder. I shrug him off.

Nan looks between us. "Well, I'm going to bed."

"Let me help," I say, reaching for her cane to pass it to her.

"No." She gives me a hard look. "I'm fine, Alice."

I pull back at her tone. I watch her until she's in the bathroom, ignoring the pressure of Charlie's gaze on my back. I stand there, without a glance at him, while Nan gets ready.

"Alice. Can you look at me?" Charlie says quietly.

I want to be mad at him. For hanging out with my grandmother without me. For the chip crumbs on the rug. For encouraging me to go on a date with his friend, and then infiltrating my mind all evening. But I don't have to dig too deep to know what's really bothering me. It's the possibility that Nan and Charlie didn't think I'd be up for a night of edibles and Ketchup Lay's. That they think I'm no fun.

"Hear me out, okay?"

I take a deep breath and turn around. He's standing far closer than I expected.

"Nan asked me to take her to the cannabis store in town after choir practice. I wasn't trying to be deceptive. She's been having trouble sleeping." I didn't know that. It explains why she's been so cranky.

"The junk food was mostly for me," he says. "I've been watching what I eat—sugar, especially—and I went a little overboard."

I take him in. The collared shirt. The tidy hair. The apology on his face. I don't know what to think about tonight. "Why are you dressed like that?" I ask instead.

He looks down at himself. "Like what?"

"Nice."

His laugh is dry. "You thought I'd wear . . . what? A bathing suit? Sweatpants? To spend the evening with your grandmother?"

He opens his mouth to say something else, but his gaze rakes over me. My cheeks, pink from the wine. My hair, tousled from the breeze off the river. I'm still wearing Harrison's hoodie. Something dark flits across Charlie's eyes. Is he jealous? A surge of satisfaction rolls through me.

"You were out late."

I shrug.

"How was the date?"

"It was nice." I lift my chin, acting with confidence I don't feel. "You were right—we have a lot in common."

Charlie has gone still, but his eyes are stormy. "Oh?"

I can barely hear over the blood pounding in my eardrums. "I had a good time."

His eyes descend to my mouth. "Cross off number five?" His voice is low, but I can hear the restraint in each syllable.

The two tumblers of wine have caught up to me. The week spent talking and swimming and staring at Charlie's chest have caught up to me. I don't think. I just lift the sweatshirt over my head and drop it on the floor. Charlie sucks in a breath, taking in the dress and my neck and shoulders. I shake my head. "No, not yet. Not with him."

"Alice." He says my name carefully, like he's keeping it safe. I find myself moving closer. We stand toe to toe, near enough for me to see that Charlie's pupils have swallowed the flecks of gold. I feel a finger coast along my thigh, and then it's gone.

"Charlie."

I set my hands on his stomach. I feel his body brace beneath my palms as he stares down at me.

"You're a bad influence," I say. "But I can be a bad influence, too."

He doesn't budge as I rise on my toes, bringing our chests into contact, soft against hard. Charlie's eyelids snap shut, and he inhales through his nose.

"Alice." He whispers my name.

"Do you want me to stop?"

My lips are so close to his that when he shakes his head, our mouths brush. I graze my nose against his and take his bottom lip between my teeth. It's not my usual opening move, but I feel as if I could devour him whole. He tastes like gummy bears. A groan rumbles in Charlie's chest, and then suddenly his hands are around my thighs and he's hoisting me off the ground. The look in his eyes is a dare and a promise and other, more dangerous things. I lock my legs around his waist and cling to his shoulders, and when he adjusts his grip, I gasp at the hard press of him against me. I move my hips, because . . .

Whoa.

"Alice," he grits out. "Fuck."

"I'm still mad at you," I say, staring into his eyes as I bring my lips closer to his. "But I'll let you make it up to me because I like you."

Charlie blinks. "I like you, too." His grasp on me loosens, and he slowly sets me back on my feet.

"Then what's the problem?"

He swallows. "We shouldn't."

"I don't understand." He was clearly enjoying himself.

"I'm sorry. It's just that . . ." He looks around the room.

I'd forgotten about Nan. "Let's go to the boathouse," I say.

"It's not that." He stares at me with tortured green eyes. "I got carried away. I shouldn't have let that happen. It's not you," he adds quickly.

"Then what is it?" My face is burning. I'm embarrassed, a little angry, and a lot turned on.

Charlie struggles to find an answer, but finally settles for, "It's probably best for us to stay friends."

I gape at him. "Friends?"

He nods, and I can't help it, my eyes lower to where there is something very unplatonic pressing up against the fly of his jeans.

Charlie swipes a palm over his head, then gives me an inscrutable look. "I'll see you tomorrow, Trouble."

25

I stow away in the boathouse the next afternoon. There are two twin beds and a large sliding door that leads to a small deck with just enough room for two Muskoka chairs. Its peaked wood ceilings are so steep you have to crouch if you're close to the sides. I've set it up like Nan did back when I was a kid, with a bunch of cheap art supplies and a plastic cloth on the table. I can't remember the last time I messed around with paint and pencils. Right now, I'm sketching the bay while Charlie stains the dock. Or at least I'm trying to sketch. My eyes keep drifting from the shoreline to him. He stripped off his T-shirt five minutes ago.

I woke up this morning with a Chardonnay headache and his voice in my ear.

Alice. Fuck.

I can't believe I threw myself at him. I've never done anything like that before. My need to touch him, to feel his body, to taste him, was overwhelming. It seemed to appear out of nowhere, an apparition that needed to be exorcised. I'm not sure I can blame the wine. We barely kissed, but I haven't been that turned on in . . . well, I don't think I've ever been that turned on.

Chewing on the end of my pencil, I watch him work on his hands and knees. He wipes his forehead, pausing to peer over his shoulder at the boathouse. I don't think he can see past the sun's glare on the window, but he looks right at me. My stomach flips.

I keep replaying the moment when I pulled his lip between my teeth, when he made *that sound*, then lifted me off the floor as if he couldn't hold himself back for another second. And then the spell broke.

It's probably best for us to stay friends.

Those words haunted me when I laid my head on my pillow, staring at the reflection of the light from his house on the water. I didn't sleep. Instead, I spent the night reminding myself why Charlie was right to pull back. I had a crush on a friend once before, and it destroyed us. And despite how mixed up I feel about Charlie, I do think that's what he's become. A friend.

I'm so deep in thoughts of Charlie that I don't hear his footsteps ascending the boathouse stairs before he knocks.

"Alice. Can I come in?" he asks from the other side of the door.

I look around for an escape route, but short of throwing myself off the boathouse deck into the water, I'm cornered.

"I know what you're thinking," he says. "And it's too shallow to jump."

I look down at myself—I've got my caftan on over a bathing suit. My standard-issue uniform this summer. I take a second to retie my hair into a neater pile on my head and cross the room. My heart is in my throat.

"Do you ever wear a shirt?" I say, holding the door open.

"I missed you, too." Charlie leans against the frame, the picture of ease, but there's a hesitance in his eyes that makes me wonder. His chest is slick with sweat, and he's breathing heavily. He looks . . . *ugh* . . . too good. "Dock's all done. Should dry quickly with this sun, but if you want to swim, you'll have to walk in from the shore until it dries."

"All right." I feel like popcorn in a microwave, nerves exploding in my chest. I know he didn't come here to tell me about the dock.

"I've never seen it in here." Charlie looks over my shoulder at the space behind me. "May I?"

I step aside. Because of the angle of the ceiling, Charlie can only stand in the very center of the room without having to duck.

"It's cozy," he says, after giving it a short inspection.

"Uh-huh."

"An ideal hideout," he says, meeting my eyes. "Since you're avoiding me."

"I am not."

His brows rise at the speed of my denial. "It's one of the nicest days of the summer, and you're hiding in here. Is this how you treat all your conquests? I feel a little used, Alice."

"Somehow I doubt that."

He shrugs. "Beside the point."

Charlie's gaze drifts to my table full of sketch pads and paint palettes, pastels, and brush sets.

"I'm just playing around," I tell him when he picks up the drawing I've been working on. "It's not supposed to be good."

"Looks pretty damn good to me." His gaze returns to mine. "Can we talk?"

"There's really no need to." I don't want to explain myself or listen to Charlie's reasons for wanting to *stay friends*. "Seriously. Don't worry about it for a second. We can move on. Pretend it never happened."

His eyes narrow, but he says, "Sure." A beat passes. "But there was something else I wanted to talk to you about. Can we sit?"

"All right," I say, nervous once more.

We take our places on opposing beds, facing each other. I bend my knees and hug them to me, while Charlie spreads his wide, hands clasped between them, leaning forward. We're so diametric, we're almost negative images. The light streams in from the windows, putting us in a moody silhouette. I'd capture it in a photo if I could.

Click.

"My mom was sick for two years before she died," Charlie says.

I blink. It's the exact last thing I was expecting.

"Her treatment was harsh, and even after all that chemo, it just . . . well, it wasn't enough." The thick swallow in his throat is the only trace of how much those words hurt. "In the end, she just wanted to be comfortable. I bought her a few gummies to try, and it eased some of her discomfort.

"I wasn't around as much as I should have been. Sam moved back home, but I was caught up in work. She died three years ago, and I'm not sure I'll ever forgive myself for not being here more." He scrapes a hand over his face, then looks at me. "When your grandmother asked me to get her something, I just wanted to help."

Before I can respond, Charlie drops his head into his palms. I stare, stunned for a moment, not sure what to do. But the sight of him crying is too much for me. I get off the bed, crouching between his knees.

"Hey." I try to pull his hands away from his face, but he shakes his head, so I trail my fingers up and down his calves, trying to soothe him.

Charlie lets himself grieve for only a few seconds before wiping his cheek with the heel of his hand. "I'm sorry. This is really fucking embarrassing."

"Oh, this is nothing," I say. "I once walked around a gallery with my dress tucked into the back of my underwear. I couldn't figure out why everyone was looking at me until an elderly woman pulled the skirt out of my butt."

He smiles. "Lucky woman."

I roll my eyes, but I'm pleased. I like making him smile. I want his dimples firmly in place.

Charlie pats the bed, so I sit beside him with my legs folded.

"I think you're too hard on yourself," I say.

His gaze travels around my face, and for a heartbeat I think he's going to argue with me, but he takes a deep breath and pulls me into him, wrapping his arms around me. I circle my arms around his waist and lean my head against his chest. He smells like sweat and sunscreen and whatever fancy soap he uses.

"What was your mom's name?"

"Sue," Charlie says, his voice hoarse. "Her name was Sue."

I hold him tighter. "I'm sorry you lost her. I'm sorry she's not here to give you a hug."

"Thanks," he whispers after a moment.

I pull my head back enough to gaze up at him. "For what?"

"For listening to me. For being my friend."

"You're welcome." I squeeze him back.

Then I climb off the mattress, holding out my hand.

"Come on. Let's go for a swim. You smell terrible."

He lets out a deep laugh and puts his palm in mine.

"You know," I say as we walk to the water, "you're a lot more high-maintenance than I would have guessed."

26

A week passes. Mid-July threatens to turn into late July. Charlie and Nan go to euchre night together and return with stories about how they trampled their competition. I throw myself into my editing backlog and preparing for Bennett's visit. In three days, Heather will drop her off for the week. I have big plans to make it a summer vacation she won't forget. Arts and crafts. Dinner at the Tavern. Cozy evenings watching movies with Nan. Boat rides.

Charlie wants to take us all out on the water. He said if Nan isn't ready to walk down to the lake, he'll carry her himself. What he doesn't know is that Nan has been practicing. She's made it all the way down and back up more than once, though the effort leaves her winded.

"Not everyone has a chance to spend time with their great-granddaughter at the lake," Charlie tells her over afternoon tea. Percy and Sam have returned to the city, but he's still here every day.

"All right, Charlie," Nan tells him. "If you must carry me, then you must." She winks at me when he's not looking.

He stays for the whole evening. The weather is wet and cool, so Charlie lights a fire while I put a chicken in the oven for dinner. We eat it with a warm bread and tomato salad, and after Charlie and I wash the dishes, we drink scotch by the fireplace with Rod Stewart on the CD player.

I photograph everything.

It's not the summer I envisioned when we arrived in June—it's so much better. I feel as though I've been wearing a heavy coat and am now finally able to take it off. I feel *lighter*.

I can't deny that Charlie is a big part of the reason. I like who I am with him. I laugh until tears stain my cheeks. I say what I think, and when he senses I'm holding something in, he tells me to spit it out. I don't have to be a perfectly edited version of myself—it's okay to have a few bumps. And I don't have to *try*. I've never felt this comfortable with a man. I'm not sure I've felt this kind of ease with anyone.

I also can't deny the way my stomach swoops when our legs slide against each other while we're swimming, or when I catch Charlie looking at me in a way that has me picturing how he lifted me off the floor the night we almost kissed. But *just friends* works. *Just friends* is all either of us is prepared to give.

Tonight he's wearing jeans and a white T-shirt. His feet are bare, and so are mine. But I've already changed into pajamas, a pretty striped nightshirt that hits me above the knee. When Nan has a piece of her chocolate and excuses herself for bed, Charlie grabs the bar and sits down on the couch beside me.

"Let's do some low-key drugs."

"You want to get high?"

"Only if you do." Charlie examines the package. "I don't think a piece of this will have much of an impact on me. It's a mild dose. Won't kick in for a bit."

"Sure," I say. "I can't let Nan have all the fun. But will you stay with me? I don't want to go on some kind of trip alone."

He laughs. "You're not going to trip, but yeah, I was planning to stick around, if you'll have me."

If you'll have me.

We each break off a piece, grinning, and cheers them together.

"I don't know if I'm high yet," I say to Charlie forty-five minutes later. We decided to start a puzzle—a unicorn drinking from a river that I found at Stedmans—and are working on it on the floor by the fire.

"No?" Charlie's lying on his side, his head propped on his hand. "You've been staring at that piece in your hand for ages."

"Oh my god, I hadn't noticed." I start giggling. "Charlie, I might be a little high."

"You might be," he says, dimples winking.

"But I don't feel *high* high."

"How do you feel?"

I look into the flames.

"Alice?"

"Pardon?" I turn back to Charlie.

"You okay?"

"I'm just thinking. I think I feel . . . kind of light and floaty? And warm, which is probably because I'm sitting in front of an actual fire. But also, just like, less sharp, you know?"

He looks at me with a soft, melting gaze. "Yeah, I know."

The firelight flickers over Charlie's face, making his hair more golden. His smile is deep. I reach out and press my finger into one of his dimples, and he arches a brow.

"Sorry," I say. "It was beckoning to me."

He laughs. "You *are* high." I move my finger to the other one. He lifts his brows again, amused. He looks so young.

"You remind me of when you were a boy."

"You didn't know me when I was a boy."

"But I can imagine it when you're like this."

"Like what?"

Sometimes I catch Charlie looking at me, or staring at the water, or studying his hands, and he seems so mournful, my entire body aches. He's experienced such profound loss. But he brushes it off whenever I ask what's bothering him.

"Happy," I tell him. "You look happy."

His grin falls. The dimples disappear.

"Don't do that." I move my fingers to either side of his mouth, trying to pull the edges back up. "Be happy."

My efforts are rewarded with a gentle smile.

"I like how your skin is smooth, but your stubble is prickly, and your jaw is so strong. And I like how you like my grandmother." I know how I sound, but I feel like human glitter, shimmering effervescence. Like nothing is wrong, like nothing *could* go wrong under this roof with Charlie. I run my finger over the bow of his top lip. "I like your mouth, too. These two mountaintops."

"Alice," Charlie says, sitting up, so that we're facing each other, legs crossed. He stares at me intensely, but it doesn't bother me that he might be able to peer into my soul. It makes me feel brave.

"Can I show you something?" I've been waiting for the right time to do it.

He frowns but says, "Of course."

I get up, jelly-legged, and dig the photo out of the kitchen drawer.

"Promise not to freak out?" I ask, holding it to my chest as I return to the floor. Charlie puts a hand on my bobbing knee.

"Not much freaks me out." He takes his hand away when I go still.

I pass him the photo, and a hurricane of emotions crashes across his face. Confusion. Disbelief. Shock.

Finally, he lifts wonder-filled eyes to mine. "I can't believe it was you."

I blink at him. "What?"

Charlie bends closer to the photo. "Of course it was you," he says to himself. "It makes sense. I can't believe I didn't figure it out."

"Charlie?"

"You took this." He fixes his gaze on me, piercing and bright. Fresh as new spring leaves.

"The summer I stayed here," I confirm.

He shakes his head, and then suddenly, he grabs his phone, thumbing through his photos. When he finds what he's looking for, he passes it to me. It's a picture of *my* photo, *this* photo, displayed on a wall in a black frame.

"It hangs in a boardroom of a bank where my buddy works," Charlie explains. "He thought it looked like me. I couldn't believe what I was seeing. It's me, it's us."

It's the print I sold back when I was a student. I blew it up more than I should have, making it slightly grainy. But I liked that. I thought it added a sense of nostalgia.

I peel my eyes away from the phone, stunned.

"You, Sam, and Percy?" I assumed it was them the night we watched the fireworks, but I want to be sure.

"Yeah." Charlie rubs his forehead. "It was so wild. My friend sent it a few years ago. It was right after Percy and Sam had gotten back together. It felt like a message from the universe or fate or some shit. Like things were as they were supposed to be." He searches my face. "You really took this?"

I stare into Charlie's eyes, and for a moment I'm entranced.

Green grapes. Kiwi fruit. Lime juice. Bands of impossibly bright light rippling across a black sky.

"Yeah, I really took it.

"This photo means a lot to me," I say softly as we study it together. "It made me think I might be good one day. It helped me get into photography school. It was the first shot I ever sold." I pause. "It changed my life."

Charlie turns to face me. "I've gone to see it," he says. "And I tried to find you, but there was no signature. I wanted to buy a print. I wanted to remember us like this, when things were simple."

"I think that's one of the reasons I feel so connected to it now," I say. "When I look at it, I feel like I'm seventeen again."

"So you do remember us?" Charlie puts his hand on my leg when it starts vibrating again, but this time it stays there.

"I remember you," I whisper.

His eyes travel across my face so slowly. I don't recognize the feeling in my chest, full yet weightless. Like there's a hot-air balloon about to set sail beneath my sternum.

"You should have said hi," Charlie says, voice low.

Time ticks by slowly. My perception shrinks to the space between us.

"I should have," I murmur. "I wish I *could* have, but I was so shy. I've always wanted to be someone different, someone who could talk to cute boys and race around in a yellow boat."

"I like the person you are. I wouldn't change a thing."

"No edits?"

"Not a single one."

I become aware of three things at once: My nightshirt is made from the thinnest of cotton, the hem has shifted up my thighs, and Charlie's hand is still on my leg.

"I can't believe it was you all this time," Charlie says. "And now you're here."

We both watch as goose bumps dapple my skin. His thumb smooths over my knee, and the touch zags through me like lightning. A whoosh of air leaves my lungs. His gaze shoots to mine.

Kiss me, I think.

I hold my breath as Charlie lifts his hand to my face. He traces my jaw. "I want . . ." he says. His eyes move to my lips, and his fingers follow, skimming the corner of my mouth. "But I shouldn't."

"You shouldn't what?" I whisper.

"Want," he says, his gaze still fastened on my lips.

"I strongly disagree." I take a breath. "I think you should."

A groan rumbles in his chest, and he brings his eyes to mine. He cups the back of my neck, fingers tangling in my hair. He pulls me closer, until our foreheads meet.

The heat of his skin, his smell, the way my blood races to the apex of my legs—it's too much to look at him. My eyelids flutter closed. We breathe each other in. Charlie's nose nudges mine, and even that innocent touch reverberates through my body.

I want to kiss him like nothing I've wanted before. I want to know how his lips feel against mine, and I want to know what he tastes like. Kissing someone for the first time is like learning a new dance, and I want to master Charlie's choreography.

"Kiss me," I whisper.

Charlie's lips coast over mine.

"Because you want to cross off number five?"

For a second, I have no idea what he's talking about. I shake my head when I remember.

"Kiss me because I want you to."

I tilt forward to close the shred of oxygen that separates us. But instead of kissing me, he leans away and I fall into his chest.

I scramble to my feet, mortified, and make a beeline for my room.

"Alice, wait."

Charlie sticks his foot in the threshold just as I'm shutting the door. I glare at him, but he slips inside and closes it gently behind him.

"Let's talk about this."

I don't like confrontation, but I'm sick of smothering my feelings all the time. "Why?" I ask. "So you can tell me we should *stay friends*? Believe me, I've got the message now. It won't happen again."

He shakes his head. "Because I care about you. You believe me, right?"

There's so much pleading in his eyes. "I believe you," I say quietly, and then we sit together on the edge of the bed.

"I didn't misread things, did I?" I ask, staring at our legs. "You were touching me, and then talking like you wanted something to happen. We were so close to kissing, right?"

"We were very close to kissing," Charlie admits.

"And the other time, we almost . . ." I stop short of saying *kissed*, because it doesn't capture where things were heading. I was seconds away from tearing off his clothes while my grandmother was in the next room.

"We almost," he agrees.

I watch him from the corner of my eye. "So what happened?"

"It seems I've developed self-control in my midthirties," he says.

I wait as he looks at me, his gaze roaming my face like he's memorizing each feature, lingering on my lips. He's still except for the rise and fall of his chest.

"I want you," he rasps. His stare makes me feel like it's an effort not to touch me, and I know he's telling the truth. "And I think we both know that if we start something now, it's not going to end with a kiss."

"That's presumptuous," I say, but my voice is hoarse.

I'm very aware that we are on a bed, that all that stands between us is a few inches of space and layers of fabric.

"Am I wrong?"

He's right. If I get my mouth on his, it's not going to stop there. I don't want it to. Our almost-kiss was mind-blowing. I can't imagine how good the real thing would be. But before I admit it, Charlie tucks a tendril of hair behind my ear.

"I don't want to jeopardize our friendship, Alice," he says. "Not even for sex."

"What about for great sex?"

He shakes his head, a smile tugging on his lips. "Not for that, either."

"What are you doing on the couch?"

My eyelids flutter open to find Nan standing over me. I'm disoriented until I remember the chocolate and the unicorn puzzle and collapsing face down on the sofa after I walked Charlie to the door.

"I must have passed out."

"Good night?"

I think of Charlie's thumb brushing my knee and asking him to kiss me.

"We got into your chocolate."

"Delightful, isn't it? Really loosens you up."

"It loosened my tongue, that's for sure."

I fix Nan her toast and my eggs, and we eat at the table together. She's quiet as we begin sewing a tablecloth, not sullen, but contemplative. I'm not much chattier. I've been thinking about what Charlie said last night about risking our friendship, and I don't think I agree with him. I've never been able to untangle sex from romance, but Charlie isn't a stranger. I'm attracted to him, and neither of us wants a relationship. It could be the first step to a whole new Alice—my hookup training wheels. Nothing complicated. No expectations. Just a fling with the boy across the bay until the end of summer.

I'm finishing the hem when Nan says, "Your grandfather was my closest friend, aside from Joyce."

"I know," I tell her. "I remember how you were together. You were always laughing when Grandpa was around."

Her eyes glisten. "I knew I'd never fall in love again, but I do miss the connection we had. I miss having him here to laugh with."

"You can laugh with me."

She puts her hand over mine. "And I'm grateful for that. Having grandchildren is a truly special thing, but it's not the same, of course."

I nod, and she studies me. "When I see you and Charlie together, it reminds me of myself and your grandfather."

"Because we laugh?" I ask quietly.

"*You* laugh, Alice. You laugh that big, beautiful laugh of yours. And you're more like yourself when you're together. You're always so busy taking care of everyone and making people happy, but you're different around Charlie. There's a lightness to you I haven't seen in a long time—like you have the freedom to just *be* when you're with him."

"That's just because I'm on vacation."

Nan slants her head. "No, it's because when you speak, he listens. When you smile, he smiles. When you need something, he offers help. When you give him something, he thanks you. You're peas and carrots—I think you've found yourself a lifelong friend."

My mouth goes dry. The connection Charlie and I have seems

special, but hearing Nan say it solidifies what I've been feeling. I'm not sure what's going to happen between us, but it's real.

"What if I wanted more than friendship? But something more . . ." I've confided in Nan about so many things—hopes, fears, secrets, dreams. But I've never talked to her about sex. "Something more casual than a relationship?"

Her blue eyes meet mine over her glasses. "I can see your wheels spinning, but try not to worry about it too much, Alice. You never know—it might turn into a great romance."

"You're just saying that because you like him so much."

"I like Charlie a great deal, but I'm saying that because I see you together, and it reminds me of what it felt like to fall in love."

I swallow, and Nan pats my hand. "Just see where the sun takes you. And don't forget: Good things happen at the lake."

27

When I park beside a black Porsche at the grocery store later that morning, what happens in my body is more than nerves and headier than excitement. I'm full of volatile energy. I've been operating on autopilot for months, and now I've been switched on. It's pure anticipation. Something I haven't felt in years.

And while I'm prepared to run into a preposterously handsome marble statue of a man, I don't expect to find him staring at the baskets of pickling cucumbers again.

"What is with you and this vegetable?"

"Technically, cucumbers are a fruit." Charlie looks down at me, his gaze fond. His hair is mussed, standing on end at the front. I almost reach out to smooth the spikes down. He hasn't shaved in a couple of days, his eyes have dark shadows beneath them, and I'm pretty sure he was wearing the same T-shirt yesterday. He's the hottest of trash.

"You look awful."

"I didn't sleep." He gives me a meaningful look that I feel low in my belly.

"Really? I had the best sleep I've had in ages. Nan found me passed out on the couch this morning."

The corner of his mouth lifts.

"So," I say, inspecting the produce. A bucket of lacy dill stalks sits on the floor with a handwritten LOCAL sign stuck in their midst. "Are you going to give any of these cucumbers a good home or what?"

"I haven't decided." He rubs the back of his neck. "My mom made the best dill pickles. I've been thinking about giving them a try, but I haven't pickled anything in my life."

He's been dipping into Sue's recipe box. After the chocolate cake, he brought Nan and me her morning glory muffins and then cabbage rolls. Both were excellent.

Charlie has his arms crossed over his chest, and he's staring down the cucumbers like he's facing an opponent in a Roman amphitheater.

I pick up two baskets and put them in my cart. "How many do we need?"

Charlie's eyebrows creep up his forehead. "Really?"

"Yeah. How hard can it be?" I choose a stalk of dill. "I'm sure Nan would like to help. She's good at this stuff." I pause at the mystified expression on Charlie's face. "Unless you want to do it alone?" Maybe the cooking thing is between him and his mom.

"No," he says, voice rusty. "I'd love the help."

When Nan and I arrive at Charlie's house in the afternoon, he's much brighter. He's taken a nap, showered, and shaved. He's even had his hair buzzed short. He helps Nan up the porch stairs, and the sight burrows into my heart so deeply that I avert my gaze.

"Would you like a cup of tea first?" Charlie asks Nan. The kitchen is covered in canning gear.

"After," Nan says, rolling up her sleeves. "Let's get these jars sterilized."

I slice the cucumbers and peel the garlic, but otherwise Nan instructs, and Charlie follows her orders. I've brought my Pentax, and I shoot a roll of black and white.

I don't realize how broadly I'm smiling until Charlie looks at me.

Click.

"Having fun?" he asks.

I am. Shooting has given me control and a sense of mastery, but it's been a long time since it's been fun.

There's one picture, when Nan is watching Charlie fill Mason jars with brine and Charlie glances at her for approval, that breaks my heart as soon as I take it, because it's late July, and summer is fleeting. I want to press pause on today, on this month, on these two people. Capture it not just on film.

Charlie puts the kettle on once they've finished, and we drink our tea on the deck overlooking the lake. The kids from the cottage next door swim over to dive off Charlie's floating raft. They have an open invitation to use it.

"What a lovely place to grow up," Nan says.

Charlie looks out at the water. "It really was."

"Though I imagine the house and the property were a lot for your mother when she was on her own," she says, and Charlie nods. "She must have been a tremendously hard worker."

"She was." He stares at the view for another moment. "I always knew that from the restaurant. But I didn't fully appreciate all the things she did for us until I moved away for university.

Cooking was a big part of that. Big breakfasts. Birthday cakes. Holiday feasts. She loved to feed people."

"Is that why you've been trying her recipes?" Nan asks.

"Maybe." He smiles. "And I love to eat. I've missed those pickles."

"Not my thing," I say, flashing him an apologetic grin.

His eyes pop. "What?"

"I don't like them."

"Me neither," Nan says. "I did all my pickling for Alice's grandfather and the church bazaar."

"We just made a dozen jars," Charlie says, glancing between us, mouth hanging open.

"I know," I say, laughing. "They'll keep, don't worry."

"No, that's not it. It's just . . ." Charlie looks at Nan and then me. He holds my gaze in a way that tells me how much I matter. "Thank you."

"You're welcome."

I feel Nan watching us, and when I peek at her, she gives me a pointed *I told you so* look.

Nan and Charlie discuss the ins and outs of pickling and preserving various fruits and vegetables, teacups between them. It's so outrageously wholesome that I'm laughing when my phone lights with a text.

A lump forms in my throat when I read it.

Heather: I'm so sorry, Ali. I can't bring Bennett up north. An important case just landed . . .

"What's wrong?" Charlie asks.

I give him a lackluster smile. "Heather and Bennett can't come. My sister has to work." I look to Nan. Her lips are pinched, the only sign of her disapproval. "She says she'll find time next month."

At that, Nan grumbles, "Always on her own schedule. What about yours?"

"It doesn't matter to me," I say, although it does. I've bought extra groceries. I've made a calendar of activities. The weather is supposed to be stunning. I was going to bring Bennett to the party Charlie is throwing for Sam and Percy.

"Well, this sucks," Charlie says.

Nan and I look at him.

"I've finished the tree house," he says. "I wanted Bennett to check it out before the big reveal on Saturday."

I didn't know Charlie was done, or that he was planning on showing my niece. I stare at him, an uncomfortable pressure building in my chest.

"Excuse me," I say, rising.

I escape to the main-floor powder room and run cold water over my hands, then press my palms against my cheeks and forehead. I miss my family.

"You're okay," I tell my reflection. "You're okay."

Charlie's waiting for me in the hallway when I finish.

"Are you okay?"

I do what I always do and pretend like I'm not hurt. "Yeah. I'm fine."

He studies me for a moment, then wraps me in a hug. "You're a shit liar."

I press my cheek against his chest and breathe him in.

"What if I drive to Toronto to get Bennett?" he says, still holding me. "I can return her to the city at the end of the week."

"You'd do that?" The back of my nose tingles. I'm not used to someone taking care of me. "It's eight hours there and back."

"Sure." Charlie lets me go. His eyes move between mine. "I'm used to the drive—it's nothing for me."

"It's not nothing." His offer means the world to me. "But my sister won't let Bennett in a car with someone she doesn't know."

"Fair enough. But if you can talk her into it, I'm game."

"Thanks," I say. But I know Heather—it's not happening. I lean on the wall, studying him. "You finished the tree house?"

"I had to bring in a couple of ringers, but yeah. I was going to surprise you. I thought you and Bennett might want to camp out for a night. Sleep under the stars." The seventeenth item on my list.

"That would have been nice," I say, my voice unsteady. "I've never slept in a tree house."

Charlie flashes me a mischievous green-eyed grin. "You're welcome to sleep in mine anytime, Alice Everly."

Alice Everly. Alice Everly. Alice Everly.

Flirting—it's the distraction I need. "With or without your company?"

Charlie's smile turns dangerous as he leans into me. I shiver at the feel of his lips grazing my ear. My heart beats harder, faster, louder. "I told you I sleep naked."

I can tell from the wry arch of his brow and the way his eyes dance that it's a dare.

"I'll come by at dusk," I say. "You can see what I sleep in."

His gaze travels around my face. "I'm not sure if you're joking."

"I guess you'll find out."

28

might hang out with Charlie later tonight," I say to Nan over dinner. She sets her fork down.

"Do you want to come?" I ask, trying to sound casual. "I think we'll probably just watch a movie."

We've made no such plans.

My grandmother surveys me with amusement. "I think I'll stay put."

A little after eight, I buckle my sandals, fingers shaking.

"Alice?" my grandmother calls before I step outside.

I pause with my hand on the doorknob.

She's sitting in her chair with a book. Her eyes stay fixed on the page as she speaks. "It gets awfully dark at night." A hint of a smile crosses her lips. "If you want to stay there instead of walking back, I'd understand." She doesn't lift her gaze to see me blush.

I wish her good night and step into the evening. The light is dim in the woods that grow around the driveway. It's slightly brighter when I get to the road. The air is sweet and warm, the sky painted in lavenders and blues. A walk through the bush on a stunning summer night should be relaxing, but I'm not sure I breathe the entire ten minutes. I'm going because my pulse hasn't settled since Charlie whispered in my ear earlier today. I'm going because I can't stay away.

The lights are on inside, their warm glow beckoning me closer. Charlie passes by the living room window wearing his gray lounge pants and a T-shirt. I'm in shorts and a sweatshirt. I didn't dress for seduction. I dressed to climb a tree.

With each step I take, my pulse becomes more urgent. I step onto the porch and put a hand over my chest to calm it down. I see Charlie again. He's sitting in the dining room, his forearm resting on the table. There's a cuff around his bicep attached to a small monitor. I take a step back, but not before Charlie lifts his head. I feel like I'm witnessing something he didn't want me to. We stare at each other.

"I'm sorry," I say, loud enough for him to hear me through the glass. "I'll just . . ." I turn to leave. I've just stepped onto the gravel driveway when I hear the door open behind me.

"Alice. Stop."

I turn around, wincing. "I'm sorry. I didn't mean to interrupt."

Charlie walks across the porch, not stopping until he's right in front of me. "You don't have to apologize. It's not a big deal. I'm supposed to monitor my blood pressure," he says. "It's been a little higher than it should be." His tone is casual, but his expression is anything but.

"Is everything okay?" I ask.

He stares down at me for an almost uncomfortable length of time, lips pressed together. "Why are you here?"

Without the buzz of wine or the toasty haze of an edible, it's hard asking for what I want. But I've come this far. "I want to see your tree house."

Charlie stares into the forest. When his eyes return to mine, conflict swirls in the shades of green and gilt. He's going to turn me away. I lift my head, set my hands on my hips, and pull my shoulders back, bracing myself for rejection.

"You look like you're about to fight me," he says.

I narrow my eyes, and he lets out an exaggerated sigh and then tips his head toward the water. "Come on, Rocky."

I follow Charlie down the hill to the edge of the bush, where we stand side by side, staring at the most stunning tree house I've ever seen. It's built over two levels. The first ladder leads to a round platform around the trunk, and a second connects it to an upper deck and the tree house itself. It has a door and screened windows and a cedar-shingled roof. Charlie folds his arms over his chest, grinning at my slack-jawed expression.

"So," he says, nudging me with his hip. "What do you think?"

I blink up at him. "Whoa."

His smile lures his dimples. "I can't take all the credit. Harrison helped me design it, and he's done the trickier parts." Charlie points to a little break in the bush at the base of the tree. "There's a path that leads to the cottage next door, the one that used to be Percy's. She and Sam would go back and forth between our house and her place all summer long. I love the idea that their kid will play here, in the spot where they became friends."

I smile into the woods, but when I glance at Charlie, he looks melancholy.

"You're a good brother."

He shakes his head. "Not really."

"And a romantic," I add, ignoring his comment.

He raises two skeptical brows. "No one who knows me would ever say that."

"Maybe they don't really know you, then."

"I'm not a very good person, Alice. I've made more mistakes than most." He takes a deep breath, then says quietly, "Sometimes I wonder if I've ever done anything good in my entire life."

"*This* is good," I say. "The way you've helped Nan and me is good." I want to tell him that *he's* good, but I'm not sure words would be enough to make him believe. So I link my arm in his. "Come on, Sad Boy. Take me up to your tree house."

"The view," I say. "It's spectacular. It's almost like we're on the water."

There's a slash of bright red running on a diagonal across the sky, disappearing behind the hill of the far shore, but otherwise the night is indigo and growing darker by the second.

"Almost as good as the view from your boathouse," Charlie says behind me. He's leaning against the door to the tree house. It's a squat, round-topped entrance, like it leads to an enchanted hideaway.

Everything about this moment is spellbinding. The pine-kissed air. The distant call of a loon. Floating high in the trees with Charlie. I look back to the lake. There's a bonfire on the beach near John's cottage. Laughter rolls across the bay. A fish jumps closer to shore.

"No, this is better. It feels like we're somewhere magical," I say.

"It does."

I turn at the tenderness in Charlie's voice. I take a step closer, and every muscle in his body seems to tense. I find his hand clenched at his side and raise it between mine. He doesn't breathe as I stare up at him and uncurl his fingers, lacing them with my own. When I bring his knuckles to my lips, a low hum vibrates in his chest. I desperately want to know all his sounds.

"Take me inside?"

His eyes sweep across my face. "Are you sure?"

"About seeing your tree house?"

"About *this*." He steps into my body, and I'm forced to tip my head to look at him. His fingers skate down my bare arm, from shoulder to wrist, and goose bumps rise in their wake.

"Are you?"

"No." His gaze darkens as his fingers continue trailing along my arm. "Even though I can't stop thinking about all the ways I could make you scream my name."

His admission lands straight between my legs. "What's holding you back?"

Charlie cups my chin in his hand, and stares at me, his gaze stormy. "I was hoping you would."

I shake my head slowly. "I have another idea."

Charlie's thumb traces my jaw. "That sounds risky."

"Maybe it is."

Charlie lowers his head to mine. My heart thrashes as his lips graze the corner of my mouth. But he doesn't kiss me. Instead, he whispers "I knew you'd be trouble" against my ear.

I shut my eyes before pulling away. "Take me inside," I say again.

This time Charlie opens the door.

I duck to pass into the space, but inside the ceiling is high enough for even Charlie to stand. I turn around in a circle. It's a small square room with two single-pane windows looking onto the lake and another out to the bush. It has that amazing fresh lumber smell. There's not much in the way of furnishings—just a bamboo-framed couch and a low table beside it. I hear the flick of a lighter and turn to see Charlie ignite an old-fashioned oil lantern. It makes the whole room glow. There are two rolled-up sleeping bags in the corner.

"Were you expecting me?" I say, gesturing to them.

He shakes his head slowly. "You are the last thing I expected," he says.

I stare at the lamplight blazing in his eyes. Has my heart ever beat this fast?

"I bought the sleeping bags so you and Bennett could camp out here," Charlie continues. "There's a blow-up mattress kicking around the basement of the house, and if you position it under the window, you'd be able to see the stars."

It's as if there are a hundred tiny fireworks exploding in my chest. I walk toward him until there's only a breath of space separating us.

"I never thought I'd be happy that my sister canceled, but I'd rather sleep under the stars with you. I like you. I like being with you." Every inch of my body feels like it's on fire. Each cell is alive. I can feel my pulse in my lips, my neck, my wrists. "And you like me."

He's deadly still. "We're friends."

"Do you think about making your other friends scream your name?"

He pauses but doesn't concede. "I started sleeping around when I was fourteen. I've made a lot of people scream my name."

He's trying to scare me off, but I won't scare easily. "That's not what I asked."

Charlie's eyes drop to my mouth, and when they return to me, there's no mistaking the desire in them. His gaze is unflinching. For a moment, we remain that way, focused on each other, chests moving with short, shallow breaths.

"No," Charlie says. "It isn't." Quivering golden light caresses the contours of his face. He steps closer, head tilted down to me. The space seems to close in around us. My stomach flips, and I think that's what he wants. He's trying to make me nervous, to call my bluff.

"I see you when I close my eyes at night," he says, eyes burning. "You fill my dreams. I think of you when I'm in the shower.

I imagine how it would be to have you on top of me, how your hair would feel falling against my chest. I've thought about how many times I could make you come with my mouth. With my fingers. With both."

My lips part. My knees go weak. "Don't stop."

The twist of his mouth becomes wicked.

"I've wondered how long I could hold out when I finally had you. And if I could make you beg for me. I've fantasized about how you would taste. How you would feel around me. Since I met you, you're the only person I've imagined screaming my name."

It is an effort not to launch myself into his arms and ask for everything he's just described.

"Can you use the rest of your body as well as you use your mouth?"

Charlie's eyes glimmer. "Better."

"And you like me." I reach up, running my fingers over his hair. The newly shorn strands tickle my skin.

Charlie takes my face in his hands. "I think I might like you more than anyone."

I turn my face in to his palm and lay a kiss there. Charlie closes his eyes briefly and inhales through his nose.

"But you deserve someone who can give you more," he says, looking at me with new determination. "You're smart and kind and funny. You're a good person and, god, you're beautiful, Alice." He tucks a curl behind my ear, his eyes turning sad. "I love spending time with you, but I'm not in a place where I can get involved with anyone. I'm not built for a long-term relationship."

Charlie is unlike anyone I've ever known. *I'm* unlike the Alice I know with him. I *want* more. And the way he's holding himself back is more exhilarating than anything I've experienced. Confused eyes follow the curve of my mouth as I smile.

"I'm not looking for a boyfriend," I say. "And in the name of transparency, I've also thought about you naked on occasion."

His gaze crackles. "Oh yeah?"

"I blame that book you gave me." I loop my arms around his neck, and Charlie places his hands at the base of my spine. It's almost like we're dancing.

"Alice Everly." He turns my name into a full sentence. "What do you want?"

"This," I tell him. "I want to kiss you, and touch you, and be touched by you. I like you, and I trust you. And neither of us wants to be anything more than friends."

What I want is to be the person who makes Charlie come undone. I rise on my tiptoes and press my lips to his neck. "I want you," I say into his skin. I whisper in his ear, "It doesn't have to be complicated. It can be just for the summer—another activity on our list. No expectations past the end of August."

He turns his cheek to meet my eyes. "I don't want to mislead you. *This*," he says, tugging my hips to his, "is all I can give you." He tips his head closer. "I don't want you to regret me."

"If you think that's a possibility, then I haven't been making myself clear." I brush my nose against his. A thread of space separates our mouths. I've never wanted to lay claim to another person's lips so badly. "It's not just your remarkable face or ridiculous body—you're pretty great, Charlie. I could never regret you."

His eyes flare. "You might be the biggest surprise of my life, Alice," he says.

And then he crushes his lips to mine.

29

t's not a kiss. Or not one that I've ever experienced. Because Charlie kisses me with every millimeter of his body. With the command of his lips, with his teeth, which coax my bottom lip from my top, and his tongue, which meets mine with confident strokes. He kisses with the tips of his strong fingers as they curve behind my ears, angling me exactly where he wants. With the arch of his back, bending over me, engulfing my senses, and the press of his knee, urging my legs apart. With each sound I make, he adjusts. Kisses me deeper, moves his hands to my waist, bringing me closer.

When his lips travel to the underside of my jaw, I tilt my head back. His groan vibrates against my chest. I feel his fingers in my hair as he releases it from its knot. Without thinking, I reach up to tidy it. Charlie's hand comes around my wrist, and I pause, meeting his eyes.

"Leave it," he says, looking at me with a hunger I don't know how to handle. "I don't think you realize how beautiful you are."

"Whereas you know exactly how beautiful you are."

Charlie's lips quirk, but his voice is serious. "I mean it." His eyes are hooked onto mine like they'll never let go. "The day we met, I thought you were the most radiant woman I'd ever seen."

I laugh. "Radiant?"

"Radiant. Dazzling. Incredibly gorgeous. Hot as hell. Sexy as fuck. Take your pick."

His tone leaves no room for argument. "Until I told you off." I wasn't exactly pleasant that day on the dock.

It's just a nice face. It's literally the last thing that would make someone attractive to me.

He grips my hips, and I can feel the heat of his hands through the thin fabric of my shorts. "When you told me off, I was ready to drop to my knees and put my remarkable face between your thighs." He pulls me against his erection, and my mouth goes dry. "That was the first time I thought about making you scream my name."

Charlie's thumbs dip under the hem of my shorts. "I guess I beat you, then," I say. I run my hands over his shoulders and arms, up and down, marveling at all that muscle at my disposal.

"How so?"

"Because," I say, sliding my hands under his T-shirt, exploring the twin divots at his lower back. He hisses when I run my nails over his skin, and clamps his bottom lip between his teeth, pressing me more tightly to him. "I wanted you when I first saw you handle a cucumber in the grocery store."

A laugh erupts from his chest as entrancing as the setting sun. "Alice." He kisses my nose, then my mouth. "I told you." Then the hinge of my jaw. "Trouble."

"In my defense, it had been a while since . . ." I don't want to say Trevor's name. "It had been a while."

Charlie studies me, sweeping my hair over my shoulder and wrapping it in his fist while he kisses me thoroughly. There's no teeth or tongue, just the tender caress of his mouth on mine. It's the sweetest way of being consumed, savored like the last bite of homemade chocolate cake. He leans back just enough to look me in the eyes when he says, "I'm going to make you come so many times, you won't remember a time when you went without."

I laugh, but it dies in my throat when Charlie's hands grip my backside, and he hoists me off the floor, guiding my legs around him.

"Show-off."

"I think you'll like all the ways I can show off for you." He lowers me slightly so that he's pressing against me in the exact right spot. I rock against him, and I wonder if he can tell how ready I am. There's fabric between us, but not much.

"I want you like this," I tell him, reaching between us for his waistband. "Now."

He shakes his head and walks us toward the sofa. "Not now."

I pull back, scowling. "I don't understand. I thought we agreed." There's a term for what this is, but I'm pretty sure my brain has relocated somewhere between my thighs, so it takes a moment to recall it. "Friends with benefits," I proudly exclaim when it comes to me.

Charlie lays me down on the sofa and then hovers over me. "I want to do this differently than I would have in the past. I want to be careful."

"Meaning what?"

"The people I share benefits with aren't typically my friends." Charlie smooths a finger over the frown lines between my eyes. "This is new for me, too. I want to go slow. Maybe we should stick to crossing off number five tonight."

Kiss a cute guy.

"I'm not sure I'd describe you as *cute*," I tell him. "And I want those five thousand orgasms you promised."

He smiles down at me, and I touch the dimple in his left cheek.

"Is this a negotiation, Alice?"

"Is this how you negotiate?"

"This and a nice tie."

I prop myself up on my elbows so I can nip his bottom lip. "Maybe we should add a tie next time."

"Trouble," he says before kissing me again. I get lost in his mouth, in the weight of him pressing me into the cushions, in his expensive smell mingling with that of the wood, wrapping itself around my memory. With one large hand on my upper thigh, Charlie pushes my legs wide enough to settle between them. My hands move to his backside, desperate to keep him close. I raise my hips and tilt my neck back, because even just this feels incredible.

"It could be fun," Charlie says. "Fooling around like seventeen-year-olds." He lowers his lips to my neck and sucks. Hard.

He presses into me, and I squirm beneath him as he continues to kiss and bite and suck my neck, and then it dawns on me what he's doing. I push him away, laughing.

"*Do not* give me a hickey, Charlie Florek."

His eyes sparkle like fireflies. "I think it might be too late." He examines his handiwork. "You have three."

"Is this what you did when you were seventeen? Go at someone's neck like a vampire?"

"No. When I was seventeen, we'd probably both be undressed by now." He huffs out a dry laugh. "Actually, we might be getting dressed again at this point."

"That sounds fun."

"I don't know," he says. "I'm having a pretty good time here at first base."

I cackle. "Oh my god. I forgot about the bases."

Charlie's smile smothers mine. "That laugh," he says, and the sound dissolves on his tongue.

I wrap my legs around his waist, and we set a rhythm with

our mouths and our hips, and I hear myself gasping. The sounds
I make are unfiltered and unfamiliar, breathy and then guttural.
I'm not thinking about what Charlie might like. I'm not performing, like I have in the past, trying to make it good for him. I'm
just me, which makes it even better. It's liberating. I'm so into it
that my kisses become clumsy, and my teeth knock against his.

"Sorry," I say when they clack a second time.

Charlie tilts my head back. "Don't apologize." He drags a
finger down my throat, and I shudder. "I like unraveling you."

He keeps his hands to my face and neck and limbs, but I'm
not going to last much longer. Desire is twisting more tightly inside me. It's a multisensory experience, almost too much with
the friction and Charlie's smell, the way he breaks our kiss and
looks at me like I'm someone important, the taste of him on my
tongue. When my legs start to shake and my breathing turns ragged, Charlie whispers in my ear, "Just like that, Alice Everly." My
skin pebbles, and then all the tension building in me shatters.

I close my eyes as Charlie brushes the damp curls away from
my forehead. He kisses me once, tenderly, and when I open my
eyes, I find him staring down at me, concerned.

"I don't think that qualified as first base," I say, panting. Not
that I'd made it even halfway to first when I was seventeen.

Charlie chuckles. "I honestly have no idea where *that* falls."

I reach between us, running my hand over the thick length
straining the soft fabric of his pants. He pulls his bottom lip between his teeth, and his eyelids flutter closed for a moment before he takes my hand in his, kissing it.

"Not tonight," he rasps.

"That doesn't seem fair," I say. "I got what I wanted."

He leans over me, resting his forehead on mine. "So did I.
And these are my favorite comfy pants. I don't want to get them
messy."

I hum. "I do believe there are options for keeping them clean." I raise my eyebrows meaningfully, and he laughs again.

He taps me on the nose. "Trouble."

Quickly, I nip the end of his finger, and his eyes widen. "You just bit me."

"Touch my nose again, and I'll bite harder."

"Is that so?" He kneels between my legs.

"It is." I sit up, and he flicks the end of my nose.

"How dare you."

But before I can react, he has my arms pinned in one hand and is tickling my ribs with the other.

I shriek his name and laugh so hard, I cry. It's not long before I'm on top of him, trying to make him laugh. Charlie isn't very ticklish, but he is smiling. I pause for a moment, touching my aching cheek.

"What's wrong?" Charlie asks.

I look down at him. "I've been smiling too much," I tell him.

Charlie's eyes flash with delight. "No such thing."

30

W ell, look at this," Nan says, holding her newspaper's arts section aloft when I shuffle out of the bedroom the next morning. "It's an ad for your show."

It's a *full-page* ad. It must have cost Elyse a fortune. Nan lays it flat on the table, taking a photo with her iPad.

I didn't sleep under the stars with Charlie last night. He asked whether I wanted to stay or if I'd prefer him to walk me back to the cottage. I chose option B. It felt like the right ending to what will go down as the most epic make-out session of my life. The stars can wait.

Now those hours kissing him in the tree house feel like a lifetime ago, as if they really did happen when I was a teenager. I fell asleep with a smile on my face, but I've woken to reality.

I look at the paper over Nan's shoulder, feeling dizzy at seeing my name listed with the others.

My dread rises. How am I ever going to back out now? Taking a stand with Willa was one thing, but disappointing Elyse is another. Her opinion of me matters. Our friendship matters. I should have told her weeks ago I was thinking of dropping out.

I haven't finished my coffee when I get a string of texts from Heather.

Nan sent me the ad! LOOK AT YOU!

I'm so excited!

Can you come back a day early so we can go shopping?

You're giving a toast, right? You can practice with me!

I watch the messages flash on my screen, then turn my phone face down on the table.

Later, after we finish the curtains for Nan's bedroom and she heads out on a walk, I take my camera and the binoculars down to the water. It's humid, almost sticky. The sun is hidden by a fortress of clouds. I want to leave my city problems behind for a little while, so I text Charlie.

Me: Thought I'd do a little bird-watching. But I haven't spotted any interesting species.

Charlie: No peacocks?

Me: Unfortunately not.

A minute later, I peer at him through the binoculars as he walks down the hill and then out to the end of his dock. He sets his phone on a small, round table, and I can see the smirk clear on his face as he raises his arms and peels off his T-shirt, and then, so fast I almost miss it, he does a flawlessly executed back-flip off the end of the dock. I laugh to myself as he climbs out of the water and gives his head a shake.

Me: Found one. Definitely male. Loves showing off.

I watch Charlie read the text and grin.

Me: Come over here. I want to tell you something.

The thrill of watching Charlie hop into his boat and travel across the bay to me makes me giddy. I shoot a few frames. I want to save this feeling.

But by the time Charlie pulls up to the end of the dock, apprehension is written on every tense line of his face. He asked me twice on the walk home yesterday whether I was okay.

"Help me in?" I ask.

Charlie reaches out his hand, and I take it to step onto the back seat. He stares at me, green eyes fastened to mine.

"Last night was the most fun I've had all year," I say. "I don't regret it."

He nods once, then lifts me onto the floor of the boat. "Let's go for a ride."

We go fast. Faster than I've ever gone. I let my hair down and smile into the wind as we soar toward the vast open end of Kamaniskeg. I photograph Charlie's hand, casually gripping the wheel. I shoot his bare feet. I capture the expression he gives me when he says, "Feet, really?"

There's a group of kids at the top of the rock, waiting to jump, and as we pass them, I lean over Charlie and press the horn.

Aaaah-whoooo-gaaaaah!

His fingers tangle in my hair, holding it out of our faces. I have the urge to kiss him, though I'm not sure if we kiss in the light of day. Last night awakened a hunger in me that we didn't come close to sating, but Charlie's not his usual flirty, quippy self.

"You have a bathing suit on under that, right?" he says, eyeing my caftan as we return to his dock.

"Of course. Do you have plans for my bathing suit?"

He doesn't look up from the rope in his hands. He seems heavy. "I'm going to teach you how to do a backflip. Number eight."

He knows that list better than I do.

"Not a somersault?"

"A backflip is *slightly* easier."

We swim out to the floating raft, where the water is deeper. Charlie stands with his hands on his hips, explaining how dangerous flips are and all the things not to do. I feel like I'm in school. He's distant. There's no teasing, no flirting. He demonstrates how to do a backward dive into the water, and we practice until I can launch myself away from the raft with enough momentum that when I hit the water, my arch continues under the surface. When Charlie finally shows me how to flip into the water, tucking his knees to his chest, I flinch, worried he's going to hit his head.

"I'm not going to do that," I say when he surfaces.

"Okay."

He swims back to the ladder and climbs up, standing a few feet away from me, arms folded and frowning. I think about the boy from my photo. How sunny he seemed. How perfect I thought his life must be. How easy. How golden.

"Sorry for wasting your time," I say.

Water runs down his nose and neck, along his torso. "You're not a waste of time, Alice."

I chew on my cheek.

"What is it?" he asks.

I want to ask about last night, but I chicken out.

"Sometimes I don't get why you want to hang out with me. We're so different."

"Are we?"

"You're this trader dude with an overpriced car that you drive too fast. You live in *Yorkville*. It doesn't make sense why you'd want to do all the things on my silly list."

"That's not who I am. That's my job, my car, my home. That's not *me*. I'm just a guy on a raft, trying to figure out his shit like everyone else."

I study him for a moment, the tension in his shoulders, and whisper, "Do *you* regret last night?"

"Of course not."

"Okay." I release the breath I was holding. "Good. You seem kind of off."

"I'm sorry. This summer . . ." He rubs the back of his neck, squints into the sun. "It's been hard for me."

"And not because of your troublesome neighbor?"

He gives me a weak smile. "No, not because of that. My dad died when he was my age. In the spring. He didn't make it to summer."

I remember how resigned Charlie sounded when he told me he was thirty-five. "Every year we get is precious," he'd said that day.

I set my hand on his arm. "I'm sorry. I don't know what else there is to say, but I'm here. And so are you. Healthy. Alive."

His gaze darkens, and he looks like he's about to say something.

"Charlie?"

I don't think he hears me, so I stand beside him, and together, we stare out at the lake.

"I've been thinking about him a lot," he says eventually. "Being back here, in his house. Driving his boat, standing on the raft he built. Sometimes, the wind will ripple across the lake in a certain way, and just for a second, I can hear him calling out to Sam and me, telling us to get our life jackets on." He peers down at me. "It's hard to believe that he's gone—that they're both gone—and now I'm thirty-five. At my age, my dad had a wife, two kids, a business he was proud of. What would I leave behind?"

"Hey. Don't talk like that. You're not going anywhere."

"I could." He swallows again. "Any of us could."

"Is that what the tree house is about?"

"My legacy?" He scratches his eyebrow. "I didn't think of it like that, but yeah, it's probably that. So fucking arrogant."

"Stop. Of course this is a hard year for you. But the tree house is an amazing thing—don't twist it out of shape."

"I'm sorry." He links his fingers behind his neck and looks up at the sky.

I don't like seeing him like this. "Everything is okay." I wrap an arm around his middle and squeeze. "We're here. On this beautiful lake. Together." I feel him take a deep breath.

"Can I help you take your mind off it?" I ask.

"I think you probably can."

I tilt my chin and catch the quickest glint of a smile before Charlie scoops me up and chucks me in the water. He jumps in beside me before I even come up for air. It starts as a water fight, splashing and wrestling and laughing, and ends with me kissing Charlie beneath the surface. When we come up for air, he gestures to the ladder. "Up."

Which is how I find myself making out with the boy across the bay on a raft on Kamaniskeg Lake. Just two people, figuring out their shit, kissing each other like there's nothing better in this world than just kissing. My tongue is buried deep in his mouth when I hear a loud clanging. I pause, smiling at the sight of Charlie's swollen lips. "What was that?"

"I think—"

He's cut off by the same *ding* of metal hitting metal.

"I think that's your dinner bell."

We turn our heads toward the cottage as Nan waves from across the bay.

31

We climb the steps to where Nan waits for us on the deck, guilty grins on our faces. Charlie insisted on coming up to "face the music," though he was laughing as he said it.

"The pair of you," Nan says, looking between us. "Necking like teenagers for everyone to see."

"I'm sorry, Nan," Charlie says. I bite my lip so I don't snort at the puppy dog eyes he gives my grandmother. "It's my fault. I—"

He's silenced. "Charlie Florek, I will not listen to you apologize for something you are clearly not sorry about."

He drops his head, and Nan winks at me.

"Come on, both of you."

Charlie holds the door to the screened porch open for Nan, and we follow her inside. She picks up her phone and punches in a number, then sets it to speaker as it rings.

"What is this?" I ask, glancing at Charlie, who looks as confused as I feel.

"I'm staging an intervention," Nan says.

The ringing stops, and Heather answers. "Hi, Nan. Do you have her?"

"I do."

"What's going on?" I say again, heart beginning to race. I

have a bad feeling that whatever is happening, I don't want Charlie here for it.

What the hell? he mouths.

I shake my head. I have no idea.

"Hi, Ali," Heather says. "I'm just going to put you on hold while I get Dad."

"I think you should leave," I tell Charlie quietly.

"Are you sure?"

I nod, and he gives my shoulder a squeeze. "Text me, okay?"

"Where do you think you're going?" Nan says.

Charlie looks at me for guidance.

"He's going home, Nan."

"Actually," she says, directing her attention to him, "I'd like you to stay. You might be able to help."

"Is he there?" Heather's back.

"Who?" our dad asks.

"Ali's cottage friend."

"Charlie Florek," Charlie says, sounding like he's in a suit and tie and not a wet bathing suit. For a second, I picture him in another life, his real life, completely in control, not a joker but a titan.

"Oh my god," Heather says. "I have so many questions for you, but we have a hard out in ten minutes, so I'm going to cut to the chase. Alice, you need to go to the opening."

"This is about the show?" My entire body runs cold.

"Congratulations, Alice," our dad says. "This is a tremendous honor, a testament to your talent, success, and hard work. I'm damn proud."

I'm aware of Charlie's gaze on me. I hate that he's here right now.

"He cried when I told him," Heather adds.

I close my eyes. She wasn't supposed to say anything. "Thanks, Dad."

"Charlie," my sister says, "I'm not sure how much Ali has told you about the show."

He looks to me, not with judgment or surprise. He looks to me so I can decide how I want to handle my sister.

"He knows the basics," I say. My rage is an icy thing, chilling my fingers and toes.

"One of Alice's photos is appearing in a group exhibition for a brand-new gallery," Heather says. "It's a very big deal. The opening is in a few weeks, but Alice doesn't want to leave the lake to attend."

"She thinks I'm too infirm to be left alone," Nan adds.

"I don't think that at all," I say.

"And that it's too much travel for me to come with her."

"I don't want you to wear yourself down."

"Alice, help me understand where you're coming from," my father says. "This is a career highlight. If your fear of public speaking is stopping you, I'd be happy to hire a coach to make sure you're prepared and comfortable. You'll be wonderful."

"It's not that, Dad." Though I do hate talking to an audience—I always freeze up. My heart rate spikes, my tongue may as well be made of concrete, and a cool, clammy perspiration chills me to the bone.

One by one, Heather and my father lay out their arguments as if they're in court. Another, stronger person wouldn't put up with this level of meddling. Heather certainly doesn't allow anyone to tell her how to manage her life. But I can only look for the nearest exit.

"We only want the best for you, Turtle," Heather says.

I'm too angry to explain myself.

"Are we done now?" My voice is barely louder than a whisper.

"What do you think, Charlie?" Nan asks.

Charlie fixes his gaze on me. "I think it's time to end this call." And then he walks over to the phone and hangs up on my sister and father.

I blink at him, stunned. It's the hottest thing I've ever witnessed.

"Are you okay?" he asks.

I shake my head. I turn to Nan, trying to keep my voice from shaking. "Why would you do that to me? I'm a grown woman. *I* make my decisions."

"I thought it would help."

"You embarrassed me. I'm trying to respect your independence and privacy when you ask me to. I've been trying to give you what you need." My voice rises in an unfamiliar way. "I'm here for *you*. Why can't you be here for me, too?"

Nan flinches, and it feels awful.

"I need some space." Without waiting, I exit the cottage and head straight for the boathouse.

Charlie gives me space for twelve minutes. When he finds me, I'm sitting on one of the beds, knees bent to my chest, crying. He doesn't say anything, just sits beside me and pulls me into his arms. Somehow, it only makes me sob harder.

"I'm here," he whispers into my hair. "You'll be okay."

Eventually the tears ebb, but Charlie keeps holding me. It's quiet except for a light rain tapping against the roof and windows. I could stay here forever.

"Alice?"

I make a mumbling acknowledgment against his chest.

"I have an idea that might cheer you up."

I gaze at him. He's wearing a green T-shirt with an image of two Muskoka chairs on a dock on the front that Nan has obviously found for him.

"Want to do some bad art together?"

Make a bunch of bad art. Number seven.

We sit opposite each other at the small table in the boathouse, blank pieces of paper and pencils in front of us.

"We're going to do blind contour portraits." I took an introductory drawing class back when I was in school, and this was the first exercise we were given.

"The way it works is that we get five minutes to draw each other's faces, but you can't lift your pencil from the page, and you can't look at what you're doing. You have to use a single, unbreaking line to sketch my face."

Charlie taps his bottom lip with a finger. "I just remembered that I don't like doing things I'm not good at."

"It's supposed to be fun. Try not to think about it too much."

He gives me a serious nod that has me grinning.

"I like it when you do that," Charlie says, his eyes locked on my mouth as we begin to draw.

"Do what?" I'm starting with his left eye, slowly forming the curve of his lid.

"Smile," he says.

Charlie's face is scrunched in a scowl of concentration, and I can't help but giggle.

"I'm trying to do your hair," he says. "If this resembles anything other than overcooked spaghetti, I'll be shocked."

When the timer on my phone rings, we're both in hysterics. I've laughed more with Charlie in the last couple of weeks than I have in the previous six months combined.

"That cackle," he says. "It's brutal. I love it."

"I mean." I hold up Charlie's portrait. I've got his left eye overlapping with a giant mouth. His right eye is somewhere up on his forehead. It's not clear what's hair or cheek or nose.

"Wow," he says. "I believe they call that an oral fixation."

"Let's see what you've got, then."

Charlie slides his drawing across the table to me. I can make out two large eyes. My lips look more like a heart than a mouth and fall somewhere near where my neck should be. My hair is all loop-the-loops, my chin a sharp V.

"It's glorious," I say, still laughing.

"It's terrible."

"I'm framing it."

The rain has begun falling harder, creating dimples in the surface of the lake. We both turn to the window for a moment.

"Do you want to talk about what happened back there?" Charlie asks, breaking the silence.

"I hate that you heard all that—the part where I yelled at Nan especially."

"You raised your voice, Alice. You didn't yell. But I wouldn't give two shits if you screamed at the top of your lungs. You have every right to be upset."

"Heather knows I don't love the photo that's been chosen, but she thinks I'm being fussy."

"It's your art. Having an opinion isn't fussy—it's your job."

"The truth is I don't want the photo in the show. But I can't back out now, so I'd rather pretend it isn't happening."

"Why can't you back out?"

"Because I'm a terrible coward."

"Try again."

I tell Charlie about Elyse—how much I respect her taste, how I don't want to let her down. "I still can't believe she wants to include me in her first show," I say. "Heather's right: It's a huge honor."

"But?"

I turn the pencil over in my fingers.

"It's just me," Charlie says gently. "You can talk to me."

It takes me a second to meet his eyes. His gaze is warm. It's as if I'm lying in a sun-dappled field in the middle of August.

"I don't think I have a piece I'd want to display right now, not something that feels true to me. I know, technically, I've improved as a photographer, but I don't feel connected to my work the way I used to."

"How did you used to feel?"

"Alive. Excited. Like I was taking someone inside my head and showing them how I saw the world." I watch water droplets trickle down the windowpane. "Since I've come back here, I've been remembering what it was like when I first picked up a camera. I took a lot of terrible photos, but I also captured shots that felt more personal, more alive than what I do now. I think I've been so caught up in building a career, in making my clients happy and working to earn my place, that I lost sight of what makes *me* happy. The balance is off."

He smiles. "It sounds like it's time to correct the balance, then."

"Just like that?"

Charlie's stare is relentless. "If not now, then when?"

Every year we get is precious.

I'm at a crossroads.

"Do you think I should drop out of the show?"

He leans back in his seat. "Listen, if someone wanted to show off my work and tell the world I'm awesome, I'd be a cocky bastard. I'd rub it in the face of all my colleagues." Imagining it brings a soft smile to my lips. "But that's *me*. You're not a self-centered ass like I am."

"I don't think you're a self-centered ass."

"That's one of your flaws," Charlie says. "But the fact that you have integrity isn't."

"I've done some work I'm not proud of because there's a paycheck attached to it," I tell him.

"You have no idea how much I relate."

"Do you like your job?"

"Most of the time, not particularly."

"Why do you stay if you don't enjoy it?" I ask. "Trading must be extraordinarily stressful."

Charlie's gaze is as direct as his answer. "I like the money, Alice. I like it a lot."

"Is that enough?"

"Sometimes. We never had much growing up. I can remember my parents at the kitchen table, sorting through the bills, so stressed. It seemed unfair since they worked so hard. They always figured it out, but I didn't want that for myself. I didn't want to be devastated by a car repair." He leans across the table. "I'm very good at what I do, and I love being good."

I digest this. "You've never really explained why you're taking a sabbatical."

There's a moment of deliberation before he answers. "I needed a break."

"How come?"

He stares at me across the table, and I can see a debate waging in his eyes.

"It's just me," I say, repeating his words back to him. "You can talk to me."

His focus drops to the portrait he's drawn, and he runs a finger over the squiggles of my hair. I'm not sure he realizes he's doing it.

When Charlie meets my eyes, his gaze is discernibly sharper, like he's locked onto something. "I bet you'd do anything for your friends."

"I'd do anything for the people who matter to me." I think he would, too.

His voice is slow, serious. "Do *I* matter to you?"

"Of course." I don't have to think about my answer. Charlie matters to me in a way that would have seemed impossible weeks ago. But the look on his face makes me question whether that's what he wanted to hear. "Is that a problem?"

"No," he says quietly. "I'm a lucky man." He sounds genuinely touched. "Earlier today, you said you didn't understand why I wanted to do your bucket list with you."

"I remember," I say softly.

"When I was young, I took shifts at the restaurant almost every evening in the summer. I didn't mind too much, because I liked the paycheck, and the place was my second home. Working in a kitchen is grueling, but there's a rhythm and a rush that's hard to find anywhere else. But I envied the cottagers having a barbecue on the deck or waterskiing just before the sun sets, when the lake is glass. Percy's family used to do puzzles and watch movies together at night." He smiles, but it's bittersweet. He looks away for a moment before turning back to me. "This time with you and Nan is exactly what I imagined it would have been like for a regular family. You've given me the summer I've always wanted."

My throat tightens. "Me too. You've given me what I wanted, too."

"Boat rides and smutty books?"

"Fun," I tell him. "That's what I was missing. Until I met you."

"That's one thing I'm good for," he says with a smirk.

Charlie may be able to read me, but I see him, too. I can tell the difference between when he's flirting because he wants to play, and when he's trying to keep his heart tucked somewhere safe. His gaze follows me as I stand and walk around the table to him. He pushes his chair back so I can stand between his legs.

"You *are* fun," I say, setting my hands on his shoulders and giving him a gentle shake. He's one of those flame-like people whom we all gravitate toward like moths, soaking in their warmth. "I haven't felt this comfortable with someone in a very long time. I haven't laughed this much since I don't know when. I can speak my mind without being afraid you'll judge me. It's so freeing. So, yes, you're fun. That's a gift, Charlie."

He looks up at me with something like affection. "I'll come to your show."

"What?"

"If you decide to do it, I'll be there." He holds my gaze.

I imagine a pair of clear green eyes in a sea of blurry faces. "*If* I decide to do it, I'll look at you when I give my speech. I'll picture you naked."

He grins. "You haven't seen me naked." His hands find my rib cage and run up and down my sides.

"Doesn't mean I can't picture it."

He pinches my butt. I swat him on the arm, but he has the reflexes of a big cat, capturing my hand and bringing it to his mouth. He sucks on the sensitive pulse point on the inside of my wrist while his other hand sneaks under my caftan and up my thigh. Higher. His fingers pause when they reach the bottom of my bathing suit top. He gazes at me, his lips still pressed to my wrist.

"Ready for second base?"

I pull my caftan over my head. "I'm ready for a home run, bases loaded."

Charlie chuckles, but his gaze has gone dark. "Trouble, and no."

I give him a look of exasperation.

"You do know that I'm not going to fall in love with you if we have sex," I say.

"You can't guarantee that." He flashes me a cheeky grin. "I'm *very* good."

I laugh. "You're something."

"Don't worry. I'll make it worth your while. Besides, I have to keep you interested somehow."

I wonder if there's an ounce of truth in his words, but then his thumb brushes across the still-damp fabric of my bathing suit top, and I shiver. Lip pulled between his teeth, Charlie pinches my nipple between his fingers.

"As good as that feels," I say, head falling back on a gasp as he rolls the tight bud between his fingers, "I'm not sure you can make it worth my while from second base."

In response, he takes my hand and slides it down my stomach to the edge of my bathing suit bottom.

I stiffen. "I've never done that in front of someone else."

Charlie looks momentarily stunned, but then he smiles. "Don't make me do all the work, Alice Everly."

I stand between his thighs, hesitating for a moment, before I dip my hand below the edge of my suit. Charlie watches, hunger darkening his stare. I shut my eyes, tipping my head back, concentrating on the feel of his breath against my stomach and the press of my fingers. A quiet sound escapes my throat, and it's all it takes for Charlie to get to his feet and carry me to one of the twin beds.

"I thought you didn't want to do all the work," I pant as he sets me down.

"I wouldn't want to be accused of being lazy," he says, before replacing my fingers with his own.

After a volcano erupts behind my squeezed-shut eyelids,

Charlie bundles me in his arms. I nuzzle into his chest, close my eyes, and breathe him in. Hot skin and that other luxurious, green scent that I find very relaxing.

My words jumble somewhere between my brain and my tongue. "What is the way you smell?"

A hand trails up and down my arm. "The way I smell?" I can hear him smiling.

"Yeah. I can't figure it out. It's expensive and plant-y."

I feel his chuckle against my cheek. "It's my body wash. Eucalyptus and lavender. I bought it at a hotel spa."

I raise my head. "That's it. You smell like a spa."

He laughs again. "Is that a good thing?"

"Very. I might need to borrow it."

His fingers move from my arm to my hip. "I want you to know that I don't think you're a turtle."

"No?"

"No. You're a Pegasus-unicorn, Alice Everly. You're one of a kind."

32

It's still drizzling when I walk Charlie to the dock. Our goodbye is awkward. I lean in for a kiss and he goes for a hug, and we end up in a weird pretzel with my lips pressed to his collarbone and Charlie laughing at me.

I watch the yellow boat cut across the bay, and then make my way up to the cottage, preparing an apology to Nan. The fragrance of onion and garlic frying in oil fills my nose when I step inside. I find her in the kitchen.

"Do you need help?"

"I'm managing," she says. "I'll let you know if I get weary. You go change into something warm."

I want to argue because she'll be tired when she's done, but I give her what I've asked for: freedom to make her own choices.

"I want to apologize for earlier," I say as we sit down to eat.

Nan makes her pasta sauce with ground beef, tinned mushrooms, and carrots, and she spoons it over naked egg noodles—everything about the dish would alarm an Italian, but I love it. It reminds me of the sleepovers Heather and I had at her house after the twins were born.

She sets down her fork and lifts her chin. "No," she says. "I owe you an apology, Alice. It was wrong of me to ask your sister to speak to you. She was adamant about bringing your father into the conversation, and I thought we could help you see what you're missing out on." She pauses. "But you're an adult, and we need to respect your decisions."

"I appreciate that." I take a deep breath. "Because I'm not going to participate in the show."

"Alice! Whyever not?"

I tell Nan everything. How, even though the photo may be one of my best, it's not one I truly love. How I'm afraid of disappointing Elyse. How my work doesn't give me the same purpose and fulfillment it once did.

"I need to recalibrate," I tell her. "I need to find my voice as a photographer again."

She takes a minute to digest what I've told her. "I'm proud of you," she says. "Knowing one's own mind is one of the secrets to a good life."

"Oh? Any others you want to share?"

She thinks for a moment. "The ability to forgive, and friends worth forgiving," she says. "Speaking of which, I'm very sorry I embarrassed you in front of Charlie. Though I'd wager it's his opinion of me, not you, that took a wallop. He was none too happy with me after you left. Told me I was old enough to know better."

I shake my head, holding back a smile. Nan begins to laugh.

"He's a bold one, hanging up on your sister and father like that. A good match for you."

I stare at her for a moment, because she's right. Charlie and I respect each other—our similarities and our differences. I don't think there's a single thing I could say that would make him turn his back on me. "As my friend," I tell her.

"Don't forget I saw you two on the raft. Friends don't kiss like that."

"Sometimes they do," I tell her. "It's different these days, Nan."

She gives me a disbelieving look but doesn't press.

After dinner, I bring her a square of chocolate, and we sit in the living room. She's reading on her iPad, and I'm on the floor with a puzzle.

"I haven't spoken to John Kalinski in more than a decade," she says.

I keep my mouth pressed firmly shut.

Nan sighs. "I *loved* your grandfather."

"I know you did."

"I was fifty-nine when he died. We didn't have nearly long enough together. I know it's not his fault that he's gone, but sometimes I get so cross with him for leaving me." She smiles sadly. "I know I've been out of sorts lately. It's hard being here without them."

"Grandpa and Joyce."

"And John, too. This place is full of memories. Not all of them good—it's where I came after your grandfather died. I was alone here for a few days before Joyce joined me." Her eyes are glassy. "When she died, I felt so lost. She's been gone for thirteen years now, but I feel her everywhere here. It's like losing her all over again, but it's also a comfort. I talk to her all the time, mostly when you're not around."

She pulls a hankie out of her pocket and dabs her eyes. "John and I stayed close after she passed away. I filled his freezer with meals. Checked in on him. He wanted me to come up to the lake. His son had lost interest, and John didn't want to come alone. But I didn't think I could be here without Joyce. Three years after her death, I changed my mind. It felt like enough time had passed, and I missed these walls, the way it smells, the view." She looks at the lake out the window before continuing.

"John and I came up together for two weeks. And it was nice—sharing meals with one of my dearest friends, watching the sun set together, *laughing*."

"I'm sure," I say. "It must have been such a relief for both of you."

"It was. I think we got caught up in it." She clears her throat. Nan twists her hands in her lap. She's nervous.

"There was just one kiss," Nan says. She looks to the rafters, taking a deep breath. "I didn't start it, but I didn't stop it, either. We both knew it was a mistake, and John wanted to talk about it, but I felt so terribly guilty. Kissing Joyce's husband under her own roof." She shakes her head.

I move to the sofa so I can be closer. "Nan," I say. "You both lost your spouses. Grandpa would have been gone for . . ."

I'm doing the math in my head when she says, "Eleven years."

"Somehow I don't think either Grandpa or Joyce or anyone could fault you for seeking comfort in a good friend."

"Perhaps," she says. "But the accusations I flung at John, the way I yelled at him, the things I said . . . it was very ugly, Alice. I insisted he take me back to Toronto the next morning. I didn't speak to him the entire drive. It was the last time I saw him."

I think of what she just told me about the ability to forgive, and friends worth forgiving. I think of how she faltered when I suggested we come to the lake until I told her John wouldn't be here.

"Charlie said John wants you to give him a call. Why don't you?"

She clicks her tongue. "It's been too long."

"You know what Charlie would say if he was here?"

She smiles at me. "What would that *friend* of yours say if he was here?"

I ignore her implication. "He'd tell you that you're lucky to be alive at eighty, and even luckier to have one of your oldest friends on this earth. He'd tell you to reach out to him."

"Funnily enough," Nan says, "that's almost exactly what he said."

33

The strangest thing happens when I find the courage to call Elyse to tell her I want to withdraw my photograph from the show.

She's *thrilled*.

"Good for you. I'm devastated I won't have one of your pieces, of course, but you have to follow your intuition."

"You're not mad?"

"Of course not." She laughs. "It's about time you disagreed with me. Although, I do wish you'd have done it sooner. And I would still love to have you at the opening."

"I'll visit as soon as I'm back." I don't want to leave the lake a moment sooner than I have to. "And I'm sorry. I know how much you love that shot, but I want to go in a different direction. I've been playing around with some new stuff, and I might be onto something." And as I say it, it's like the click of a shutter. I *am* onto something—something I want to keep chasing.

"Obviously I'm intrigued. You'll show me when you're ready?"

I promise I will.

"It sounds like this summer has been good for you," Elyse says before we hang up. "You sound different."

"I feel different," I tell her. "I feel like I've woken up."

Charlie and I spend our days together, floating on the lake, racing around in the boat, jumping from the rock. We discover a boulder on the other side of the boathouse, flat enough to lie on together, that's very private. A secret spot. He leaves Nan and me to our sewing but comes back in the evenings for cards, puzzles, and one impassioned game of Monopoly. He's as ruthless as a real estate mogul. We stay up long after Nan goes to sleep, talking until the moon hangs high above the water like a disco ball.

On Friday evening, I sit between Charlie's legs on the boulder, looking over the water, my back resting on his chest. I turn my head to kiss him and find hesitation in his eyes. It's often like this. He'll pause for just a second, long enough that I know he is considering exercising restraint. But he never does. He'll blink and press his mouth to mine with an urgency that's almost staggering. Tonight, his lips move from my mouth to my shoulder as he draws lazy circles over my bathing suit top, then lower, with a maddeningly relaxed pace, slowing even further when I get close, until I'm shaking, almost in tears, whispering his name over and over.

We haven't had sex. Charlie wants to *take things slow*, and I know it's because he's afraid of breaking this delicate thing we have. I won't admit it, but it's been kind of fun dragging it out. It's sneaky and silly and just like I'm seventeen. Not that I was kissing anyone at seventeen.

But everything changes on Saturday. It's Percy and Sam's party, and things suddenly feel grown-up. I've pushed the adult world and the city aside, but now the city is coming to us.

I don my armor. I straighten my hair, securing it in a sleek ponytail at the nape of my neck, and it hangs to the middle of my back in a shining rope of auburn. I wear my tortoiseshell glasses and a black short-sleeved silk jumpsuit. I paint my lips and nails red.

When I examine my reflection in the mirror, I see a confident, stylish woman. The Alice I am when I'm shooting. But it feels like a mask.

"You should let your hair down," Nan says as I'm buckling my sandals, the ones with a chunky heel and straps that wrap around my ankles in a way that is both complicated and decidedly sexy. They're comfortable, and I have two pairs. I'm picky, but when I find something I love, I buy multiples. I go all in on everything, including footwear.

"Do you mean that literally?" I ask.

"No," she says. "But now that you mention it, why do you have it pulled back so tight? You haven't worn it like this all summer."

"Does it look bad?"

"You look beautiful, Alice. You always do."

"Thank you." I unslouch my shoulders to mimic hers. "It would be a good night to use that phone." I've written John's number on a piece of paper and left it on the counter. "You'll have privacy," I add.

"We'll see."

I pour her a glass of scotch. "Here." I set it on the table next to her chair. "Call your friend."

I kiss Nan on the cheek and hoist my bag over my shoulder. I'm glad I offered to take photos. I need a camera in my hands tonight. I stride out the door with a confidence I don't feel.

On the walk there, I focus on my breathing, on the crunch of pebbles beneath my feet, on the scent of pine that fills the evening air. But there's a pit in my stomach I can't get rid of. A house full of strangers. People who mean something to Charlie. And Charlie himself. We haven't discussed how we'll behave together. Am I supposed to pretend that I haven't spent hours making out with him in the tree house?

I'm okay. It's just a job.

I repeat it to myself, but it doesn't feel true.

As I approach the house, I'm so nervous, I barely register my legs. I feel like a teenager in the worst way—self-conscious and terrified I'll fade into the background. I pass cars parked along the side of the narrow road, and when I get to the Florek drive-way, there are so many vehicles it's like a parking lot.

The windows of the house are wide open, and music and laughter drifts out in greeting. Paper lanterns are strung every-where. They crisscross over the path to the front door and drape the perimeter of the porch.

Percy answers before I knock.

"Oh my god, Alice!" She yanks me inside. "Hi! I almost didn't recognize you. You look so different. In a good way, I mean. You look *hot*." Her eyes expand. "I'm sorry, that was weird. I'm a little overwhelmed with all this." She waves her arm around. Music plays, but it's the volume of the crowd that's deafening. Even the entrance is shoulder to shoulder.

"The party?"

"Yeah. But it also just really hit me on me on the drive up here today." She leans closer like she's telling a secret. "I'm hav-ing a baby. I'm going to be a *mom*."

I laugh, feeling my anxiety ebb like it often does once I'm doing the thing instead of thinking about it. "That's the rumor," I say. "And thank you. You also look different. Also hot."

Percy's hair falls in tousled waves to her shoulders, parted in the center, with curtain bangs framing her lovely brown eyes.

Her makeup is rosy and natural looking, but I bet it took ages to get right.

"I'm sweating like you wouldn't believe," she says.

"One of the perks of being pregnant is that we call it *glowing*."

And she is. Her dress is a pretty periwinkle blue with a square neckline, a fitted bodice, and a skirt that's draped over her waist, falling elegantly to the middle of her calves. She's wearing sandals similar to my own, with a solid heel that won't sink into grass, except they're silver and even higher.

"Anything you can do to make sure I'm not excessively *glowing* in the photos would be much appreciated," Percy says as I take my cameras out of my bag. I'll shoot mostly digital, but I've also brought my Pentax and rolls of black and white, my preference for parties. You can strip away the noise of color and the busyness of the room and focus on the action and emotion. Hopefully there'll be enough light to work with.

"Don't worry about that," I tell her. "Just have fun. Pretend like I'm not even here."

She raises her eyebrows. "Oh, I don't think so. You and I haven't spent nearly enough time together." She walks toward the kitchen, gesturing for me to follow. "Come on. I think he's been waiting for you. He keeps looking at the door."

We squeeze our way through the kitchen to the deck. My eyes find Charlie immediately. He's leaning against the railing, a bottle of beer in one hand, gesturing with the other, holding court with Sam in a large group. He's clean-shaven, dressed in a crisp white shirt and a pair of black dress pants. His dimples are showing off. I fiddle with my Pentax because he looks incredible, and I need to find calm.

We're a few feet away when he glances at me, and then does a double take. I raise my camera on instinct, before I can unpack the look he gives me.

Click.

Through my lens, I watch his mouth break into a dazzling smile, as bright as late July sun.

Click.

"I told you," Percy says.

Sam wraps his arm around her when we reach them. He whispers something into her ear that makes her chortle. Charlie tugs on my ponytail by way of greeting.

"This is different. The glasses. The lipstick."

"It's my work uniform."

"I've always loved a woman in uniform," Charlie says, giving me a wink. I shake my head. The man can't help himself.

He leans into my ear close enough that his lips brush my skin. "You look unbelievable. Like always."

If anyone else sees the way he's staring at me, they're going to figure out just how much we're benefiting from our friendship. Charlie clearly doesn't care, and the feeling of holding his attention in such a large crowd is almost drugging. It's all I can do not to turn my cheek and kiss him. But I pull back and give him a once-over. "You look fine, I suppose."

"I look *damn* fine."

I roll my eyes, but I'm smiling. My nerves have evaporated. I've coated myself in all my protective layers, but they aren't what makes me safe. It's Charlie. I don't need to be in-command photographer Alice or obliging daughter Alice or perfect girlfriend Alice. I can just be me. A woman at a party, trying to figure out her shit like everyone else.

I'm introduced to Julien, a longtime friend of the family and the chef and owner of the Tavern. I meet friends of both Charlie's and Sam's and their partners. I meet Percy's parents. When Harrison joins the group, I notice Charlie takes a step closer to me.

At one point, Percy lets out another loud laugh, and Charlie and I turn to see her and Sam cracking up about something. I glance at Charlie, and I'm hit with a sense of déjà vu. It takes me a moment to figure out why, to place the familiar expressions: Percy's big smile, the way Sam is focused on her, and Charlie, watching his brother with a delighted smirk. It's how they were in my photo.

I snap frame after frame, and then Percy pulls me over to ask me what shade of lipstick I'm wearing. And soon we're talking about makeup and magazines and art directors we both know. I glance at Charlie when I hear his laugh, and I see him and Sam sharing some kind of inside joke.

And it dawns on me.

This is *exactly* where I wanted to be when I was seventeen, but it's also exactly where I want to be now.

Percy, Sam, and I are deep in a conversation about the manuscript she's working on when I feel a hand on my back.

"What can I get you to drink?"

I pause and look up at Charlie.

"And why are you smiling like that?" he says.

Because for once in my life, I don't feel like I'm on the sidelines. For once, I'm in the photo.

"I'm having a good time," I tell him. "Sparkling water would be great, thanks."

"Really? I hired a bartender. She'll make anything you want."

"I don't drink while I'm working."

"All right," he says. "One sparkling water, coming up."

"What do you think of the tree house?" I ask Percy and Sam once he's left.

"We haven't seen the finished product," Percy says.

"Charlie's being dramatic," Sam adds. "The official unveiling is tonight."

"It's pretty incredible," I tell them, and they share a look. I get the feeling Percy and Sam can communicate without speaking. "It's come a long way since you were last here."

Percy's smile grows. "He's let you in it, then?"

Her question is a loaded one, and I look around, hoping Charlie will return and rescue me from what I'm almost certain is about to become an interrogation. But he's nowhere in sight.

"He has," I say slowly, knowing I'm turning a vibrant hue.

Sam arches a single brow and takes a sip of whatever brown liquor is in his glass.

"I'm going to pop inside," I tell them. "I want to get shots of your guests."

I slip away but not before I hear Percy telling Sam, "You owe me twenty bucks."

Thirty minutes later, I feel a hand on my shoulder. "There you are. I've been trying to find you." Charlie passes me a glass. "You get what you needed?"

"For the most part." I'd like to take a few more of Percy and Sam, but otherwise I think I've captured enough crowd and detail shots.

"Want to put the cameras away for a while? Enjoy the party?"

I shake my head. "I'm better with them."

"They look heavy. Don't you get sore?"

"My neck and my shoulders do, but I'm used to it. Don't worry about me."

"Not worried. Just checking in. I want you to have fun."

"I am having fun. This is a great party, Charlie."

I take a moment to peek around the living room. It has a large stone hearth in the middle, grander than the one at our cottage. The mantel has a display of photos of Charlie and Sam as children. I've already inspected them all. There's one of their parents on their wedding day. Sue reminds me so much of Charlie, sunny and dimpled. Sam looks more like his dad. There's another in a pewter frame of Sam and Percy sitting on the end of the dock, wrapped in towels—they're young, barely teenagers. And another of them on their wedding day. Percy's gown is lacy and elegant. She looks at the camera while Sam stares at her, the way he does in my photo.

There's a DJ in one corner of the room and a bartender in another. She's wearing a bow tie and suit, and she's making non-alcoholic Persephone Spritzes and whiskey Sam Sours. The music is a curious mix of old country songs, Motown, and pop, but somehow it works. The room is still bursting with people. It's an attractive crowd. I wave to Harrison, who's chatting with a gorgeous redhead and Percy's best friend, Chantal, a stunning woman with waist-length box braids. Both are looking at Charlie with narrowed eyes.

"Exes of yours?" I ask. He lets out a snort.

Guess that's a no.

"I met Chantal earlier, but who's the other one?"

"Delilah."

I glance at Delilah, and she catches me looking. She makes her way over.

She's wearing a red dress that shows off her little waist and generous curves. Her hair is a deeper shade of auburn than mine, brighter, bolder. She's like human fire, my opposite. I peer at Charlie. *They* would look good together.

"Charlie, hey," she says.

"Good to see you, Delilah."

She offers me her hand. "Delilah Mason."

"Alice Everly," I say. "How do you know Sam and Percy?"

"I've known Percy since elementary school, but I met the

Florek boys when I was fourteen or fifteen. I had a bit of a crush on this one," she says, tilting her head at Charlie. His mouth is arranged in a wry grin.

"Don't worry," she tells me. "He never showed me a second of interest."

"Why would that worry me?"

She looks between us. "Oh, I'm sorry. I assumed you were together. He's been looking at you like you're some kind of snack."

Charlie lifts his brows at that, and I will my face not to heat. "We're good friends," I tell her.

"Okay." Delilah laughs, and I think she may have had one too many Sam Sours. "I know what being *friends* with Charlie entails."

Charlie's spine straightens just as Chantal comes to Delilah's side. "Sorry about her," she says to me. "She thinks she can hold her liquor."

As Chantal yanks a giggling Delilah away, I turn to Charlie. "What was that about?"

He takes a swig of beer. "History."

34

Sam was right about Charlie being dramatic. The entire tree house is draped in an enormous cloth—I can't imagine how he found it or got it up there. The sun has set, but Charlie has lanterns down here, too. About twenty of us have peeled away from the party for the big moment. Percy stands with her back resting on Sam's chest, both their hands on her belly. Charlie's shirtsleeves are rolled up—he looks like a cologne commercial. Harrison is a few feet away, holding a length of rope.

"I'm going to keep this short because I know you'd all rather get back to the fun than hear me speak," he says. "Plus, I think I told every embarrassing story I have about Sam at the wedding."

"I have a few more," Percy adds, and Sam shakes his head, smiling.

"I've never been happier than the day I found out I was going to be an uncle," Charlie begins. He pauses, looking at his sister-in-law. "Pers, I know you're worried about . . . well, absolutely everything parenthood involves, but anyone who knows you knows that you'll be a wonderful mom." A murmur of agreement runs through the crowd.

Charlie sets his eyes on his brother.

"I love you, Sam." For a second, I think Charlie may cry. He takes a steadying breath, looking up at the trees. "You're going to be a great father. I wish Mom and Dad were here to see it."

"Me too," Sam says, his eyes watering. Percy whispers something in his ear, and her father puts a hand on Sam's shoulder.

I weave my way to Charlie's side because I want him to know he has someone here for him. He looks down at me and takes another deep breath.

"Okay, let's do this." He turns to Harrison and nods, then Charlie unites two extension cords as the cover falls to the ground. A gasp runs through the group, followed by applause.

The tree house glimmers with thousands of white twinkle lights. They glow on the railings of the two decks, wind their way up the trunks of the two trees the fort rests in. They line the pitched roof, and the frames of the windows and the door.

"Jesus," I hear Sam say.

Percy starts to cry.

"You really do like showing off," I murmur to Charlie.

"I like seeing them happy," he says to me. Then louder: "Cut it out, Pers. You haven't even seen inside yet."

"This is over the top, even for you," Sam tells Charlie, pulling him into a hug. "Thank you."

I slip away, giving them privacy.

I share a drink with Harrison, and chat with Percy's parents on the porch. I lose track of time, and when I finally make it back inside, the crowd has thinned. Percy is sitting on the couch, with Delilah and Chantal. All three women have kicked off their shoes.

"I'm going to head out," I say to Percy. "But I wanted to say goodbye to Charlie. Have you seen him?"

"He was in the kitchen a while ago," Chantal says.

"I saw him sneak back toward the tree house," Delilah adds.

"I'll walk you there," Percy offers. "I need to stretch. I'm not comfortable in one position for very long these days."

She doesn't bother putting her shoes back on before leading me outside. A veil of stars covers the sky, and we take a moment to stare at them.

"You can't see them like this in the city," Percy says.

"I don't think I've ever seen so many," I say.

She hums. "I love it here."

We follow the path down the hill, but then Percy stops to face me.

"I know you and Charlie say you're just friends," she says. "And you're free to tell me to mind my own business, but I think you would be good for him. I think you could be good for each other. He really does have a big heart. You probably know that already, but it can be hard to see beyond his joking."

"I do know that." I'm glad he has other people in his life who recognize it, too. "But we *are* just friends. It's not going to turn into anything more than that."

She bites her lip. "Okay, I get it. And if Sam were here, he'd be gesturing for me to stop talking, but he's not, so . . ." She shrugs. "You're not like the women he usually spends time with. He looks at you differently, too. I think it could be more. I think maybe it already is."

I start to argue but Percy laughs. "Come on, Alice. Did someone else give you that hickey?"

I touch my neck, immediately flushing. I thought my collar covered it. Effing Charlie.

"That's what I thought," she says, as smug as the man himself. "Just try to stick with him, okay? He's a real pain in the ass, but there's so much good there."

I stare at her, not sure what to say. But I don't need to say any-thing because Percy links her arm though mine and leads me along the path. Just as we reach the ladder, she asks for my phone.

"I'm texting myself," she says. "So we have each other's con-tact info. Get in touch whenever you want. It'll be nice to have a friend who can put up with the Brothers Florek for an evening."

She passes my phone back and returns to the house in her nice dress and bare feet.

35

The tree house is silent when I knock.

"It's just me," I say, opening the door slowly. I expected to find Charlie with a joint and a few friends, but he's sitting on the couch, head tipped back, eyes closed. "Hey."

Seconds pass, and Charlie says nothing.

"Are you okay?" I ask.

He replies without moving. "I slept with her."

My body freezes.

"Delilah?"

Charlie sits up slowly and looks at me.

"Percy," he finally says. "I slept with Percy."

I feel like I might vomit. It takes a moment to force out, "When?"

"A long time ago." His voice is as cold and quiet as a frozen lake. "The summer before she and Sam started university. I was twenty."

I sit on the couch beside him only because I'm not sure my legs will hold me.

"They were in a bad place," Charlie says. "Sam was away at some science workshop. He was pushing her away, telling her he needed space but hanging out with other girls. Their relationships status was questionable—Percy wasn't certain they were together."

"Why?" It's the only thing I can think to say.

"I thought Sam was being a dick. I thought he was ungrateful for what he had." He swallows thickly. "I thought I might have been in love with her."

Blood rushes to my ears. "And were you?"

He rubs both hands down his face. "I don't know. I had feelings for her, yeah, but I think I was mostly jealous and lonely and wanted what they had."

Charlie leans forward, hands clasped between his knees, looking at me from the corner of his eye. "They didn't speak for more than ten years. It messed them both up. Percy spent more than a decade punishing herself for what happened. Sam hated me. He closed up again, just like after our dad died. The light Percy brought into his life vanished. And Mom was so disappointed. It was worse than her being angry." He shakes his head. "Aside from losing my parents, it was the worst time in my life. Fuck, that sounds so selfish. It was worse for Percy and Sam."

"Why are you telling me this?" I ask quietly.

He straightens, pinning me with a venomous green gaze. "I want you to know what being friends with me entails." He echoes what Delilah said earlier.

I stare at him, trying to pull my thoughts together, to separate what I know about Charlie from my shock and disappointment, and swallow back the bitter snap of envy. "You were twenty," I say slowly. It would have been the summer after I stayed here.

"Old enough to know better."

"Maybe." I think of myself at twenty, hopelessly in love with Oz and wholly unable to tell him how I felt. "But young enough to struggle with complicated feelings."

He tilts his head to look at me more fully. "Why are you going easy on me?"

"Do you want me to tell you that what you did was shitty and wrong and hurtful?"

He swallows. "Yeah. Get mad at me, Alice—I deserve it."

I could. I feel unreasonably jealous and betrayed in a way that confuses me. I'm angry with Charlie for laying this on me after he's made me like him so much. And he wants me to lash out at him, to walk away.

"I'm not going to give you that," I say.

Charlie's jaw clenches, but he doesn't speak.

"You made a bad decision about who to sleep with when you were twenty. You already know that. Now I do, too. But you weren't the only one at fault."

He doesn't respond.

"Sam has clearly forgiven Percy. They're disgustingly in love. They've moved on. They're married. They're having a baby."

Still, he says nothing.

"And I know that's not who you are, Charlie."

"That *is* who I am," he says, eyes wide. "Why can't you see that? I'm the guy who slept with the love of his brother's life."

I shake my head. Charlie deserves to have someone in his corner. "Screw that."

He blinks at me.

"Maybe we wouldn't have gotten along when we were younger," I tell him. "Maybe I would have been too shy, and you would have been too full of yourself. But I'm not friends with the person you were then. I'm friends with *you*."

I give him a moment so it sinks in, but there's only a slight change in his posture as he glances around the room.

"*You* built this magical tree house for your niece or nephew," I say. "You made the best birthday cake I've ever tasted. You take my grandmother to choir practice and make me laugh harder than I have in my entire life. You care about people, and you're far kinder and more considerate than you give yourself credit for."

Charlie has gone still, but he hasn't taken his eyes off me. He's listening. He's always listening. But I hope he's hearing me, too.

"I'm not friends with the person you think you were in the past. I'm friends with you now. And I like that man." I rest my hand on his knee. "Even if he's high-maintenance."

Charlie lets out a short, disbelieving laugh but quickly falls serious again. "I'm still selfish, Alice," he says, his voice rough. "I still want things I shouldn't."

Charlie's gaze drops ever so slowly to my mouth.

Laughter and music carry on outside these walls, but all I hear is the beating of my heart.

"Why shouldn't you?" I whisper.

His eyes land on mine, and there's nothing but him and me together in this oasis in the treetops. The lamplight blankets us in gold, and Charlie's smell mixes with the wood, like the most luxurious forest.

"Charlie," I say quietly when he doesn't answer.

He gives me a long look and says, "Fuck it."

I'd smile, but his mouth is already on mine. His tongue parts my lips, greedy. It's unhinged, the way he devours me, growling dirty things against my skin. Where he's going to put his tongue. The parts of his body he wants to see covered in my red lipstick. What he thought about in the shower this morning. How he wants me to keep my glasses on. I scramble to unbutton his shirt. We're going to do this. *Finally.*

Charlie curses my name as he wraps his hand around my ponytail and pulls my neck to the side so he can kiss his way down my throat to my collarbone.

"I like how desperate you sound," I murmur.

"You have no idea."

He guides me onto my back, and hovers over me, spreading my legs with a knee while he works at the buttons at the top of my jumpsuit. His shirt hangs open, and I smooth my hands over his chest.

"I might have some sort of idea," I say, tilting my hips to meet his. He's already so hard.

Charlie laughs, then pauses to meet my eyes. "You're incredible."

He lowers his lips to mine, but this kiss is gentle and sweet. Something precious.

"You make me feel incredible," I tell him. "You make me feel so good."

His hands find mine, and he laces our fingers together on either side of my head.

I'm so lost in the slow glide of our tongues, the caress of his thumb on the back of my hand, that I don't notice the door to the tree house opening until I hear "Sweet Jesus."

I bolt upright, bashing my head into Charlie's, holding the top of my jumpsuit closed. Sam stands in the doorway, his eyes on the ceiling.

He lets out a long-suffering sigh. "I *really* should have known better."

36

Charlie: How are you this morning?

Me: Still embarrassed.

Charlie: Don't be. Sam didn't see anything.

Me: You were ON TOP OF ME.

Charlie: Thirty seconds later, and it would have been worse.

Me: Ugh.

Charlie: And Percy's thrilled. She woke up singing, "I knew it, I knew it, I knew it."

Me: UGH!

Charlie: I'm sorry, Alice. It's my fault.

Me: Yes, I blame you entirely. I'm completely innocent.

Charlie: So what you're saying is?

Me: No regrets.

37

By the time the first week of August comes, we've fallen into a rhythm. Nan and I get our town gossip on Mondays at the hair salon. She's driving short distances now, so on Tuesdays she takes herself to physio, and I delight in someone else having to listen to her gripe about the exercises. We go for walks through the bush and turn the cottage into a flowering garden with our sewing machine. During her naps, Charlie and I swim or take a ride in the yellow boat, but since the night of the party, we haven't so much as kissed. It feels like something has shifted between us, but I'm afraid to ask.

He insists on bringing Nan to choir practice, and when I ask him why, he gives a vague answer about enjoying the music. But all is revealed when the Stationkeeper Singers perform at the Barry's Bay Railway Station over the long weekend. I almost fall out of my chair when Charlie joins Nan at the front of the room. He has more enthusiasm than talent, and I bite my cheek to keep from laughing.

Charlie's here for afternoon tea and often stays for dinner. One night, he takes us to the Tavern for pierogi, sausages, and braised red cabbage. After we eat, he darts back into the kitchen to help clean and returns with Julien. We stay late into the night, long after the restaurant closes, listening to the chef's stories about Charlie, Sam, and their parents. Julien teases Charlie relentlessly, but it's clear there's love between them, that they're family.

We hear about Charlie's first shift working the deep fryer and the time Julien caught him making out with a server in the walk-in refrigerator. When Julien turns serious and tells Nan and me about how proud Sue was of her sons, I reach under the table and squeeze his thigh.

I'm here for you, I'm saying.

Charlie's hand finds mine.

I know.

We stay like that, fingers wrapped together, for the rest of the evening.

The next day, he and I return to the cottage after taking the Jet Ski to the jumping rock, and find Nan on the phone, speaking in hushed tones. She called John the night of the party. She's said next to nothing about their conversation, only that she's glad they connected. I'm certain that's who she's talking to now.

Charlie and I creep back outside and return to the shore, sitting on the sand in our bathing suits, our legs extended in the water. I have my big straw hat on, but Charlie puts extra sunscreen on my back and shoulders. I'm still as pale as a boiled pierogi, whereas his tan is deeper than when we met, his hair spun with blond.

I close my eyes and lean back on my elbows, a smile on my face. Today was a very good day. The bathing suit photos ran in

Swish over the weekend, and this morning, Willa sent me an email saying the response has been overwhelmingly positive.

> I hate admitting when I'm wrong, but here we are. I
> hope you'll consider shooting for us in the future.

"Still gloating, I see," Charlie says.

I laugh. "I'm not gloating. I'm basking."

"As you should be." He clears his throat. "Listen, I have to go to the city Thursday. But I'll be back Saturday."

That's the day Heather's finally bringing Bennett to the lake. I crack open an eye. "What's happening in the city?"

"I have an appointment."

"How mysterious."

Charlie taps his foot against mine, and I straighten, looking into his eyes. They're like gemstones, sparkling in the bright afternoon sun.

"It's a doctor's appointment, and I'm going to have dinner with some people from work."

I stare out at the lake, the sun glittering on its surface, the water-skier who's zigging and zagging across the wake of a speedboat, the break in the bush around the bay, where the Florek house sits perched on top of a hill. I look at Charlie's feet in the water next to mine.

There are only three weeks of August left—our time at the lake is running out. I'll miss him. I'll miss *this*.

"Give it to me," Charlie says.

I squint at him. "What?"

"Whatever it is that's on your mind."

"I'm going to miss you when you're gone. That's all. I'm getting used to having you around."

He gives me his sad-boy smile. "I'm going to miss you, too."

~~~~

Charlie shows up the next evening to take Nan to euchre. I watch them pull away in my car, a sinking feeling settling in my chest again. He's leaving for Toronto tomorrow morning, and while he'll only be gone two days, I'm dreading the time without him. I can feel summer slipping away, and there will never be one like it again. John has decided to put the cottage up for sale next spring.

Even if Charlie and I stay in touch in the city, it won't be the same. It can't be. Our relationship is defined by warmth and water. We'll be busy with work, living in different neighborhoods. I've filled roll after roll of film, as if I can keep time from its forward march. But the days will soon grow short, and the snow will come.

I sit on the deck with my notebook. I'm not much of a writer, but I want to capture more than images this summer. I want to remember how it's felt to be here with Nan and Charlie. I want to remember the raccoons in the outhouse, and Charlie's letter, and the way he and Nan became fast friends. I want to remember what it feels like to let loose.

I've written a couple of paragraphs when I hear a car in the driveway. I rush around the cottage, worried that something has happened to Nan. But the passenger seat is empty.

"What's wrong?" I ask as Charlie climbs out and strides toward me. He's wearing jeans and a T-shirt and a look that robs me of breath. He wraps one hand around the back of my head and another around my waist and brings his lips to mine. The kiss is a demand, a claiming, a brand. His tongue is hot on mine, his grip firm on my middle, flattening me to him.

"I'm sorry," he says against my mouth. "I wanted you too much."

I don't know if he lifts me off the ground or if I climb him like a tree.

"No such thing," I tell him, biting his bottom lip. "Although I hope you didn't leave my grandmother on the side of the road," I say. "I'm somewhat attached to her."

"She's playing cards. I'll pick her up in a few hours."

"And do you have any ideas for how we should spend that time?"

"I just wanted to hang out with you," he says. "Before I go."

Putting on a movie and making out like teenagers on the couch would be fun enough, but tonight I want to behave like the thirty-three-year-old woman I am. I unwind myself from Charlie, thrill bubbling beneath my skin. "I have a better idea," I tell him, taking his hand.

I'm going to see if I can find the limits of Charlie's self-control.

I pull my shirt over my head as I walk down the stairs to the lake. The water is quiet. The sun has dropped beneath the hill. There's no one around to see what I'm about to do, but my heart is hammering in my chest.

I reach around my back to unhook my bra.

"What are you doing?" Charlie says from behind me.

I look over my shoulder instead of responding and drop it on the dock.

"Number ten?" he asks, his voice thick.

"Number ten," I say, turning back to the water. "And twelve." If this isn't reckless, I don't know what is. I slide my sweatpants down my legs. I hear Charlie suck in a breath. We haven't seen each other undressed.

I walk to the end of the dock, slip off my underwear, and stand, naked, at the edge. Somewhere behind me, Charlie swears.

I take a moment to look back at him. His chest rises and falls as his gaze journeys from my shoulders, down past the flare of my hips, lower, lapping up every inch.

"Eyes up," I tell him.

"You're playing dirty." He looks to the sky and whispers a few words I cannot hear.

I turn back to the water and breathe in the crisp evening air, letting it caress my skin, and then I dive in. I've never gone skinny-dipping before, and I can't believe how good it feels. I swim beneath the surface as far as I can before coming up for air, and then turn to find Charlie on the dock, staring at me in wonder.

"Are you coming?" I ask.

I see the flash of hesitation.

"I thought you were supposed to be shy," he says.

"I thought you were supposed to be bad," I fire back.

He closes his eyes, tilts his head to the heavens, and laughs. *Click.*

"You're even more trouble than I thought," he says, and then, looking me square in the eyes, he pulls off his shirt and unbuttons his jeans.

From here to the end of time, the image of Charlie Florek standing naked in midsummer twilight will be one of my most prized possessions.

I paddle a little closer, drinking him in. He watches me watch him, smug as a person who looks as good naked as he does ought to look.

"Are you coming in, or are you just going to stand there showing off?"

"I'm just trying to remember the moment," he says.

"What moment is that, exactly?"

Charlie dives in, and I watch him glide underwater until he reaches me.

"You," he says, standing in front of me. His head is above the surface, while I have to tread water. "And me." He looks around him. "This."

I've never been so aware of my skin—the water touching every inch, the clean air against my face, the tight pinch of my nipples. I eye the beads of water that slide down Charlie's chest. My leg brushes against his hip, and his gaze returns to me.

"Let's swim," he says.

So we do, in a slow crawl deeper into the lake. I try to memorize the sensations—the sounds of our bodies swishing through the water, the slippery feel of our legs sliding against each other, the smile Charlie gives me when I turn onto my back, arms splayed. The happiness that spreads through me when he does the same and our fingers find each other. I'm not sure how long we float before we swim back to the dock. I pounce on Charlie as soon as the water is shallow enough that he can stand, wrapping my arms around his neck and legs around his middle.

I kiss him with a hunger that grows every second. I wanted to make Charlie fall apart, but I didn't anticipate how good this would feel—our slick skin and the cool water. Charlie meets every searching stroke of my tongue, but I can feel the tension in his body. He holds me tight so that I'm clamped against his waist.

I bring my mouth to his torso, collecting a droplet with my tongue and following its path up to his collarbone. He tilts his head back so I can taste the skin at the base of his neck, hissing when I pull his ear between my teeth. My nipples graze his chest, and I moan. His grip on me falters, and I slide down his hips. We both groan at the feeling of the hard, hot press of him between my legs. Charlie swears, then walks us to where it's not as deep, so that my upper half is out of the water. His mouth drops to my breast, flicking his tongue over a tightened, aching peak, then the other, drawing it into his mouth.

"Is this what you want, Alice?" he asks, moving to the other nipple.

I shake my head, and his hand finds the swollen flesh between my thighs. We stare at each other as he strokes me slowly.

"This?"

I shake my head again, then gasp as his fingers plunge inside me. I hold on to his shoulders for balance.

"Better?"

"Much."

But it's not enough for Charlie. After I shudder around his hand, biting my lip to keep myself from calling out his name, he pulls me out of the water, and we dart into the boathouse. We're kissing before we have the door open.

"There's something I want before I go," he says, sitting me at the end of one of the beds. He kneels at my feet, and with both hands on my legs, pushes them apart.

Charlie kisses the inside of one thigh, and then the other. He looks up at me from under his fair lashes, and his palms smooth over the backs of my calves. His pupils have almost swallowed up the green. I try to squeeze my thighs together, but they meet Charlie's shoulders. His eyes flare.

"Impatient?"

"No," I say, although *impatient* doesn't begin to describe how badly I want Charlie's mouth on me.

Charlie's tongue travels up my inner thigh, and then moves to the other leg. I squirm, and he sits back on his heels, surveying me. He wraps a fist around himself. "This is what I do when I think about going down on you."

"Charlie." I'm seconds away from tackling him to the ground.

He hums, and then dips his head between my legs. With no searching, he brings his mouth exactly where I want it.

This time, I let myself scream his name.

We're curled together on the sofa on the screened porch, my feet in Charlie's lap, listening to loon calls. We have about thirty minutes before he needs to pick up Nan, and we're mostly sitting in cozy silence. My hair is still wet, dripping onto my sweatshirt. His is dry. The way it's buzzed so close to his head emphasizes his jaw, and if I didn't know him better, I'd find him intimidating. But now I know there's no reason to be intimidated. His tenderness coincides with all the hard lines and wisecracks.

Charlie's looking at his phone, and I'm fiddling with my camera. He doesn't even blink when I take his photo anymore. I'm not the only one who's grown more comfortable this summer.

"What are you looking at?" I lean closer and find him slowly scrolling through my Instagram. I know he's seen what I've posted from the lake, but watching him study my work so closely stirs up a specific concoction of nerves and squeamishness. I care about what he thinks. It's an effort not to put a pillow over my head.

"Fuck, you're good," Charlie murmurs, and my cheeks go hot. "Look at this."

He holds up a shot I took a few years ago of a florist in Leslieville. She'd asked me to take photos of her and the space for her website after she redecorated. This was my favorite. She's arranging flowers at a large table, and the surface and floor are carpeted with petals and twigs and leaves. Her hair is braided in a crown around her head, and it's a little mussed. Hazy light streams through the window, and there's a timeless quality to both the subject and the shot that I love.

Charlie scrolls some more. He's going deep.

"You have no photos of yourself," he says after a little while.

"Why would I?"

"Why wouldn't you?"

"It's a professional account. I'm not going to post selfies." Yuck. "And I *hate* having my photo taken."

Charlie grins. "Isn't that a cliché—the photographer who can't stand being in front of the camera?"

"Shut up." I poke his leg with a toe. "What's on yours?"

He looks at me, eyebrows raised. "You'd know if you followed me."

I can't quite explain why I haven't. Maybe I'm afraid to see Charlie's life beyond the lake.

"Fine." I send him a follow request, and he immediately accepts.

"See," he says as I look through his photos. "It's a bunch of random shit *and* selfies."

Photos of the lake and the boat. Most are of him with friends. There's one of Charlie with his arm around Sam on what is clearly his wedding day. Both are dressed in suits. Charlie points to himself. "Sexy as hell."

"You know, I've met professional models who aren't as confident about their looks as you are."

"I could be a model."

I laugh. "You're too old."

"Fuck off."

I peer at the side of his head. "I think I see some silver in there."

"You do not."

I don't.

"Yeah, right here." I run a finger over his ear, and he turns his head quickly, capturing it between his teeth.

Somehow I find myself on my back with Charlie straddling

me. He locks my wrists above my head with one hand, while he reaches for my camera.

"Put that down, Charlie Florek," I say. "You don't even know how to use it."

"I'm getting better." I've been showing him a few basics. "Come on. Just one. You've spent the whole summer getting shots of other people. Why not one of you, too?"

"I never let anyone take my photo."

"Why?" Charlie shifts off me. I right myself, legs folded underneath me so I can face him.

"It makes me extremely uncomfortable."

He sets the camera down and holds up his phone. "Would this be easier for you? I don't have any of you, and you probably have thousands of me by now."

"All right," I huff.

I watch him focusing on whatever he's doing with phone settings. He's so handsome.

"Are you ready?"

"No." But I smile my cheesiest, toothiest smile.

"Beautiful," he says when he's finished.

That night, after Charlie has brought Nan home and we wish him a safe trip to the city, I get a notification: charlesflorek has tagged me in a photo. My chest tightens as I study it. Charlie must have been shooting before he asked if I was ready. It's me, staring at the camera, staring at him. There's a gentle smile on my mouth, and my eyes are warm. I look happy—no, it's stronger than happiness. I look like I'm at peace.

The caption is short. He's only used one word.

Alice.

38

I meet the rising sun on Saturday with a sense of hope and purpose. The reflection from the lake dances on the ceiling of my bedroom, and the living room is cast in deep yellow. Nan is still asleep, so I fix myself coffee and head down to the dock with my notebook. Charlie has been gone for two days, and I've missed him like a rib. Too much, maybe. But he'll be back today, and Heather and Bennett are arriving this afternoon. I'm counting the minutes until they get here.

Steam from my mug curls into the air. I take in the silent stillness of morning for a few minutes before opening my notebook. I've spent much of the last forty-eight hours writing down all the strange and surprising and meaningful things that have happened so far this summer. I'm almost up-to-date—recounting the events of Percy and Sam's baby shower bash. How nervous I was, and how included I felt. The speech Charlie gave before revealing the tree house. I stop, flip back to the bucket list I wrote at the beginning of the summer. It seemed frivolous then, but now I see how I tricked myself into taking risks, into stepping outside of my comfort zone.

I look across the bay at the yellow boat. The one I've now spent so much time in. I'm not the girl I was at seventeen. I'm thirty-three-year-old Alice Everly, and I can do hard things. Jump off cliffs. Kiss cute guys. I can't backflip into the water, but I can say no to opportunities that don't serve me. And I can make Charlie Florek blush. I can still feel my legs circled around his hips in the water.

My sister and niece pull up to the cottage shortly after two.

"What happened to you?" Heather says, giving me a hug, and I breathe in her perfume. It's an almost masculine scent—smoky and dark, bold like she is.

"I can't remember the last time I've seen your hair like this," she says, holding me out with both arms.

I've worn it down and let it air dry after my swim. It's a tor-nado of curls.

"It's my lake look," I say as Bennett climbs out of the car and bounds over to me.

"I wish I had hair like yours," Bennett says, giving me a hug. She smells extra sweet, that artificial sugar candy smell of thirteen-year-old girls.

"Ditto," I say, pushing a strand of her long, dark hair away from her eyes. She's tall like my sister, but she's constantly trying to make herself small, crossing her arms over her middle and rounding her shoulders. She reminds me so much of myself at thirteen.

"Come give your great-grandmother a hug," Nan calls from the door, and Bennett rushes to greet her. Nan is standing straight—no cane in sight.

"I'll give you the grand tour," I hear her say as Heather and I carry Bennett's things inside, including two canvas bags full of her books.

"I'm worried about her," Heather says to me quietly as Nan takes Bennett out to the deck.

"Really?"

"She's watching all these makeup tutorials."

"You were getting into Mom's makeup when you were four."

"It's not just that." Heather looks at me with horror. "She has a crush on a boy."

"Oh?" Bennett has been a bit of a late bloomer.

"Anthony. I looked at her diary."

"Heather!"

"What? She's become so secretive and even more self-conscious."

"Do not read her diary," I hiss. "Don't you remember what it's like to be thirteen?"

"Yes! That's why I'm worried. Thirteen *sucks*." My sister is as tough as nails, except when it comes to her daughter. Wherever Bennett goes, she carries a piece of Heather's heart in her pocket. While the differences between my siblings and me are plentiful, this we have in common: The Everly family loves big, and it loves hard.

"I can try talking to her if you want," I offer.

"Please do. I need her to turn out like you."

"You just want her to stay a virgin until she's twenty-two."

"Thirty-two, actually."

"Bennett has a good head and a good mom. She'll be okay." Heather takes a deep breath. "You're probably right."

I put my arm around her waist. "You know what you need?"

"A martini."

"I got you gin, but no." I kiss her cheek. "You, my dear sister, need a ride on a Pegasus-unicorn."

Bennett, Heather, and I are drifting on the inflatable loungers while Nan watches from the deck with a cup of tea.

My niece wears a loose T-shirt over her bathing suit, even in the water. It reminds me of the summer I spent here. Mom had taken me on a shopping trip before I left, a rare occasion when it was just the two of us. I was giddy, hopped up on sugar from the milkshakes we'd eaten in the food court, and picked out my first two-piece bathing suit, a tankini that showed the smallest sliver of stomach. By the time I got to Barry's Bay, my confidence had evaporated. I wore it under a terry cloth dress that I removed a second before I jumped into the lake and shoved back over my head as soon as I was out.

Heather, on the other hand, is wearing a magenta-pink one-shouldered suit with cutouts at the waist and has the poise of someone about to board a yacht. Everything about her says, *Notice me*, though Heather doesn't care about what anyone thinks of her. Kind of like Charlie.

I haven't heard from him since he got back today, if he's back, and my gaze keeps traveling to his house.

"Forget the martini," Heather says. "I need something with an umbrella in it. This is divine."

"I wish you could stay for the week, Mom," Bennett says.

Heather's face is guilt-stricken. "I wish I could, but I've got . . ."

"I know," Bennett says. "Work." She doesn't sound bitter, just bummed. I'll remind Heather later what a gift it is that her teenage daughter wants her around.

"I have some news," I say to change the subject. "I've decided not to participate in the show. I pulled my photo."

Heather looks at me, aghast.

"Give me a second," I say, before she launches into an opening argument. "I've been shooting while I've been here. It started out as just for fun, but I think some of what I've done might be good."

Over the last two days, I've combed through what I've shot digitally. The photos are much more relaxed than my typical work. More natural. There's one of Nan, a teacup and saucer in her hand, her head thrown back in a laugh, the afternoon sun slanting over her face. She's utterly captivating. Charlie isn't in the frame, but he was the one making her smile.

There are dozens, possibly hundreds, of photos of him, too. But I scrolled through them quickly. I was afraid of missing him even more if I lingered too long on the light in his eyes or the way he grins at me through the lens.

"Actually," I amend, "I think they might be great."

Heather blinks at me for a moment, and then she claps her hands. "Tell us everything."

I explain to Heather and Bennett how I feel like my job has become almost entirely about getting someone else's version of the ideal shot. I tell them I've been so focused on pleasing clients and photo editors that I forgot how to please myself along the way.

Heather gives me a look, and I know exactly what she's thinking. I'm thinking the same thing. An entire conversation passes between us without speaking. The way I've approached work is just like how I've approached relationships.

"But something's changed since I've been here," I say. The photos I've taken at the lake are so much looser. There's skill in what I can achieve with a set, a lighting assistant, hair and makeup.

But there's an unscripted kind of magic in shooting from my heart. I follow my instincts, not a meticulously planned brief. And, sure, some of the shots aren't any good, and they're far from flawless, but even the mediocre images are rich with emotion. Photos of Nan. The water. Charlie's yellow boat flying across the bay. Memories of this second golden summer.

It feels like I've come full circle.

"Wow," Bennett says when I finish speaking.

Heather lets out a whoop and gets to her knees, shimmying on the Pegasus-unicorn and clapping her hands over her head. "I haven't heard you talk so passionately about your work in ages," she says.

"I wouldn't have thought she'd be able to do that on there," I say to Bennett.

"Nothing keeps Mom from her victory dance."

I laugh, but then I see a familiar figure across the bay, and heat washes over my body. My heart begins to trip over itself. He waves, and I wave back.

Heather follows my line of sight. "Is that *him*?"

"Is that *who*?" Bennett asks.

"Auntie Ali's new boyfriend."

My head snaps in her direction, cheeks flushing. "He is *not* my boyfriend."

My sister and niece share a wide-eyed look, and they both begin to giggle.

Heather cups her hands to her mouth and yells, "Come meet the family, Charlie," then waves her arms over her head.

"Are you as much trouble as Alice?" he calls out.

Heather casts me a look that lets me know she's going to be asking what that means later.

"So much worse," she yells back.

I imagine Charlie laughing to himself as he steps into the boat.

"Do not embarrass me, Heather."

She puts her hand to her chest. "Me? I would *never.* And especially not in front of your . . ." She glances at Bennett, and they both sing out, *"Boooooyfriend."*

"He's just a friend."

"Sure, sure."

I look at Bennett. "He's just a friend."

"Then why are you so red, Auntie Ali?"

Heather begins to snicker, and the yellow boat's motor rumbles to life.

"Yeah, Ali," Heather mimics. "Why are you so red? Is it because your *boooooyfriend* is coming?"

Bennett laughs.

"Stop," I say, though I've started laughing, too. I can't remember the last time my sister and I were goofy together.

When Charlie's boat approaches and Heather begins to sing, "Alice and Charlie sitting in a tree," I lean over the side of the moose, putting my hand in the water to splash her, but I lose my balance and tumble into the lake.

The first thing I see when I poke my head out of the water is Charlie, standing in the boat a few meters from us. He's in a teal bathing suit and a white shirt, and something in me eases, knowing that he hasn't returned from the city any different.

"Good to see you, Trouble."

I stare up at him, my lips curving into a grin that matches his own.

"Hi," I say.

"Hi," he says back, his eyes softening with his voice.

Behind me, Heather clears her throat.

"Charlie," I say. "This is my sister Heather and her daughter, Bennett."

"Good to meet you in person," he says to Heather. "And nice to meet you, Bennett."

Bennett looks at him from beneath her eyelashes while Heather mouths, *Oh my god*, to me.

"I'm taking the boat out," Charlie says to my niece. "Would you like to come?"

She nods, tongue-tied.

"Heather?"

She grins between Charlie and me. "You couldn't keep me away."

"Think we can convince Nan to join us?"

My niece shakes her head.

"She was too tired to do the stairs today," Heather says.

"I can help with that." Charlie calls to where my grandmother sits on the deck, "It's time to get you out on the lake, Nan."

Even if I didn't photograph it, the image of Charlie carrying my grandmother down the thirty-two wooden steps to the dock will be permanently etched onto my brain.

Nan sits beside Charlie in the passenger seat, and Heather, Bennett, and I sit up front. Tears stream down Nan's cheeks as we sail across the water, and I'm not sure if it's from the wind or whether she's caught up in the moment.

I commit it all to film, and every so often, I find Charlie looking at me with a smile as lethal and magnificent as the sun.

We travel to the southern end of the lake to the narrow mouth of the river, and when we pass a couple on a Jet Ski, he presses the horn.

Aaaah-whoooo-gaaaaah!

Bennett cracks up, a gasping-for-breath laugh that has Heather smiling at her daughter with wonder. I can almost hear what's running through her mind—that if her kid can laugh like that, she's doing okay.

I make my way to the back of the boat and sit behind Charlie. We don't talk; I just want to be close to him.

"How do the Everly women feel about grabbing a bite?" Charlie asks when we approach the Bent Anchor.

"Pro," says Heather.

"Alice?" He looks at me over his shoulder.

"I didn't bring my wallet."

His gaze dances around my face. I missed that naughty grin. "Then I guess you'll owe me."

I take photos of everything. Charlie escorting Nan to the patio, her arm in his. The oversized pours of white wine. The basket of fries and platter of nachos. Charlie listening to Nan describe what Heather and I were like as children. Charlie looking at me. I shoot until Heather confiscates my camera and passes it to him for safekeeping.

Bennett and I sit on the end of the restaurant's dock when we're done, waiting as Charlie pays the bill. We're not saying much of anything, just kicking our toes in the water, watching a group of teenagers jump into the river from the nearby bridge. She leans her head on my shoulder, and I wrap my arm around her. I hear the click of my camera.

Bennett and I both turn around. Charlie is holding my Pentax up to his eye.

"You won't want to forget this," he says. "Smile."

But I'm already smiling. I let Charlie take my picture.

"Bennett, come here for a sec," Heather calls from the boat, and my niece pops to her feet.

"One more," Charlie says, crouching beside me. He turns the camera around, an old-fashioned selfie.

"Really?" I ask him.

"Really."

We're still looking at each other when he presses the shutter.

Once everyone is piled in to the boat, Charlie steers us toward the bridge. There's a line of kids waiting to jump.

"Let's do that another time," I say to Charlie.

"Why not now?" he asks.

"Well, this I've got to see," Heather says.

Charlie drops the anchor, and we swim to shore, climbing our way up to the bridge and taking our place in line behind two tan girls who are probably eighteen or nineteen.

"You guys go first," they tell us. "We've never jumped before."

"Me neither," I say, giving Charlie a nudge.

He shrugs and climbs over the railing to the top of a concrete pillar. I hear one of the girls asking her friend whether she thinks he's too old for her.

And then Charlie turns around so he's facing me, winks, and then springs backward off the platform, flipping in the air before slicing into the lake.

"Whoa," I hear the girl say.

I climb over the railing, and before I jump, I look at her over my shoulder and say, "Sorry, that one's mine."

39

Okay, tell me everything." Heather stares at me as she takes a sip of her martini. "And I'll smell it if you hold out on me."

I knew this was coming. That's why I suggested we sit out on the screened porch, even though Nan and Bennett have already gone to bed. It's also why I'm drinking a strong cocktail from an old-fashioned juice tumbler—the cottage has fifteen mismatched mugs but not a martini glass in sight.

I take a sip and cough. "This tastes like hellfire."

"Stop delaying." Heather pulls her legs up, facing me with them crossed beneath her. I do the same. We're wearing similar pajamas, except mine are blue and hers are pink. It feels like we're kids again, sharing a bedroom, though back then, it was Heather describing her latest crush.

"Umm . . ." I don't know where to begin.

"Fine," she says. "I'll tell you what I like about him." She holds up a finger. "One, he threw himself into the middle of three generations of Everly women like a champion. He got Bennett to talk to him at lunch, and he carried Nan like the precious cargo she is." A second finger rises. "Two, it takes balls to hang up on Dad and me the way he did last month. I respect that. And three, he kept his shirt on."

I sigh, remembering how on the boat ride back, Charlie cut

the motor in the middle of the lake so we could jump off. Heather went first, and I followed. Bennett was hesitant, so Charlie offered to jump with her. They stood on the end of the boat, both in their T-shirts, and cannonballed into the water. Charlie rarely wears a shirt on dry land, let alone in the water.

Heather clears her throat. "And four, well, look at him. The way that shirt stuck to his abs. Give me another martini, and I might fight you for him."

I laugh.

"And five . . ."

"Wow, this is a long list."

She gives me a meaningful look. "He adores you."

I study my drink, feeling the blush creep across my cheeks.

"And he makes you laugh. Like really laugh—that scary witchy cackle of yours."

"Yeah," I murmur.

"Have you had sex?"

"What?" I squeak. "No."

"Lie," Heather says, voice flat. "Your face is bright red."

"We're *friends*."

"Lie."

"We are, Heather. That's the truth."

"Please. You ogled him like you've seen him naked."

"Well . . ."

"I knew it!" she cries, slapping me on the arm so that my drink almost spills. "Describe everything to me. Length. Girth. Curvature. Leave nothing unaccounted for."

"Absolutely not, you psycho."

She sighs. "You're no fun. But is it good? I bet it's good. He looks like a man who can f—"

"We haven't had sex," I say before she can go on. "We've done . . . other stuff."

"I love how uncomfortable you look right now. What other stuff, Ali?"

"Like, third base?"

Heather laughs so loud, I'm sure it can be heard around the bay.

"Shhh." I kick her. "And we *are* friends. We just also happen to be physically attracted to each other, so we're going with it. We're having a summer fling. Nothing complicated. Neither of us is looking for a relationship."

"You're going with it?"

"Right."

"Turtle, you haven't *gone with* a relationship your entire life."

"I'm trying something new," I say. "We genuinely like each other. We respect each other. We have fun together. It's refreshing."

She presses her lips together as she studies me, the way she does when she's going into lawyer mode. "What do you like about him?"

What don't I like about him?

"He's . . ." I look out at the lake, thinking about when I first realized there was so much more to Charlie than provocation and pectorals. "He's different from me—more outgoing, more confident, not shy at all. But we're similar, too. He's really attuned to people and takes care of them in his own way. We can spend hours and hours together, talking or not talking, and we don't get sick of each other. He's funny, but he's also incredibly thoughtful. I can be myself when I'm with him. And I've never had so much fun. With anyone. Ever."

I look back to my sister. Her mouth is hanging open.

"Oh my god. You're in love with him."

"I'm not," I say quickly.

"You are, Ali. I haven't heard you talk like this about anyone since Oz."

My stomach drops. Nothing good came from the way I felt about Oz, but the setup is strikingly familiar. Gorgeous man. Strong friendship. Oz and I finished each other's sentences. We encouraged each other. I told him almost everything I was thinking. We used to lie on opposite ends of his futon, my feet by his head, and talk all night. A few weeks before we slept together, he'd said to me, "No one understands me the way you do." The night he took me home, I let myself believe he'd been waiting just like I had. I shake my head slowly. I can't make the same mistake I did with Oz.

Heather sets her drink down and puts both hands on my knees. "I think it's different this time. Oz treated you like a groupie. Charlie looks at you like he'd follow *you* anywhere."

"What Charlie and I have now works for us," I tell Heather firmly. And it *is* different than it was with Oz. This is not a years-long unrequited crush. Charlie and I have been open about where we stand.

"And what is that exactly?"

"Friendship. I don't want it to go further than that."

She looks at me with abundant skepticism.

"I can't, Heather. I think what Charlie and I have might be rare. I don't want to ruin it. Relationships are too risky. Look at Mom and Dad. They wasted all those years on each other, and then Mom fled to the other side of the country." I avoid bringing up my sister's gut-wrenching divorce.

"Mom did not *flee*," Heather says. "She's always wanted to live in British Columbia, and now she's making it happen. She's happy."

"I know." I picture Mom on the first day I visited, rosy cheeked and sipping on a cup of rooibos tea. We'd gone to a hot yoga class and then her favorite café. She looked blissed out in a way that I'd never seen. Even her movements were less frantic. I thought it was the yoga, but she was like that the entire time I was there. At peace.

"I think relationships can change," Heather says now. "And they're not always easy. After everything, I still believe in love. I just don't have the time or energy to offer another person right now." She stares out at the lights of the far shore for a moment. "I don't think Mom and Dad consider the years they were together a waste, either. Nothing lasts forever, Ali."

"Right," I say. Case closed.

"Right," she repeats. "That's why you should grab onto whatever makes you happy now and hold on for as long as you can. Life's short."

I shut my eyes for a moment. It sounds like something Charlie might say.

40

t's the longest, fastest week of summer. Each day begins with Charlie teaching Bennett and me how to water-ski. She gets up on day two while I continue to face-plant. When I finally manage it, I shout with joy, then go skidding across the water like a skipped stone. Charlie takes us on boat rides in the afternoon, and sometimes Nan joins. When Bennett complains about the cottage's DVD selection (heavy on Bond films), Charlie brings over a box of old horror movies from his basement. I question whether *The Blair Witch Project* is appropriate for a thirteen-year-old but am met with three sets of rolling eyes. Sometimes Charlie joins us, and he and Bennett have fun trying to pry the pillow from my face during the scary parts.

The days pass without a moment for Charlie and me to be alone. The need to feel his lips on mine, to taste him, to press my nose into his neck and inhale is a specific brand of torture I've never experienced. Sometimes I catch Charlie looking at me, and I think he feels it, too. One night, when Bennett has fallen asleep on the couch, he and I creep out to the screened porch, and I twist myself around him like climbing ivy. But as soon as our lips meet, I hear Bennett shift inside, and we separate with comical speed. I cannot get busted by my niece.

"You sit over there," Charlie says, pointing to one end of the sofa and then the other. "And I'll sit here. I need a few feet of space between us. I don't trust myself not to touch you."

The way he's staring, eyes glinting like emeralds, ignites warmth in my belly.

"Don't be dramatic," I tell him.

We nestle at opposing ends of the sofa, a blanket over our legs. I have the feeling that we go together, fit together, despite our differences. He makes me bolder, and I make him softer. He makes Bennett bolder, too.

Bit by bit, Charlie manages to coax her out of her cocoon, either by teasing me or making fun of himself. Each hour, she unfurls a little more. One day, when I'm bringing lunch down to the dock from the cottage, I hear her telling Charlie about a boy she thought liked her until she saw him at the movie theater with someone else. The kid ignored Bennett when she said hi. They don't see me, so I stay very still as Charlie gives her a short speech about not putting up with crap from guys.

"My mom always said that trust and friendship come first," Charlie tells her. "And it doesn't sound like he's been a good friend," he adds.

Bennett sighs. "No, he's been a bit of a jerk."

"If he's smart, he'll come around. And if he doesn't, he's not smart enough for you."

She nods, and I begin to make my way to them.

"One quick swim before lunch?" he asks her. "I bet I can make a bigger splash than you."

She smiles up at him. "You're on."

They both charge to the end of the dock in their bathing suits and T-shirts, tucking their legs up as they cannonball into the water. They come up laughing. Charlie's eyes meet mine, and I stumble.

"Get in here, Alice," Charlie calls. "Biggest splash you can make."

"I'm good. I don't want to get my hair wet."

The two of them give each other a look, and then Charlie swims to the ladder and pulls himself out. He stalks toward me. I set the tray of sandwiches and iced tea down.

"No," I say, seeing the look on his face. "Don't even think about it."

With a grin, Charlie scoops me up. "Too late."

"I hate you," I say as he carries me to the edge of the dock, my arms around his neck.

He smiles at me, water running down his face in glistening rivulets. "Nah," he says. "You love me."

And then he drops me in the lake.

That evening, after we FaceTime my mom and Bennett gives her a detailed play-by-play of how she got up on water-skis, my niece and I arrive at Charlie's house in our pajamas with bags of chips, candy, soda, our toothbrushes, and more books and magazines than we can possibly read in one night. Charlie has the tree house all set up for us, with two sleeping bags and pillows on an inflatable mattress pushed under the window so we can sleep under the stars (number seventeen).

Bennett marvels at the view, the twinkle lights, and the arched doorway, and Charlie looks like he might float away with pride. He leaves us to ourselves. Bennett and I eat and talk and read and then eat and read some more until she can't keep her eyes open. I tuck the sleeping bag around her shoulders and quietly sneak out of the tree house with my toothbrush.

The house is in darkness, but Charlie has left the porch light on and the door unlocked. I sprained my right wrist in a water-skiing mishap this afternoon, so I'm brushing my teeth with my left hand. I hear the floor creak behind me. I meet Charlie's eyes in the mirror. He leans on the frame. No shirt. Pajama bottoms.

"Did I wake you?" I whisper, even though there's no one here but the two of us.

He shakes his head. "I was watching TV in the basement. I heard you come in. Where's Bennett?"

"Sleeping."

"Do you need help?" he asks, stepping inside the bathroom.

"With brushing my teeth?"

His gaze lands on the smudge of toothpaste that's landed on my top.

I scowl. "It's hard with my left hand."

Charlie holds out his palm, and I raise my eyebrows. "Seriously?"

"I'm always serious."

I hesitate for a moment, then hand Charlie the toothbrush. I stare at him, suddenly feeling more vulnerable around him than I have in a long time.

"Open up," he says, gently taking my chin in his hand. He starts with the bottom molars, completely focused on doing a good job. When his gaze flicks to mine, an all-too-short shock of green, my chest squeezes. Charlie Florek is brushing my teeth, and it's possibly the most intimate experience of my life. I grip the counter behind me because my legs are beginning to hollow out.

"You know what I was just thinking?" he says, voice low.

I shake my head.

"After tonight, we will have finished everything on your list."

My eyes go wide.

"As long as you've taken one good photo, it'll be done," he says. "Minus the backflip."

"Wow," I try to say, and Charlie smiles.

"Spit," he says. And I do.

He takes my chin again, moving to the upper teeth.

"I missed you last week." His voice is rough, scraping down my body like a calloused palm. He's still concentrating on the task at hand, and I can't reply. "I couldn't wait to get back. I didn't stop the entire drive here. I felt like I'd left my family behind when I was in the city." His eyes find mine. "You're important to me, Alice. I just wanted to say that in case you don't know. This year has been hard, and I'm not sure how I would have coped without you this summer."

I let Charlie finish, and take a moment to wash my face with cool water. I meet his eyes in the mirror. "You're important to me, too."

With a hand on my shoulder, Charlie turns me to face him. He tucks a stray curl that's fallen out of my bun behind my ear.

"I don't want the summer to end," I tell him.

"We can pretend it won't." His tone is casual, but his gaze is heavy.

The air shimmers around us. We stare at each other for one charged breath, and then we collide like knights on a battlefield. We kiss and bite and taste each other. Our mouths are ravenous. And so are Charlie's hands, which move over every inch of skin he can find. Mine track his ridges and valleys. My shirt is off. His hands are on my waist, lifting me up. I sit on the counter, legs spread, reaching for his pants as he's sliding off my pajama shorts.

He swears, bringing his mouth to my chest. I lean my head back against the mirror, naked. He curses again. "I missed you so much, Alice."

We freeze at the sound of Bennett's voice.

"Auntie Ali? Charlie?"

"One sec," I call. "Just brushing my teeth."

I rush to get my jammies back on, glaring at Charlie, who's doing his best not to laugh.

My heart doesn't return to a normal rate until Bennett and I are back in the tree house and she's fast asleep. But then I remember Charlie's voice.

I missed you so much, Alice.

My pulse begins to soar once more.

41

'm fixing tea the day after the tree house sleepover while Nan is on the phone with John. They've been talking a few times a week since the night of the party.

"That would be lovely," I hear her say. "But I don't have a way to get there."

"Get where?" I ask when she's hung up.

"John's invited me for lunch, invited us all for lunch, actually, but it's too far."

I search for directions to Ottawa on my phone. "It's only two hours away."

"What's two hours away?" Charlie asks. He and Bennett have just come back from a Jet Ski ride.

"Ottawa," Nan and I reply.

"What's in Ottawa?" Bennett asks, walking into the cottage in flip-flops and a wet shirt.

"My friend John," Nan tells her.

"Let's take a road trip," Charlie suggests. "You're closer here than you will be in Toronto, and I've been meaning to visit John all summer."

"I want to come," Bennett says, and we all glance at her. "I've never been to Ottawa."

Charlie looks to me. "What do you say, Auntie Ali?"

I turn to Nan. "Let's ask John if he's free tomorrow."

Charlie and I formulate a plan that night over text. We'll take my car. I'll drive there, and he'll drive back.

Me: I think we should give Nan and John some time alone tomorrow.

Charlie: Sure. We can grab a bite downtown and take Bennett to Parliament Hill while they talk.

Me: Thanks for doing this with me.

Charlie: You don't need to thank me, although there are other things I'd rather be doing.

Me: Care to enlighten me?

Charlie: Did I ever tell you that you're trouble?

Me: If you're not in the mood for trouble, I'll just have to read page 179 again.

My phone rings seconds later. "Why don't you read it to me?"

~~~

Nan barely speaks the entire drive to Ottawa. When we pull up to the modern cube of a home where John lives, she peers out the window.

"This isn't where I pictured him ending up."

The house is owned by John's son, and it's one of those multi-level flat-roofed concrete-and-glass structures.

"Are you all right, Nan?" Bennett asks. Charlie and I share a glance.

"Not really," she says. "Let this be a lesson to you all: Don't let wounds fester. It only gets harder to repair them."

With that, she steps out of the car. Charlie offers her his arm, but she shoos him away. We hang back, giving her space.

Nan rings the bell, and the door swings open. I hear John say my grandmother's name before she steps forward into a long embrace. When they part, Charlie shakes John's hand, giving him a warm pat on the shoulder.

"My goodness, Alice," John says when he sees me. "You've grown up."

"You did, too," I say, giving him a kiss on the cheek. John's salt-and-pepper hair has gone white. He wears his trousers high on his waist in a way that I thought was funny when I was younger, and now looks rather stylish. His eyes still twinkle behind his wire-rimmed glasses, the way my grandfather's did. John is a couple of inches shorter than Nan. So was Grandpa. They were best friends, two scrappy short dudes with a passion for fishing and pranks and poker.

"John, this is my great-granddaughter, Bennett," Nan says.

John studies Bennett, who's doing her best to maintain eye contact. He extends his hand. "It's an honor to meet you.

"Would you like tea? Coffee?" John asks, leading us through

the white space. It reminds me more of a gallery than a home. I like how clean it feels, how free of baggage, though it strikes me that John looks out of place. It's very different from the Tudor he and Joyce lived in, with its dark wood, brocade, and knickknacks.

"Thanks for the offer," I say. "But we're going to take Bennett downtown while you two catch up." Nan has agreed to this plan, but now she looks at me, wild-eyed.

"We've got tickets for a tour of the East Block," Charlie says. "Bennett wants to see the historic rooms. We'll be back around three, if that's works."

John glances at Nan and then straightens his shoulders. "We'll see you this afternoon. Have fun, kids."

We eat on the patio of a pub in the ByWard Market before heading to the imposing Gothic castle–like fortress that is the East Block of the Parliament Buildings. Charlie is hooked on the tour guide's every word, and at one point raises his hand to ask a question about its restoration.

I snap a photo and then whisper "Nerd" in his ear. He tucks me under his elbow and tousles my hair before smacking a kiss on top of my head. Bennett stares at us, mouth agape, and we both freeze.

I smooth my palms over my shorts when Charlie releases me.

"We're just kidding around," I say to Bennett.

"Whatever." She rolls her eyes. She's never looked like such a teenager.

"Not whatever," I say.

"Auntie Ali, please. I'm not stupid. You two are obviously doing it."

My mouth: open. My face: scarlet. My ability to speak: zero.

My niece—whose diaper I changed not that long ago!—is talking about sex.

Charlie puts his hand on my shoulder, squeezes, and then lets go. "Bennett, your aunt and I are good friends. We're not a couple. And apart from that, it's none of anyone's business." He says it in that easy way of his, with no hint of reprimand, but there's no mistaking that he's telling her to back off.

I hold my breath, waiting for Bennett's face to crumple, but she nods. "Okay."

Later that afternoon, we return to John's house tired from an afternoon of wandering in the city and sticky with sugar and cinnamon from the BeaverTails we ate in the car. No one answers when we ring the doorbell. The three of us stand on the step looking at each other, and then we hear my grandmother's laugh. We follow the sound to the backyard, which is much the same as the front. Ornamental grasses in right-angled beds, a concrete block patio. Nan and John sit at a table across from each other, each with a cup of tea. They're laughing. I raise my camera.

Click.

I don't want to interrupt them, but Nan hears the shutter.

"Oh," she says. "Is it three already?"

We stay for a round of iced tea, and when we say our goodbyes, John is unabashedly teary, pulling a hankie from his trouser pocket to blow his nose.

"We'll keep in touch?" he asks as Nan climbs into the back seat.

She nods once. "Yes, we'll do that."

Charlie pulls away from John's house, and Nan waves at him out the window. I have my grandmother and my niece in the back seat, and Charlie beside me. I sigh.

Charlie casts me a quick look. "What's that sound?"

"Just happy."

"Me too."

"Me three," Bennett chirps from the back.

"Me four," Nan says. "Thank you all for coming with me. It's a day I won't forget."

"Did you tell John about our cottage makeover?" I ask.

"Oh lord, no. I want to see if he even notices."

"Oh, he'll notice," Charlie says. "It's impossible not to. So many flowers."

"You don't like them?" Bennett asks.

"I don't like them," he says, looking at her in the rearview mirror. "I *love* them."

Just before we hit the highway, Charlie turns the music on. I start laughing as Rod Stewart's voice rasps over the speakers. I crank the volume, and we sing our hearts out to "Forever Young." Nan is the only one who can carry a tune, and Bennett only knows the chorus, but it's the best rendition of the song I've ever heard.

We make our way through Rod's hits as we drive. I can't help but stare at Charlie. The late-afternoon sun brings out the flecks of gold in his eyes, making them appear even more feline. The light catches on his lashes and hair, creating a halo around him. He looks not of this earth.

We're almost home, careening up and down over the giant hills in Wilno, Rod Stewart having been replaced with Shania Twain, who I've learned was one of Charlie's mom's favorites. We're singing about men's shirts and short skirts, even Bennett, who has the lyrics on her phone.

The sun has dropped into our eyes. Charlie lowers the shade visor, and I fish out his sunglasses from the center console. They're aviators with silver frames, and there's a subtle designer

logo etched into the arm. I slide them onto his face, and he
thanks me without taking his eyes off the road. He has one hand
on the wheel, the other tapping on his thigh as he sings. And
even though I love being here with Nan and Bennett, I'd like to
drive somewhere in Charlie's fast car with the windows down
and the music up. Just him and me. I wonder if the Porsche is big
enough inside to do bad things.

"What are you thinking?" Charlie says, glancing at me. An
eyebrow tilts.

"Nothing."

"It's not nothing. You're blushing."

He reaches over and ruffles my hair, and I swat his hand away.
"I was thinking I want you to take me for a drive in your car."

"Oh yeah?"

"Yeah. Let's add it to the list."

"We finished the list," he says.

"Maybe we should make a new one. One we can take to
Toronto."

"What are you talking about?" Bennett asks, leaning forward.

Charlie flicks his eyes up to hers in the rearview mirror.
"Nothing."

I watch my niece's smile grow. "Oh my god," she says. "You're
talking about being a couple, aren't you?"

I'm about to remind her of our conversation earlier today
when Charlie shakes his head. "No."

"But you should *totally* be a couple, right, Nan?"

My grandmother stays quiet.

"We wouldn't be good together, would we, Alice?" Charlie
says, offering me his dimples.

I can feel everyone in the car looking at me, but I don't reply.
The longer it takes me to respond, the harder it gets to speak. I'm

not good at lying. And the truth is glancing over at me, lowering his sunglasses. I swallow back the lump in my throat.

"*Awkwaaard,*" Bennett sings quietly, and Nan shushes her.

Charlie's grin falls. "Alice?"

I shake my head, sinking down in my seat a few inches.

Charlie reaches for my hand, but I don't want him to touch me. I pull away, feeling his gaze on me.

And then I see it on the road.

Everything happens so quickly.

I scream Charlie's name.

A squeal of tires. The slam of brakes. And then I'm thrown against the side of the car.

42

A re you sure I shouldn't come tonight?" Heather asks.

I'm in a bed in the Barry's Bay hospital emergency room with a splitting headache and three fresh stitches above my right eyebrow.

"I don't want you driving in the dark," I tell her. "And Bennett and Nan are fine." Shaken, but unharmed.

The fox is okay, too. Charlie swerved to miss it, then swerved again to move out of the way of an oncoming car. He slammed on the brakes just as we were about to hit the ditch. All in all, it was an impressive feat of emergency driving, but I bashed my head on the door frame in the process, blacked out briefly, and woke up to Charlie frantically calling my name and pressing his balled-up T-shirt to my brow.

"I know they're all right," Heather snaps. "Bennett called me right away. I'm worried about *you*."

"They don't think it's a concussion," I tell her. "The doctor and nurses have checked me out. You'll be here tomorrow, anyway."

I glance up and find Charlie lingering at the edge of the curtain around my bed. I insisted he take Nan and Bennett home to the cottage. I didn't want them waiting around the hospital. Charlie stares at my stitches, deep grooves between his brows. He must have made a pit stop at his house—he's wearing a T-shirt that's not covered in my blood.

"I gotta go," I tell Heather. "Please don't tell Mom and Dad. I'm fine. I'll see you tomorrow."

She sighs. "I love you, Turtle."

"I love you, too."

A nurse slides past Charlie, telling him to take a seat.

I avoid looking at him as she asks me a series of questions.

Am I dizzy? No.

How is my headache? Bad.

Am I nauseated? No.

Any ringing in my ears? No.

She examines my eyes again, and then excuses herself to go talk to the doctor on call.

"Alice?" Charlie's voice sounds like a metal scrape.

I fiddle with the ID band on my wrist. "Nan and Bennett are okay?"

"They're worried about you, but yeah. I put a frozen pizza in the oven and poured your grandmother a scotch. They'll be waiting for you."

I nod.

"Alice?"

Reluctantly, I lift my eyes to Charlie's. He's pale. Anxiety radiates from him in waves. We stare at each other, but then the nurse pops back in and announces that I'm okay to go home. She says to continue monitoring for signs of a concussion and then lists symptoms that would require me to call an ambulance.

"You look out for her, Charlie," she says, giving him a pat on the shoulder. They're about the same age.

"I will. Thanks, Meredith."

Neither Charlie nor I speak as we walk across the parking lot, my arm looped through his to keep steady.

"I'm so sorry," he says once we're in the car. "I can't believe I hurt you." He's staring out at the farm on the other side of the road, and the lake beyond.

"It wasn't your fault."

His eyes swing to mine, full of disbelief. "I wasn't paying attention. And now look at you." He lifts his fingers toward my temple, and I flinch. He drops his arm. "I could have lost you."

I steel myself against how wrecked he sounds, reminding myself of what he said in the car.

We wouldn't be good together, would we, Alice?

"It's just a few stitches. It's nothing."

"You'll have a scar."

I shrug. "A tiny one." The doctor said it should fade to almost nothing.

He runs his hands over his face. When he looks back to me, I can tell he wants to talk more, but I hold up my hands. Whatever he wants to say can be saved for later—my brain feels like mashed bananas.

"Can you take me back to the cottage?" I ask. "I just want to put on some clean clothes and see Nan and Bennett."

Charlie nods and starts the engine.

"I'm spending the night with you," he says a few minutes later as we pull into the driveway.

"That's not necessary."

"It's not optional, either. I said I'd look out for you."

He shuts off the car and faces me.

"I don't want you to stay," I say.

Charlie blinks, and I know I've insulted him. It's not intentional—but I need space to untangle my feelings.

Just when I think he's going to relent, he straightens his spine. "Too bad."

I let Nan and Bennett fuss over me and fix a cup of chamomile tea while Charlie sits in the corner, watching us in uncharacteristic terse silence. By ten, I'm exhausted and announce that I need to go to bed. When I'm done brushing my teeth, I find Charlie in my bedroom, his jeans exchanged for pajama bottoms.

"What's this?" I point at the wooden rocking chair he's moved into the corner.

"That's where I'm spending the night."

I look at the size of the chair and the size of Charlie. The two are incompatible. "I don't need you to watch over me."

"Please just let me do this," he says. "I promised Heather."

"You spoke to my sister?"

"I wanted to apologize for putting you all at risk."

I'm too tired to argue, so I pull back the sheets, flick off the bedside lamp, and lie down. It's not the most comfortable mattress, but right now it feels like heaven. I hear the creak of the rocker as Charlie sits.

"I can't sleep with you staring at me like that," I say after a few minutes. He's lit by the moon, hands between his knees, wide awake. "Just go home, Charlie."

"Not happening."

"Fine. Then get in bed. It'll be less creepy than you sitting there."

"I'm afraid I'll fall asleep if I lie down."

"You should fall asleep," I tell him. "I won't tell Heather you slacked on the job."

The mattress dips with his weight. I'm several degrees warmer with Charlie lying there, face tilted to me. I stare at the ceiling, hands behind my head, wishing I could pretend that he's not here, that what he said in the car didn't hurt.

It's so much darker here than in the city, but Charlie's presence cuts through the black. It's awkward, him and me, lying together in my bed.

"I reek, don't I?" I didn't have the energy to shower, and Charlie smells so good.

"You're fine."

I make a dubious noise, and Charlie leans over, giving my armpit a good sniff. "Better than fine."

I push him away. "Gross."

He turns to me, resting his chin on his hand and trailing a finger over the inside of my upper arm. "Nothing about you is gross."

I shiver, and despite the headache, despite good sense, my body sparks to life.

Charlie's finger drags back and forth across the sensitive skin, down toward my armpit and back up to my elbow. His mouth follows a minute later, leaving kisses behind. While his lips caress my arm, then my ear, his fingers journey south, along my side, over my stomach, slipping beneath the waistband of my pajama shorts.

"I don't think we should do that," I say.

His fingers still. "I want to make you feel good. After today, I owe you that at the very least."

I shake my head. "It's too dangerous. Nan, Bennett . . ." But it's also me. I need to make sure I've got any squishy feelings in check.

Charlie pulls his hand away. "I don't have anything else to give you, any other way to say I'm sorry."

I frown. "Sex isn't the only thing you have to offer."

He turns back to face the ceiling. "I know a lot of women who would disagree with you."

I don't have patience tonight. "That's because you purposely seek out partners you know won't ask anything more of you."

"What do you really think, Alice?" His tone is light, but I feel him looking at me intently.

"I think that one day, when I don't feel like my head is being crushed under a giant's foot, we're going to have a real conversation about your relationship baggage."

He knows mine. I've told him about Oz and Trevor, and the boyfriends in between. I shared my theory that lifelong love is mostly a scam. He didn't agree.

Charlie doesn't speak for a long moment. "One day," he says eventually. "But not right now."

He extends an arm around my shoulders, giving me a nudge. I relent, settling my head on his chest, and he rubs his hand over my back.

"Alice, I don't know what I would have done if you'd been badly hurt . . . or worse."

I shush him. "Don't think like that."

"I feel better now that I can touch you," he says. "I think it helps get the message to my brain that you're okay."

"I *am* okay," I whisper, shutting my eyes. My body is leaden. "But let's rest now."

I fall asleep to the beat of Charlie's heart and even breaths. A lullaby that's specific to him, to this night.

43

I sleep a long, dreamless sleep, and when I open my eyes, I'm lying in the same spot on Charlie's chest. I have fuzzy memories of him trying to rouse me throughout the night, checking to make sure I was okay, and me telling him off.

"I've learned a lot about you in the past nine hours," I hear him say now. His voice has been sanded down from sleep. I feel his fingers playing with strands of my hair. I'm only half awake, and I make a grunting sort of noise by way of reply.

"You told me you hated me no less than four times," he says.

"I regret nothing," I mumble.

"You're impossible to move. I tried to roll you off me once I lost feeling in my arm, but you kept rolling back."

"You're the one who put me here."

"And." I can hear him smiling. "You drool."

I sit up straight, and stare at the damp spot on Charlie's gray shirt where my mouth had been. He laughs. I meet his eyes for the first time this morning. He's wearing a lazy smile, and his cheek is lined with pillow creases.

"Good morning, Alice."

There are a few glorious seconds where I stare at Charlie, when all that matters is how handsome and cozy he looks. But then what he said in the car yesterday comes reeling back.

We wouldn't be good together.

It's like being dropped into glacial waters.

"It's not a big deal," Charlie says, mistaking my expression for embarrassment. He tugs me toward him. "Come back. Is it always this chilly in here in the morning?"

I shake my head. "We should get up," I say, climbing out of bed. "I'll make breakfast for everyone."

Charlie sits as I rush to pull on a sweatshirt and a pair of thick socks.

"No one's awake yet. What's wrong?"

I pause to look at him. "Nothing. I'm sorry I drooled on your shirt."

"I don't give a shit about the shirt. What's going on right now?"

I close my eyes briefly. I don't want to admit what's wrong, not to Charlie, not even to myself. We agreed on an easy, breezy summer fling. On friendship. I went into it with eyes wide open. He made no promises. But his comment hurt. Even in the light of a new day, it hurts. Because I think in some other world, if we decided to be together, we might be better than good. We might be great.

"I need some alone time," I say. I'm not going to dump everything that's running through my mind on him before I've had a chance to figure it out for myself.

Charlie's gone still the way he does when he's trying to contain himself, when he's not sure how to act on whatever is happening in his body and mind. "You're angry with me," he says. "About the accident."

I'm angry with me, I think.

"That's not it. You just said it yourself: It was an accident."

"But you're angry. I can tell."

"I'm tired," I tell him. "I need some quiet."

He studies me, frowning. "Are you sure?"

"Yeah. Just leave me to myself for a bit."

I turn my back as Charlie gets dressed.

Then I watch him leave.

Heather arrives that morning in a cloud of perfume and dust from her speeding car.

She squeezes her daughter so hard that Bennett tells her she's hurting her. I get a similar rib-crushing hug, followed by an interrogation about how I'm feeling. Physically, I'm fine. The stitches are barely noticeable. My headache is much better. Otherwise, I'm garbage.

"How's Charlie?" Heather asks when we're alone. "He sounded like he was in shock when I spoke to him yesterday."

"I think it scared him more than it did the rest of us."

"Because he's in love with you."

"He's really not," I say.

"Oh please. He looks at you like you're a scoop of ice cream on the hottest day of summer."

"Just drop it, Heather. I don't want to talk about Charlie."

For once, Heather drops it.

She and Bennett leave after lunch. On a different day, I'd wish my sister could stay another night, but I'm grateful for the peace.

"Do you want to talk about what's bothering you?" Nan says as we watch Heather's car pull away.

I shake my head, and Nan puts her arm around me.

"When you're ready, then."

"I think I might go back to bed." I want a break from my mind.

Nan looks at the dark clouds that lurk in the distance. "Good day for a nap," she says. "I might do the same."

It's suppertime when I wake. I have three missed texts.

Charlie: Can I cook dinner for you and Nan tonight?

Charlie: I'm making my mom's pierogi.

Charlie: Don't make me eat all of them on my own. I have to maintain my figure.

As much as I want to spend the night with him, Nan, and a giant plate of dumplings, I need space more.

Me: Just woke up from a long nap, and I'm still zonked. Rain check?

Charlie: Are you okay? How's your head?

Me: I'm fine. I promise. I just need to chill tonight.

Charlie: Do you want company? I'm very chill.

Me: I think I need a night off.

Over the next minute, several three-dot text bubbles appear and disappear, until finally: I'm sorry, Alice.

I put my phone away and leave my room to find Nan. She's in the kitchen, heating up a can of Heinz tomato soup and making grilled cheese. It's what she used to make when I was sick. I put my arms around her waist and kiss her cheek. It's exactly what I need.

"Thank you."

"You're welcome." She tilts her head to the ceiling. "Do I know our girl, or do I know our girl?"

I'm not sure if she's talking to Grandpa or Joyce, but I guess it doesn't matter.

Nan tells me about her afternoon with John over dinner. She apologized to him for being absent. He apologized for kissing her all those years ago. They both agreed it meant little more than friends trying to cope with grief. I can see that she's shed an incredible weight. She's moving better. Smiling more. Telling jokes at John's expense.

"You seem more like yourself," I say, sopping a crust in the last of the soup. It tastes like I'm seven years old. What I wouldn't give for a glass of apple juice right now.

"I *feel* more like myself." Nan sets down her spoon. "I know I've been short with you at times, and I'm sorry. Usually, I still feel like I'm forty, at least in my mind. But the hip replacement threw me for a loop—I really felt my age. I love this cottage, but it's also been a reminder of how much past is behind me, and how little future is left."

My throat tightens. I can't imagine a world without Nan. "I'm sorry," I whisper. "I hope it wasn't a mistake to come here."

"Not at all! I'm grateful to you, Alice. Reminiscing with John put things into perspective. I'm lucky to have so much past, so many memories. It's a gift to age." She looks at me over her glasses. "Even though sometimes it really sucks."

I laugh.

"It's also been a treat having so much time with you," Nan says. "You've flourished this summer."

My eyebrows rise. "I've done nothing all summer."

Nan gives her head a sharp shake. "You've been tremendously happy."

I blink, but tears spring to my eyes as though they've been waiting there all along.

"And now you're not," Nan says.

I stare at my empty bowl. "I don't know what I am."

I hear Nan's chair move, and then feel her hand on my shoulder. "Let's have a talk."

Let's have a talk.

I've heard Nan say those words dozens of times. When I learned Mom was pregnant with the twins. When my friend told the boy I liked that I had carrot-colored pubes. When I stopped talking to Oz. When my parents announced they were splitting up. When Trevor dumped me.

Nan eases herself onto the sofa and pats her lap. I lie down, my head on her lap, and I cry. They're heaving, ugly sobs that grow even heavier when I feel Nan's hand running through my hair. My dad used to do the same thing when I'd had a nightmare or a bad day. I wonder how many generations of Everlys have been comforted in the same way.

"I think I have feelings for him," I say when the tears have stopped. I want to deny it so badly, my stomach aches. "And I don't want to. I'm trying to fight them. I just want to stay friends." The thought of not having Charlie in my life—in pushing him away like I did with Oz all those years ago—it's unbearable.

"Well, you can try all you like, Alice, but I expect it will be next to impossible. You feel things deeply. You always have."

I wipe my cheek. "I hate that about me."

Her laugh is kind. "It's one of your best qualities. In the long run, it will be more difficult to keep pushing your feelings aside than it will be to stare at yourself in the mirror and accept who you are and what you want."

"But what if what I want gets me hurt?"

"There are no guarantees in this life. But I'll be proud to have a granddaughter who is brave enough to follow her heart."

"I think you're a lot stronger than me."

She scoffs. "Just older. I don't have many regrets." After a moment, she says, "But I do wish I hadn't run away from John. I wish I'd stuck around long enough to talk to him about what had happened, even though it would have been difficult. All those years we lost."

"I'm scared."

"Yes, I imagine you are." Nan pats me on the shoulder. "Falling in love is terrifying."

I spend three days avoiding Charlie. I tell him I have some last-minute edits to do for a client. It's not a lie, but it takes me under an hour. I send one-word answers to his text messages, decline his invitations for Jet Ski rides and movie nights. He asks if he can take me to the hospital to have the stitches removed, but I don't reply until after they're out. I stay in the boathouse when he comes over one afternoon for tea.

"You're torturing that poor man," Nan says when Charlie drops her off after euchre. "He's not daft. He knows you're giving him the runaround. I don't think he's shaved all week, poor thing. He's looking rather mangy."

"I'm trying to sort out how I feel," I tell Nan, and she replies with amused silence.

"Okay, I'm avoiding him." I throw up my hands. "I like him!"

Nan laughs so hard that she has to dot away tears with her embroidered hankie.

"You're priceless," she says once she's collected herself. "But you'll have to face the truth—and Charlie—sooner rather than later."

I barely sleep that night. I stare at the light from Charlie's house. I imagine how I'll possibly keep a seal on everything that's brewing inside me. I'm a human kettle on high heat, and I don't want to see him until I've cooled to a simmer.

But I don't have that luxury.

The next morning, Charlie fills the doorway to the cottage, arms folded across his chest, looking thoroughly unimpressed. Nan was right—he hasn't shaved. Charlie has the beginnings of a beard, but it's not mangy.

He glances at Nan over my shoulder, and she passes him a tote bag. Before I can ask what's inside, he lasers his eyes on me.

"You're coming with me."

44

Please tell me we aren't breaking into your old high school."

Charlie and I are parked outside of a large brown brick building. I'm sitting on my hands to keep from fidgeting. I don't know what his plans are, but I'm nervous. It feels like we're on the brink of something, but I can't see whether what lies ahead is treacherous or wonderful, or whether it's both.

"We aren't breaking into my old high school." It's the first thing he's said in fifteen minutes.

"So what are we doing at your alma mater?"

"If I told you, it wouldn't be a surprise." Charlie reaches for the tote my grandmother gave him out of the back and opens his door. I watch him get out of the car, baffled.

"What's in that?"

Charlie ducks down, one arm on the frame. "If I'd known all it would take to get you to speak to me was a surprise, I would have done it sooner."

"I wasn't not speaking to you. I texted. I said hello when you stopped by."

He raises an eyebrow. "You know you can't tell a lie to save your life. Come on."

I climb out of the car and follow him up the concrete stairs to the entrance. A man in a janitor's uniform opens one of the glass doors. He's a big guy with glasses, probably in his late sixties. Charlie shakes his hand.

"Good to see you, Tony. Thanks for doing this."

"Not a problem. I'm here all week anyway with school starting soon."

"I appreciate it all the same. This is my friend Alice."

"The photographer," Tony says, shaking my hand. "Nice to meet you."

"You too," I say as we step inside. The lobby of Madawaska Valley District High School looks like that of any high school: Speckled shining floors and fluorescent lights. Glass cases of trophies and photos. A set of doors that leads to what I assume is the cafeteria, with its long, uncomfortable-looking tables. I feel immediately out of place, the same as I did at Leaside High.

"I'll leave you to it," Tony says. "I'm sure you remember the way." He gives me a stern look. "Make sure he stays out of trouble. I've taken care of enough of Charlie Florek's messes to last a lifetime."

"You're famous in this town, huh?" I say as we walk down a dim hallway lined with blue lockers. He's dressed in shorts and a hoodie, and it's easy to imagine him walking in this same spot twenty years ago.

"It's a town of twelve hundred people. Everyone's famous."

I hum. "I get the impression you're special."

Charlie stops in front of a door and pulls a single key from his pocket.

"What is this?" I ask when we step inside, though it's clearly the art room. A space not so different from this one was my sanctuary as a teenager. The chairs sit, overturned, on large tables. There's a sink and tall storage cupboards with stacks of paper and canvas stretcher bars on top. The walls are covered with color charts and posters detailing two-point perspectives. Drying shelves, wooden artist mannequins, canvas rolls. The smells of my youth come flooding back to me: freshly sharpened pencils, oil paints, turpentine.

"This," Charlie says, watching me take it all in, "is my apology for putting you and Nan and Bennett in danger."

"You've already apologized."

"Not well enough."

He takes a step to the side, and I follow his focus to the door at the far side of the room. There's a light box over the top, the words IN USE written in red.

My jaw drops. "There's a darkroom?"

"Yeah." Charlie holds out the tote. Inside is my box of film. All the rolls I've shot this summer. "You're free to use it as much as you'd like before the year starts."

"How?"

"Because I'm famous in this town." He smirks. "And the art teacher here, Olive, is the daughter of one of my mom's good friends."

I stare at Charlie, speechless and enormously touched. He knows that I miss using a darkroom. My heart feels too big for my chest, like it might crack right open. I'm smitten. I'm struck. I'm crushed by the totality of Charlie. This complicated, kind, infuriating man.

"I also promised to buy Olive a bunch of supplies for her classroom."

"Thank you." My voice catches, and I blink away the stinging in my eyes. "No one has ever done something like this for me before."

Charlie brushes this off with a wave of his hand. "Text me when you're done, and I'll come pick you up."

"You're not staying?"

"Nah. I don't trust you to keep your hands to yourself in that tiny room. I'm irresistible in red light."

"You've been in there before?"

"Yep."

"With a girl?"

Charlie winks. "With more than one."

And with that, he turns and walks toward the door. "I'll see you when you're done," he calls over his shoulder.

I stare at the darkroom door, a smile unfolding on my lips.

My first task is to take an inventory of the equipment and orient myself. This darkroom isn't set up for color developing, but there's plenty of black-and-white film in the bag Charlie brought. After giving myself a Google refresher, I begin mixing the developer, stopper, and fixer chemicals, pouring them into separate cylinders.

The vinegar smell transports me to a time when my world narrowed to another small room like this one. I used to spend hours upon days to get the perfect print, making contact sheets, testing and retesting the exposure to nail the contrast. Then doing it all over again with a single negative, enlarging it and running test prints, searching for the exact right balance of light and dark.

I turn on the red light so I can get a roll out of its canister. I won't develop any photos today—the negatives have to be processed first. I steady my hands as best I can and manage to get the film onto a reel and into the developing tank without scratching it. I triple-check the amount of time it needs in each solution and how often I need to turn it over to agitate the chemicals.

There's a scientific quality to this work that I find soothing. About ten minutes later, when I'm adding water to the developing tank to rinse off the chemicals, my face is scrunched in concentration, but my soul is singing. I should probably stop at one roll in case I've botched it, but I'm enjoying myself too much. I move on to a second.

When I'm ready to leave, there are three strips hanging to dry. I clean up, feeling lighter than I did when I entered the room. I've made art for nobody but myself. Even if there's nothing here deserving of a gallery wall, that's worth something.

My face is flushed with pleasure when I exit the school. Then I spot Charlie.

He's leaning against his car, watching a flag flap in the breeze. When he sees me, his face tilts in my direction, and even from this distance, I can see his eyes flash. A smile grows on his lips, mirroring my own.

This, I think. *This is worth something, too.*

"I'm going to come back tomorrow," I tell him on the drive to the cottage.

"I'll give you the key." He glances at me. "Olive asked if you'd consider coming back to talk to her students in the school year."

"Tell her I'll think about it. Would you want to come with me? Make a road trip out of it?"

Charlie stares at the road ahead. He takes a deep breath. "I'd like that," he says slowly. "If I can make it work, I'll be there."

"I'd love to see it here in the winter."

"It's beautiful. Sam and I usually try to get a rink going." He sounds wistful.

I picture us having hot chocolate by a fire. Skating on the

lake. Cold pink noses. Bright blue skies and evergreen branches crusted in glittering white. Charlie and me. Sam and Percy and a newborn baby.

"Stay for lunch?" I ask when we turn onto Bare Rock Lane.

"Boat ride after?"

"How about the Jet Ski? Let's go jump off the rock."

I know I need to tell Charlie I have feelings for him, even if it ruins everything. Just not yet. I want to wrap my hand around the last strands of summer, to enjoy what we have for a little longer.

But the next day, as I stand in the darkroom looking at the print I've spent the morning developing, I realize my time is up.

It's the second photograph that will change my life.

45

Charlie stares straight at me in the photo. His cheeks are dimpled, his smile lit with wonder. But it's the look in his eyes that leaves me breathless. It's one I've seen before. It's how Nan looked at Grandpa. It's how my parents used to look at each other. It's how Sam and Percy gaze at one another. I know the expression in my bones.

My heart hasn't slowed since I examined the negative. I don't know how I've failed to notice it, because the same look appears on Charlie's face in at least half a dozen of the images. Maybe it was so fleeting I missed it, or maybe the camera kept the truth hidden from me.

I took this photo the day we made pickles with Nan. She's in the background of the shot, an unfocused figure at the sink, and Charlie is in the fore. I think I'd just made a joke—something juvenile about his expert handling of cucumbers. He'd glanced up at me with what I thought was surprise.

Click.

But it's not surprise on his face. Or that's not all it is.

I press my palm to my cheek, feeling how hot it is, while I wait. I texted Charlie ten minutes ago. When I hear his knock, I jump. Slowly, I tear my gaze away from the photograph and go to the door.

Charlie's smile drops as soon as he sees me. "What's wrong?"

I shake my head. "Nothing . . . you just startled me." God, I'm nervous. "I thought you might like to see what I developed."

"Absolutely."

I lead Charlie to the darkroom and stand beside him.

"It's a really good shot, Alice."

"There are better ones," I say. Some might even be great.

Charlie looks down at me, his mouth hooking upward. "Then why did you choose this one?"

I'm not sure whether he can't see what I do, or if he's in denial like I was. I straighten, hoping that standing tall like Nan will trick me into being brave.

"We met over the cucumbers," I say.

His gaze melts—the same as in the photo. Just like it did yesterday afternoon before we jumped off that granite cliff into the lake, and again when we sat on his floating raft after we'd returned, feet dangling in the water. A monarch butterfly had landed on my finger. I raised it to my eye, telling it how pretty it was, then looked at Charlie, who was staring at me with the same bare adoration.

"So sentimental," Charlie says now, but his voice is thick.

I meet his eyes, my pulse thundering. "This has been the best summer of my life," I tell him. "These last two months have meant everything to me. I want to show you how much they've meant. How much you mean."

His fingers brush against mine. "Alice." My name falls from his lips like a plea. I see the tension in his neck, his shoulders.

"I want you," I whisper. Charlie's gaze darkens, not moving an inch as I rise on my toes and lean into his ear. "I want all of you."

His face turns to me, green lightning flashing in his eyes. Before I've even set my heels back on the floor, Charlie's hands are on me, lifting me clean off the ground. His mouth finds mine, a growl rumbling deep in his chest. His tongue is wanting, his sounds as desperate as my own.

"You have no idea," he says, his lips skating down to my neck, "what you're asking for."

"I know *exactly* what I'm asking for," I say, tilting my chin back as he tastes my skin. Charlie flicks a switch, and the room goes dark except for the red light glowing over his face. Our lips collide again, frantic.

Charlie sets me down on the edge of the sink, stepping between my thighs. I reach up, pulling his face to me, taking his bottom lip between my teeth, hard enough that he hisses and then tugs my hips against him, letting me know how much he wants this.

"Don't you dare hold back," I say.

He groans. The word *trouble* vibrates in his chest.

I feel his fingers working at my bun, and then my hair falls over my shoulders. I reach for the fly of his pants as he slips the straps of my dress off my shoulder, the material puddling at my waist, leaving my breasts exposed.

"Fuck, Alice."

I don't know if he's swearing because I didn't wear a bra today, or because I have my hand around him. His fingers tease my nipple, a firm, rolling grip that has me tilting my head back. Charlie's tongue finds the opposite breast, flicking in a way that has my legs squirming. We both moan as he pinches and sucks. My heel connects with something on the shelf below, and it crashes to the ground.

He pushes my dress up my legs, presses his thumb against the already damp fabric of my underwear, and I buck again, then hurry to push his jeans fully down his hips. "Now," I tell him. "I want you now."

We've already had the talk. He's clear; I'm clear. Birth control? Check.

I lift my hips to pull down my panties, but Charlie rips them off.

I blink in shock, then laugh. "Always so dramatic."

He grins as he pulls off his shirt, and the look is mischievous and sexy and wholly Charlie. The sight of his absurd body, how impressively large *everything* is, in the red light of a darkroom, is so filthy I'd laugh if I weren't about to combust.

"You're so hot," I tell him.

His gaze travels over my body slowly, and he grips himself with his fist. He strokes himself as he presses a finger inside me, and then another. "So ready."

"You have no idea," I say, repeating his words back to him.

He moves his fingers, slowly, torturously, in and out. His eyes are locked on mine.

"Please," I say. "Charlie."

His grin is wicked, a promise of things to come. "Say it again," he grinds out, taking my hips in his hands, pulling me so that he's right there.

"Charlie," I say as he pushes inside.

I gasp at the size of him, and he stills, eyes searching mine. "You okay?"

I nod. "Everything," I tell him. "Please."

He slowly presses, giving me time to adjust. But I don't want time. I don't want to adjust. I want him, and I want him now. I wrap my legs around the backs of his thighs, trying to pull him into me. "All of you," I tell him. "Hurry."

He kisses me, hard, then he lifts me, and with one strong thrust, he's there. I gasp his name.

"Don't stop," I say. I try to rotate my hips, but his grip is too strong. He holds me in place.

"I need a second, Alice," he grits out, forehead on mine. "You feel too good."

He inhales through his nose, and then his eyes find mine. A tremor runs through me at what I see there. He presses his lips to my scar and then to my lips. It's the sweetest of kisses. My back meets the cool brick of the wall. His smile is quick, and then he's moving with strong, unrelenting thrusts that steal my breath. I begin to squeeze my eyes shut, but I hear Charlie say, "Stay with me."

"Too good," I manage to say. Charlie is hitting me in the exact right spot, and everything inside me is coiling tight.

"Not yet," Charlie says. "I'm not even close to being done with you."

He gathers me up and drops onto a rolling stool. His mouth closes around one of my nipples, his hips still. My legs are spread over him, but my feet don't reach the floor. There's nothing for me to use as leverage. I'm at his mercy.

Charlie hums against my skin, his tongue finding the tightened flesh. His hand comes between us, and the feeling of his lips and his fingers is almost too much—and then his hips begin to rock. My thighs start shaking, and Charlie eases off. I growl.

"Stop showing off," I pant the third time he brings me to the edge. I can feel my pulse all over my body, hypersensitive.

He gives me a half smile, his bottom lip held between his teeth, and grinds out, "This is nothing."

I roll my eyes, and he nips at my earlobe. "Wait till I get you in a bed," he growls against my neck, and a thrill runs through me.

"Tonight," I say.

He nods. "Tonight."

He positions me so I can sink on top of him, my knees around his thighs. Like this, I can move. Being on top has always made me feel vulnerable, nervous, like I might do something wrong. I circle my hips once, tentatively. I look between us, feeling awkward, and then back to Charlie. I don't have to say anything. One hand curves around my waist to guide me. Still, Charlie lets me take the lead, feel what works for me. He stares up at me, murmuring praises, saying my name, and any trace of self-consciousness vanishes. I can be myself with Charlie. Even like this, he only wants me as I am.

I can tell he's struggling to keep his eyes open, to keep himself from taking over. His fingers are between my legs, urging me closer. He pulls his bottom lip between his teeth again, tendons in his neck straining, and the sight of this man coming undone beneath me is intoxicating. I'm not sure I've ever felt this powerful.

When I cry out, white-hot pleasure ripping through me in shuddering waves, Charlie brings my mouth to his. Our kisses are deep, our tongues searching, and when he begins to pick up his pace, my nerve endings tighten and ripple once more. One orgasm is about to roll into another, or maybe it never ended. I'd be surprised, except this is Charlie. He can play my body like it has black and white keys.

I tell him I'm still coming, and he smiles against my lips. Charlie watches me, grinning that sexy, smirky grin of his. He doesn't let up until I go limp, and I collapse against his chest, trying to recapture my breath.

His hand traces a path up and down my spine, tangling in the ends of my hair. The contrast of how big he is and how gentle his touches are brings goose bumps to my arms.

I press my lips to his chest. Sample it with my tongue. Hum at how much I like the salt of his skin. I move to his shoulder. His neck. Jaw. Tasting. Kissing. Sucking. Biting.

"I could make a meal out of you," I murmur.

Charlie laughs. "I think you already are."

I move on to his mouth. "This is my favorite part."

"Kissing?"

"Your lips." I suck on his bottom one, releasing it with a pop. "The way they flirt and smirk and tease." I trace the arches of his top lip with my tongue.

His whole face smiles back at me, not just the curve of his mouth. Dimples. The lines at his temples. The glint of his eyes.

"I must be slipping if my mouth is still your favorite part."

I grin. "Maybe you need to try a little harder. You just made me do all the work."

I've barely finished the sentence when Charlie has us both on our feet. His hands skate over my arms and he drops a kiss to my neck.

"You trust me?"

"I trust you." I'm trembling with anticipation as Charlie turns me around and bends me over the counter.

I trust him more than anyone.

I can't stop smiling. Charlie and I parted hours ago, and the giddy grin hasn't left my face.

"Would you like to tell me why you look like the cat who ate the canary?" Nan asks as we sip tea on the deck. Charlie had plans with Harrison this afternoon, but my gaze keeps drifting to his dock, waiting for a glimpse of him. "Or shall I guess?"

I don't reply, just lift my mug to my still-swollen lips.

"Tall, handsome, and strong as a grizzly?" Nan looks at me over her glasses, and my smile grows.

"Face like a movie star? Voice made for the radio? A backside that could crack a walnut?"

I choke on my tea.

"Shall I go on?" Nan says as my phone buzzes.

Heather: Yesssssssss!!! GET IT, ALI!

Heather: Tell me EVERYTHING. When? Where? How was it?

Heather: GIRTH!!!!!

More overexcited messages follow. I couldn't hold it in. The best sex of my life with a man I've come to care about deeply. I had to tell someone.

Strangely, my first instinct was to call Charlie as soon as we kissed goodbye.

"Can you believe that just happened?" I wanted to say. "Can you believe how good it was?"

Heather was my next option.

I dash out a reply.

Me: Today. Darkroom. Exquisite. Can't talk now. Call you later.

Heather: YESSSSSSSSS!!!!!!!! TREVOR, WHO!?

I laugh, then turn my attention back to Nan.

"Do you mind if I spend the night at Charlie's?"

"Of course not," she says, setting her cup down.

The next time my eyes travel to the Floreks' dock, I see him standing there. Charlie waves, and we wave back.

"I told you," Nan says, smiling over the water.

"What's that?"

She glances at me. "Good things happen at the lake."

46

Charlie brings Nan takeout from the Tavern for dinner. He tells her our plans for the evening as he piles her plate high with braised red cabbage, mashed potatoes, and pork schnitzel. According to him, he's teaching me how to make his mom's pierogi. Nan and I exchange doubtful looks.

"We're cooking?" I say on the way to his house.

"Oh, we're cooking." He flashes me his sex eyes, and I snort.

I'm wearing my slinky green dress and have packed nothing but a toothbrush and tomorrow's clothes. I didn't even bring my camera. I've been waiting all afternoon to get my hands back on Charlie. For all his talk about bedroom moves, I doubt I can wait to get upstairs. But then he leads me inside, straight to the kitchen. There's a five-pound bag of potatoes and a sack of flour on the counter.

I glance at him. He's wearing jeans on his bottom half, a T-shirt on the top. His lips are still a little swollen and his face is a lot smug.

"We're actually making pierogi?"

"Like I said." His gaze tours the length of my body, and when it returns to my face, it's dark with promise. "Though I didn't tell your grandmother my other plans."

"Which are?"

"Eat. Swim. Et cetera."

"I thought you needed to wait thirty minutes after eating before swimming."

He stalks across the room toward me. "I didn't say what I was eating."

I pull a face despite a singular throb of desire between my legs. "You're terrible."

"You have no idea." Charlie kisses me once, quick, his thumb skimming over my bottom lip before he moves around the counter. "You peel the potatoes."

My hands tremble as I work. Charlie is kneading dough, his forearms flexing in a way that would make me think of naughty things if I weren't so tightly wound. I can't keep pretending. I need to tell him how I feel. It's not fear that's making me antsy. I've seen how Charlie looks at me. I'm nervous, but I'm also excited.

"We're going to end up with a restaurant's supply of pierogi," Charlie says as he covers the dough. "Maybe we can freeze some for you to take back to the city."

I hum. We're cooking together, talking about freezing leftovers. We're friends, but we're already so much more.

Charlie has music playing over the speaker on the counter— his dock rock mix. Classics that my friends might play ironically but that Charlie embraces. He doesn't like anything ironically. He's singing out of tune, and I realize that this is something else I admire about him. He's unapologetically him. He catches me staring and winks.

"Forever Young" begins to play, and I laugh. Until the end of time, I will associate Rod Stewart with this summer, with this night.

I'm finishing the potatoes when I feel Charlie at my back. He kisses my neck, slips the strap of my dress down my shoulder.

His lips follow. A hand coasts over my waist. Lower. I prod him with an elbow.

"We're cooking, remember?"

"Sorry," he says, though I can hear him smiling. "I love this dress. And I've been thinking about you all day."

"Same." I turn my cheek to look at him. "I wanted to call you. I wanted to talk to someone about how great it was."

His eyes soften. His smile is golden. It's the look from the photo. The one I've failed to recognize until today.

"You could have," he says. "I'm happy to talk about my sexual prowess any time. Angles, depth, speed, favorite positions."

I laugh and elbow him again, and he spins me around, kissing me so deeply, I drop the vegetable peeler on the floor. Charlie groans into my mouth. It sounds like relief and longing and hunger. Usually our kisses grow more and more frenzied, until we're clamoring for each other, but this one moves the opposite direction. Charlie holds my face between his hands. I open my eyes to find him staring at me in the way no one has before.

Only him.

He taps my hip, smiling. "Back to work, slacker."

We set about boiling the potatoes and frying the onions in butter, their fragrance filling the kitchen with something that smells a lot like home. When the dough is ready, Charlie rolls it out until it's a thin, smooth sheet. Charlie looks at me, watching him with my mouth hanging slightly open.

He chuckles. "Impressive, right?"

"I want to say no, because the last thing your ego needs is further stroking. But yeah, impressive."

"Sometimes I helped my mom with them if she was short on time. Rolling out the dough was her least favorite part of the process." He shrugs. "I didn't mind it, and I liked being in the kitchen at the Tavern. It made me feel closer to . . ." Charlie stops speaking, and I put my hand on his arm.

"Your dad."

He nods. "We didn't talk about him at home after he died. But at the restaurant, I could feel him there. When my mom wasn't in earshot, Julien would tell stories about him, mostly trash talk. And it felt normal, I guess. Sam never really liked working in the kitchen. Couldn't wash a dish to save his life. But for me, that place, the people there—it was my family."

He's quiet as he cuts the dough into circles. I add a spoon of potato-onion mixture and then he shows me how to pinch the dough closed, making a crescent with folded edges. It takes me half a dozen tries to get it right, Charlie working three times faster than I do.

I glance at him after I've done one properly, but he's staring at my hands, his jaw tight.

"Charlie? Are you okay?"

He gives me a weak smile. "Yeah. Just went back in time for a sec."

"Want to tell me about it?"

"It's nothing," he says. He inspects the dumplings in front of me. "You've got the hang of it."

"Not bad, right?"

"No," he says, kissing my temple. "Not bad at all."

We go for a boat ride before we eat. The sun has sunk below the hillside, leaving the horizon streaked in blush and blue. And even though the sight of Charlie on this picture-book evening is one I want to remember forever, I don't itch for my camera. I'm in the moment, at the center of the action.

I release my hair from its elastic, and Charlie grins, then presses the throttle down. We soar across the lake, and I try to soak in every last detail. The rumble of the motor, a sound I can distinguish from all the other boats on the lake. My hair lashing against my cheeks. The softness of Charlie's pullover against my skin. The goose bumps on my legs. The cool wind on my face and the fresh air in my lungs. The reflection of the sunset on the lake, like we're sailing through the sky.

And Charlie.

I never want it to end.

But eventually, my teeth begin to chatter. Charlie takes off the jacket he's wearing and throws it over my legs, and we head home. I tackle him as soon as we're on the dock, braiding my arms around his neck. He stumbles back. "Caught you," I sing.

Charlie lifts an eyebrow, then picks me up off my feet and throws me over his shoulder.

"Caught *you*," he says, and carries me up the hill.

"Turbulent ride, but I like this view." I pat his butt.

He plants a kiss on my hip, not setting me down until we're in the kitchen.

I put my hands on his chest. "Show me your room?"

"Trouble," Charlie says, but he takes my hand and leads me upstairs.

"I can't believe I haven't been up here before."

Charlie points to a door. "Sam's old room." I stick my head inside. Other than a crib, it looks like a teenage boy's bedroom. A bookshelf is stuffed with comics, Tolkiens, and textbooks, and there are two posters on the wall. One for the movie *Creature from the Black Lagoon* and another of an anatomical heart.

"Sam and Percy stay down there," he says, gesturing to the end of the hall. "And this"—he nods to the room on the other side of the hallway—"is my room."

I step inside. It is very much *not* a childhood bedroom. There's a large bed with a low headboard that's upholstered in black fabric. I run my hand over it. Velvet. From the art on the walls to the sleek desk, everything is sumptuous and new and expensive-looking.

I walk to one of the two large windows that look over the water.

"You can see John's cottage from here," I say.

"I can." Charlie stands behind me. I keep my gaze on the lake as he shifts my hair and kisses my neck.

"It's a good view," I murmur.

"It is." One of his hands sneaks under the sweatshirt, sliding over the silk of my dress. I lose the sweatshirt, and I feel his smile against my skin, right between my shoulder blades. "Although I prefer this one."

I pull the dress over my head and hear him hum in approval. A finger runs down the center of my back, and I shudder. Charlie reaches around me, resting his hands on the window frame, caging me in. He brings his lips to my ear. "Is this how you want it, Alice? Up against the glass?"

I make a noncommittal sound, though I'm almost vibrating at his words, at the feel of his clothing against my bare skin.

"I don't think so." I turn to face him, lips parting at the need in his gaze, the flush of his cheeks. I sneak my hands under his shirt, laying them against his stomach. "I seem to recall you talking a big game about a bed."

Charlie's dimples flare, and then he picks me up and lays me across the mattress. "Fair enough."

It's after midnight when Charlie fixes us each a plate of pierogi. I watch him cook in only his underwear, and I eat sitting on the kitchen counter. I've barely chewed my last bite before we're kissing again. The moon is full—its glow envelops us like an ethereal blanket, until we eventually fall asleep, Charlie's body curled around mine.

I dream of waking in my Toronto bedroom and finding Charlie sleeping beside me. His lips are pursed, his forehead slightly creased. It's so vivid, I can smell him. I can feel his stubble when I skim my palm over his jaw. His eyelids flutter, his lashes catching the first of the morning sun that slips through my window. Charlie stretches an arm over his head and then wraps it around me, hugging me close. His eyes are closed, but he's smiling. He presses a kiss to my forehead. "I'm still sleeping." But then he rolls me on top of him, and I stare into a pair of remarkable green eyes. I kiss him, slow and decadent. "As much as I'd like to lie here," I say, "we did agree to host my entire family for lunch today, and there are pierogi to be made." He sweeps the hair back from my face. "Let's stay in bed for a little while longer." His hand travels to my shoulder. And even though I'm vaguely aware that I'm dreaming, I feel his touch, back and forth, along my arm, and I moan.

"Good morning, Alice," I hear real-life Charlie say.

I blink awake.

I'm in his bedroom. Bright light pours through the windows. The reflection from the water shimmers on the ceiling. Charlie's body is curved around mine, his fingers trailing the length of my arm.

"Good morning," I whisper, smiling. "I just had a very good dream."

"Oh?"

I turn in his arms, and Charlie pulls me against his chest.

"Me and you in my bed in Toronto."

"Sounds hot."

"It was. But it was also . . ." I shift so that I'm propped on my elbow. Sunlight kisses his cheeks and eyelashes, casting him in gold. "It was nice."

He gives me a sleepy smile. Waking up next to him like this is even better than in my dream.

"Charlie?" I say, tracing his jaw.

"Alice?" His eyes are incandescent.

I know exactly what I want. And the time has come to tell him.

"When we go back to the city," I say, running my finger over a dimple, "I think we should do this for real. You and me—I'd like to try."

Charlie squints like he's not sure what I've said. "Try?"

"Yeah, see where it goes," I say. "I know it's not what we originally planned, but we're so good together. It's weird how much we make sense."

I pause, because Charlie has gone eerily still. Suddenly, he sits up, and I hurry to do the same.

"Alice." I'm not sure how he can put so much weight into a name, how he can fill two syllables with so much frustration and sorrow. His eyes plead with me. Everything I've wanted to say turns to ash on my tongue.

Charlie runs a hand over his head. "I need coffee." He practically leaps out of the bed. "What would you like for breakfast?"

I pull the sheet around myself as he throws on a pair of track pants. He peers at me over his shoulder and pauses. "I'm useless before I've had coffee."

"Sure." I sound deflated.

Charlie sits on the bed beside me. "Please, Alice. Can we just go downstairs and wait to have this talk until we've both woken up?"

I stare at him. "It's a pretty straightforward conversation."

"Please," he says again.

So I wait while Charlie fixes the coffee and cooks me scrambled eggs with toast that I can't force down my throat. I set my fork on the plate, and Charlie winces into his mug. I wait for him to take his last sip, and then I tell him the truth.

"I have feelings for you," I say.

Charlie opens his mouth, but I plow ahead. "And I can't pretend that's not the case. I won't."

"Alice." He's shaking his head, his eyes cast downward. "Alice, I can't."

My frustration rises.

"What do you mean, you can't? Of course you can. We have the best time together. We fit. I want more nights like last night. I want more of everything. Would you please look at me?"

It takes him a moment before he raises his eyes. I can see the apology in them before he speaks. "I told you I'm not in a place where I can get involved."

"We're already involved, Charlie. What we've been doing this summer . . . that's a relationship. And you're *good* at it."

"I can't do this in the long term." He looks away. "It wouldn't work."

"How can you possibly know that?" My voice breaks.

Charlie rises, coming around the table and crouching in front of me. He wipes the tears away from my face. "Please don't cry. I care about you. I care about you so much." He's almost as upset as I am. "I'm just not built for a relationship."

"You are built for ME."

"Alice." His voice is pure anguish.

"Don't pretend that you don't agree or that you don't have feelings for me. I've seen it, Charlie. I know you."

We stare at each other for seconds, and then his face goes blank.

He stands, giving me his back. "This was a great summer,"

he says slowly. "I wish it could stay like this, that I'd stay interested longer than a couple of months. But I'm me and you're you. We're too different. It would never work. I'd get bored."

"I don't believe you," I whisper. But now I'm not sure. Maybe I've deluded myself, just like I did all those years ago with Oz. "Look at me, Charlie."

When he faces me, I've never seen him so closed off, so impenetrable. His eyes are cold, his jaw tight. His voice sounds like it's being scraped over shards of glass. "I'm doing you a favor, Alice. One day you'll see that."

I stand, forcing the tears back, and look him straight in the eye. "You know what I think? I think you're a fucking coward. I think one day you're going to realize that for all the shit you say you've done, *this* is your biggest mistake."

Hurt flashes in Charlie's gaze. I give him one more moment, but his eyes drop to the floor.

"I thought you were better than this," I tell him. And then I go.

I don't let myself cry again until I see the cottage, and my sobs come in loud, painful gasps. I double over, not sure I can take another step. But then Nan opens the door and holds out her arms.

47

MONDAY, AUGUST 25
THE LAST DAY AT THE LAKE

I spend two days in a numb fog, wishing I never came to the lake, before I pull myself out of it. And then I block his number. I refuse to see him. There's a full week left of August, but Nan and I are going home early.

I pack our things into the car and take one last look around the cottage. I say goodbye to the view, to the curtains and pillowcases and tablecloths Nan and I made this summer, to the jar of matchbooks and the shelf of Harlequins. I say goodbye to my bedroom. I leave the key in the outhouse. But I don't say goodbye to Charlie.

I spend my first week in the city focused on creating a new routine. I find a darkroom to rent. I carve out time in my schedule to work on my own art. I pick a date to meet with Elyse to show her my new photos. And every morning, I swim.

Today begins the same way as the previous seven. Shower. Swim cap. Goggles. Climb onto the diving platform and slice through the water. Twenty laps. Thirty. I don't stop, don't slow, don't think. I breathe and kick and count, a crystalline clarity smoothing the sharp angles of my pain. Forty. Fifty. I get to sixty faster than I did yesterday. But there's no pleasure in it. Like every other day, I'm not even out of the water before reality crashes into me.

I've never borne this type of heartbreak. It's both the loss of what I had with Charlie—our unlikely friendship and connection, the ease of being with him—and the loss of what could have been. I've done my best to cope, throwing myself into a new project, spending hours in my studio, and then retreating to the solace of my condo. I used to find calm in the cool polished concrete floors and clutter-free surfaces, the gleaming marble and spotless glass. But after being at the cottage with Nan and Charlie, it feels lonely. The sleek furniture Trevor picked seems even more alien. And despite the clamor of sirens and horns and garbage trucks outside, it's too quiet.

I stand next to the pool, hands on my knees, bent at the waist, breathing heavily, fighting back tears.

"You're okay," I tell myself. "You're okay. You're okay."

I feel a hand on my back. "Do you need to sit?" A woman's voice.

I'm making a scene. Amazing. "Yeah," I say. "I think I overdid it."

"Here. Let me help."

The stranger puts an arm around my shoulders and a hand on my waist and guides me to the bench. I pull off my goggles and take a few more breaths with my head between my knees.

"Thanks," I say, straightening. I find myself looking into the big brown eyes of an extremely pregnant woman in an orange bathing suit. Her hair is twisted into a knot at the top of her head. "Percy?"

She blinks at me. "Oh my god, Alice. I didn't recognize you. Are you here a lot? I started coming when I got pregnant. I was on the swim team when I was a kid, and Sam thought it might be a good way for me to cool off and move a little, even if I'd rather be sleeping in on a Saturday morning." She lowers her voice. "Are you all right?"

I feel the tears welling again as I remember Charlie saying how much Percy talked. "Yeah, I'm okay," I lie. "Thanks for giving me a hand."

"I heard about what happened with Charlie. At least, I heard a brief version from Sam that involved some choice profanities. I'm so sorry."

"It's fine," I tell her. The last thing I want is for her to feel bad for me.

"I can tell it isn't fine. Don't forget, I saw you two together." Percy chooses her next words carefully. "This year has been hard for Charlie, worse than any of us could have anticipated."

"You mean because of his dad?"

"That's part of it. I know Sam isn't looking forward to his thirty-fifth birthday, either. But there are other things you don't know," she says quietly. "Sam and I have tried to get Charlie to be more open about it. I think he . . . well, it doesn't matter what I think. Just please have some patience. I'll keep working on him."

"Don't bother," I tell her, sounding stronger than I feel. I grab my goggles off the bench and stand. "It was nice to see you. Enjoy your swim."

"Alice," Percy calls when I'm almost at the changing room. She walks toward me slowly, a hand on her stomach. "I understand if you don't want to talk to Charlie, but could we stay in touch? We could come for a swim, get something to eat after?"

I frown at her. "Why?"

She laughs. "Because I like you. Do I need a better excuse?"

For some inexplicable reason, the back of my nose stings. I shake my head.

Percy smiles, big and broad, the kind of smile that warms you right through. "Good. Next Saturday? I'll text you."

I sit in the quiet of my condo with a peppermint tea, blinds closed to the September sun. I'm shaken by what Percy said this morning. It takes everything I have not to call Charlie and ask him about it. But I plan to hold on to my last sliver of dignity. I told him what I wanted, and he rejected me. I let him see me, the real me, not some kind of constructed, unblemished version. I showed him who I was, and it wasn't enough.

But I miss him. His smirk. The firefly flicker of his eyes. His voice and laugh and teasing. The way he listens. I don't know whether there's a place in my heart for him as just a friend, but I don't know if I can cut him out of it entirely, either.

"You're okay," I tell myself. Just like I have after every other disappointment and heartache. I will not think about how I felt so much more for Charlie after just two months than I ever did with Trevor. I will put my head down and focus on the work that I love. I'll buy myself the floor lamp I've been eyeing. Maybe repaint my bedroom. Sink back into the life I've made for myself, comfortable and safe.

I spend the rest of the day curled on my couch with my laptop, looking through shots of Nan from the summer. It's not until my stomach voices its discontent that I peel myself away from the screen, eyes dry, neck aching. There's not much in my fridge. I should have gone to the store, but I lost track of time. I've avoided opening my freezer all week, but I'm desperate.

"You're okay," I say, taking out one of the Tupperware containers Charlie dropped off at the cottage the day before we left. I'd stayed inside, listening to him plead with Nan to see me. I'd told her what happened, my head in her lap, her hand running through my hair. She hadn't said much, but before she sent Charlie away, I heard her use the words *disappointed in you*. It made me feel worse. They'd been friends, too.

I prepare the pierogi the way Charlie did, boiling them first and then frying them in a pan until they're golden brown. I don't have sour cream, so I put a little grated cheese on top. They don't taste as good as they did that night with Charlie. Nothing tastes very good right now.

I look around my living room. The neat stacks of art magazines are just where I left them; so are my throw pillows, fluffed and propped to magazine-worthy standards. The couch and dining chairs that I hate. I bought new scented candles for the coming autumn, but no one has been here to enjoy their spiced-apple glow. I've been too down to connect with friends, and I haven't seen my family since I've been home. Heather and Dad have been busy with a case. Lavinia is stressing over an audition, and Luca rises an hour before his night shift at the bar. I haven't wanted to bother them. I called Mom, but I'd caught her as she was heading out the door for yoga, and I was in the darkroom when she tried me later. I call her again now, but it goes directly to voicemail.

And while I like my own company, it isn't what I want. I need Everlys around me.

I write a text to the family group chat. I waver for a moment, and then I press send.

I've been going through something, and I could really
use you guys. Are any of you free to come over tonight?

The effort of asking anyone to put down what they're doing
and help me is exhausting. I don't realize I've fallen asleep on the
couch until there's a loud knock.

"Open up, Ali." Heather.

"We have tequila." Lavinia.

"And cake." Luca.

I open the door, rubbing my eyes, and my siblings engulf me
in a storm of perfume and sequins and kisses.

"I didn't think you'd come," I say when we pull apart. My
siblings give me the same scrunchy-faced look. Heather's wearing a pink lounge set. Lavinia's in a glimmering dress and tippy
heels, and Luca's in the tight white tee and suspenders he wears
for work. The three of them are all dark-haired, but the twins
have Nan's blue eyes.

"That might be the most Turtle thing you've ever said," Luca
says, setting a cake on the counter. It's in a plastic grocery store
container, chocolate, the words "Happy Birthday" in pink frost-
ing on top.

"Of course we came," Lavinia says. "You asked us to."

"And you never ask, Ali," Heather adds.

My eyes begin to water, and I'm quickly in the middle of another Everly tornado.

"What's going on?" Lavinia asks, ushering me to the couch
and petting me like I'm a kitten.

"The real story," Luca says, dropping down beside me and
putting his feet on my coffee table, knocking over the magazines.

Heather clatters around the kitchen and brings us each a

glass of tequila, swearing as one splashes onto my cream wool rug. "Sorry, Ali. At least it's clear."

"It's fine," I tell her. For once, I don't mind the mess.

We clink our glasses together, and then Heather looks me in the eyes. "Tell us everything."

"Quick," Lavinia says.

"Before Dad gets here," Luca adds.

Our dad arrives thirty minutes later in a suit and bow tie. Everything about Kip Everly is big—his mustache, his personality, his reputation as a litigator.

"Welcome home, Alice," he says, kissing my temple. "It's good to have you back in the city."

Heather plies everyone with more tequila, and Lavinia and Luca recap what happened with Charlie for our father in under two minutes, and in a manner that will not cause him to worry about me. The way they tell it, it was a summer fling gone wrong. The way they tell it, it's kind of funny.

Dad laughs in the right places at the twins' rehashing, but I can tell they aren't fooling him. He puts an arm around my shoulders, and I lean against him.

"Want me to kick his ass?"

"Yes." I let out a long breath. "But he's pretty strong."

My dad squeezes me. "So are you."

When the buzzer rings, I peer around the room, puzzled. We're all here. I see Luca and Lavinia exchange a glance. I look through the peephole and gasp, swing the door open, and throw myself into my mother's arms.

"How are you here?" I say, tears already running down my face.

"Nan thought you might need me."

I bury my face in her neck and breathe in the sweet fragrance of lily of the valley. Her hair is cut even shorter, and she isn't as soft as she used to be, but she smells just like my mom.

~~~~

Mom and I eat chocolate cake in our pajamas the next morning, surrounded by the aftermath of last night's gathering.

"Do you want to tell me what happened?" she says. "The real story—not whatever yarn Luca and Lavinia were spinning last night."

"I might cry," I warn her.

"Then you'll cry."

As we eat, I tell her about the summer—the good with all the misery.

"I wasn't ready to fall for him," I say, adding another damp tissue to my pile.

She hums. "It sounds like he wasn't ready to fall for you, either. But maybe the story isn't over yet."

Mom laughs at the surprise on my face.

"What, can't a sixty-year-old divorcée believe in romance?"

"Is that what you're looking for out west? Love?"

"I'm looking for a new beginning. It's not easy being alone after all these years. To go from having a big family under one roof to just me . . . well, I didn't like it. If I could have kept you all at home with me, I would have."

I blink at her. "Really? You always seemed so stressed."

She laughs. "I was! But I felt like I had a purpose. I felt needed. Nothing made me happier than when we were all together. The Christmas mornings. The dinners when your dad was home early enough to eat with us. Those vacations. Remember Florida?"

"The twins weren't even potty-trained yet." They screamed the entire plane ride, and threw a tantrum at every shop, every restaurant.

My mom smiles at the memory. "You and Heather became a little duo that trip."

My parents had rented a house with a pool, and she and I

spent a lot of time underwater, escaping their noise, thumbing through magazines on lounge chairs when they napped. Heather let me borrow her lip gloss. I was elated that my big sister had deemed me cool enough to hang out with.

"I was happy back then," my mom says. "It was madness, Alice. But it was a beautiful madness." She sighs. "But this city makes me feel caught in the past. I need some time away to get unstuck. To discover who I am when I'm not a mother or a wife. It won't be forever."

"Good," I tell her. "I still need you. I can't believe you all showed up like that. I can't believe you flew across the country for me."

"Really?" She tilts her head. "You know, you were such an independent child. I was so busy with the twins and putting out Heather's fires, and when I think back, I know I missed when you needed extra support." She reaches across the table and puts her hand on mine. "I see the incredible woman you've become, but that doesn't mean you don't need help. I'll always be here for you, Alice. I will always show up for my daughter."

"Okay," I whisper, my throat thick. I didn't know how much I needed her to say it.

She squeezes my hand and then straightens. "You work so much, and I know you like your space. I try not to bother you. The last thing I want is to be a burden to my children."

I study my mom. I didn't know she felt that way—the way I have for so long, allergic to being an imposition. We text more than we talk these days. I thought it was because she was busy with her new life out west, not because she thought I was busy with mine.

"You're never a burden, Mom," I say. "You can ask us to show up, too. You can always call me."

She waves her hand in the air. "Don't worry about me. I can take care of myself."

That sounds like something I'd say, too.

"But you don't always have to. I'm here."

She smiles. "I know you are."

48

Something changes the day after I cry into my cake with Mom. It happens when I'm swimming, like an epiphany. I'm doing laps, and instead of telling myself that I'm okay, I tell myself that I *will* be okay. Maybe not today, but I'll get there. I repeat it in my head, over and over.

I'm in the changing room, about to dry my hair, a process that takes a good thirty minutes, when I pause. I *hate* the blow-dryer. I despise the straightener. I'd rather put my time to better use. I step into the late summer sun with my hair damp, curls already springing up at the nape of my neck.

Things I want begin to fall into my mind, like a drizzle that becomes a downpour. I want to get a comfy couch and dining chairs that I like, and then I want to have my friends over for dinner. I want more time with my niece and more sloppy nights with my family. I don't want to run anymore; I only want to swim. I want to visit my mom in BC again. I want to do more sewing projects with Nan. I want to work hard, but I want more fun. More mess. More people I love.

What I want when it comes to Charlie is less clear. I want him back in my life. I want to never talk to him again.

I get my film developed, and see that look in his eyes, over and over and over. I meet Percy at the pool in mid-September and we go for brunch afterward. I tell her I feel certain Charlie felt something for me beyond sex and friendship. She says she thinks so, too. She tells me to unblock his number, to give him a call. And I almost do. I want to tell him how mad I am. I want to compose a powerful speech, one that encapsulates how shattered I feel. I want to scream it into his voicemail so he can listen to it over and over. But whenever I try to figure out what to say, I start with "I'm so mad at you," and what comes next is "I miss you."

I throw away Trevor's box of things. I host a small dinner party. I order takeout instead of fussing like I used to. And I don't mind cleaning up by myself when I kick everyone out at one in the morning. I like it when my home is loud and full of people, but I like it when it's quiet and just me, too.

I have Bennett come for a sleepover. I bring Nan to her first dance class since having surgery. She's almost completely healed, and when "Dancing Queen" begins to play, we laugh so hard we both have to sit on the floor.

I spend a few days taking stock of my freelance work and make a conscious decision to scale back my list of clients so I can make time for my own work while still paying the bills. It's easy determining who to weed out: From now on, I'm only going to work with people I enjoy working with. So I send a note to the art director at Percy's magazine telling her I'd love to shoot for her again, and when I get an email from Willa, asking if I'll take on another assignment for *Swish*, I politely decline.

But I'm surprised when Willa replies saying that she understands and asks if she can take me out for a drink. We go to a cocktail bar near her office, and she apologizes for what happened with the bathing suit photos.

"It was a new job," she says. "I was under so much pressure from my boss, and I was worried about impressing him."

I tell her I can relate, and that I'll give her a second chance.

I meet Elyse to share what I've shot over the summer, and she gasps.

"I'm working toward a solo show," I tell her, and ask whether she would consider hosting me at her gallery.

The question is only half out of my mouth when she screams, "Hell, yes!"

By the end of September, I'm more than okay.

But I still miss Charlie. I want to see him again. I want to yell at him.

I just don't know what comes next.

The first day of October is a Wednesday. It's a classic fall day. The sky is blue, the sun a plump marigold yellow. Every greengrocer has displays of chrysanthemums and pumpkins and gourds on the sidewalk. The coffee shop beside my studio has put out bales of hay for benches. I'd love to spend the day there, reading the sequel to *Ruling the Rogue* I bought at the drugstore yesterday, but I'm shooting a holiday entertaining story for *Swish*.

It's a long day and a full set—Willa, models, hair, makeup, two assistants, food and prop stylists—and we've just wrapped when my phone rings. I frown at the name on my screen. Percy always texts.

I step out into the hall, shutting the door behind me, my stomach already twisting.

"Hello?"

"Alice, hi. I have some news about Charlie. Are you sitting down?"

49

I take a cab to the hospital. I don't trust myself to drive. I could barely process what Percy was telling me beyond the words *open-heart surgery* and *intensive care.*

"He's okay," I tell myself. Because that's what Percy told me. I keep saying it, even when the driver looks at me in the mirror with alarm.

I walk as quickly as I can through the lobby, and then I start to run. I get lost in my panic. I spin around, trying to find the room number, and then I see a pregnant woman at the end of the hallway. Percy's in a yellow hospital gown and mask, talking to a doctor, her hands on her lower back. As I get closer, I realize the doctor is Sam.

She raises her hand when she sees me, and I know how I must look, red-faced and tearstained, mascara running to my chin.

"He's fine," she says, hugging me around her belly. "Right, Sam?"

"I'm not sure how happy he is with you, Percy." Sam turns to me. "But yes, he's fine, given the circumstances. Ross procedures are major cardiac surgery, but Dr. Lim is one of our best, and she's pleased with how it went. He's more than twenty-four hours post-op and recovering well."

"I would have called you sooner," Percy says. "But they're strict about visitors the day of surgery. I know this must be a shock. We wanted him to tell you. Sam tried to convince him, but he's been adamant."

I stare at her, open-mouthed. This was scheduled. Charlie knew all along he was having heart surgery. I put a hand on the wall.

Sam looks apologetic. "He didn't tell us at first, either. Fortunately, this is my hospital, and there was no way he could have kept it a secret. But I'll let him explain himself." He gives Percy a meaningful look. "Another day."

"There's a nurse in with him right now," Percy says. "He'll move out of the ICU to the surgery unit tomorrow morning."

I can barely process what they're saying.

"He knows you're here, and I'll show you to the room when he's ready," Sam says. "But do you want anything in the meantime? Water? Maybe a Kleenex?"

Over the next half an hour in the cafeteria, I listen to Sam explain that Charlie had a stent in the spring in addition to yesterday's surgery. I type *aortic valve stenosis* and *aortic coarctation* into my phone so I can look them up later.

"It came out of nowhere," Percy says. "Sam forced Charlie into seeing a doctor back in March after he complained about being out of breath at the gym."

"He'd been feeling faint, too," Sam says. "His blood pressure reading was high, and his doctor found a murmur."

I think back to the fear in Charlie's eyes when he grew winded that day working on the dock, and to when I'd seen him through the window, with the cuff around his arm. He'd said his blood pressure had been a little high. I hadn't given it much thought. I assumed it was related to work stress.

Sam tells me that the conditions are congenital, that they're most often passed down from fathers to their children. "We assumed Dad died of a heart attack, but there wasn't an autopsy. He likely had the same conditions. In severe cases, left untreated, they can cause sudden death."

I look at Percy's stomach.

"The baby's okay," Percy says. "The prenatal ultrasounds have all been good—it's less common in girls."

"A girl?" I muster a smile.

"A girl." Percy smiles back.

But then I look at Sam. He seems so together, despite all of this. "What about you?"

"I did the screening after Charlie's diagnosis. I'm clear."

"It's been a tough year," Percy says. "But Charlie's going to heal, and we're going to have this little girl. It's going to get better." She looks to Sam. "Right?"

He kisses her forehead. "I swear." And then he glances at the clock. "You should be good to see him now, Alice. Are you ready?"

I take a deep breath and nod my head. "Yes."

Before Sam leads me to the elevator bank, Percy gives my hand a squeeze. "Thank you for coming."

I squeeze back. "Thank you for calling me."

"You might find it hard to see him like this," Sam says as I'm putting on a gown. "He'll be groggy. His throat is sore—he may not be able to talk much."

I nod.

"I didn't want to go into everything in front of Percy, because it makes her queasy, but I think it's important to know what he's been through," Sam says. "The surgery involved making an incision and separating his breastbone. His chest will hurt. Actually, everything will hurt."

It's hard to breathe. Charlie spent the summer waiting for this. I think of how lost he sometimes looked, how sad. And now I know why he wanted a seventeen-year-old summer, too.

"It's a complex surgery. His aortic valve was replaced with his pulmonary valve, and a donor valve was put in its place. During that time, his heart was stopped. There was every reason to be confident it would go smoothly, but . . ."

Sam looks away. I can tell he needs a moment to hold it together.

I nod again. It's hard for me to speak, too.

"He's no longer intubated, but there are a lot of tubes—in his arms, his torso," Sam says gently. "The room is full of equipment. There are several monitors and beeping. It might be overwhelming."

"You're telling me not to freak out."

"I'm asking you to try." Sam places a hand on my elbow. "But it's hard to see people we care about like this. Do your best."

My nose stings at the kindness in his eyes, the way he knows that I care. I care so much. I look at the ceiling, blinking the tears away. I'm going to see Charlie after he's had cardiac surgery, and I need to stay calm.

"Sorry. I'll be okay," I tell Sam.

He studies me. "Would you like me to come in with you?"

I shake my head. "I can do this."

"Then I'm going to take Percy home to rest, but I'll get her to text you my number. If you have questions after you see him, or anytime, just give me a call, okay?"

"Thank you."

He turns to leave.

"Sam?"

He pauses, meeting my eyes.

"Who else has been to see him? Who else have you called?"

He pulls his mask down his chin, giving me a soft smile. "Just you, Alice. I think you probably know that."

And with that, Sam leaves me alone in the hall outside of Charlie's room.

"I'll be okay," I tell myself. And then I open the door.

Charlie's eyes are closed. His hair is longer now, and his skin has lost its summer glow. He's lying down, a blue gown loosely draped over his upper half. There are all manner of lines going into his arms and neck, along with IV bags and screens, just like Sam said. I ignore everything. I focus only on Charlie.

Not wanting to wake him, I quietly move to the chair next to his side, watching his chest rise and fall, blinking back tears.

Charlie hasn't opened his eyes when he speaks. "Stop staring at me, Alice." Every word sounds pained.

"How do you know I'm staring?"

"Because you can't help yourself," he croaks.

Slowly, he tilts his head toward me. Stunning green eyes meet mine, and I can't help it, tears roll down my cheeks, dampening my mask.

"I'm so mad at you," I tell him. "And I've missed you so much."

He swallows, his own eyes beginning to well.

"You shouldn't be here," he rasps.

"Shh. Of course I should be here."

Charlie's fingers twitch as if he's trying to move them toward me. I lean forward in my chair, setting my hands on his upper arm, away from all the gear he's hooked up to. He closes his eyes again.

"You look good in yellow," he mumbles.

Moments later, he's asleep.

50

S am texts me the next morning to say that Charlie has been moved out of the ICU. He tells me he'll be in the hospital for another week but that he's doing well. I ask Sam if I can come in the evening after I'm done with work. He begins to type out a reply, but then my phone rings.

"Hi, Alice." He hesitates before he says, "I'm sorry, but he says he doesn't want you to visit again."

I stand in the middle of my kitchen, an icy chill trickling down my spine.

"He said he doesn't want to waste your time."

Before this summer, I might have agreed to keep my distance. But I know Charlie, and I don't believe that's what he really wants. It's not what I want, either.

"Well, too bad for Charlie," I say to Sam. "Tell your brother I'll give him a couple days to catch up on his beauty rest, but that I'll be there on Saturday."

"Good," Sam says. I can hear his smile. "It's about time Charlie met his match."

I arrive at the hospital on Saturday with a bouquet of balloons and an envelope.

Charlie is sitting up, his color far better than it was a few days ago. He's in a private room, whether by luck or Sam's intervention, I'm not sure.

I stand in the doorway, our eyes locked together.

"I meant it when I said you shouldn't be here," he says. His voice is clearer than it was earlier in the week.

"I won't stay long," I tell him. "But I won't stay away, either."

"I don't want you seeing me like this. There's a reason I didn't tell you." He closes his eyes briefly, gathering strength.

"We don't need to talk about that today," I say. "But you can't stop me from worrying or wanting to help. You need support, Charlie. You need your people, and like it or not, I'm one of them."

Charlie stares at me. He doesn't argue.

"All that matters right now is that you get better. And then I'll yell at you."

His lips curve. "Fair enough."

I hand him the envelope. "These are for you. So you don't forget."

His eyes move between mine. "Forget what?"

"Us."

I visit Charlie every day for four days. I don't mention the photos I gave him, and neither does he. Instead, he tells me about the day last spring when he walked into his doctor's office, thinking

Sam was making a big deal about him being short of breath, and walked out in shock. His doctor had heard a heart murmur. More tests led him to a cardiologist's office and the diagnosis of two heart conditions that could prove fatal. The first condition, an aortic coarctation, was taken care of with a stent soon after.

"A stent isn't even considered a surgery," Charlie says. "Doctors do them all the time, and I was in and out the same day. But there were still risks. And even though Sam is a cardiologist and assured me that I was getting the best care, I could tell even he was getting anxious as my surgery date got closer."

Charlie tells me the surgery means he has a normal life expectancy. He's healing as he's supposed to, but it will take a few months until he's fully recovered. He won't be able to return to work right away, but he's not sure he wants to go back at all. He tells me how his diagnoses threw him, how worried he was when they waited for the results of Sam's screening, and how anxious he's been about the baby.

I bump into Sam in the hallway, and his hair is smooshed up on one side, like he's been running a hand through it. Stress radiates from him—his daughter is coming any day. I ask what I can do to help, and he gives me the keys to Charlie's condo.

I fill Charlie's fridge with obnoxiously healthy foods; sort through his mail; water his single plant, a fiddle-leaf fig; and put fresh sheets on the bed.

The day before he's released, we walk the halls of the hospital together.

"I couldn't focus at work," Charlie says as we turn back toward his room. "Recovery after the stent was straightforward, but waiting for this surgery really threw me. There was no reason not to work, and I was supposed to stay active, but I couldn't bring myself to care about my job, so I took the sabbatical."

"That sounds like it was the smartest thing to do," I tell him. "Getting some time away to think, to relax."

He looks at me, his eyes dancing. "Until I met a very troublesome redhead."

"Careful," I tell him. "I'm still furious you didn't tell me."

We reach his room, and Charlie's voice softens. "You would have wanted to take care of me. You would have worried."

"Yes."

His eyes search my face, and even if I hadn't told him how I feel, he would see it now. "You would have stuck with me, through all of it."

I lift my chin. "Yes."

"And I couldn't ask that of you. You've given so much of yourself to other people. You told me once that you lost yourself in your last relationship. I wanted you to have the freedom you deserve. It wouldn't have been fair to ask you to be tethered to someone like me."

"Someone like you?"

"I'm broken, Alice."

When Charlie said he's not built for relationships, he meant it literally.

"I'm sorry," he says, eyes pleading. "For everything I said that morning. I just couldn't bring myself to tell you the truth. I didn't want you to feel like you had to stand by me because of pity or a sense of loyalty."

"I could never feel sorry for you," I try to joke.

But Charlie steps closer, eyes darting between mine. "What if something had gone wrong? Or what if something does go wrong in the future? It's possible. There could be complications. I may need another surgery in twenty or thirty years, and I won't be as strong as I am now. I watched what losing my dad did to my mom." He looks to his feet. "I'm not worth that kind of pain, Alice."

"You can't live in the what-ifs, Charlie. You're here. I'm here. I wish your mom were here, too."

His brows knit together. "Why?"

"Because I think she'd tell you how wrong you are. I think she'd tell you that all the pain and grief were worth every minute she had with your dad." I put my hand on his cheek. "You're worth it, Charlie. Whether you believe it or not."

The next day, I get a phone call from a frantic-sounding Sam. "Alice? Hi. We're on our way to the hospital."

I jump to my feet. Charlie is being released today. "What's happened? Is he okay?"

"Yes. Shit. Sorry. Percy's water just broke, and her contractions are only a few minutes apart. We're not going to Charlie's hospital. We're on our way to Mount Sinai." Percy lets out a string of profanities in the background. "I'm supposed to pick Charlie up in thirty minutes," he says, panicked.

"I'll be there," I say. "Don't worry about any of it."

"Thank you. I owe you."

"Take a deep breath, Sam," I tell him. "You're going to be a dad."

I hear him breathe. "Thanks, Alice. I'll keep you posted."

I find Charlie in his room. In the days he's been here, his hair has become shaggy. He has a beard. He's wearing the clothes I packed for him to come home in—his favorite comfy pants and a loose-fitting buttoned shirt that won't aggravate his incision site.

"Upstaged by your niece, huh?"

He smiles—a gorgeous, golden Charlie smile. "The nerve of that girl."

"Complete monster," I agree.

"I was hoping she'd arrive on my birthday. I had big plans for an annual October sixteenth party."

"I know. But you'll only be a week apart. I'm sure you can split the difference."

"Thank you for coming," he says.

"I told Sam we should just put you in a cab, but he was insistent."

Charlie laughs, and I pick up his overnight bag. "Come on. Let's get you home."

51

Charlie and I step into his stunning condo. He has a penthouse suite on the twenty-eighth floor, with an astounding panoramic view of the city. Everything is glossy black and brass, with just a few modern dashes of pale oak, and high coffered ceilings. Even the kitchen is black on black. But the space is still warm with light gleaming off the surfaces. There are soft velvet pillows and leather seating and a thick rug in front of a glass-surrounded gas fireplace in the center of the living room.

It's photo shoot–ready, but it also felt a little lifeless, so I put flowers in the kitchen, the living room, and beside his bed. I've placed tiny white pumpkins down the center of his dining table. I bought a few magazines and books I thought he might like and arranged them on his coffee table. I didn't need to clean. The place was spotless.

"Thank you for the flowers," he says. "And the pumpkins." Charlie opens the fridge and shakes his head. "And all of this." His voice is thick.

"I figured it was the least I could do given everything you did for me and Nan. She'd like to come visit, by the way. When you're ready."

"I'd really like that." He turns to me, eyebrows lifted. "What do you think of it?"

It's another thing we haven't spoken about—that I've spent hours in his home without him. His building is far nicer than mine. It has an art deco vibe, and the lobby looks like a five-star hotel's. There's an indoor pool on the second level and a lush garden with bubbling fountains on the fifth. Even the hallways are elegant, with wainscoting and sconces that cast flattering dim light.

"It looks like a high-end porn set," I tell him. "I was surprised your bed wasn't circular."

He laughs, then winces at the pain.

"I'm kidding. It's a very swanky bachelor pad. It suits you."

Charlie studies me, frowning slightly. "It's weird to see you here. You're out of context."

"You'll get used to it, but I'll take that as my cue. You need to rest. Call me if you need me." I unblocked his number eight days ago.

I lean in to kiss his cheek goodbye, and just before my lips brush his skin, he turns his head. His eyes lock on mine. "Stay."

I hesitate.

"You can sleep in the guest room. I don't want to be alone. I don't want you to go."

"I don't think so," I whisper. I want to be a good friend, but spending the day and night together, even in separate rooms, doesn't feel right. "I don't think I can go that long acting like things haven't changed." And I want to give Charlie time to heal before we talk about us.

"It's never going to be like it was in the summer, is it?" There's so much despair in his voice, I almost change my mind.

"No, it isn't," I say softly. I walk to the entrance. "I'll come back tomorrow after work, okay? Let me know as soon as you hear any news about the baby."

Charlie nods. "I'll text you."

I close the door behind me.

52

'm almost at the elevator bank when I hear his voice.

"Alice. Stop." I turn around to find Charlie in his doorway.

We are at opposite ends of the hallway, but even from this distance I can see how lovely his eyes are. My chest tightens at the hope I find in them.

"I opened the envelope."

"Oh?"

There were seven photos inside. Some color. Some black and white. Some were taken with my digital camera. Some I developed myself.

Six are of Charlie. Charlie holding a chocolate cake, glitter on his cheeks, a tiara on his head, staring at me as he sings "Happy Birthday" off-key. Charlie floating on the Pegasus-unicorn. Charlie and Nan chatting that first day, she in pearls, him in a bathing suit. Charlie making pickles. Charlie at the foot of the tree house at Percy and Sam's party. Charlie in the yellow boat. In each of them, he looks directly at the camera, through the lens, and right at me.

The seventh is the photo he took of the two of us on the dock at the restaurant the day we went with Bennett, Heather, and Nan. And while the image isn't perfectly focused, it's so clear.

Charlie walks toward me, and I meet him halfway.

"Just this morning," he says. "All of them. I tried to look before, but I couldn't."

"Why?" The question comes out as a whisper.

Charlie brushes a curl away from my temple. "Are you sure you want to know, Alice? Are you really sure?" There's more vulnerability in his gaze than I've ever seen. "Because I've been trying to do something right. I want better for you than me. I want you to have a life full of freedom and joy and glitter and art. An endless bucket list."

He stares into my eyes, and it's the look from the photos. The look artists write songs and poems and books about. It's the look I saw that day in the darkroom.

"Tell me what you saw in the photos, Charlie," I say.

His gaze sweeps across my face, and when his eyes find mine, there's something new there. A solid, unrelenting focus that roots me in place.

"I saw a man who couldn't keep his eyes off you. A man who hasn't looked so happy in a very long time. I saw a man who finally found the kind of person he always wanted for himself. A best friend. A smart-ass. A brilliant, talented, caring woman, who deserves so much more than me."

Charlie's eyes glide over my face like a gentle caress, and he takes my hand. We stare at each other.

I want what happens next, I want so many moments with Charlie, but standing on the precipice with him right now, about to take a leap together, is one of the most wondrous experiences of my life.

"I saw something else in those photos," Charlie says.

And then he goes for it.

"I saw myself falling in love with you."

My heart is racing and my throat is too tight to speak.

"I'm in love with you, Alice," he says. "I knew the day you crashed John's boat that you were going to be trouble for me. I should have kept my distance, but I couldn't stay away. And the more I got to know you, the more beautiful and terrifying it became. Until I knew I'd finally found the person I've been waiting for." He puts his forehead on mine and closes his eyes.

"But I thought that asking you to be with me was too selfish, even for me. I thought I could give you what you wanted— friendship and sex—and leave it at that. I would care for you, and you would care for me, and we'd hang out and kiss all summer and that would be enough. And one day, when you found someone who could guarantee the happy ending you deserve, I'd learn to be happy for you."

My vision of him blurs with tears.

"When you told me you had feelings for me . . . I'm so sorry, Alice. I'm so sorry for everything I said. I just—"

I put my hand over his mouth. "Let's leave the groveling for when you have more energy, and back up to the part that came before."

Charlie smiles beneath my fingers. "The part where I tell you I love you?"

"Yes, that part. I liked that part a lot."

Tears fall down my cheek, and Charlie kisses them away. I'm already smiling when he says, "I love you, Alice Everly."

Alice Everly. Alice Everly. Alice Everly.

"I want to make you laugh that witchy laugh. And I want to be there for you when you cry. I'll bake all your birthday cakes. I want to tell you dirty things and watch you blush. I want to see every photo you take and tell you how brilliant you are. I want to get to know your whole family. I want to hear all of your jokes. I want to spend summers at the lake with you and winters in the city. I want to run your errands, and buy you expensive soap, and pose nude for you."

I laugh.

"There it is," he says to himself. "My Alice has the best laugh."

"'My Alice'?" I say, grinning.

"I hope so. I want that," he says. "I want you more than anything."

"Good," I tell him, setting my hand on the scruff of his jaw. "Because I love you, too, Charlie Florek."

His smile grows. It's sunshine shimmering over the water. It's permanent summer.

"I love you so much it's a little embarrassing," I say.

His green eyes sparkle. His pretty mouth smirks.

My Charlie.

"*Whoa*-level embarrassing? Or crash-your-boat-into-a-rock-level embarrassing?"

"Much worse," I tell him. "It's so much worse."

I kiss him once, carefully.

"You can do better than that, Alice."

"I'm afraid of hurting you."

His fingers thread into my hair. "It'd be worth it," he says, and then Charlie takes my mouth with his.

It feels like all the greatest kisses in one. Like kissing your high school crush, and the best friend you've fallen in love with, and the person you want to stand beside for as long as time will let you. It's the starting gun and the finish line. It's a surge of pleasure and satisfaction and rightness that reaches deep into my soul. And even when a neighbor opens the door to their apartment and gasps, we don't stop kissing. But eventually Charlie pulls away with a groan.

"I knew it would have been smarter to keep this to myself."

"Why's that?"

"Because I still have at least another week before I'm cleared to have sex."

I laugh. "Typical. You always want to take things slow."

"I'll make it up to you," he says. "I'll make it up to you for a very long time."

53

FRIDAY, OCTOBER 10
SUSIE'S BIRTHDAY

The next morning, we're woken by Sam calling to let us know that the baby was born in the early hours of the day. Both she and Percy are healthy. They've named her Sue, after Sam and Charlie's mom, but they plan to call her Susie. Sam sends us a dozen photos, and everyone looks tired and happy and snuggly.

Charlie and I lie in bed, marveling at the pictures, and after breakfast, he asks me if I'll help him shave—he's supposed to be careful with raising his arms. I sit on the marble counter in his bathroom, and he stands between my legs. As I carefully run his razor over his cheek and jaw and neck, he apologizes for our last conversation at the lake, for pushing me away, for saying he wouldn't stay interested, that it wouldn't work, that he'd get bored.

"They were lies, Alice," he says, while I scrape the blade over his throat. "It was the only thing I could think of in the moment to protect you. I didn't want you tied down by me. But I regretted it as soon as you left. I don't think I can ever express how sorry I am."

For the next week, we're inseparable. Apart from when I'm shooting or running errands, we're together, in Charlie's home. I know I'll have to come up for air soon, go back to my condo, return to the pool. And I will. But not yet. Right now, we're greedy for each other. It's not like it was in the summer. It's heady and earnest. There are no more barriers to what we share. Charlie is still full of teasing and smug grins, but there's no joking when he tells me how much he loves me. I feel cherished and safe, but I also feel like I'm flying.

Charlie's birthday falls on a Thursday in October, seven days after he's released from the hospital. As soon as my eyes meet his in the morning, I can tell something's changed. There's a lightness in his gaze I haven't seen since the lake.

"Happy birthday," I say, my fingers skating over his cheek as we stare at each other in the pale morning light. "You're thirty-six."

His smile takes my breath away.

"I made it," he says.

And I know exactly what he means. Past thirty-five. Past the age his dad was.

"You did."

"And now you're here. I must have done something right in a past life," he says.

I kiss him. "You've done plenty right in this one."

The more I've gotten to know Charlie, the clearer it's become that for all his talk, he doesn't think very highly of himself. So that morning as we face each other in bed, I tell him everything I love about him. There are the things I knew before. How kind he is. His smile. The way he pokes fun at me but knows when I need to be taken seriously. His aurora borealis eyes. The way he speaks to my grandmother. The time he hung up on my dad and sister. The bow of his top lip. How he follows his mom's recipes. His honesty. His tree house. His kisses.

And there are the things I'm learning about him now. That he makes his bed every morning. That he comes to life after three sips of coffee. How he organizes his ties by color, has a large collection of fancy cookbooks and a weakness for kids' cartoons. That he sings in the shower. That he talks to Sam every day.

"That's a very long list," he says. "I'm not sure it will ever sink in. It seems impossible that you could feel that way about me."

"Then I'll tell you over and over until you believe me."

I'm on set until midafternoon. When I'm done, I make a quick run to the grocery store before returning to Charlie's place. His mouth is on mine before I've taken two steps inside. It's a demanding, knee-weakening kiss.

"I got some good news from the doctor earlier," he says as he unbuttons my coat and drops it on the floor.

I glance at the clock. Sam and Percy have been resting at home with the baby, but they're coming for dinner tonight for Charlie's birthday. We paid them a visit when they got home from the hospital, but only stayed for a little while. Susie and I were the only people in the room who weren't completely exhausted. She's almost totally bald, but she looks so much like Sam.

"It's super annoying," Percy had said, smiling.

"We only have an hour before they'll be here," I tell Charlie. "And I still have to cook."

He winks. "I can work with that."

Charlie leads me to the bedroom. The curtains are closed, and the space is illuminated with dozens of candles.

"What is all this?" I turn toward his bed, gawking at what's scattered on the gray velvet coverlet. "Are those rose petals? This is not what I'd expected."

"Wait for it." Charlie gives me a grin as he reaches into his pocket and pulls out his phone.

Seconds later I'm doubled over, cackling as Rod Stewart's rendition of "Have I Told You Lately" plays over the speakers.

Charlie shuts off the music, and I straighten, still laughing.

"God, you're beautiful."

"God, you're cheesy," I say, cheeks straining.

"You like it."

"I love it," I correct. And then Charlie kisses me so deeply and thoroughly, I link my wrists around his neck to stay balanced. He pulls back an inch, staring at me in the flickering glow, and the seriousness in his gaze makes my stomach twirl.

"I wanted to do something more romantic than a darkroom."

"I liked the darkroom."

"I know you did. But I can do better. With everything. I'm in this, Alice. I'm so in this."

"I know."

I know that he's worth so much more than he thinks he is. I will give him everything I have—my time and my devotion and my heart. And I know he'll give it right back to me. Because I know Charlie. The incorrigible flirt. The human beam of sunlight. The man I love.

He's my best friend. And he's remarkable.

EPILOGUE

stare at the photo, and just like that, I'm seventeen.

I hear them across the bay. For a moment, I'm lost in the golden glow of a summer long ago. The laughter of three teenagers. The rumble of a familiar motor. A camera between my hands.

And then I feel him standing beside me—his warmth, his smell, the hand that settles on my lower back. I saw him across the room earlier tonight, but we haven't had a chance to speak. He looked as proud and puffed up as a peacock. I was in the middle of a conversation with a collector, and he raised his glass, tossed me a wink, and mouthed, *Later.*

"I've been waiting to corner you," Charlie says now. "You're a very popular woman this evening."

I tilt my head and find a pair of gleaming green eyes. "I can't believe how many people are here," I say. The space is packed, the music barely audible over the noise of the crowd.

"I can," Charlie says. A hand skims down my arm, and his

fingers knit through mine. "I've never believed in fate. But it's hard to argue with this."

We turn and study the three teenage faces in front of us. Charlie, Sam, and Percy in the yellow boat. My name on the wall beside them.

I've spent time at Elyse's gallery during the show's installation, but walking into the space earlier this evening, when it was still empty, surrounded by my photos, affected me in a way I didn't anticipate. I was glad I came alone, that I'd asked Charlie and my family to wait until the crowd began to arrive. I sat on the floor in the middle of the exhibition, soaking it in.

There are twelve large-format photographs in *Alice Everly: Seen.* In one, Nan and John sit on a bench in the backyard of his home in Ottawa. It's called *Reunion.* In *Unstuck,* my mother tromps through rows of grapes in muddy galoshes, her cheeks a windswept pink. There's one of Percy, pregnant, in her orange bikini, pouring a cup of coffee, morning sunlight streaming in through the window. I named it *Coming Soon.* And then there's *Falling*—the photo of Charlie I developed in his high school darkroom last summer. *One Golden Summer* hangs in the back corner.

"A lot of people can't stand their early work, but I still love it," I say to Charlie now. "It feels timeless."

Charlies leans toward my ear. "That's just my good looks." I snort, and he adds, "And your exceptional talent."

He plants a soft kiss on my cheek. "I know we're here celebrating your work, but I think it's important we also celebrate those pants." His gaze drops down my body, bottom lip between his teeth, and I laugh.

I didn't straighten my hair but am otherwise dressed in all my armor—glasses, red lipstick, chunky heels, a black silk blouse—but I'm also wearing a pair of leather trousers the old Alice wouldn't have dared to pull off. Charlie had me up against the door when I tried them on for him.

"At the risk of swelling your ego to an unbearable degree," I say to him, "I'm not sure *remarkable* quite covers how you look tonight."

Charlie also bought a new outfit. A charcoal herringbone jacket and pants with a snug cream cashmere turtleneck underneath. He looks as hot as he thinks he does.

I run my hand over the lapel. "I love this."

"Yeah? More than the suit and tie?" Charlie's city uniform has changed since quitting his job in the spring. He joined a prestigious foundation that raises money for heart disease research as CFO a few weeks ago.

"I do love the suit and tie," I tell him. "But this isn't as stiff. You seem more like yourself."

Charlie's surgery was only a year ago, but it's hard to remember him as anything less than healthy and happy and light. Every room he enters glows with his warmth and ease.

Not that it surprises me. I fall more in love with Charlie with every joke, every laugh, every evening he leaves me alone to go to choir practice with Nan, every morning he struts around the apartment with his shirt off, every kiss I press to the scar that runs down the center of his chest.

I moved into his place—*our* place—in the spring just as he gave his notice. Charlie took the summer off to decide what he wanted to do next and to work on John's cottage. We still call it that, though it's ours now. Percy and Sam insisted there was enough space at the house after Susie's arrival, but that's not why Charlie bought it. He wanted a new beginning, a cottage to fill with memories of our own. I spent the summer traveling between Barry's Bay and the city. I hung out with Percy and Susie, while Sam and Charlie attempted to update the cottage kitchen. They called Harrison for backup after the first weekend. It's a major improvement, though the curtains Nan and I sewed remain.

"You've made Charlie the best version of himself," Sam said to me one of those weekends. We were sitting on the dock with Percy, while Charlie was in the water beside us, taking Susie for a swim. She has both her father and uncle wrapped around her finger.

"He was always this version," I told Sam.

He was just waiting for someone to see and love him for who he really is, same as I had been. We're opposites in so many ways, but underneath, we're so alike.

We watched Charlie swirl Susie's chubby legs in the water, and then Percy turned to me. "This might sound weird," she said, and Sam started to chuckle. She glared at her husband before turning back to me. "But I had this feeling that things weren't complete until you showed up. It's like you were always meant to be here, Alice."

At that, Charlie's eyes swung to mine. "That's because she was."

We brought Nan back to the lake with us, too. She spent a week with Charlie and me, more cheerful and agile than the previous summer. Her hip is better than it was before the surgery. She was at the cottage to witness the biggest argument of our relationship thus far: I want to paint the wood walls white, and Charlie is adamantly opposed. We were in the kitchen, washing dishes, both of us in bathing suits, me with dish gloves on, and what started as a conversation became a full-out battle that was only broken up by Nan laugh-crying from her armchair.

"John and Joyce used to have this debate every summer," she said when we joined her in the living room. "It's nice," she said, "that so much has changed, but so little has, too."

I loop my hands around Charlie's neck now, barely aware that I'm in a room full of friends and family and colleagues. He sets his hands on my hips.

"Have you looked at it yet?" I ask.

"I have."

I took the final portrait in the show just one month ago. I sat on a stool in my studio. No makeup. No sleek ponytail. No clothes. I stared into the lens and took my own photo. The plaque hanging beside it reads:

I hate having my photo taken. But as I began to assemble images for this show, I was inspired by the courage of my subjects. I decided it wasn't fair of me to ask for their vulnerability without confronting my own. It's one of the most terrifying things we all do—allow people to see us without all our protective layers.

It's the only photograph I didn't show Charlie before tonight.

"What do you think?" I ask him now.

Charlie's cheeks have turned pink, and I'm suddenly worried I've gone too far. It takes him a moment to answer.

"It's beautiful, Alice," he says, his voice hoarse with emotion. He kisses my cheek. "The photo. You. The entire show. The way you throw yourself into everything you do."

Before he's finished speaking, I pull him tight to me and he whispers, "I love you," in my ear.

"It's almost time," I say, releasing him.

"Are you ready?"

I look around the room, and then Elyse raises her hand, ushering me over. I take a breath. "Yes."

"Because if you're still nervous, I can strip right down. Save you from having to imagine it."

"I know you would," I tell him. "But I'll be okay."

He squeezes my hand. "You'll be brilliant, Alice Everly."

I stand at the front of the room, listening to Elyse's opening remarks. When I take the microphone, I scan the faces staring back at me. Heather and Bennett and Mom. Nan and my father. Luca and Lavinia. Sam, Percy, and Susie. My friends. So many people I've worked with over the years. But there are also collectors and journalists and people I don't recognize. My throat begins to close. I'm cold with nerves.

And then I find Charlie. He's off to the side, and from where I'm standing, *One Golden Summer* hangs in the background over his shoulder.

I love you, he mouths to me.

I look into those extraordinary green eyes. And then I begin to speak.

ACKNOWLEDGMENTS

This book would not exist without the tremendous outpouring of passion from the fans of my first novel, *Every Summer After*. Thank you for putting my hometown on the map! To the readers who've waited patiently for Charlie's happy ending: Thank you for loving him as much as I do.

Thank you to the unstoppable Amanda Bergeron and Taylor Haggerty, publishing's ultimate power couple.

Thank you to Jasmine Brown, who in the dwindling weeks of 2020 rescued the manuscript for *Every Summer After* (then called *Swear On It*) from the slush pile.

Thank you to Deborah Sun de la Cruz and Emma Ingram, my Canadian dream team.

Thank you to Christine Ball, Anika Bates, Craig Burke, Kristin Cipolla, Kristin Cochrane, Beth Cockeram, Erin Galloway, Ivan Held, Jeanne-Marie Hudson, Sareer Khader, Bonnie Maitland, Vi-An Nguyen, Bridget O'Toole, Chelsea Pascoe, Theresa Tran, and everyone at Berkley and Penguin Random House Canada who touches my books.

Thank you to Heather Baror-Shapiro, Hannah Smith, and my editors and publishers around the world.

Thank you to Carolina Beltran and Jamie Feldman, two of the nicest, smartest people in LA.

Thank you to Elizabeth Lennie for another gorgeous cover painting. This one made me gasp.

Thank you to my friend, photographer Jenna Marie Wakani, who answered every one of my out-of-the-blue text messages about cameras, film, and terminology, and who gave me the idea for a steamy darkroom scene. Thank you also to photographer Erin Leydon, who graciously shared the ins and outs of her career with me.

Thank you to Meredith Marino for being my number one fan and dearest friend. I can't put into words how much your support means, which is why I spent a revolting amount on our Taylor Swift tickets. Jay, thank you for loaning your wife so she can come on book tour with me, and for your inspirational Charlie Florek cosplay.

To my friends Sadiya Ansari, Ashley Audrain, Lianne George, Heather Lisi, Courtney Shea, Rosemary Westwood, and Maggie Wrobel: Thank you for being there.

I've always known Charlie had a heart condition, but I had no idea what it was until I spoke with cardiologist Dr. Beatriz A. Fernandez Campos. Bety, thank you for being game to diagnose Charlie and for taking me through the ins and outs of Ross procedures, stents, recovery, and the stress and anxiety Charlie would have faced. Any mistakes are my own.

Joanne Olsen is the finest physiotherapist in Barry's Bay and an active member of the Station Keepers, a group of volunteers who make the community more vibrant. (If you ever come to town, make sure you check out the Railway Station Museum and the nearby Water Tower Park.) Joanne is also a member of the Station Keeper Singers choir (as is my mom). Joanne, thank you for your help understanding Nan's recovery and for everything you do for the Bay.

Thank you to Neil and Connie O'Reilly, former owners of the Barry's Bay Metro, who went above and beyond to stock copies of my books at the store back in 2022 and worked my first book event at the Barry's Bay arena. I once volunteered as an elf for Santa photos at the store, so I think we're even now. Congratulations on your retirement!

Thank you to my mom and dad for your encouragement, answering my Barry's Bay fact-checking questions, and your constant ribbing. Like the Floreks', the Fortune family's love language is teasing. But there's no joking when it comes to how much I owe to you both.

Max and Finn, the time we spend at the lake as a family is the most cherished of all my summer memories. I love you.

Marco, by the time this book comes out, we will have celebrated twenty years as a couple. What the hell? When I close my eyes, I can picture the first time you visited me in Barry's Bay. I was standing in the lobby of the inn, and you walked across the lawn in your brown Wilco T-shirt, and I watched with a huge smile on my face. I couldn't believe that my journalism school crush was my boyfriend and that he'd driven from Toronto to see me. Two decades later, our love story continues to unfold, but you'll always be my happy ending.

ONE GOLDEN SUMMER

Carley Fortune

READERS GUIDE

BEHIND THE BOOK

My first novel, *Every Summer After*, was published three years ago, in 2022. That spring, I watched in overwhelmed awe as the conversation around the novel shifted during its earliest weeks, from "Looking forward to reading this one" to "This is the book of the summer!" to "Is this book worth the hype?" *No!* I thought to myself. *Lower your expectations! It's just a book!* It was a startling introduction to authordom, to say the least.

I wrote *Every Summer After* during the pandemic, and it's a book about where and how I grew up. I channeled all of my teenage angst and insecurities into Percy and Sam, and through them, I was able to relive the summers of my youth in Barry's Bay. Writing it was a project I took on for myself, and it was an escape as much as it was a revelation. I'd been a journalist for fifteen years, but in the pages of *Every Summer After*, I learned that I was a novelist, too.

I'm so glad I had no idea that the book would find its way into so many readers' hands and go on to become such a hit. I doubt I would have had the courage to put so much of myself into the story had I known. Some of those pieces I'm happy to talk about—like my childhood on Kamaniskeg Lake, working at my parents' restaurant, my cousins' yellow speedboat, and the Jumping Rock—and some of those pieces are mine alone.

And although I've been thinking about writing a story about Charlie since before *Every Summer After* was published, I couldn't have anticipated how many times I'd be asked for it. Readers wanted more Percy and Sam. Readers wanted a happy ending for Charlie. Readers wanted more Barry's Bay.

At an event during my publicity tour for my second novel, *Meet Me at the Lake*, two young women waited at the end of my signing line. I looked up at them with a smile, but they were not smiling. "We have a bone to pick with you," they said. I looked around the auditorium, hoping for an escape. "We *need* Charlie's happy ending," they said. "Justice for Charlie!"

The more people requested Charlie's love story or another book about Percy and Sam, the more daunting it felt. I didn't want to write a sequel. At the time, I'd left Percy and Sam where I wanted them to be. But Charlie lingered in my mind. I had more to say about who he was, and, like many readers, I wanted to know how his love story unfolded. That meant I needed two things: a heroine and guts.

Because what I had learned in the spring of 2022 is that once a book is published, it no longer belongs to just me. It's yours, too. It belongs to the reader. Like Alice, I'm so grateful I spend my days doing the thing I love, but there's a particular kind of magic in creating art for oneself, without worrying about the expectations and judgment of others. That's especially true for the Alices and Carleys of the world: We care what people think. Our audience matters.

To write the best story I could for you, I needed to be confident enough not to fret over how you would respond. I had to shut you out as much as I could. I turned my focus to inventing Alice. I auditioned many characters before I found someone who was both the ideal fit for Charlie and had a compelling journey in her own right. And while I hope anyone who wanted more Sam and Percy enjoyed the glimpses of their married life, I wanted this book to be about so much more than dipping a toe into their world again.

Every Summer After leaned heavily on autobiography as I explored what Kamaniskeg Lake meant to me as a teenager. But *One Golden Summer* allowed me to examine what returning to the lake means to me as an adult. Through Alice, Charlie, and Nan, I was able to explore how being immersed in nature, far from the city, can give us literal and figurative distance to reflect on our lives. *One Golden Summer* is a story about how we sometimes need to go back so we can move forward. We are, in many ways, exactly who we were as teenagers and yet wholly different people—something both Charlie and Alice discover in this book. This is a story about two people who are afraid of letting themselves truly be seen. It's also a book about perfectionism, regret, and the march of time. And, of course, it's a love letter to the place where I grew up. As Nan says: Good things happen at the lake.

xo,
Carley

ONE GOLDEN SUMMER
DISCUSSION QUESTIONS

1. Alice spends two transformative months on Kamaniskeg Lake when she's seventeen. Do any of your summer vacations hold a similarly important role in your memory?

2. How do you relate to Alice's struggles with people-pleasing and perfectionism?

3. Do you think "friends with benefits" is ever a good idea? Why or why not?

4. Charlie's true motivation for pushing Alice away isn't revealed until later in the story. What did you think was behind his refusal to enter into a relationship with her?

5. In our society, aging is particularly fraught for women. But Nan tells Alice, "It's a gift to age." What do you think?

6. Alice finds joy in taking photographs just for the fun of it while she's at the lake. When was the last time you took on a creative project for your own pleasure?

7. Family dynamics are explored in this book. Alice is the "turtle" of her family. Charlie is the "joker." Who are you in your family?

8. What are the top five things on your ideal summer bucket list?

QUESTIONS FOR
EVERY SUMMER AFTER FANS

1. *One Golden Summer* takes place three years after the events in *Every Summer After*. Are Percy and Sam where you expected them to be?

2. How have your feelings about Charlie changed—or not—between reading that book and this one?

3. How does Alice compare to who you pictured as a partner for Charlie?

BOOKS I READ AND LOVED WHILE WRITING *ONE GOLDEN SUMMER*

Good Material by Dolly Alderton

In Exile by Sadiya Ansari

The Ministry of Time by Kaliane Bradley

This Is It by Matthew Fox

The Husbands by Holly Gramazio

The Love of My Afterlife by Kirsty Greenwood

The Most Famous Girl in the World by Iman Hariri-Kia

The Life Cycle of the Common Octopus by Emma Knight

The God of the Woods by Liz Moore

A Love Song for Ricki Wilde by Tia Williams

CARLEY FORTUNE is the #1 *New York Times* bestselling author of *Every Summer After, Meet Me at the Lake,* and *This Summer Will Be Different*. She's also an award-winning Canadian journalist who has worked as an editor for Refinery29, *The Globe and Mail, Chatelaine,* and *Toronto Life*. She lives in Toronto with her husband and two sons.

VISIT CARLEY FORTUNE ONLINE

CarleyFortune.com

CarleyFortune